The Living

Published by Hesperus Press Limited
28 Mortimer Street, London W1W 7RD
www.hesperuspress.com

First published by Hesperus Press Limited, 2012

Copyright © Живущий / Анна Старобинец. – M: ACE 2011

English language translation © James Rann, 2012

Designed and typeset by Fraser Muggeridge studio

Printed in Jordan by Jordan National Press

ISBN: 978-1-84391-377-1

The Living

Anna Starobinets

Translated by James Rann

Welcome to Renaissance, the global historical databank.

Caution!
This box contains only private
correspondence and documents.

This box has been leased for 120 years, with optional
extension on request.

Access to this box is only available to the leaseholder.

Access to this box is not available to
leaseholders under the age of eight.

Please enter your incode.

Thank you,
incode accepted.

Please place your plastic incode e-card against
the illuminated section of screen.

Thank you,
e-card accepted.

Please place your left hand against the illuminated
section of the screen.

Identification failed.

Caution! Please try again, ensuring that your palm
is in full contact
with the illuminated section of the screen.

Identification failed.

You do not have access to this cell.

Renaissance will inform the SPO regarding
your attempt to...

Caution!

Your session has been suspended.

You have entered the Level 1 SPO access code.

Level 1 access code accepted.

Level 2 access code accepted.

Level 3 access code accepted.

The triple SPO code is being processed...

This box contains only private correspondence
and documents.

Renaissance is not responsible for the accuracy
of information contained in this box.

Triple code processed.

Triple code accepted.

You may now access this box as *guest*.

Thank you for using Renaissance, the global
historical databank.

Please enjoy your reading experience.

There is no death.

Part 1

Hanna

September 439 Anno Viventis
First day of the waning moon

...The doctor who did my analysis was not too worried at first. He just said that the connection can malfunction, so he'd have to do everything again, sorry that I'm making you wait. He froze, not blinking, looking past me, through me. His pupils were narrowing and widening spasmodically, in a sort of jerky rhythm. Then, once the rhythm was established, he shut his eyes for some reason. As if he couldn't hold three layers... but that never happens with medics... So, he must have gone deeper; but why? The office smelled strongly of sweat, and I held my breath. I noticed that his eyelids, his forehead and his nostrils had a wet sheen. I thought: something's wrong with him, this doctor, it's him that's malfunctioning, the connection's working fine... When he opened his eyes again his face looked as if he had just seen the incode of the Butcher's Son, or maybe not just the incode, but the Son himself, with his weary workman's smile and his foul-smelling axe, covered in blood, just like in The Eternal Murderer.

'I need to perform the procedure again,' he said, and I noticed that his hands were shaking.

'For a third time?'

He did not say anything in reply, just detached one sensor from my stomach and attached another identical one.

For about a minute we sat in silence: me in that huge cold chair and him opposite me. I thought, if there, inside me, there is someone from the Blacklist, some maniac like the Butcher's Son or Rotten Rick, then I won't get to see him, I won't see him even once, and they'll keep him in a House of Correction, in solitary, and they'll feed him three times a day and not say a word to him, they won't say a word to him until the day he dies, and he'll never know what for. I thought about how hypocritical it was to call them Houses of Correction. No one has ever tried to correct anything there. They just keep them there. Stuffed and silent...

Then the sensor squeaked, and the doctor read off the result again; everything seemed to suggest that it was exactly the same as before.

I asked, 'Is there something wrong?'

He said nothing.

'Is there something wrong with my baby?'

He got up and paced around the office. 'His father...' The doctor's voice rattled like a beer can skittering along the road. 'Do you know him?'

'No. It's a festival baby.'

'Get dressed,' he looked past me, 'and wait out there in the corridor. I've called the SPO.'

'Is he abnormal?'

'What, sorry?'

'The baby. My Darling. Is my Darling on the Blacklist?'

'Ah... no...' He finally looked at me, but the way he looked was somehow strange, as if from afar, as if through binoculars, as if I were hovering somewhere on the horizon, as if I were in *socio* and not there in front of him. 'No. Your Darling is not on the Blacklist.'

'Then why the SPO? What have I done? What is the nature of my violation?'

'I'm not authorized to say,' he said absent-mindedly and at that moment stopped noticing me. He was clearly occupied by some other conversation in a deep layer.

The SPO officer did not hurry. He appeared after about forty minutes, and I spent all of those forty minutes in the corridor, watching the females going through various office

12

doors, all stressed, irritated, accustomed to the terror of the discovery that awaited them, trying to prepare themselves for the worst, but all the same stubbornly clinging on to the best. Hope. Hope glowed on them like radioactivity. Waves of toxic hope flooded the corridor. Please let it be sorted. Please not now. Please let me be empty.

They are different when they come out of the offices. The empties move with the smooth and swift gait of dancers, as if they have become slimmer, as if they have been made lighter by the emptiness swirling round inside them. The others step heavily, as if they have put on weight instantaneously. Their gaze is turned inward; oh, that well-known humble gaze, that evaluates, that tries to examine and understand the useless little thing growing inside them. Humility, responsibility, duty – that's what their psychotherapists will say to them tomorrow. Humility to Nature. Responsibility to your Darling. And Duty to the Living. Yes, it's hard. These three elements of harmony will cause you some difficulties. But you will find consolation in the other three. Pleasure, stability and immortality. And now let's all stand in a circle, take each other by the hand – anyone who wants to can put on contact gloves – and repeat together: 'The Harmony of the Living is formed of six components: humility, duty, responsibility, pleasure, stability and immortality.' And all together now: 'The Harmony of the Living depends on me personally.'

My psychotherapist reckons that tactile contact and group repetition is absolutely perfect training. Painful, but helpful. He says that dancing in a circle and singing in a choir is a sort of model. In the circle you understand way more clearly than in *socio* that you are part of the Living... In the circle you feel more protected. In the circle you're not even afraid of the Five Seconds of Darkness.

'...No death!' the planetman slumped heavily into the empty chair next to me and placed a square black briefcase by the legs; the mirrored mask stuck to his face was a little bit murky and covered in blotches. 'It's hot today...'

'What is the nature of my violation?'

'There was none.'

'Then why do you want to interrogate me?'

'It's my job.' The planetman looked at me intently and, as far as one could tell by the expression on his mask, squeamishly. 'Please, put this on.'

He held out another mirrored mask, which was also less than spotless.

'Is using a "chatterbox" compulsory?'

'The conversation device is compulsory.' He shook the proffered mask impatiently. 'Put it on. It's completely sterile on the inside. Like that, thank you, Hanna... It's just a conversation. Nothing like an interrogation...'

The mask was cold. Cold and sticky, like the touch of some deep-sea creature.

'Now I am going to connect your mask to the conversation device... Mm-hm... and mine too... There we go. It's just so our conversation will be recorded, that's all.'

Beneath the mask his voice suddenly changed horribly, turning into a sort of monotonous buzzing.

'On completion of our conversation you will receive a copy of the transcript. The conversation device cannot cause any harm either to you or your...er...er... foetus. It is made of ecologically sound...'

'What is the nature of my violation?' I also buzzed like a defective electric doorbell.

'There was none.'

'I don't understand what's going on.'

'Me neither,' he smiled with his mirror mouth. 'I don't understand either. That's why you are required to tell us everything relating to your...er...er... foetus in as much detail as possible.'

'It's a festival baby.'
'I said in detail...'

Would you like to suspend session with document No. 1?

Yes no

Document session suspended

Move to new document or terminate session with this box?

Moving to document No. 3 ...

Document No. 3
(Transcript of conversation between leaseholder and SPO officer, dated 10.09.439 A.V.)

SPO officer: You are required to tell us everything relating to your foetus in as much detail as possible.

Interlocutor 3678: It's a festival baby.

SPO officer: I said in detail.

Interlocutor 3678: Today, on the first day of the waning moon, I appeared at Medical Centre No. 1015 in relation to the law on monthly population control. The doctors established that I was pregnant...

SPO officer: Had you previously attended the Centre regularly?

Interlocutor 3678: Yes, of course. I come here every month.

SPO officer: Have the doctors at the Centre ever established that you were pregnant before?

Interlocutor 3678: No. This is the first time it's happened.

SPO officer: Have you not had sexual contact before?

Interlocutor 3678: I have.

SPO officer: Did you have fertility problems?

Interlocutor 3678: No.

SPO officer: Then why is this your first pregnancy?

Interlocutor 3678: I took precautions.

SPO officer: That is forbidden.

Interlocutor 3678: I have permission.

Interlocutor 3678 rummages through her handbag. The sensor shows rise in body temperature of 0.3°, increase in pulse rate to 130 beats per second, pupil dilation to 6.3mm – 2.8mm over the norm for given lighting conditions.

Interlocutor 3678: Here you go.

Interlocutor 3678 shows a document to the SPO officer: a permit for the use of contraceptives, issued on the basis of medical opinion confirming the Interlocutor's marginally sub-normal mental development.

SPO officer: Tell me about the festival in more detail.

Interlocutor 3678: The child was conceived at the regional Festival for Assisting Nature during the last new moon, as part of the population control programme, in accordance with the law about planned...

SPO officer: Could you identify the father?

Interlocutor 3678: Are you making fun of me?

SPO officer: I am doing my job.

Interlocutor 3678: How could I identify the father? I keep telling you: the baby was conceived at the festival, how could I know which of...

SPO officer: How many partners did you have at the festival?

Interlocutor 3678: Five... Seven... I don't know.

SPO officer: According to our data, the Reproduction Zone at the last Festival for Assisting Nature was visited by 1,352 men. We will bring them to you for identification. Will you be able to recognise your partners amongst them?

Interlocutor 3678: I don't know. I'm not sure... I am not obliged to do that. The law on the confidentiality of sexual relations isn't going anywhere.

SPO officer: Naturally, you are not obliged. It is only a request. A request from the Service for Planetary Order.

Interlocutor 3678: I'll grant your request, if you'll explain to me what is going on.

SPO officer: OK, I will try and explain it to you. At the Festival for Assisting Nature, in which you took part, the existence of 610 people was temporarily terminated in the Pause Zone. Simultaneously, in the Reproduction Zone, 611 people were conceived. Of these, 610 are the direct incarnation of those who had been in the Pause Zone – all the incodes match perfectly. And only one, your festival baby...

Interlocutor 3678: Is that the reason you've frightened me so much? Fofs![1] That's just hilarious! It has been proven that for festival children only in ninety-five per cent of cases do the pausers undergo stable reproduction, and in the remaining five per cent the incodes can come from whoever. So what? You stuck this thing on me just to tell me that my Darling's incode doesn't match one of the pausers'? Well, so what? I really don't care whose incode the kid has, smin,[2] the main thing is that it isn't some criminal's... He's not a criminal, is he?

SPO officer: I don't know.

Interlocutor 3678: Well I do know. The doctor said that my Darling is not on the Blacklist.

SPO officer: That is correct. The incode of your foetus does not appear among the incodes on the Blacklist.

Interlocutor 3678: Then what's the problem?

SPO officer: The problem is that the incode of your foetus... the incode of your Darling does not appear anywhere at all.

Interlocutor 3678: I don't understand. What do you mean by that?

SPO officer: Exactly what I said. His incode does not have a counterpart code in any of the codes stored in the global database: not a single one in three billion. In essence, your future child does not have an incode at all. Instead of an incode both of the devices used for your intrauterine scan read 'Void'.

Interlocutor 3678: Void?

SPO officer: Void. Zero. He has no in-history. Your Darling has had no previous lives.

Interlocutor 3678: So then... but... how then... whose place has he taken? I mean, has one of the livings temporarily ceasing to exist not been reproduced? They've disappeared? Is that what's happened?

SPO officer: Far from it. No one has disappeared. Someone new has been added.

Interlocutor 3678: That's impossible! You're an SPO officer – you should be ashamed of yourself! Are you in one of those sects or something? What is this heresy? For it is written: 'The Number of the Living is unchanging, the Living is three billion livings, and neither by one shall this number be diminished, nor by one shall it be increased, for eternal rebirth...'

SPO officer: Don't get worked up, I've read the Book of Life too and learned the key passages off by heart. But a fact is a fact. The population of the Living has changed and is now three billion and one. And that 'one' is your Darling with his 'void' incode. I am afraid you have no idea how serious this is. So far no one does.

Interlocutor 3678: He... my Darling could be a risk to the harmony of the Living?

SPO officer: We can't rule it out.

Interlocutor 3678: Will they put him in a House of Correction? Why are you shaking your head? He'll be... They won't let him be born? Will I have to have an abortion?

SPO officer: It's not up to me to decide these things. Over the next seven days 'the Zero problem' will be examined at the very highest level. For the duration of this period you will remain in hospital under observation. You do not have the right to leave the confines of the ward until such time as a decision has been made by the Council of Eight. Tomorrow you will be sent the first 300 men who took part in the festival, for identification. Is that all clear?

Interlocutor 3678: Yes.

SPO officer: I have one last question. If you have permission to use contraceptives, why did you not take precautions at the festival?

Interlocutor 3678: Because I wanted to conceive.

SPO officer: What do you mean by that?

Interlocutor: Exactly what I said. I wanted a child.

SPO officer: Explain that.

Interlocutor 3678: My medical certificate allows me to take precautions, but it does not absolve me of my duty to the

Living. I carried out my duty. Do you have a problem with any of that?

SPO officer: Nothing of the kind. Your position deserves every respect... Thank you for the conversation.

(end of transcript)

<u>Move</u> to new document or <u>terminate</u> session with this box?

> *cerberus:* fancy a beer?

Caution! You must <u>move</u> to another document now or <u>terminate</u> your session with this box.

'Oh, come on, enough is enough, Ef, terminate. Let's go and have a beer. This bloody bank is as stuffy as the Living's backside. And this bloody mask will melt right here on my face if I'm not chugging on a cold one soon.'

<u>Move</u> to new document or <u>terminate</u> session with this box?

'Alright. You've talked me into it.' Ef jabs sluggishly at 'terminate' with a bandaged hand. 'Let's go and have a beer.'

The Man with No Face

There is no one on the street. It has not yet got dark, but the golden glow of the little lights built into the paving slabs already illuminate the evening mist and the delicate pink surface and fine white veins of the marble.

cleo: no death ef all of a sudden you're here

Ef's boots leave black tracks of grime on the marble; an electronic wonder-cleaner, who stands frozen by the pavement wearing a bikini and rubber gloves, turns herself on with a quiet click, gets down on all fours and sets to work wiping off the marks. She crawls after them quickly, thrusting her rear in the air and making quiet, monotonous groaning noises. Clearly ones like her are meant to arouse a desire in passers-by to procreate and multiply.

Cerberus turns around and spits on the pink marble with relish. The cleaner dutifully drags herself towards his spittle with a cloth.

'Get lost!' Cerberus laughs and gives her a slight kick to the face with his sharp-toed boot. The cleaner freezes and, not unclenching her plastic lips, makes a sultry 'mmmmhhh': that is how she has been programmed to react when touched.

cerberus: they've got decent beer in this place round the corner

cerberus: hear what i'm saying?

cerberus: ef!

'They've got decent beer at that place on the corner with Harmony Avenue,' Cerberus says out loud. 'What, you offline or something?'

ef: no sorry just got distracted. ok. let's go to Harmony

They turn left. Harmony Avenue is empty; the concretal sculpture – an enormous bronze-coloured palm – looks lonely, as if waiting for a handshake that it will never receive... Only half-mad Matthew, a tall, scrawny old man, is there, wandering around at the base of the concretion, shaking his little bell and crying determinedly: 'He died for us! He died for our sins! Died for us!'

cleo: everything alright?

'Do we have a violation here?' Cerberus snaps at him. 'Are we using certain words?'

'Oh, he is the beginning and the end,' Matthew howls. 'And his name is... Zero! He died for us! He was burned in the sacred fire...!'

cleo: i get worried when you're grey for ages ☺

'He died, died for us!'

'Silence!' barks Ef. 'You're lucky I want a beer. If not I'd have had you straight off to Correction!'

'You, you blood-soaked hounds of hell! Acolytes of the devil! Men with mirror faces! Men without faces! Men without voices! Tremble, for he cometh! And his kingdom cometh! And his will will be done! Thus is thine twine swine! For you shall be cast down! And you shall be cast out! For he died for us! For he is the Saviour! And his name is...Zero...!'

cleo: maybe something's up with your connection?
i'm going to get tech support

...The beer has a hint of iron about it. It's either the beer itself or the mask that's stuck to his nose and lips that gives the drink this metallic taste. Ef runs the tip of his tongue around the inside of his cheek. No, it's not the mask. His cheek, smashed from the inside against his teeth, is bleeding, that's what it is.

Cerberus returns with a second mug of beer, falls heavily into the chair opposite, sucks up a third of his beer in one go and goes back to staring at him with the soft blank ovals of his mirror eyes. These eyes reflect Ef's mirror eyes, which reflect those eyes which reflect... Ef starts to feel queasy, as if he were seasick; he lowers his head and looks into his glass. The foamy surface of the beer does not reflect anything.

cerberus: did he say anything, that zero, before he...

Cerberus looks at the empty tables around them and moves closer just in case.

... before he... you know... destroyed himself?

ef: listen i just want to be like everyone else

cerberus: what do you want ef?!

ef: me?:–) i want to sleep. but that zero, before he died he said 'listen I want to be like everyone else

cerberus: don't talk like that!!

'Don't talk like that, Ef!' Cerberus has clearly got nervous. He is so nervous that even the measured buzzing that the chatterbox makes from his voice sounds a tone higher. 'Don't talk about death. There is no death.' Cerberus nods pointedly at the chatterbox under the table and points at his temple as if to say, 'You idiot, everything's being recorded.'

'There was death for him,' Ef says wearily. 'For Zero. You know very well he was born without an incode. And yesterday he died. He blew up a wonder-sunshine and died. There will be no more "voids", Cerberus. He won't be continued – it's been confirmed by all the population control centres. It wasn't a pause. It was death.'

> cerberus: the one thing i don't get is how he could crush a wonder-sunshine in his HAND?? it's not humanly possible... maybe he wasn't a human at all?
>
> ef: all biological signs suggest he was a human ☺ i think he just dug into it a bit before and twisted something... or it was just broken that also happens sometimes...
>
> cerberus: well anyway it's all for the best basically. for the Living.

Cerberus stretches his mirrored lips, still wet from the beer, into a smile and buzzes evenly: 'The number of the Living is unchanging. The Living is three billion livings, neither by one shall it be diminished, nor by one shall it be increased...'

> and no more voids. aren't you happy?

'Yes,' Ef says. 'Very happy. It's just I'm awfully tired. And my hands hurt.' He struggles to waggle his bandaged fingers.

'It burned you pretty bad?'

'All the skin's come off.'

> cerberus: fofs... and your face?

ef: not my face you know i was wearing my mask it's fireproof

cerberus: show me

ef: show you what?

'Er, your face. And you keep touching your cheek. Maybe you're burned all over. Take off your mask, I'll have a look.'

Ef jumps out of his seat. Then sits back down.

'Officer Cerberus. You have just suggested that I break Service for Planetary Order regulations. Your words have been recorded by the conversation device, and I will take full responsibility for…'

SPO_service: third level access: processing signal: do you wish to make an official charge?

ef: not yet

'OK, OK, what did you jump up like a flea for? It was just a little test. A joke!' Cerberus buzzes apologetically.

'So was it a test or a joke?'

cerberus: gopz![3] a friendly joke of course!

Ef examines his reflection in Cerberus's mirrored features and feels another wave of nausea. He knocks back some beer. Closes his eyes. It gets worse.

Darkness does not come, instead of darkness there is *structure*. It's as if he was nestling his face in a squidgy termite mound… Hundreds of tiny rounded boxes, a mobile, porous mass. Most of the boxes are dripping with light – busy or available – and pulsing gently. The rest, murky-grey and immobile, seem abandoned. Cerberus's box also gives the impression of being uninhabited...

> *cerberus:* stop that you've known me a hundred years!

> *ef:* ok let's just leave it

> *cleo:* ef!!

One of the available boxes swells up and bursts open, as if transformed into a greedy mouth.

> *cleo:* ef i know you're there

He opens his eyes. Cerberus's mirrored mask reflects his own mirrored mask which reflects Cerberus's mirrored mask... His jaw drops and his tongue lolls out. He jumps up.
'You what?'
'I am going to be sick.'

> *autodoctor:* relax. deep breath. and ou-u-u-u-t. in –
> and ou-u-u-t. you are overtired. you need to sleep.
> alcohol is not recommended. take plenty of fluids and
> get some fresh air.

'So, has it passed?' Cerberus asks with heartfelt interest. 'Another beer maybe?'
'I am overtired,' says Ef. 'I need to sleep. Alcohol is not recommended. Fresh air is recommended... No death!' He goes towards the exit.
'No death,' Cerberus replies and belches carefully, covering his mirrored lips with his hand. The chatterbox turns his belch into a brief despondent howl.

re: chain letter
from: dissenter

You've got a stupid job, before the pause you had
a stupid job, and after the pause you'll have a stupid
job. But you want to be a screenwriter or a designer.
Follow Zero: he has come to change your life.

!caution! this may be spam
*mark this message as spam? **yes** no*

Ef marks it as spam, though there's no point: 'the letter of
joy' has already been sent to a dozen friends from his address.
It's impossible to stop the process. He already knows that.

At that moment a new message comes:

re: important
from: a dissident well-wisher

Don't believe the lies. The Leo-Lot ray works in both
directions, backwards and forwards...

Ef reads the letter to the end and notices that there is
another layer between his face and the mask – a cold film
of sweat. He marks the letter as spam, then deletes it, but
memorizes every word. His heart beats in his fingertips, in his
ears, under his Adam's apple, as if it has burst into a hundred
miniature hearts and his blood has scattered them through
his body.

perhaps you are frightened?

– the autodoctor chirps up.

Perhaps. But that's none of your business.

When Ef turns on to Harmony it starts to rain – suddenly, without any warning splashes, as if an automatic disinfection shower had been turned on to full power.

The pale pink marble is soaked and turns the colour of raw liver. In the light of the pavement's built-in lamps the raindrops look like clouds of golden insects swarming together at the scent of blood.

> *cleo:* tech support checked the link you're just in invisible

The raindrops tickle the naked plastic bodies of the electronic cleaners, and the cleaners groan dutifully. The raindrops drum softly against Ef's mirror mask, bringing no relief. Bringing no freshness. If only he could take it off. If only he could take it off and feel the cool moisture...

'Tremble, for he cometh... Tremble, for he cometh... Tremble, for he cometh...' Lanky Matthew shuffles from one bare foot to another right on top of a lamp, in a golden column of light. Streams of gold pour down his face, his long grey matted hair and neck.

'Men without voices!' The old man comes to life when he sees Ef. 'Men with mirror faces!'

Ef slows down.

'No death, Matthew. You're all wet. Go home.'

He would like the words to sound soft, but the chatterbox chews them up and spits them out as an order.

Matthew opens wide his misty blue eyes and bursts out in squeaky laughter, revealing his teeth, which are long and rotten like a horse's. Then he whimpers and squats down. He trails a bony finger across the wet shiny marble:

'Do you see what colour the ground *really* is? Do you see what colour it really is?'

'Go home,' Ef says again. The he turns off his chatterbox and adds, 'I see.'

    cleo: why are you like this?

'There are voices inside you,' Matthew whispers, and his gaze clears up for a moment. 'Other people's voices, right?'
'Yes. Of course.'
'They are demons!' Matthew clasps his knees in his arms and sways from side to side. 'They are demons. Disconnect. Demons. Disconnect. Demons. Disconnect...'

    disconnect from socio

    are you sure you want to disconnect from socio?

    yes *no*

    confirm:

    ef: yes

    caution: when in disconnected mode you cannot see your list of socio *contacts, or use* socio *to chat and find and share new information. Continue with disconnection?*

    yes *no*

    caution: when in disconnected mode you will not be an active part of socio. *Continue with disconnection?*

    yes no

Yes

you are no longer in socio

Don't worry, you can reconnect to socio at any time.

Connect: interrupting connection with socio *for longer than 30 minutes is not recommended. If you do not re-establish connection independently, mandatory remote connection will take place after 40 minutes.*

Zero

...I just want to be like everyone else. I don't have ideas above my station. I want to be like everyone else. I can't now, so it'll have to be later. After the Pause. Hey, you! Hey, you there, in the future! I hope you will actually exist. I hope that you will be me. I hope that I will exist. If you are my continuation, if I am you, then sorry for this stupid incode that you've got from me... Personally, it ruined my life, but I really hope you find a way to deal with it somehow. That I'll deal with it somehow there in the future. In eight years' time... Because you're eight, aren't you?

It's probably cowardice. It's running away. It's not fair. But if you will exist, if you do exist, forgive me for what I'm about to do. Sorry if I've ruined your (or should I say 'my'?) mood. Sorry if I've created any problems for you (ha-ha, for me!!). I want you to understand. I'm planning on killing myself – yes, yes, sorry about that, sorry once again, I shouldn't say that, I should put it differently. I'm planning on 'temporarily ceasing to exist', 'taking a pause', but I'm no fool, I know: they all get pauses, but all I have is a 'stop'. So if you do exist, if you will exist, then glap[4], we've won, you and me, because it means that we're like everyone else. I'm like everyone else. I am a part of the Living.

And if you're not there, if you just don't exist, if I am no more, if I am going to disappear, I'll die forever, like people used to, before the birth of the Living... Well, then I'm a mistake of nature. A genetic malfunction. A sickness. A tumour on the body of the Living. So it'll be better without me. More correct. Simpler. Basically, however this ends – it'll be better than it is right now....

I always wanted to be like everyone else. But they have made me a god. They have made me a devil. They have made me a fruit fly for them to do experiments on. They have made me very dangerous. They did not even know what they were doing.

They have forced me into a corner. They have left me completely alone.

Today he will come again. Ef, the man in the mask. To look for defects, to ask nasty little questions, to start digging about inside me like I'm a heap of common property.

And then I'm going to set myself on fire. Then they'll all see how a wonder-sunshine burns!

I'm sure you want to understand. If you are me, you'll definitely want to understand… I always really wanted to.

I'll tell you everything I know. Because you need to know.

Because I need to know. I will need to know everything.

My mother was called Hanna. I won't say that she's gone because we're not allowed to talk like that. Because, of course, she is still around. She has continued to live on… All I'll say is – I miss her. I miss her like she's gone – ever since she went into the Pause Zone at the Festival for Assisting Nature.

Hanna was her temporary name. Her eternal name is Mia 31, but I don't like it, it sounds like a type of washing machine. She didn't like it either and always introduced herself as Hanna. What name she likes to introduce herself by nowadays, I don't know. And I don't want to know.

She had incredibly pale skin. Pale and so clear it was almost transparent, which is rare for globaloids.

Her eyes were velvety, like the wings of a tortoiseshell butterfly.

At night she would always sing me a lullaby – you know, that old one about animals, it's still part of the range of programs in A Living Childhood. It gets installed at, I think, about age three. You'll probably remember it:

Sleeping are the calves and lambs,
Sleeping are the newts, the rams,

Cows and lizards, hares and sheep,
Dreadful dreams disturb their sleep.
Dreams of waters dark and slow,
Dreams of bitter, future woe.
Dreams of drifting, crewless boats,
Dreams of floating, faceless ghosts...

I was already nearly nine, but I always asked for that song. I refused to go to sleep without it. Hanna said that I shouldn't, that big boys like me don't need songs, big boys like me shouldn't really live with their mothers anymore, they should live in a boarding house, and there aren't any lullabies there.

'But I live with you,' I said.

'You do,' Hanna agreed.

'So sing then.'

And she sang. She had a beautiful voice:

Wolves are howling to the sky,
Cats are weeping where they lie,
Snoring horses, groaning sheep,
Dreadful dreams disturb their sleep.
Dreams of waters dark and slow,
Dreams of bitter, future woe.
On the shore so cold and high,
Beasties sleep and time runs by...

'You're not going to send me to a boarding house are you?' I asked.

'I'm not,' Hanna said.

'And we're going to be together forever?'

'That doesn't happen, Darling,' Hanna said.

She didn't call me by my name – later I realised why: it frightened her, it forced her to look into the abyss, into that nothingness, into the white emptiness surrounded by the black circle... She didn't call me Zero. She just called me Darling.

'Why?' I snivelled. 'Why can't we be together forever? We're immortal, aren't we? Let's just agree: when one of us di...'

'Darling!'

'I meant to say, when one of us temporarily ceases to exist, then the other one will just look for them, and everything'll be like it was before.'

'It doesn't work like that, Darling,' Hanna shook her head.

It doesn't work like that. She turned out to be right. I didn't believe she was right until Ef agreed to take me to see her. Turns out I had no need for the fat little girl that she had changed into. And she had absolutely no need for me either.

No one needs anyone, pal. You don't mind me calling you 'pal'? I hope you don't think it's over-familiar? At the end of the day I'm talking to myself. Or maybe I'm not talking to anyone at all...

'Tell me you love me,' I asked Hanna.

'There's no point, Darling.' She suddenly went tense all over.

'Why?'

'I've already told you. The Living is full of love and every part of him loves every other part equally.'

'So does that mean you love me?'

And she said:

'Yes.'

And then she added so quietly I could barely hear her:

'I love you as much as I love any other part of the Living.'

'You love me as much... as much as you love crazy Matthew who goes down the street shouting?'

She didn't say anything. I got angry.

'Tell me you love me more than anyone!'

She didn't say anything.
'So sing then.'
And she sang:

On the shore so cold and high,
Beasties sleep and time runs by...
Time runs by and night descends,
We can't help our little friends.

On the day when I saw her for the last time, on the day when Hanna went to her last Festival, she said that I should go to bed on my own. She said that she'd be back too late. And so she'd sing me the song earlier.

For the cats and for the deer,
For them all the end is near.
Only you can slumber there,
Smile, and know no care,
For, my Living, little guy,
You will never, ever die.

'No death!' she said as she left.
'No death!' I replied.
'I love you,' she said. 'I love you more than anyone.'
She was thirty-four.

For a whole year more she had the right to visit the Reproduction Zone at the Festival for Assisting Nature. The reproductive period officially ends at thirty-five.

It would have been another eleven years before she would start receiving messages from the local Centre for Population Control with the gentle suggestion that she visit the Pause Zone. Messages like that start coming at forty-five.

It would have been another sixteen years before she would start receiving messages from the local Centre for Population

Control with the strict recommendation that she visit the Pause Zone. Messages like that start coming at fifty.

She could have lived for another twenty-six years until a Compulsory Pause. This measure applies to those who are over sixty and do not want to comply with the suggestions voluntarily.

For a whole year more she had the right to visit the Reproduction Zone at the Festival for Assisting Nature.

But she went to the Pause Zone.

She did it because of me. Because they hadn't taken me into the boarding house and had left me with her. Because she had sung me songs. Because she loved me more than anyone.

The Man with No Face

Nothing extravagant, that's what he had thought. An SPO officer's living quarters should be strictly functional.

'Strictly functional,' that's what he had said to the decorator, 'Stylish minimalism.' He did it all up in *socio* tones: walls à la inviz and safety furniture in the colours 'available' and 'busy'. There wasn't a lot of furniture, Ef had insisted on that, just what was absolutely necessary. The only extravagance was in the bathroom – an expansive terrarium for his Pet. But his bedroom was pretty much empty – just a soft aquasleep floor-covering with maximum surface tension. Ef had preferred maximum for a long time now, because, maybe other people don't like it, but personally he was not a fan of waking up with the feeling that he was stuck up to the waist in his own floor. Not to mention the fact that sleeping on something flat is better for the spine…

…He sits on the floor, pulls off his mirror mask, realises that he still needs to get up, go and wash in cold water, change the bandages on his hands which had got soaked in the downpour and feed his Pet – but a dream still shackles his arms and legs. It's not even a dream, but the sort of germ of a dream. He's dreaming of a river. Or something that was a river once, or is going to become one…

> *39:50*
> *independent connection is not operational*
>
> *39:51*
>
> *39:52*

…Animals appear at the river, or maybe they're plants – something alive, but not yet fully formed, he tries to give them all shape…

39:53

39:54

39:55
independent connection is not operational

He thinks: his dream should be like a garden where he can grow miraculous herbs...

39:56

He thinks: his dream should be like mud and sand which he can make into a castle...

39:57

He thinks: someone is watching him. But at that moment he lets the thought go and it floats off downstream...

39:58

39:59

He thinks: he doesn't have much time and the river is flowing fast...

He thinks about the weed in the river...

40:00
...compulsory connection to socio *is underway...*
we're back!

It was like the river, his thoughts, and the weeds, were all clumped together and chucked away. As if a tablecloth had been yanked away, and beneath it there is a mushy termite mound. Hundreds of little oval cells, a porous writhing mass. Ef is inside it. Inside one of the cells.

It clings tightly to him, like a cocoon; Ef twists and turns, instinctively trying to tear through it.

> *ef:* help:

The walls of the box respond to his movements, obedient and moist. They don't break – they stretch. They give way, freeing up space for him. Now he is inside a ball.

> *ef:* settings:
> *ef:* details:
>
> *disconnection from* socio *led to the automatic deletion of personal settings*
> *at the current moment standard* socio *settings are in operation: null interface*
> *restore saved cell settings ef?*

> **yes** no

Ef gets up and goes over the soft floor to the bathroom. Seeing him, the mantis stands on its hind legs and scrapes the wall of the terrarium with his front legs... Ef taps his fingers on the glass – the mantis folds his hands together solemnly, as if praying, begging for food. One leg is bent, broken...

Wash. Wash and drink, drink, drink cold water... He rinses his face and takes a few greedy gulps, but it doesn't get any better. The water seems warm, horribly warm, imperceptible. Ef lifts his head and looks at himself in the mirror: murky drops run down his mirrored mask, which is reflected in the mirror, reflected in the mask, reflected in the mirror...

What the hell? Did I not take my mask off?

He reaches for the soft edge under his chin: the mask doesn't give. Like it's stuck to this skin. He pulls at it again.

invalid request

He pulls with all his might.

it looks like you are trying to do something slightly incorrect
do you want to upload a new userpic for ef?

yes no

The front door turns out to be locked from the outside. He shoves it with his shoulder.

invalid request

it looks like you are trying to do something slightly incorrect

ef: i'm trying to leave the house!!!

...processing request...
invalid request

you are currently in sleep mode
do you want to wake up?
yes *no*

autodoctor: waking up is not recommended at this time of day. for full recuperation of energy you should sleep for another 4.5 hours

do you want to wake up?
yes *no*

warning: socio *continues to operate in sleep mode.*
you can see your list of contacts in socio, *chat in* socio,
receive information in socio *and share it with other*
socio *users. do you want to wake up?*
yes *no*

autodoctor: information about unusual interruptions in
your sleep will be sent to the SPO medical department

do you want to wake up?
yes **no**

caution: you are now in sleep mode...
you have 3 new socio *messages...*

ef: open

1

while you were away from socio, *you missed the daily trailer*

attention: trailer loading...

...Every day after sunset we watch our favourite series: 'The Eternal Killer' and 'Festival Passions'! in the next episode of 'The Eternal Killer': the Butcher's Son has broken free again! He's looking for a new victim! Seventeen-year-old Kate has no idea that she's got an early, painful pause ahead of her! But then, who does... Super-sleuth planetman Pete is already on the trail of the Butcher's Son. He'll stop at nothing to catch this correctee! in the next episode of 'Festival Passions': socio-*designer Don has not appeared in the Reproduction Zone at the appointed time. Disappointed Anne plans to give herself to three strangers. Who knows, maybe one of them will treat her to a world of unforgettable sensations...*

which show would you like to watch today?
The Eternal Killer *Festival Passions Both shows*

2

while you were away from socio *information was collected for you regarding your search request 'cleo' what would you like to do with this information? open in viewing mode* **save in memory**

3

While you were away from socio, *user cleo invited you to meet on* socio

43

what would you like to do with this invitation?
accept invitation *decline invitation*
do you want to meet cleo right now?
yes *no*

Zero

From the age of five I visited the local natural development group: Hanna took me to a shining round building, which looked like a ball of natural cheese, with oval holes for windows. Of course, no one did any developing there, that was just a name. But I liked it. I liked the cheese house. I liked the poor kids, who since birth had had neuron chains that didn't join up right, making it impossible to install SDP, the Standard Development Program, or anything else for that matter. They had ugly faces with big foreheads and tiny chins, they had drooling mouths, they had eyes weeping with sores, but their gaze fascinated me – it was direct and intense, tenacious, not like other people's.

They looked at me in amazement. I was absolutely healthy. I could have had SDP installed without any problems, if it weren't for one 'but'.

I was dangerous. So they wouldn't hook me up to *socio*. At all. The decision was made at the highest level.

I was dangerous. I was surplus to requirements. I was unknown. I might violate something somehow... Of course they didn't mention any of this to Hanna. They just announced that an additional cell would be required for me to be hooked up to *socio*. 'Unfortunately, the creation of an additional cell could lead to a malfunction in *socio*.' I remember her face when she got the message. Or I think I remember, I was very little – in any case, I'm sure that that's what her face looked like at that moment. Frozen, grey. Like it always was when one of the departments contacted her about me.

I liked talking to the other children from the development group – they didn't know who I was. And if they had known, they would not have understood. I liked lying. I lied and said that I had known my incode for ages, that I knew everything about myself, that I had managed to listen in to the adults talking. And I liked listening to them lie too... We told each other cock-and-bull stories about our lives before the Pause, in which we were all heroes and were all awarded the Order of the Living; we chose the most prestigious ranks and professions for ourselves: we were all secretaries of the Council of Eight, architects, entomologists, or farmers or fruit growers.

And so I was a farmer. When they gave out the little boxes of natural food (I don't know how it is now, but at that time children under nine were given a hundred grams of natural animal food produced by a Farmer of Merit in that region, it was part of the Programme for Assisting Nature), I said that the little chunks of meat which were inside, they're actually from my farm, before the pause I had a farm, and I kept pigs there, yep yep, real pigs, I saw them up close, and they weren't scared of me at all...

We all adored these little boxes of happiness with their multi-coloured stamps: 'Region EA 8_milk', 'Region EA8_egg_hen', 'Region EA 8_ meat_pig'...

'You're lyin'!' said a little boy with envy. He had a crooked face and piercing eyes. 'You're lyin', aw uh a-imals are scaye' o' duh Wiving!'

'Gopz,' I said. 'They're not scared of me. They can sense a Farmer of Merit.'

...I liked our teacher; she was elderly, only two years to go until a compulsory pause. She would close her eyes and tells us about the Living and about what the world was like before His birth, in ancient times. She would put on these programmes from A Living Childhood – non-*socio* versions, they don't make them these days – and we'd watch them on an old Crystal Xo, like the ones you get in branches of Renaissance, just three times bigger. Most often she'd switch on Baby Bubbles. You know, about those amazing round creatures – if you're eight, you'll remember – Monkles, Mousie, Duckles, Fishie, Wolfie and the rest – they stand in a circle and dance round, quicker and quicker all the time, until they all get stuck together into one big multi-coloured ball. His name is Livvles. His pink mouth smiles and says, 'There is no death.' And that happens before every episode.

We knew that all the normal kids, all the ones who had had A Living Childhood installed, took part in the circle dance. I hope that you've had better luck than we did. I hope that when you were five you danced around in a circle with Duckles and Mousie, that you merged together with them into a big shining ball… We didn't. We just looked on from the outside. We were outcasts. We couldn't feel like we were part of the sphere. Part of Livvles… But our teacher still reckoned that Baby Bubbles was the best material for us. And the most forgiving. Simple. The shape of a sphere: you'd get it even if you didn't have any neuron chains at all. The shape of a ball. Unity.

I remember one of the episodes very well. It was called 'The Pause: It's Great!' In it Wolfie accidentally eats a poisonous berry and struggles back to her little house and lies down in bed. Her friends come and sit with her. They're all really sad, because Wolfie isn't feeling well. Then Fishie says, 'Do you want us to help you, Wolfie?' Wolfie nods and her friends carry her out to the lake and put her right in the water. She sinks down to the bottom. A couple of big bubbles and then you can't see her anymore. Her friends stand in a circle and smile and start to clap their hands. But Monkles doesn't want to clap. He runs round the lake shouting, 'Where are you, Wolfie?' His friends explain to him that Wolfie has temporarily ceased to exist. Then Monkles cries, bright blue tears fly all around. His friends look around and stand in a circle. They dance round and round until they form one big bright ball. It's Livvles. He explains to Monkles that it's bad to cry at times like this. That it's ugly and stupid. That there is no death. That it's just a pause. He promises that Wolfie will come back and that she will be happy. She will be happy, as if there had never been a poisonous green berry… In the end the friends go back to Wolfie's house, where there is a surprise waiting for them. Wolfie is alive – but she's absolutely tiny, and not blue, but pink... They all hug and turn into a big bright ball... The Pause: it's great. At that moment I believed.

Maybe if they had let me be part of their dance, part of that ball, then I would have kept on believing in it. But I wasn't a part of it, I watched on from outside. And when Hanna went to her last Festival for Assisting Nature, when she went and never came back, I behaved badly. It was ugly and stupid. When I found out that I would not see her again, I turned into that crazy Monkles, I cried and howled, I refused to eat, I hugged her black dress and started biting whenever anyone tried to take it off me... I covered my ears when they said it was only a pause, that Mia 31 would live forever, that there was no reason for tears... I didn't want to hear it. I was unnaturally inconsolable. I exhibited a pathological reaction.

Paradoxical grief. That's what it's called.

At first I liked him. Ef, the man in the mask. He didn't look at me with the same mixture of squeamishness and surprise as the others. I simply couldn't see the way he did look at me. And his voice: it was a mystery what he actually sounded like. All I could hear was an even, automatic buzzing, nothing fake about it, in fact no intonation whatsoever.

I thought: I'd like to hide under a mask like that too.

He sat down next to me and said, 'I know that you don't like hearing that there is no death, that Hanna didn't die, because her incode is eternal, that in nine months' time she will be born again inside some little baby, that eternal rebirth is the secret of the Living...'

He said, 'I'm not going to tell you all that again.'

He said, 'Let's discuss this like grown-ups. But to do that you're going to have to calm down and stop wiping your snot everywhere.'

So I stopped. For the first time since I had been told that she would not be coming back, I washed my face and brushed my hair. And got ready to listen. I thought that he would tell me that there was no reason to hope. That I was right, that there was no point in them comforting me, that she was no more... I wanted him to take away my hope. The hope which they had, despite themselves, planted in me, the hope they tortured me with every day. The hope that she would come back. With a different face. In a different body. I thought that he would tell me: life goes on without her. I was ready to accept it.

But he told me something else. He said, 'You have DCIV. My condolences.'

'No,' I said. 'Gopz. I haven't got an incode at all.' He stretched his mirrored lips into a smile.

'Gopz... But I like you, kid. Don't be scared.' The corners of his mouth slowly slunk back. 'If you like I can read the note on your medical records.'

I nodded. He started right away, without a pause – his connection was excellent.

'"...Intensely expressed negative emotions in regard to pause of his biological mother. Multiple episodes of paradoxical grief. Outbursts of aggression. Attacks do not respond to standard unit of therapeutic methods..."'

He gave off a measured buzzing and I thought: I wonder if he closes his eyes, there, behind his mirrored muzzle? Probably not. Definitely not. Why should he? Of course he doesn't close them. He's a planetman after all. They say they can hold five layers... Or is it six? I wonder how many layers they can hold. Hanna held three with no effort, she had a great memory. I could have taken pride in that, but instead it saddened me. It'd have been better if she shut her eyes, like all normal people. In third layer most of the messages that came to her were about me and I'd have preferred not to see her glassy gaze. It would have been better if she'd shut her eyes. I wonder, before she... did she close her eyes? And what exactly happened there? A pill? An injection? Some sort of gas? An electric shock? Later, after the pause, after the Five Seconds of Darkness, no one remembers how exactly it happens... But everyone is sure that it doesn't hurt.

It doesn't hurt. It doesn't hurt.

She wasn't in any pain. They told me: she wasn't in any pain...

'"...emotional condition could be classed as not conducive to the harmony, peace and integrity of the Living. Likely presence of destructively criminal incode vector (DCIV). Provisional potential threat coefficient (PTC) of 7, which matches the PTCs of persons with DCIV, observed over a period of more than five reproductions..."' He broke off. Something in my expression probably confused him. 'If you don't understand something, ask. You're only nine, but this is a grown-up conversation.'

'How did it happen?' I asked.

'How did they calculate the coefficient? It's simple. They take...'

'No. How did it happen, the... pause? You're a planetman: you must know?'

'Of course I know. And you know too: it doesn't hurt.'

I wanted to scratch his mirrored mask with something sharp. So that there would be a screech: metal on glass. And blood would come out of the slash.

He stood up and took a couple of steps back, as if he'd guessed what I was thinking.

He buzzed:

'I would like to hear questions that are relevant. Relevant to our conversation.'

I suddenly got bored.

'No questions. I understand.'

'What do you understand?'

'They think I'm a criminal.'

'No. Absolutely not!' Judging by his gestures, he was talking very animatedly, however, the buzzing remained just as sleepy. 'Having a destructively criminal incode vector is not a crime. People with DCIV are not criminals. That's very important. What's also important is that some of those people with DCIV – most of them – would immediately become criminals if the Living did not look after itself. It is thanks to this constant care that you're being sent to a House of Correction for people with DCIV.'

I get a ticklish feeling in my stomach, as if someone is stroking me on the inside with a cold little paw.

'Is it forever?' I ask, but it sounds more like a confirmation. The paw starts wriggling again.

'...I've been sentenced to life imprisonment?'

'Three mistakes straight off in such a short question. For one, DCIV is not a sentence. It's more like a diagnosis. A warning sign. You can work on it, it can be fixed. That's why it's called a House of Correction. No one's being punished there, there are no prisoners, there are correctees. They are provisionally innocent and working on staying that way in the future. And finally, imprisonment for life... That's just a joke! What can be for life in your eternal life? I hope that everything'll be sorted after the first pause.'

The first... I suddenly wanted to bite him. Hard, so I could hear the crunch of his shattered bone.

'You think I don't know that my first pause is probably going to be my last? Why are you lying? Don't you know who I am?' I almost shouted. I think I stamped my foot.

'No one knows who you are,' he buzzed calmly. 'I don't know either. But I do know something else. If you don't want your first pause to be your last, if you want to stay with the Living, then your anger is unacceptable. The Living is full

of love, and every part of him loves every other part equally...
You have fifteen minutes to gather your things. You will be
picked up. I'll come and visit you every week. There is no
death.'

The Man with No Face

ef: no death
cleo: glap you're here! why didn't you reply
i was worried
ef: sorry
cleo: ok you coming in?

open cleo's cell

ef: enter *cleo's* cell

cleo: you like it?
ef: yeah of course it's nice here
cleo: no i mean the dog you remember it was you
who sent me the link so i hooked myself up a dog

cleo has updated her status: **dog-owner**

she's already learned to get excited when guests come
look how happy she is that you've come do you like
her?
ef: i don't know
probably
have you ever seen real dogs?
cleo: no
oh well fine you don't like her...
all for nothing
it's a really interesting program you can train her
the dog can learn twenty commands and then if
for example you give her a bone then take it away
she bites you it's really funny
want to give her a bone?
ef: no

cleo: fine i'll do it myself

command *heel*
command *chew bone*

tell me about it
ef: what?
cleo: you know
in *socio* there was an announcement that zero
stopped living
you were with him
tell me about it
ef: why do you want to know?
cleo: come on please i want to know
ef: he set himself on fire
cleo: but are you ok?
ef: yeah got a little burned but nothing too bad
cleo: is it true he didn't get reproduced?
ef: it's true
cleo: fofs! and that they're closing his file now?
ef: that's classified
cleo: ok fine
ef: why do you ask?
cleo: you know it's just
ef you're weird somehow
are you sleeping alright?
ef: yeah and you?
cleo: me too
what do you dream about?
ef: i have bad dreams
cleo: like what?
ef: about animals probably cos of your dog
by association
cleo: and what do the animals do?

ef: should i tell you the dream?

cleo: ok then

ef: in my dream i'm at a farm

it's dark i can't see anything i feel my way but i

know that it's a farm because they are screaming

they're frightened i feel their fear i'm frightened too

the thing we're afraid of is here at the farm

it's alive

i have to find it i know it's hiding in one of the cages

i feel for the iron bars with my hands until i find the

right cage

i just know it's there behind the bars

it's quiet it isn't screaming

in my hand i've got a key

i have to open the door and go in inside

i turn the key in the lock...

cleo: no don't go in

ef: i have to

cleo: ef it's just a dream

you shouldn't go in there

you're probably sleeping in an uncomfortable position

got a crick in your neck or something

that's why you're having nightmares

try and move or say something out loud in first layer

so did it work?

ef: yes thanks

cleo: they say that dreams are memories from your

past maybe you once looked for something on a farm

in a different reproduction

some sort of violator

ef: yeah could be

cleo: you were a planetman before weren't you?

ef: and what do you dream about?

cleo: you

such a strange dream
it's like me and you are in first layer at the festival
in the reproduction zone...
we're not wearing any clothes
not even contact underwear or gloves you're hugging
me from behind
and it's nice
weird right?
ef: what's weird?
cleo: you know that in dreams strange things like
that can seem nice
skin to skin
without contact underwear
i can't even imagine it!
sometimes even with underwear i feel awkward
ef: you don't like festivals?
cleo: of course not who does?
i mean what normal people
it's too rough
physiological
of course you need to put up with it for the sake
of the living
but liking that sort of thing when you've got access
to *luxury*?
do you like festivals?
ef: no of course not
but it is our duty
cleo: ok let's not talk about duties now ☺
i've got altogether different plans ☺

connect to luxury...
invite user ef to participate in an act of luxury...
invite other friends to participate in this act? yes **no**

cleo: come to me
i've missed you
ef?
ef: the dog... i don't like it when she's watching
cleo: oh sorry ☹

*temporarily turn off **dog** app*
invite user ef to participate in an act of luxury...
come on ef!!!
ef: accept invitation

Cleo

NB! This entry should not be read by those under the age of 12.

Dog freezes with an expression of shocked reproach on her face. But then she disappears, and at the same time all her accessories are deleted from the cell: bowls, bones, toys, little rugs, a medal, her lead and her collar... It's like she was never even here. I tell myself: as soon as he leaves, I'll reconnect with saved settings. **Dog** won't understand anything, she'll think she just fell asleep then woke up. But all the same I feel bad. She'd already got used to it here. It's like I've kicked her out...

But I've got to be easy-going. Especially now. Ef is losing interest in me. He never responds to my approaches, doesn't say anything, he doesn't trust me anymore.

They say that there's no better way of getting close to someone than in *luxury* mode.

They say that there's no better way of getting to know someone.

His fantasies are usually as simplistic as he is. In the early stages he liked chasing me, he liked to feel like he was pursuing me. He *creates* something like a jungle for the chase, with long, moist inviz-coloured plants. He puts me in a tacky short 'busy'-coloured dress. I agree to be the victim, to be pursued, and run from him through the 'jungle'. I part the grey stalks with my hands, they're slippery and cold and dead – but I breathe life into them. I paint his dull jungle in the brightest shades of 'I'm feeling lucky'. I fill his plants with warm, sticky moisture, I make them move, make them wind round my naked legs and creep up under my dress.

The slippery stalks stroke me as I run... Ef is getting closer, I can hear him breathing hoarsely, he shoves me and I fall down face first. He turns me onto my back and tries to push my legs apart but I squeeze them tightly together. So tightly that the stalks crawling between my legs snap – they're filled with sticky moisture. He leans over me and I look into his mirrored mask...

I never see his face. Not just in *luxury* – never at all. In first layer he has to wear the mask the whole time, but that doesn't really matter, we hardly ever meet in first layer. What matters is that he doesn't have a face in any layer. He has that same mirrored mask in *socio*. It's a mystery. Even if you assume that his face is deformed, in *socio* he could choose any user pic.

What would you have to be like to wear a mirror mask in all layers? What would you have to be like to dress strictly in inviz not only in first layer, but in *socio* too? What would you have to be like to turn your *socio* cell into this copy of a standard first-layer living quarters? I've been to his cell a few times. A bleak place. So bleak it's as if there's no *socio* at all... The first time I even tried to drink water from the tap. To check. Ef watched me and seemed flattered. He said, 'This is my living quarters in first layer – an exact copy.'

He said, 'A real planetman's cell should be strictly functional.'

What must you be like to drag all the poverty and simplicity of first layer into a world where nothing is impossible?

You probably have to be obsessed.

...I never see his face, but in *luxury*, glap, I can choose what I see for myself. I can make a face for him...

Luxury is one of the Living's greatest *socio*-sacraments. A garden of delights in which the fantasies of every participant in the *act* let out shoots and blossom. They get woven together these fantasies, they grow into each other, become one... 'Absolute unity – that's what brings us joy,' as it says in the *socio* settings. 'In *luxury* mode you share all of the five senses you have access to with your friends.'

It doesn't say in the settings that *luxury* mode activates the part of the brain known as the nucleus accumbens. But I know something about it. As long as the *act* is going on, everything you see, hear, smell or touch with your tongue or skin, excites your pleasure centre.

...I make a face for him. It's different every time, once I even tried my own. He doesn't see himself, but he can feel the transformation, he can feel that he is losing control over what is happening. Then he shakes off the face I've made, and takes me to a different location with a jerk. Normally it's something like an abandoned building site or warehouses in some wasteland. Bits of stones, the rusted skeletons of cars, concrete blocks... Solitude. I've named this place the Wastes of Solitude. He leaves me there alone – to wait until he appears.

In first layer (after the *act* I always check the chronometer in the settings) only a couple of minutes pass, but here in *luxury* it lasts a thousand days – that's what his fantasy is, that's his move, and whatever I do, however much I try, I'm not able to reduce this period. Maybe it's all because of the depression which takes hold of me in the Wastes, or something else, I don't know – but here he's always stronger than me. If I make any attempt to leave, to change the setting or wind time forward he responds the same way – he puts me back in the Wastes of Solitude. And starts the count again from zero.

I wait for a thousand days. There's nowhere for me to go, nothing to think about and no one to talk to. I can't invite any of my other real friends to visit me in the Wastes – Ef only likes *luxury* for two, and group *acts* are blocked in his settings. Sometimes I *create* phantom friends for myself in the Wastes. Ef doesn't touch them, doesn't react, but I soon cancel them myself anyway. They always end up somehow flat and boring, with indistinct narrow faces, with movements that aren't quite right and a wooden gait. They give voice to my thoughts with my words, they seem to me like hungry ghosts, heralds of my madness. I *cancel* them and wait for Ef. I'm powerless. I only have one way out – leaving *luxury* mode, one-sided termination of the *act*.

Only once, on one of the first times, did I do it. I broke off the *act*. Ef was furious. He left and didn't appear in my cell for a few months. He said that he couldn't bear it when the *act* was broken off without his knowledge... With arguments, pleading and promises I tempted him back. I swore that I'd be a good girl from now on. That I'd never break off the *act*. That I'd wait for him in the Wastes of Solitude. What else did I have left? *Luxury* is the best way to get close to someone. *Luxury* is the best way to draw out someone's secrets.

I wait for a thousand days. I sit on my haunches and I am filled with a sadness that's so penetrating that it's nice even. I am alone. My phantom friends tell me, 'You're alone here, Cleo.' 'You can't carry on, Cleo.' 'You can't stand this any longer.' 'This is torture.' I close my eyes. I pray, I dream about this monster coming quicker. He is my saviour, my hope, my reward. I'm waiting for him. I can't carry on without him. On the thousandth day he comes, and I let him do whatever he wants to me. He is my lover. My saviour. I am happy to do anything, as long as he stays with me.

And then, while we're still in *luxury*, but after the *act*, when he's knackered, happy and trusting, when he is in sleep mode, that's when I ask him a couple of questions and he answers them. And I note down his answers in a file called 'Nameless'.

...That's what it's normally like, but this time everything is different. There's no jungle, no Wastes, no red dress. We stay in my cell and he hovers about stupidly then sits on the edge of the sofa. He's completely passive, he is expecting something from me – I try to figure out what exactly. I ask him.

cleo: you want me to do everything myself today?
ef: yes

This is a new one. This puts me on my guard.

I make us some jungle with long, moist plants in all shades of 'feeling lucky'. I put on a short, 'busy' dress... Something's wrong with *luxury*. His reaction is paradoxical. I don't feel any pleasure from his side. He carefully probes an oily liana, covered in sap, with his finger. He *cancels* it and pulls his hand away sharply when the plant disappears. He turns his face towards me, examines my dress. I can feel the hem creeping downward, the synthetic cloth catching on my uneven skin, tickling my legs. It's nice... He laughs suddenly. He changes the cut and the colour and the material. Now I'm wearing a long black silk dress.

So we stand there. Among the lianas, in the bright jungle. He's obviously not planning on chasing me. He grudgingly, lazily, *cancels* another couple of plants...

I say to him,

> *cleo:* do you want to go to the wastes of solitude?
> *ef:* lovely name
> *cleo:* thanks i thought of it myself
> i think it suits it
> *ef:* yes i like it
> i want to go to the wastes please
> *cleo:* you want to go to the wastes yourself?!
> *ef:* yeah

Finally I realise. He wants to swap roles: not be the torturer, but the victim. He wants to feel what it's like for me, sick bastard.

> **Subject: chain letter**
> *You want a dog. A real, living dog in first layer. Follow Zero, and animals will love you like they love him* ☺
> **!warning! this may be spam**
> *mark this message as spam?*
> **yes** *no*

I form the Wastes – I don't manage to reproduce it absolutely accurately, I can see myself that certain details are missing, but overall it's the same. He looks around with interest, he likes his new role. I say 'wait' and leave him there for a thousand days.

Where does he normally go when he leaves me here alone? I don't know; personally, I *create* a fantastic little house for myself with a swimming pool on the roof. And there on the roof I install a telescope pointed at the Wastes of Solitude... I lie in the water, my arms and legs thrown out like a starfish. Hundreds of ticklish streams envelop me like cold, restless tentacles. I enjoy the touch of these tentacles. I enjoy the sensation of weightlessness. And I like the fact that I have a hostage. From time to time I get out of the water and observe him through the telescope.

He's sitting on the ground, his head in his hands, rocking slightly from side to side. He looks despondent. He doesn't try to change anything, or cancel it or reconfigure it... I enjoy the feeling of power. I like keeping him there. I say to myself: it's not like I've got a cruel streak. Far from it. I'm full of mercy, like any part of the Living. It's just that *luxury* is designed to excite my pleasure centres.

On day three I get bored and I just wind forward a couple of weeks – just for me – hoping to discover some interesting shifts in the Wastes. I look through the telescope: what I see exceeds my expectations. The Wastes are not there anymore; in their place is a river with muddy banks overgrown with brown shrubs. Ef is sitting by the river, leaning back on some sort of dark formless heap which I can't make out. He holds his face in his hands, something about it has changed, but for the first few seconds I can't figure out what. Then I realise – his pale skin is showing through his fingers. He's taken off his mask. For the first time in all this time he's taken off his bloody mask.

I cancel my little house with the swimming pool and the telescope. I delete the thousand-day waiting period. I can't miss this. I go up to him, squat down next him, and carefully take his hands from his face.

He doesn't resist. His face is the face of a child, but it's changing constantly. He seems like a twelve-year-old boy, then an eighteen-year-old girl, then a complete baby. He has full, disconsolate lips and eyes the colour of bitter chocolate. He's crying.

I suddenly see what the shapeless heap he's leaning against is. The body of an elephant. The elephant is not alive. The beads of tears have frozen in his dull amber eyes.

You get the feeling that Ef is weeping for this unliving elephant. You get the feeling that he can't control his metamorphoses. The only thing which doesn't change in his face is the expression of grief. He's whimpering quietly and inconsolably, almost to the point of tears. His shoulders are shaking. They're so broad, they don't fit at all with his swollen, fluctuating child's face.

Something's wrong with *luxury*. I don't feel any pleasure anymore. I feel like I'm hurting a child's feelings.

I say to him,

> *cleo:* ef, what is it, ef, calm down!

His chocolate eyes open wide, and he looks at me in shock: it seems like he's only just noticed that he's not alone anymore. His face freezes – somewhere between eight and twelve, then rapidly starts to mature, simultaneously becoming overgrown with that familiar mirrored encrustation.

> *ef:* you left me here on my own
> *cleo:* you've done that to me lots of times
> *ef:* awful feelings. i was scared like when i was a kid.
> like i was of the five seconds of darkness
> *cleo:* why that elephant ?
> *ef:* i don't know. i wasn't feeling well

He hurriedly *cancels* the elephant.

> *cleo:* tell me, how did Zero die?

I can physically feel his mistrust.

> *ef:* why do you want to know?
> *cleo:* everyone wants to know. natural curiosity
> *ef:* you're lying
> *cleo:* you're insulting me
> *ef:* i can see right through you
> *cleo:* and what do you see?
> *ef:* a ray
> *cleo:* ?
> *ef:* the directed leo-lot ray

From surprise, almost as a reflex, I become inviz. As if an invisibility cloak will protect me... He smiles. He reaches out his hand and calmly feels my invisible face. He kisses me politely on the forehead with his mirrored lips, and silently, without saying goodbye, leaves *luxury*. I'm left alone. I feel fear pouring down me in icy streams, all over my body, and it's like it's coming from the place on my forehead which he touched with his lips. The Leo-Lot ray... He's figured it out. Of course he's figured it out. He is going to destroy me. Lock me up in a House of Correction until the end of time.

Only in *luxury* can fear be so thrilling. Somewhere by my solar plexus the streams of fear get warm and pour down past my stomach in thick, hot waves... I decide to stay on in *luxury* for a little while to enjoy this feeling of fear.

It's not like I'll get any pleasure from it when I'm out of *luxury*.

The Scientist

Document No. 23 (leaseholder's private entry) –
access through SPO guest entry

3rd September 451 A.V.

Yesterday I visited the regional Farm with a group.

I don't like going out to the Farm. Two trips a year would be, I know, an unrealisable dream for most people, but personally I prefer working in the lab. I've never asked Lot if he likes it at the Farm: we rarely discuss things that aren't directly connected to our project, but a few times I've noticed something in his expression, something... like disgust. So I think that he's also less than thrilled about these trips.

It's all about fear. You can sense it from a few kilometres away, in your nostrils, in the pores of your skin and in your hair; the air is saturated with fear, like an electric shock, and there are no words to describe its nightmarish essence. The closer you get to the Farm, the more the fear thickens, until, finally, it turns into a warm stench cloud which is very easy to describe – the evaporated fumes of animal urine, animal blood and sweat... We wait by the gate in the wall. It's made of concrete, four metres high and half a metre thick. I can't imagine that any of the animals here would suddenly take it on themselves to try to get over this barrier – but nevertheless, according to the Farmer, there have been incidents where their instincts stopped working, and, as they tried to escape, cows and goats hit the wall, ramming into it on the run, again and again, until... until it was all over. So now as well as the wall they've installed an electromagnetic barrier too.

We wait for the Farmer to let us in, he turns off the electromagnetic barrier for a short time and opens the gates.

And lets us onto the domain of death. The domain of the mortal.

Lot and I always tell the correctees that these visits are part of their nature therapy. Studying nature, contact with living creatures unlike ourselves is an ancient form of relaxation. An extremely effective method for persons with destructively criminal incodes: it helps them develop empathy for the weak. Promotes kind thoughts. Creates a good constructive background... That's what we always say.

But it's all lies.

In actual fact we bring the correctees to the Farm to arouse entirely different emotions in them. Persons with DCIV are often inclined to perceive an animal as a potential victim (which can be explained by the fact that the animals fundamentally behave like victims), which is to say, an animal is, in this case, a PIA – a potential incitement to aggression. We test the correctees for cruelty. We want to know to what extent the cruel tendencies of those that gave a positive result last time round have progressed in half a year. And whether any such tendencies have emerged in those who reacted negatively before.

For thirty minutes the correctees have the opportunity to observe the animals through the metal bars. The correctees are sure that their *socio* has been switched off for the duration of their visit to the Farm. We tell them that this is necessary for their therapy to be maximally effective, so that they are not distracted from visual contact with the animals in first layer. This is true to a certain extent: the correctees can't be distracted from first layer – we block all the signals going in. But second layer is active. We record all the signals coming out in second layer. We calculate their potential threat coefficient, PTC, in this specific situation and determine the nature of their reaction to a PIA.

So that I will understand later on, I'll list a few examples.

The standard signals for a low PTC are like this:

> *'a real chicken!'*
> *'the goat is ugly'*
> *'the pig isn't pink like on the pictures, but dark-inviz'*
> *'it's lucky i'm in the house of correction, other people don't get to go to the farm'*
> *'the dog is drooling'*
> *'after the pause i'm going to tell everyone i saw a real live horse'*
> *'i heard that before the nativity of the Living people and animals were friends'*

Those are negative reactions to a PIA.

With an average PTC we observe transitional reactions. Characteristic for this condition are the following signals:

> *'why do they squeal like that?'*
> *'what is death?'*
> *'i wonder if they know that they don't get reproduced?'*
> *'the Living is stronger than these creatures'*
> *'of course, they're afraid of the Living'*
> *'i heard that before the nativity of the Living people killed animals, cut them up into pieces and sold them in shops'*
> *'when i was little i was given little boxes of meat made at this farm. i wonder if the Farmer killed the animals himself, or whether some machine did it, or if the animals stopped living by themselves?'*

High PTC, examples of positive reactions to a PIA:

> *'squeal, squeal, squeal, squeal louder!'*
> *'i wish they'd let me grab that bunny by the ears'*
> *'tear off their fur…'*

'if i cut off the tail the blood would flow for ages'

High PTC, examples of maximally positive reaction:

'i want to strangle the dog'
'i want to throw stones at them'
'i want to tie the pig to the bars and jab it with a stick'

On contact with the animals some correctees produce mediated signals as a reflex action. They tend to be quotes from the Book of Life or from various educational and developmental programs:

'the cow gives milk'
'snoring horses, groaning sheep'
'time runs by and night descends, we can't help our little friends'
'the Living is the friend and protector of the animals'
'for the cats and for the deer, for them all the end is near'
'our poor unfortunate brothers'

Mediated signals prevent us from accurately determining the nature of the reaction to the PIA. In the absence of other signals, we classify this reaction as transitional, but we take into account that it could also belong to either the negative or positive type.

The above is just a short professional digression. I'm trying, as I did in my previous reproductions, to pay a little attention to scientific aspects. I hope that at eight years old digressions like this will be interesting and useful and help me make my choice of specialisation...

Now I'll go back to yesterday's visit to the Farm.

Lot and I had brought a group of fifteen correctees. Among them was Zero – the very same. The person with no incode.

I don't know if I was expecting something special, but he turned out to be a completely ordinary eleven-year-old boy. Nothing remarkable about his appearance: in the evening when I went through what happened I tried to imagine him and I couldn't. I only got flashes of different fragments of his face, like pieces of a picture in third layer that's not loading. A lock of dark hair on his forehead. Narrow hazel eyes. Frowning brows. It was his first visit to the Farm.

He kept himself apart from the group, but when people talked to him his reaction was entirely friendly. Lot and I registered only one vaguely positive signal from one of the teenage correctees (*naked tail like an earthworm if i cut it off i wonder if it would crawl off or not*), the majority of signals were standard (*rats are gross*) or mediated (*before the nativity of the Living rats lived in people's houses and carried all sorts of diseases*).

From a distance of several metres correctee Zero looked at the rats with something like interest, but what real conclusions can you make about someone when your only basis is observation in first layer?! Zero is not connected to *socio*. As a part of the Living, I realise that this is correct. I recognise the full extent of the danger of connecting him... But as a scientist I'm full of regret that I don't have the chance to observe his behaviour in deeper layers... With all my respect for the Council of Eight's decision, by not connecting Zero to *socio* we have, in essence, turned down a chance of understanding him, and, consequently, of controlling him.

Then we let the group get up closer to the cages. The rats, as always, shrank back against the back wall, huddling together into one huge tangled ball, which trembled, squeaked and bit at itself. Several wounded rats fell out of this ball onto the bottom of the cage and at that moment froze and curled up, paralysed by fear. Then one of them convulsed and ceased living. None of the correctees, luckily, understood – we didn't register any signals of alarm, for the most part they thought that the motionless animal was '*tired*'. Except perhaps Zero... if anyone might have guessed what happened to the rat, then it would have been him. He looked at it, only at it, with an expressionless stare. Even when everyone else went over to the cage with the cows, he stayed standing there. I called him over but he didn't even turn round – I had to lead him away by the hand. His hand was cold and damp, and I barelymanaged to put up with touching it. At that moment the thought struck me that I'd missed something important. Something was wrong, not how it should be, when he was standing there and looking at the rats. Something was wrong with the rats. I led him by the hand and tried to think about it, but disgust stopped me concentrating and the thought slipped away.

I realised what was going on only when we got to the dogs.

I know: what is a dog? Something very different from the creature whose image opens along with the file 'Ancient domestic animals' after you have had A Living Childhood installed. Something very different from the thing I can download in a *socio*-game. One ear hanging down sweetly, the other standing up, its face tilted to one side inquisitively, the shaggy tail making circles in the air... That's just a reconstruction. If you believe the documentary evidence that has come down to us, this is more or less what a dog looked like before the birth of the Living. I repeat – if you believe it.

Real dogs are different. Gruff beasts with bared teeth, ears sticking close to their heads, wrinkled noses, and lumps of dried foam around their dirty mouths. And the stink of them. I can't imagine how once they could have lived in houses, how mankind managed to breathe the same air as them... After visiting the dog cage we always give out special respirators to the correctees, but even they can't entirely block out the unpleasant odours... For this reason correctees rarely go up close to the cage. Zero went up close.

He went right up to the bars, and then I, at last, realised what was going on. I remembered that ball of rats, which had fallen apart and crawled off in different directions when that little boy had been left alone with them. I remembered the cows and the pigs – so subdued and quiet (before I hadn't thought that they were even capable of being silent). I looked at the dogs... They were not afraid of him.

But if the rats, cows and pigs simply ignored him, then these dogs – however fantastical this may sound – actually made contact with him.

Yesterday, in the heat, their smell was particularly disgusting. The correctees kept their distance from the cage. All of them, except Zero. He stood, his face pressed against the bars, and watched the dogs wheezing and barking manically, as if they were trying to cough out their stinking fear which was tearing them up from the inside. Then he started to whistle something, the lullaby about animals, I think – and then I saw it. One of the dogs leapt forward towards the bars, to where Zero was, and froze half a metre away in a strange pose: its spine bent, the front half of its body pressed against the ground, but the back legs at full stretch and the tail up. Like it was trying to bow to him. Like it was begging him for mercy.

Unbelievable. He stretched his hand out to it through the bars and it came up to him. It sniffed his fingers and then went frightened back to the pack. I had to lead him away again, but I couldn't bring myself to touch his hand. Dog saliva glistened on his right palm.

Lot and I carried out a disinfection. Then we forwarded a message about what had happened to the SPO and the Service for Assisting Nature. We requested all the data about similar cases, we called up all the available archives in fourth and even fifth layers, but, as I was expecting, no one had ever witnessed a reaction like this from an animal.

Animals have always been afraid of the Living. That's a given, it's axiomatic. The animals were not frightened of correctee Zero. They didn't recognise him as the Living. What can we conclude from this?

There are actually two options.

Option No. 1. Zero is a neoplasm. A sort of a poor-quality, alien cell in the organism of the Living. In this instance, his confinement to a House of Correction is a completely natural step and a very sensible measure. In the human body alien cells are also put 'in quarantine' and isolated by the immune system. Then, ideally, if the cell cannot prove that it's harmless, it commits apoptosis – self-destruction, so it doesn't harm the organism. If this does not happen, the outsider has to be destroyed by the immune system's 'army'. When the immune system is weak, the outsider wins. It multiplies, infects healthy tissue, takes honest soldiers and 'drives them mad'... In our case there is no risk: the organism of the Living is healthy and strong, and the poor child is weak and confused. And anyway it's just a metaphor.

Option No. 2. Zero is a useful reverse mutation. Maybe he's carrying a retrogene and the animals recognise him as 'ancient man', whom they weren't afraid of. The proliferation of this mutation might be very useful for the Living (in which case Zero's isolation is a dubious measure). First, it opens up the long-awaited possibility of the domestication of animals. Second, we should note: correctee Zero has a phenomenal first-layer memory – according to surviving sources, just such a memory was a distinguishing feature of 'ancient man'. Bereft of *socio*, and therefore, of all the educational programs installed as he grows up, Zero nonetheless demonstrates that he is extraordinarily well-informed about various things; he can read, write, and knows how to count; the speed of his reactions and his ability for logical and abstract thought are outstanding. If this mutation were to proliferate we could expect an increase in the extra-*social* intellect of the Living even in the near future, and, consequently, an increase in interest in first layer. Interest in first layer would be a natural stimulus for the reclamation of new territories, the further development of engineering and instrument-making, the transformation and study of the environment, travel, personal appearance, physical fitness, and the proliferation of the species. An active first-layer life would help us solve the problem of early-onset obesity, thrombosis, strokes and heart attacks.

And finally – if I can dream a little bit? – extra-*social* curiosity might reopen the Living's path to the stars. Before the Nativity ancient man was actively pursuing expansion into space; it is very regrettable that this sphere remains absolutely undeveloped in our time. Who knows? Maybe the Living is not alone in the Universe...

...But I've got sidetracked.

I will strive to have Zero included in the list of correctees taking part in our experiment. In his case incarnational retrospection using the Leo-Lot ray may give tremendous results. I suggest that we simply must do this. To figure out what he means for us: 'harm' or 'benefit'. I really do hope that the boy has come to us bearing gifts.

As far as I can tell, this Ef, the SPO officer looking after Zero, is prepared to be of assistance to us in this endeavour. He was very impressed by our report about the visit to the Farm, and is petitioning for his charge to be included on the list.

Zero

I was eleven when the dog at the Farm licked my hand. The scientist who was there at the time said that there had never been anything like this anywhere. The scientist was called Leo. He was glowing with pleasure all over.

He seemed to be disappointed by my reaction: I was not happy.

He tried to gee me up a bit; I probably seemed a bit slow to him. 'Animals are afraid of the Living,' he explained slowly, as if I was mentally retarded. 'We are trying to change that situation, but so far without success. That dog... she went up to you on her own. A unique case. Do you realise? Your case is unique!'

I realised that my case was unique. I'd realised that long before my conversation with Leo, long before the Farm. But there, at the Farm, I realised that I was screwed. That dog: it was like it had marked me. Left the sticky mark of death on my hand.

Animals are afraid of The Living: it's always veeb that way. Since the Nativity, That's what our elderly teacher said in the natural development group. I remembered that lesson well.

'...Nine months before the Nativity, at the beginning of the Great Reduction, all over the world the human population fell into headlong decline. Epidemics, wars and natural disasters ended thousands of lives every day. A panic began: people did not understand that... the Reduction did not mean their destruction at all, but... the opposite, it heralded the birth of Eternal... the Living. Everyone was still mortal, they didn't know that soon... they would become part of Him...'

I noticed that she was having some difficulty talking: she was short of breath. It was like she didn't have enough air, as if she was talking on the run:

'...And we all know don't we – all together now! – the number of the Living...is unchanging, the Living...is...three billion livings, and neither by one...'

She was constantly quietly clearing her throat. She was nervy, although she tried not to show it. It was her last day before a compulsory pause.

'...shall it be diminished, nor by one shall it... be increased, for... eternal rebirth is... the secret of life...'

She could have taken a day off, but she came in anyway. She told us it was a farewell lesson. That she was being transferred to a different region.

She did not tell her pupils about the pause: she was ashamed to have lasted right up to a compulsory, and didn't want to be a bad example. But we knew. In the last month her health had deteriorated a lot, it was as if she had suddenly got old and started mixing up her layers. It looked like she had the beginnings of introverbalia: at break times a few times we heard her talking out loud in deep layers. That's how we found out about her pause. She sat at her desk, hunched over, resting her head on the glass table top. Her face was reflected palely in the glass and it was like she was talking to her reflection.

'...Before the pause you have the right to take a holiday of one to seven days in duration. Do you want to take a holiday? Yes. No,' she said in a metallic voice that was not her own. 'No,' now in her own, ordinary voice. 'Are you sure? Yes. No.' 'Yes. I don't need a holiday. It's only a pause, right?' 'Correct. It is only a pause. But any living has the right to take a holiday in order to get their affairs in order at this stage in their life.' 'I prefer to go to work. It's easier that way. It takes my mind off it.' 'Takes your mind off what? Are you experiencing unpleasant emotions regarding the pause? Yes. No.'

She fell silent. Then started rapping her words out metallically again: 'Are you experiencing fear regarding the pause? Yes. No.'

She sat up straight and covered her face with her hands. She sat there a little while in silence, then opened her hands slightly and then slapped them back, as if she were trying to hide. As if she thought that she would become invisible if she couldn't see. But the thing she was trying to protect herself from was inside her. Barely audibly, her face nestled in her hands, she replied, 'No. Of course not. It's only a pause.'

...At that goodbye lesson she was telling us about animals. She snatched at the air with her mouth. Her every word was seared on my memory.

'Nine months before the Great Reduction mankind extermi-nated practically all of its livestock and pets, as well as a large number of wild animals and birds. Scientists of the time based their argument on the mistaken hypothesis that animals were carrying deadly viruses, leading to human pandemics... By the time of the Nativity of the Living many breeds of animals and birds had disappeared forever from the face of the Earth. The numbers of those still left were reduced to critical levels. Surviving individuals migrated to mountainous and forested zones, uninhabited by man. They were pursued and there... The new-born Living stopped the senseless process of the extermination of innocents as soon as He became conscious, as soon as it became clear that the number of the Living was henceforth unchanging forever. Now the Living is the friend and protector of the animals. But He is forced to pay for other people's mistakes, mistakes made when He did not yet exist. Animals' fear of the people that exterminated them was too strong; this fear is passed down at the level of genetic memory. Unfortunately animals are not capable of realising that the all-merciful Living has come to replace prehistoric man. Unfortunately, animals are afraid of the Living. Afraid of you and me. But in time the Living will probably manage to tame them and win their trust...'

I remember after the lesson I went over to her just to say 'no death'.

'No death,' the teacher nodded and closed her eyes, and I noticed how limp her eyelids were and how they shivered weakly. Like moths. Like the crumpled wings of a butterfly that lives only for a day. I should have just gone, but I suddenly got the urge to cheer her up, to say something life-affirming, something reassuring.

'The Pause – it's great,' I informed her. 'The old and weak acquire new life. You will become young and strong again...'

She suddenly burst out laughing, so unexpectedly and shrilly that I got goose bumps. Through her laughter she said, 'Do you know why animals are afraid of the Living?'

I thought she had probably decided to give me a follow-up test and I answered: yes, I know. It's because animals are simply incapable of understanding that ancient man has been replaced by the all-merciful Living...

'Lies,' she said. 'It's because they do understand. Animals can see the Living. A three-billion-headed monster, eternally young and strong. Killing its old so that the young can grow up in their place...'

She sniggered again and I noticed that there was something wrong with her eyes. Her pupils narrowed and then widened – not simultaneously, but one after the other.

'...And insects?' She raised her voice. 'Bees, wasps, ants and termites – why aren't they afraid of us?'

'Because ancient man did not exterminate insects...'

'No, that's not why...!' Her pupils suddenly froze, with one big and the other small, and she calmly and gently said, 'It looks like you are trying to do something slightly incorrect. Do you want to switch to sleep mode? Yes. No... Automatic transfer to sleep mode is underway...'

I watched her sleeping peacefully, her head lolling to one side. Then Hanna came and took me away, saying 'Teacher's just tired.'

I remembered that lesson well. Animals are afraid of the Living.

There, at the Farm, the dog licked my hand, but I wasn't happy about it. I had gone up so close to the cage because I wanted them to be scared of me. I wanted them all to be scared of me. Because animals are afraid of the Living.

Report

(Transcript of conversation between correctee Foxcub and SPO officer, dated 17.07.471 A.V.; extract)

SPO officer: You were a witness to a very serious incident. You must tell us everything that you saw and heard that day on the Green Terrace. In as much detail as possible.

Foxcub: I haven't done anything wrong. Smin, it wasn't me! I've got nothing to do with it.

SPO officer: No one is accusing you of being an accomplice. You're just a witness. For now. But the harmony and stability of the Living depends on your answers. Do you want to help the Living?

Foxcub: Yes. I really love the Living and would do anything for it. Smin.

SPO officer: I'm glad you say so. You're right. You're a good correctee and I'm sure that soon you'll be entirely corrected. Plus, I see we've got a celebrity here today! I saw your performance on FreakTube.

Foxcub: Really?

SPO officer: Of course. And the other planetmen saw it too. Your singing was great... So, tell us what happened!

Foxcub: I heard shouting from the Available Terrace. And... I got a bit scared, but I was curious and I asked my friends what was going on up there...

SPO officer: Could you be a bit more precise there. Which friends did you ask? How did you ask them?

Foxcub: I asked in *socio*, you know, in second layer, I mass-mailed our whole group.

SPO officer: Did you get any replies?

Foxcub: Yeah, Triton and Gerda replied.

SPO officer: The text of the replies?

Foxcub: Shall I look in my memory?

SPO officer: Yes.

Foxcub: Triton: 'that psycho o is planning on destroying himself and looks like he's also planning on burning down our termite mound freak'. And Gerda... Gerda said... Sorry, I've wiped her reply.

SPO officer: Why?

Foxcub: We had a row yesterday. Because she said that the Planetman off of The Eternal Murderer is acting like an idiot and can't even find the crim when he's right under his nose, but I really like the Planetman, I reckon he's great... So me and Gerda were fighting and I got mad and *deleted forever* our whole chat history. Is that really bad?

SPO officer: Never mind, it's your personal cell, you have the right to delete whatever you want from it. Just tell us what Gerda said.

Foxcub: I don't remember.

SPO officer: In your own words.

Foxcub: I, honestly, don't remember... Fofs! I don't know how to put it in my own words. I never remember messages, they're all in my memory anyway... I haven't done anything wrong, have I? I'm not the only person who doesn't remember them.

SPO officer: Don't worry, you haven't done anything wrong. Just tell us what happened next.

Zero

'…Because there are no criminals in the world of the Living!'

'…Because they keep us in a House of Correction!'

'…Because each one of us can be corrected!'

Three 'becauses'. Every day, morning and evening, in unison. I fell asleep and woke up to this refrain. And I was myself a part of that choir: I shouted out the answers to the questions resounding in their heads. Cracker said the questions out loud for me. I never asked him to, he just liked doing it.

'Why are there no crimes in the world of the Living?' he would whisper animatedly.

…Because there are no criminals in the world of the Living…

'Why are there no criminals in the world of the Living?' he flashes his eyes in surprise.

Because they keep us in a House of Correction…

'Why is a destructively criminal incode vector not a sentence?' he giggled ticklishly in my ear.

…Because each of us can be corrected…

He liked it. He liked the questions themselves. But his responses were different. Like the other correctees he hadn't had the Living Fingers educational program installed, but he had learned to write with his hands in first layer and scrawled out his answers on scraps of paper:

'Because in the world of the Living crimes are referred to as "maintaining harmony".'

'Because in the world of the Living the criminals are in power.'

'Because the day will come when we break free.'

Cracker was two years older than me. A big forehead and small, dull eyes. Slender limbs, sharp at the joints like a spider. His right eyelid twitched like he was winking all the time. No one ever went up close to him. Everyone knew that he was crazy. I knew too, but it didn't put me off.

In fact they recoiled from him for another reason. They were afraid. They were almost as afraid of him as they were of me. Everyone knew why Cracker was there in the House of Correction. Everyone knew what it was he'd done a long time ago, many pauses back. I also knew, but that didn't put me off. I was the only one who would talk to him and listen to him. He didn't present the slightest threat to me. Nor I to him.

This sense of mutual harmlessness – that's what united us. During the day we usually stuck together. At night we slept in neighbouring beds and the two other beds – on both sides of us – were empty. We were not friends because we were both outcasts. We were friends because we weren't afraid of each other.

To start with it was difficult for me to sleep next to Cracker. He would lie on his back, pass out almost immediately and start snoring loudly straightaway. I needed a lot more time to fall asleep and I never managed to switch off before the noise started. Sometimes I lay for hours without sleeping and in the morning I would be exhausted and unrested. Later I learned to get into the rhythm of his breathing. Rumbling was replaced with silence at even intervals. I would pretend that his snoring was a piston moving up and down, blocking and then freeing up my way through to sleep. I learned to scurry forward until the piston came down for the next time. I loved this nightly game and got used to it, like it was a lullaby.

Once I started telling him about Hanna. About how we lived together, how she sang, and how she left. He didn't ask me to say anything – I just got the urge to get it off my chest, and I would never have found someone else to listen to me. My mother probably meant nothing to him, but Cracker listened very attentively and didn't interrupt me once. He quietly scratched the red patches on his neck with his slender fingers and occasionally gave a barely perceptible nod. When I had finished, he didn't tell me – he was the only person to hear

Hanna's story who didn't – that there was no reason to be sad, that she was alive and healthy, that there is no death... he didn't say anything at all. But from that time on he started showing me the forbidden notes with his responses.

He would only show them to me. Then he would hide them. He rolled them up with his spidery fingers into tiny little tubes and jammed them into different cracks. He set up hidey-holes everywhere – he even hid them in the terrariums with the pets: he would push the little tubes into the dried out wood and bury them in the wet sand.

Sometimes – rarely – Cracker would discover 'other people's' hidey-holes: with a faint smile he would pull a stiff tube of paper from some dusty hole, hurriedly unroll it and show it to me: 'Because in the world of the Living crimes are called the maintenance of harmony... Because in the world of the Living the criminals are in power... Because the day will come when we break free...' I would ask, 'So what? Wasn't it you who wrote that?'

Cracker would nod his big head and smile enigmatically:

'Let's go and see the Butcher's Son!'

The Butcher's Son was on the Blacklist. He was kept in the Secure Unit, on the minus second floor, in a transparent conical correction chamber. The chamber was exhibited for all to see in the centre of a brightly lit oval hall. Cracker and I sat right on the floor, facing the Son. The floor was clean and white. And so were the rounded, sparkling mica walls. The oval of the ceiling was one huge flat lamp. No windows, no corners, no shadows – nothing to hide, nowhere to hide away. Artificial midday. Direct, honest, correcting light.

It would be hard to imagine a less secluded place, but none-theless it was here that we normally used for our private chats. Every now and again tour groups or scientists would come in, and at those times there was no way of elbowing your way through the crowd on minus two, but as for ordinary days, hardly any of the correctees came close to the Son's chamber, apart from Cracker and me. They weren't afraid of him: they were afraid of his smile.

A Blacklister's smile was believed to be a bad omen or even a curse: it was like it was capable of 'casting a spell' on the correctee and stopping the correction process forever. But Cracker and I weren't superstitious. What is more, the Butcher's Son didn't know how to smile. He was twenty-three. He spent most of the time sucking and gnawing at his fingers, picking his nose or watching the way his multi-coloured uniform glowed and flashed iridescent in the light. The Son had his clothes changed every day, a collection had been developed for him consisting of seven outfits in 'feeling lucky' style – with sequins, gold brocade, light-inserts and a full range of colours. This fancy dress of his seemed to be part of some *socio* advertising campaign. Be that as it may, his 'feeling lucky' clothes clashed with the stark, penetrating sterility of the place. In his garish suits, in his transparent house, the Butcher's Son was like a pet. He was like a speckled butterfly in a sound-proof bell-jar.

…We sat on the white floor facing the Son. Cracker turned over the note from the hidey-hole in his spidery fingers. The Butcher's Son was licking the pads of his fingers, then putting them up against the glass and looking at the marks they left.

'So, you're saying that it wasn't you who wrote them?'

'Look.' Cracker pushed the note right up in my face with such a sharp movement that the Butcher's Son shuddered and pulled his slobbery hand from the glass. 'Look, it's completely different handwriting. Not to mention the fact that it wasn't my hidey-hole…'

He had already said that before. About the different handwriting and it being someone else's hidey-hole. But I didn't find it very convincing. I didn't see the difference in the hand-writing (a scribble is a scribble), and Cracker had so many hidey-holes that he could have just forgotten.

'You could've just forgotten.'

'Of course,' his eyelid twitched, or, perhaps, he really did wink at me. 'Of course I could have forgotten. I must have forgotten. No one would be able to remember where he had stashed a scrap of paper before the pause...'

Cracker was convinced that he had hidden notes like this in all his previous reproductions. He first found a hidey-hole with a note in it when he was eight. He found it and started doing the same: continued his 'project'...

'Where do you get the idea that it was you who left the note? It would be too big a coincidence. That you were reproduced in the same region... And ended up in the same House of Correction...'

'Nothing strange about it,' Cracker snapped back. 'At forty all correctees go to the Festival for Assisting Nature, right? To the Pause Zone, right? which gives a big chance of being reproduced there, at the festival, in the Reproduction Zone, right...?'

He was talking so quickly that he was tripping over his words. I watched his eye twitch. And red patches appear on his chalky-white skin, down by his throat. Whenever Cracker was telling me something he would pick at his neck the whole time; it was like he was coaxing out the ends of the phrases that had got stuck in his throat.

'...So people like us often stay in the same region. And end up in the same House of Correction... Of course, it suits *him* that way! That way it's easier for *him* to control us...'

'Who's "him"?'

'The Living.' Cracker winked again. 'Right, little fellow?' He drummed the knuckles of his fingers lightly against the Son's transparent chamber, then pushed his face against the glass. '...Right, little fellow? It suits you, doesn't it, keeping us all in the same jar...?'

The Butcher's Son gazed spellbound at Cracker. For a second I even thought that he really had heard him... But no. As far as I could tell, it was Cracker's nose, flattened against the glass that had caught his eye. A couple of times the Son poked his fingers against the glass, trying to touch this amazing 'snout', but then he got bored and started rocking from side to side...

The Butcher's Son didn't hear us, but we heard him. Sometimes we saw his lips moving as if he were talking, but I don't think it was coherent speech. He hadn't had a single educational program installed and no one ever communicated with him in first layer. Perhaps he was just humming something or repeating fragments of phrases he had heard in second layer... All the correctees had restricted access to *socio*, but the Butcher's Son's was minimal: only second layer, only music and entertainment programs. I don't know if they cut him off from *socio* during showings of The Eternal Murderer out of ethical or educational considerations... I suspect not. He didn't understand what it was about anyway. He didn't understand that it was a series about him.

...I was not connected to *socio* and could not watch The Eternal Murderer, but Cracker always told me what happened. I liked following the story. But above all I liked the preamble, the short story which began every episode. Cracker said it was sort of flashes of scenes a second long, and a voiceover reading out a text. I asked Cracker to repeat that text again and again. I learned it off by heart:

'This story takes place in the time of the Great Reduction, while epidemics were taking millions of lives every day. People did not know then that the birth of the Living was coming and mistakenly blamed their illnesses on their domestic animals. And at this time there lived a Butcher. When an epidemic began in his village, he took his axe and in one day he killed all the cows, goats, sheep, rabbits, chickens, dogs and cats in the area. Then he threw his bloodied axe down onto the ground and, exhausted, went off to bed. While the Butcher slept, his son picked up the axe. At first he hacked his mother and father to death, then his sisters and brothers, and then set off to his neighbours. The Butcher's Son spent all night killing people. He drenched the village in blood, left no one alive, and the next night he set off on a journey. The Butcher's Son went through villages and cities: every night hundreds of people died under the blade of his axe. Only after the birth of the Living were they able to catch the madman. He was sentenced to a public pause by hanging, and after reproduction the infant was confined to a prison...' At that moment, Cracker said, complete darkness fell, and there was a roll of thunder – kkrrboom! – and the voice came back: '... Our era: The Living is all-merciful, so there are no more prisons, there are only Houses of Correction. In one of these Houses lives the cruel Butcher's Son. Until, one night, he manages to escape...'

That's why I loved The Eternal Murderer. One night he managed to escape. Those words gave me hope. At the end of every episode they managed to catch up with him: but the hope... The hope stayed with me.

'...Why is a destructively criminal incode vector not a sentence?' Cracker finally unstuck himself from the glass and looked at me. 'Have they explained to you why we have to answer that question every day?'

'Yes,' I said. 'They explained. To get a positive boost.'

Cracker giggled:

'You could say that as well... But do you know why we don't get full access to our cell in Renaissance? Why they only let us read letters from our immediate inc-predecessor?'

'Ef says it's because every earlier predecessor is a step closer to the original Criminal. Letters from early predecessors could harm the correction process...'

'Your mate Ef is lying to you. They're not planning on correcting anyone here. They don't let us read letters from early predecessors so that we don't go mad. Because all our predecessors rotted away in Houses of Correction. All of them, get it? I was here before the pause and I'll come back here after...'

'Stop it.'

'There's no escape from this place!'

As if to confirm what Cracker was saying the Butcher's Son started banging his forehead against the see-through wall. It was one of his favourite pastimes.

'I know a lot. I have a letter from my inc-predecessor,' Cracker turned away from the Son; he was unnerved by the silent blows. '...Very boring. A run-through of the day, re-telling of episodes, remarks about the weather, quotes from the Book of Life, "fifteen signs that I'm correcting my vector well" and stuff like that... But it's a code. I immediately realised it was a code. And Cracker can always break a code – especially if he made it himself...'

'You're crazy.'

'...Cracker can break any password. Cracker can break through any defence. Cracker can write any program. My monster must die...'

'Shut it!'

'My monster must die...'

'Shut up, Cracker! You, what, want to get locked up in solitary like him?' I jabbed the glass with my finger. 'That phrase is forbidden. Especially for you! That's from the Frankenstein Message!'

'The Frankenstein Message,' Cracker whispered dreamily. 'Someday I'll finish it.'

He stuck his nose back against the Son's chamber. To make the piggy snout. The Butcher's Son stopped beating his head against the wall and froze.

'I know it's not your fault, little fellow,' Cracker said, not taking his face from the see-through surface. 'It was Him who made you do it. He took away your reason. And then locked you up here forever. But I'll take care of you. Cracker will take care of everyone, right, little fellow…? I'm a piggy!' Cracker wrinkled his nose and started grunting jokingly. 'Look what a piggy I am!'

'He must be twenty or so. Why do you keep calling him "little fellow"?' I asked.

'Because that's what I called him when he was little. Last time. In my inc-letter it says he liked it. And this too: "I'm a piggy, I'm a piggy. Oink-oink!"'

The Butcher's Son examined Cracker's flattened face thoughtfully. And then smiled.

His smile was utterly childlike.

Report

(Transcript of conversation between correctee Foxcub and SPO officer, dated 17.07.471 A.V.; extract)

Foxcub: Then, I reckon, I ran towards the Green Terrace.

SPO officer: You 'reckon'?

Foxcub: Well, I don't remember running that well because I was really worried… And when I got to the Terrace, there was no one there because everyone was in the termite room.

SPO officer: Do you remember who else was there?

Foxcub: Loads of people. I think the warders were there, the entomologist, correctees from different groups… There was a planetman there too: one like you, in a mask. And Zero. Zero was holding something in his hand. Shiny. Like a battery. And he shouted out that he wanted to… oh, I can't say that word…

SPO officer: You can now.

Foxcub: Really?

SPO officer: The Service for Planetary Order has given you permission.

Foxcub: He shouted out that he's going to die, that he's going to set himself on fire. And the planetman also shouted out, telling everyone to leave, because it was dangerous. And the entomologist shouted out that the termites would die if there's a fire and that he's not going to let… Fofs… I'm probably telling it all wrong?

SPO officer: Carry on. You're a good lad, keep going, it's going great. So you all left?

Foxcub: I don't remember… Yeah. Or no. Probably not. Because we saw what happened next…

SPO officer: What happened next?

Foxcub: Next… Next he… Correctee Zero… He started shouting something weird. That he wanted to be like everyone else or something like that, I didn't quite understand. And then he did something with this shiny thing and this fire appeared, and then straightaway there was a lot of fire, and then he started burning, all over, right there in his clothes. He burned really fiercely. Brightly.

SPO officer: Correctee Zero was shouting? Running around the place?

Foxcub: No, I don't think he was shouting at all. Or maybe I just couldn't hear. But he definitely didn't shout. When he went up in flames, he raised both his arms in the air and became like a blue pillar of fire.

SPO officer: What steps did the SPO officer take at that time?

Foxcub: The SPO officer… took steps to… I don't remember. I was just looking at the pillar of fire, because it was really bright.

SPO officer: Alright. What happened then?

Foxcub: Then… I reckon, the glass started breaking, including the glass outside the termite mound, and it also started burning and some other stuff started burning too... and then the fire safety system kicked in and this liquid came pouring out which puts out the fire... And all the fires went out. The pillar went out.

SPO officer: And then?!

Foxcub: And then we went to look at Zero and the termites, but there was nothing left. Just this soggy black dust. And it smelled really bad. They led us away.

SPO officer: Who led you away?

Foxcub: I don't remember. I reckon it was one of the warders.

SPO officer: And that SPO officer, you don't remember what he was doing?

Foxcub: I definitely don't remember. I reckon he was helping the warders.

SPO officer: Good. You're a good lad, the Service for Planetary Order would like to express its gratitude. If there is nothing you would like to add to your report, then no dea...

Foxcub: I have something I'd like to add!

SPO officer: I'm listening.

Foxcub: I want to add that... about our termites. I think, we all think, that it was really harsh to them. Zero was really mean to the pets. We always had a direct feed from the mound, usually I didn't keep it in my memory, because video files take up too much space, but the last few minutes... The way the soldiers stuck their heads out of the termite mound to try and stop the fire getting in. The way the workers crawled on top of the queen, trying to cover her enormous body under their bodies, protecting her from the fire. And the way the nymphs gnawed off their beautiful wings before they ceased living... for no apparent reason. Maybe in despair. Because they realised that it was already too late to save themselves.

SPO officer: You put it very nicely, Foxcub. It's not for nothing you're such a hit on FreakTube.

Foxcub: Yeah, I... Thanks. It's from our 'Eulogy for the Termites'. We really miss them.

Zero

Our group was taken for the experiment a few days after the visit to the Farm. There were five of us: me, Cracker, two correctees I did not know (one pre-pauser and one from the middle group) and the Butcher's Son. They brought him in literally chained to the chair, with metal cuffs on his legs and arms, which were attached to the arms of the chair by long shining chains. It was there in the white-tiled corridor that we first saw the Son so close up and not through glass. He smelled like an infant from the group of recently reproduced correctees: of milk, wet wipes and urine.

He played with his chains. He obviously liked them, the way they shone and especially the way they sounded, so he shook them with his arm and then his leg and froze in excitement, listening intently to the metallic sound. He was wearing a three-coloured *socio-maniac* suit and when he jerked his leg, his wide trouser legs hiked up a little, uncovering his ankles – incredibly thin, as if they belonged to someone who never walked anywhere. Cracker and I came to the conclusion then that the chains were mostly just a show for the lab workers. So that they could see that the terrifying monster had been tamed and was no longer a threat. So that they would not be afraid that it would suddenly take a turn for the worse like in an episode of The Eternal Murderer, that the Butcher's Son would take advantage of the situation and run off. Cracker even asked the planetmen accompanying us (including Ef) about the chains, but they did not reply: they pretended that they were busy in deep layers and did not hear us. Anyway, we understood without any planetmen: the Son could not have run off anywhere on such hopeless thin legs.

Back then we did not know much about what the experiment was about or what it was for: all sorts of different rumours were doing the rounds. For instance, the pre-pauser who was waiting his turn with us in the corridor kept assuring us that they were going to shine special 'correcting ions' on us to cure us. He was a little slow, this pre-pauser, the whole time he kept repeating that after treatment with the ray even in our next reproduction our PTC would be cut in half, then in half again, then again, and so on after every pause – our potential threat coefficient would be halved...

'So, for instance, if my PTC is twelve, then in my next reproduction it'll be six, then three, then...' He suddenly wrinkled his brow, and his face started showing signs of intense mental work, then surprise, and then, finally, pure agony.

'There will always be a half of a half left,' he told us despondently.

The one from the middle group gave a nasty chuckle: 'That can't be. Count again.'

He himself held firmly to the opinion that they were planning to 'roll out' some experimental new features in *socio* on us. These 'roll outs' were indeed carried out regularly, but to Cracker and me it was entirely obvious that they would never have got either the Butcher's Son or me to take part in that sort of experiment.

Cracker kept insisting that, whatever the goal of the experiment was, it would certainly put us all on pause.

I asked him where he got that idea from and he replied in his usual manner, 'I had a quick look in the cell of that beardy, you know, professor, while he was taking us round that Farm. He's researching the Five Seconds of Darkness... So draw your own conclusions.'

Cracker often mentioned, in passing somehow, that he'd 'taken a quick look' in someone's cell. And it was absolutely impossible to tell by his blank face whether he was being serious or just messing around.

'You're lying,' I said. 'You couldn't have taken a look anywhere. They cut off everyone's *socio* while we were at the Farm.'

'But I am Cracker. And Cracker can break any password. Cracker can break through any defence...'

I think, before I continue, I should explain to you who Cracker is. You probably know full well anyway, but just in case you don't, it will make more sense if I explain. It'll make more sense for me. I have to understand everything. Cracker isn't just any old correctee, you know. Cracker is a genius.

Cracker invented *socio*.

Well, not exactly in the form in which *socio* exists now – the first version was a lot more primitive – but it was Cracker who developed the program which allowed us to get rid of our bi-pads and cerebrons and set up a B2B^5 connection without using external transmitters. Cerebral installation.

Everyone was connected. Mass cerebral installation took place nine months before the Nativity of the Living.

He could have become a happy, decent part of the Living, my poor friend Cracker. After the Nativity, they invited him to join the Council of Eight with the eternal nickname 'Founder'. After the Nativity he should have become the heart and soul of the Living, its apostle, its viceroy, its wise defender... But he refused. Cerebral installation coincided with the beginning of the Great Reduction – and this coincidence damaged Cracker's judgment, ruined his life, changed his invector. The thing is that for some reason Cracker blamed himself. That's right, he thought that he was the reason for all those wars, epidemics, murders, terrorist attacks... Cracker got it into his head that the cerebral installation developed by him – and applied across the world – had begun the Great Reduction. And led to the birth of the Living.

How are the Great Reduction and the birth of the Living linked? I guess if you're already eight you must know: the Living is our Saviour. He came into the world to conquer death. With His birth he put an end to the Great Reduction... You also know that the secret of the birth of the Living is one of the greatest mysteries in the universe. You know that we don't need solutions or answers, all we have to do is believe that His birth is a life-giving miracle...

You know all this. Every living knows this... But Cracker – the genius, the creator of *socio*, the heretic and madman – this Cracker, he turned everything inside out. For him the link between the Reduction and the Birth was obvious – but obvious in a different way, not like it is for the rest of us. He did not think the Living was our saviour. He thought he was a monster. He supposed that the Great Reduction was a sort of gestation period. The period when the embryo is being formed... The embryo, in his opinion, came about as a result of the *fusion*, and the fusion – you've guessed it already – happened as a result of mass cerebral installation. That is to say, Cracker thought that his work had personally brought the Living to life.

And he also used to tell everyone that the Butcher's Son was not to blame for his crimes, that the Butcher's Son was obeying the will of the embryo, and that all his murders were just part of the Great Reduction.

Nonsense, right? Just absurd. Don't give it a thought. I just want you to realise how stubborn Cracker was. Cracker carried all this – his absurd sense of guilt, his absurd theory about the Great Reduction, his lack of respect for the Living, his confidence in the correctness of his own ideas – through the centuries, through many pauses and reproductions, through many bodies... And brought it to me.

He shared his theory with me during therapy on the Available Terrace.

Have I not told you about the Available Terrace? It was our second secret place, besides the hall with the Son's chamber in it. Officially it was called the Green Terrace, in the old style, but this magnificent name had not caught on among the correctees, so we just gave it an ordinary name. As silly as this sounds, the Green Terrace wasn't available-coloured (pink tiles with a black design on the floor, walls made of pinkish glass) – the name, as the warders explained to us, had survived from those distant times when the colours 'available' and 'busy' had additional symbolic meanings. 'Busy' was, for some reason, associated with physical drives ('passion') and 'available' with nature. In a word, the Terrace was called available because that's where the terrariums with the pets were. Every correctee had two or three little friends each, which they looked after: the warders thought that insect-therapy helped with correction. We had to feed our pets, clean their cages, change their water, sand or earth (depending on the little friend's habitat), and, as well as this, according to some sort of unwritten rule, it was customary to chat to them.

It wasn't that there was some rule which said we had to talk to them, no, it was just that certain correctees who were genuinely attached to their little friends always got the urge to coo at them a bit; the rest thought that silence would be interpreted as indifference or hard-heartedness, whereas a tender word addressed to a dragonfly or a caterpillar could only be a plus... There was no sound recording on the Available Terrace and the warders only occasionally observed us through the glass walls, but we knew that if we didn't communicate with our pets the warders would know about it. 'Get corrected: tell your warder everything,' 'Get corrected: help a friend with his correction,' 'Correct yourself: don't hide anything' – Cracker said that these banners kept flashing up for all of them. Informing a warder about suspicious behaviour is natural. Every word said to a warder can only be a plus. But silence will be interpreted as complicity.

Basically, there were always correctees milling about on the Available Terrace and their voices – monotonously encouraging, breaking into a falsetto with tenderness, be it fake or genuine – merged with the buzzing, squeaking and chirping of their pets. It was certainly impossible to cut oneself off or get some quiet, and that was why the terrace was our secret place. In the crowd where everyone was saying something to their pets Cracker and I could discuss pretty much anything we liked in a whisper without drawing any attention to ourselves or arousing any suspicion.

...It was there, on the Available Terrace, something like a week before the experiment, that Cracker unfurled one of those soft little paper tubes, placed it on the palm of his hand and whispered, seemingly not to me, but to his pet, 'Take a look, I've done a little sketch...'

Cracker had a big, podgy, slender-legged spider that was the absolute confirmation of the belief that pets resemble their owners. Cracker and he looked alike, they loved each other, they interacted well, during therapy Cracker always used to pick his pet up and stroke his matt, rounded body, and the spider would shiver in bliss. Cracker's second pet was a snail: a nice, inoffensive creature with touching little twitching antennae, but Cracker despised her and didn't take care of her properly, and she often got ill and would leave a murky, slimy trail behind her on the glass as she moved.

'...It's the history of our world,' Cracker said, seemingly to the spider. Uninterested, the spider trampled over the half-worn little square of paper and wandered higher up Cracker's arm, towards his elbow.

On the piece of paper there were a series of rough drawings linked by short curved arrows. I remember it all well. Several separate little men (the scrawled caption: 'ancient man') – arrow – a person's head with a nasty dark dot in the region of the forehead (caption: 'cer. installation') – arrow – a small incomprehensible little doodle ('the embryo starts to form') –

arrow – something like an egg with busy-coloured lines inside ('growth of embryo = great reduction') – arrow – a funny many-headed, many-armed monster with a rattle in one of its hands ('birth of the monster = number of livings becomes unchanging').

'Throw away that horrible piece of crap right now,' I said quietly and sweetly, as I would if I were talking to my pet. 'Get rid of that piece of paper, you poor idiot. Put it in with my termite, he'll gobble it up in no time…'

…At first, when I had only just been put in the House of Correction, I looked after a mosquito and a fly. I didn't like them. The fly annoyed me with her random movements, her inability to concentrate on any specific aims or make a choice. After I fed her her dry feed – little beige balls that had a rich, rotten smell – she circled the cage for a long time, unable to decide which of the little balls to start her lunch with… I didn't know what to talk to her about, so I normally just told her I hoped she had a nice meal and said 'no death'. She didn't feel anything for me either and, unlike the other correctees' flies, she never sat on the glass between us if I came over. The female mosquito behaved differently: when she saw me she always got notably more animated, she liked my blood and, probably, liked me too. I didn't get any particular pleasure from contact with her, but I never refused her her pleasure and did what she craved so much: I pressed the back of my hand or my cheek to the side wall of the cage. She acted with tact and care and didn't take more than two portions of blood at a time. After her therapy two little soft pink raised mounds would be left on the surface of my skin; I rubbed them with a special cream which the entomologist gave me and they barely itched at all and disappeared completely after about three hours.

After a year Ef said that he was glad that I was taking good care of my two pets. I had shown myself in a good light and now I had earned some encouragement: he would let me choose a third pet myself. Any of the species offered on the Available Terrace, it was up to me.

Of all the pets on the terrace the only one I really liked was a stag beetle that was the little friend of one of the pre-pausers, and I wanted to ask Ef to bring me one like that or, perhaps, give me that one when his owner temporarily ceased to exist... But instead I announced that I wanted a termite. 'One?' Ef asked unpleasantly and I said, 'Yes.' I still don't fully understand why I asked for a termite. Probably just out of curiosity. Or maybe to restore some justice.

The termite colony was considered the pride and glory of our House of Correction (these insects often did not take to life in captivity); there was a whole special room dedicated to their needs, next to the Available Terrace, weakly lit and full of the smell of plastic and rotten wood. There, in the half-light, in the huge terrarium made of darkened plastic, half-filled with earth, the termite mound rose up. It reminded me of a castle, ravaged by winds and battered by time, built before the Nativity of the Living and inhabited by invisible ancient spirits. To my great disappointment, it was not possible to see the architectural details of this castle through the murky plastic. As for the 'spirits' that lived there, the termites never emerged outside, they were always hiding behind the castle walls, and of all the correctees – and this is what I thought was unfair – I was the only one who was not able to see the way they lived. The termites were never looked after by anyone except the staff entomologist: he had installed a lot of mini-cameras inside the termite mound on all the levels and in every section, which were directly linked to the correctees' *socio*. So that they could always watch everything live in second layer. I didn't have *socio*. Perhaps that's why I wanted to have *my own* termite.

'Termites are social insects,' Ef said then. 'But I figure that if we give you one, it will be a useful experience for you. I'll discuss this issue with the management of the House of Correction and the entomologist.'

They obviously discussed it immediately in deep layers: the staff entomologist appeared about ten minutes later and set off for the termite room. He looked away as he passed me. He looked annoyed, almost angry. The entomologist soon came back, holding a small cylindrical plastic container with a single termite inside. He set it up on the Available Terrace, next to my mosquito's cage. Still not looking in my direction and twisting his mouth in irritation, he told me that the termite ate cellulose, that the termite was blind and asexual, that the termite could not tolerate sunlight and that the termite was a social insect. He told me everything I needed to know about my new pet. Then the entomologist gave me the feed – a silvery packet filled with damp shavings that smelled of mushrooms and woodland. I asked about the light – wouldn't my termite suffer in his transparent container on the Available Terrace – and he explained with hostility that the walls of the container were made from a special light-filtering material. Then he left without even saying 'no death'. I was surprised: before the entomologist had got on well with me and always been pleased with the health of my pets.

I remember how, after he left, a crowd of correctees gathered on the terrace and swarmed round the container with my new pet – it struck me that the container was a little like the Son's transparent chamber. I remember they were all silent for a long time, either shutting their eyes or looking round in agitation, discussing my insect on *socio*. And a correctee with the nickname Foxcub – he was pretty dumb and couldn't keep second layer well, often verbalising his deep answers – exclaimed in a loud, monotonous voice, 'Poor soldier!'

A week later I understood everything: their looks, Foxcub's outburst, and the entomologist's irritation, and what Ef had said about 'a useful experience for me'. The termite that was entrusted to me had been a member of the 'warrior' caste in the termite mound. The upper part of his body was encased in a hard brown shell, as if he were fitted out in armour like a knight. For a weapon he had huge sickle-shaped mandibles the same size as the rest of his body – so enormous that they prevented him from feeding himself. He spent the whole week in an awkward defensive pose, his blind, armoured head turned to face me and his back to the termite room, as if he were hoping to ward me off and save his home castle. He ceased living on the seventh day, from hunger, on a heap of the aromatic food shavings which I had, without fail, continued to throw into his container all this time... Cracker said that he had been doomed from the start, my new pet.

Cracker said that there, in the mound, worker termites would feed soldier termites like that with the contents of their intestines: they would carefully place digested cellulose right into their mouths.

Cracker said that every correctee knew that, anyone who had watched the live feed even once – anyone, but me.

Only then, as I looked through the transparent plastic at my unliving pet, did I realise that Ef had, of course, known in advance how me looking after this termite would end up. And the entomologist knew too – that's why he had got angry, he had felt sorry for him... Ef wanted to teach me a lesson: loners are doomed. They can't survive outside the mound.

They can't survive outside the Living.

I learned my lesson well. I felt humiliated, pitiful and helpless, like that soldier that could not swallow his own food. When Ef came to visit me a day after the end of the termite, I couldn't bring myself to look at him: not because I was offended, but because I was ashamed to see my reflection. And when Ef, in a conciliatory, almost affectionate way, offered to let me choose a third pet again ('I think you like that stag beetle, don't you?') I was horrified to hear my own reply: 'I would like a termite.'

'You clearly haven't understood,' Ef buzzed monotonously. 'Termites are social insects, you should look after a...'

'A termite,' I said. 'Just not a soldier. I want a termite from a different caste.'

They gave me a 'nymph' – a delicate, fragile creature, vaguely reminiscent of a winged ant. Her wings looked like the slender petals of a fantastic translucent daisy. In contrast to the soldier she had a sex (the entomologist, it's true, didn't want to tell me which, but I was sure that she was a little girl) and could see. For the first three hours she fluttered about the container full of joy, then settled down on a wall and gnawed off both her wings. Once they had fallen to the bottom of the container they stopped looking like silvery petals, but grew darker and started to look like husks. Her wingless body reminded me of the body of the soldier, except without the mandibles and the armour. She refused food, and I got a bad feeling, and Cracker told me that in the termite mound nymphs like this are also, just like the warriors, fed digested cellulose by the workers. But I tried to convince myself that this time everything would work out. I kept repeating to myself: there are no mandibles blocking her mouth, nothing except stubbornness and laziness is stopping her from taking some food. She'll get hungry and then she'll eat... She ceased living five days later from hunger, surrounded by the cellulose, like her predecessor the warrior.

As he took the corpse from the container, the entomologist told me that nymphs cannot feed themselves either, because their intestines lack the bacteria *Trichonympha campanula*, *Leidyopsis sphaerica*, *Trichomonas* and *Streblomastix strix*. Without these the termite cannot digest food. These bacteria only live in the intestines of worker termites.

'So, have you figured it out finally?' Ef asked, looking at the empty container.

'Yeah,' I said. 'I've figured it out. I would like a worker...'

They died, one after another. They would die and I would weep for them and ask for new ones. The correctees (all of them, apart from Cracker – he understood) saw my termites as martyrs and saw me as a crazy murderer. The entomologist stopped talking to me entirely. The psychologist checked my PIA every other day (the result was negative). The House administration sent official complaints to the SPO and asked for Ef to be relieved of his duties (reply: 'declined'). Nothing changed. A termite would die, I would ask for a new one, and Ef would force the administration to fulfil my request. Why? He was as stubborn as I was. He wanted me to be the first to break.

They could not survive outside the termite mound.

I had a worker termite that on the very first day covered the inside of the plastic walls of the container with something like cement; it must have made this substance in its intestines. When he was finished with the walls, he did the ceiling, which the air came through, too. He ceased living from lack of oxygen.

I had a worker termite who built a strange thin tube in his container, leading from the floor to the ceiling, and walled himself in inside it.

I had a worker termite that at first ate well, but then stopped and died, seemingly from sadness.

I had a worker termite that ran away during feeding and died from the light – they found him unliving by the entrance to the termite room.

I had a worker termite that died for some unknown reason, instantly.

I had a worker termite that died for some unknown reason, having first suffered for a long time.

They kept dying, but over time I started getting slightly longer lives from some of them. Twelve days. Eighteen. Twenty-four. A month and a day. A month and two days...

'...Put the piece of paper in the container,' I cooed. 'If you don't want to end up in solitary like the Butcher's Son.'

'...Give my diagram to a termite? So I'll have to digest it first you mean?' Cracker chortled. 'And then he'll choke and die. Your termites can't even eat right!'

'Idiot!' I took offence. 'I've only had workers for ages now. They eat perfectly. And this one,' I tapped my finger lightly on the wall of the container, 'this one, if he does cease living, it'll be from old age.'

The termite that was my pet at that time had beaten all records. An unassuming worker, he had been living in the container for nearly half a year already. At first – like many of his predecessors – he had just moped around. But after a couple of weeks he found himself something to do. He started building something like a column out of sand, shards of wood, spit and faeces. When he was finished with that, on top of the column (it reached about halfway up the container) he built something like a bit of a slanting palace arch, something like a fragment from the architecture of the termite mound which he, as far as I could see, imagined was a sort of long-range addition to his home castle. At the very least, this rough arch, riddled with holes, divided the container on the diagonal and was directed towards the termite mound. The top of the arch leaned against the wall of the container in such a way that you could draw a perfect line across the Available Terrace between it and the dome of the termite mound. If the termite had had an opportunity to continue his work, that's what he would have done... When he had finished the arch, he plunged back into despondency – however, I figured out a way to cheer him up. I just rotated the container slightly in a clockwise direction, so that the piece of arch made by my pet would be aimed not at the termite mound but past it. He set to work eagerly destroying what he had created and crafting a new arch, pointing in what was, for him, the only right direction... And so he kept on living with me, happily, month after month, endlessly building, destroying and rebuilding his section of the castle.

The termite had an excellent appetite: I had no doubt that he would gobble up Cracker's piece of paper in about fifteen minutes, or at the very least grind it up and put it to use in his construction. But Cracker dug his heels in.

'There's important information on that,' he muttered. 'I should hide it... in a safe place... in a hidey-hole...'

A hidey-hole. I've already mentioned the fact that Cracker set up hidey-holes everywhere. He even hid his notes in the cages with the pets: he would push his little tubes into the dried wood pulp and bury them in the wet sand... Of course, it was forbidden. It was against all the rules. He thought that they couldn't touch him because he set up the hidey-holes so skilfully... But I knew: if they wanted to find them, then they would find them. There was only one reason why they had not put Cracker in a correction chamber in the Special Unit like the Butcher's Son: out of respect for his previous achievements. He had created *socio* after all. It would be unseemly to lock up the creator of *socio* in a glass jar, like a blind, asexual termite.

Nevertheless, Cracker was teetering on the brink: his crime was too serious. That is, his first crime, the original sin which had made him fit for the House of Correction. He had tried to destroy the results of his work. A year after the Nativity he had started writing the Frankenstein Message – a virus which was meant to uninstall *socio* and kill the infant Living.

This message began with the words: 'My monster must die.' Glap, the *socio* sysadmins traced the source of the potential threat to Cracker's IP address in time. Actually, at that time, he had a different nickname: *Founder.* But after the sentence was announced – life imprisonment – they gave him a new *socio* name.

Then after a hundred years, when there were no prisons anymore, Cracker was moved to a House of Correction.

He was stubborn. He was a bad correctee. After every pause his PTC kept growing, but this did not bother him. He was teetering on the brink. He told everyone that the Butcher's Son was innocent of his crimes.

And that diagram of his... I remember when I saw exactly what it was he decided to hide and I thought, this time they'll definitely get him. Unfortunately, I turned out to be right. His crime was too serious. He should not have been taking risks and aggravating the situation. He should have been working on reducing his PTC.

The Scientist

Document No. 24 (leaseholder's private entry) –
access through SPO guest entry

4th September 451 A.V.

Five Seconds of Darkness – it sounds beautiful, but in essence it doesn't mean much. No one knows what actually happens: whether it's dark or light or just inviz. When an ordinary person hears the phrase 'five seconds of darkness' he imagines something dreadful. But at the end of the day it's just a technical term referring to the period of time when the *socio* dispatcher can't see the incode of the person who has temporarily ceased to exist in the population control system. In other words the Five Seconds is the 'pause' itself. It is then followed by reproduction: the *socio* dispatcher re-establishes the incode and registers the geographic position and personal data of the newly conceived person.

The Five Seconds of Darkness is a practically unresearched field. As we know, it is this 'blind alley' which is the main barrier to us carrying out complete incarnational retrospection and detailed examination of pre-pause conditions in the individual. Hitherto only the Roberts random flare method has been widely practised in pre-pause immersion therapy. We have created a special compound which makes the biological organism more sensitive to Roberts radiation. One injection could be enough to transform the random flashes into a directed ray. In this way, we have reason to believe that our breakthrough will radically alter the current state of the field.

Laboratory experiments on social insects (bees, ants, termites) exposed to the directed Leo-Lot ray have shown that:

a) our hypothesis about the continuity of social insects' life is correct (if this were not the case, our experiment would not have proved successful);

b) the directed Leo-Lot ray is capable of crossing through the Five Seconds of Darkness and penetrating the pre-pause zone (experiments with *Heterotermes indicola* termites gave record-breaking results – consecutive immersion to a depth of twenty-six reproductions!).

In the event of a successful experiment on humans the Leo-Lot ray will allow us to move beyond the random flare method, which will open up a broad vista of possibilities in the field of incarnational retrospection and guarantee good penetration depth.

Our method allows us to run a session of simultaneous immersion into the subject's pre-pause zone for both the subject and the experimenter.

In light of the above, we request that you present us with the following correctees from House of Correction No. 3578 ('Harmony') for voluntary participation in our first experiment with the directed Leo-Lot ray:

1. Correctee Butcher's Son, current physical age – twenty-three years.

   Reasons for participation in the experiment:
   – incarnational retrospection on the planet's cruellest criminal is of particular scientific significance for researchers and psychiatrists; our method offers us the possibility of tracing the history of the correctee's psychic illness not from the dry statements in his personal file, but directly, 'live';
   – the correctee's ability to perceive and interpret the immersion in any way appears doubtful; however, we do not see any reason not to demonstrate the immersion to the correctee.

2. Correctee Cracker, current physical age – thirteen years.

Reasons for participation in experiment:
– the correctee's continually increasing PTC; the correctee lacks any motivation for correction; a session of incarnational retrospection might be exceedingly useful for understanding mistaken and unproductive attitudes of this kind;
– incarnational retrospection on one of the planet's most famous inventors and criminals would be of particular value to scientists.

3. Correctee Ivanushka, current physical age – forty years.

Reasons for participation in experiment:
– in this instance incarnational retrospection may prove to be an example of a beneficial supplement to the psychotherapy of pre-pausers; a small percentage of people of a pre-pause age experience nervousness tension and alarm in connection with the forthcoming Five Seconds of Darkness. We propose that immersion in previous reproductions will considerably enhance pre-pausers' sense of immortality, harmony and continuity, and relieve them of many of their neurotic reactions.

4. Correctee Joker, current physical age – thirty-one years.

Reasons for participation in experiment:
– in this instance the subject was selected at random; there are no particular reasons for this correctee to volunteer for this experiment; at the discretion of the management of the House of Correction, he may be replaced by any other volunteer, preferably middle-aged.

5. Correctee Zero, current physical age – eleven years.

Reasons for participation in experiment:
– in light of the absence of in-history an attempt at incarnational retrospection in the case of this correctee is a bold and even desperate step, but one which nevertheless seems to us to be the only appropriate and correct course of action. The directed Leo-Lot ray is the only means currently available to us of shedding light on the 'Zero problem'. Hitherto we have had no conception of the genesis of this correctee, and the mechanism by which an 'additional physical person' appeared is entirely unclear. We do not know whether correctee Zero is a part of the Living, or how serious a threat he presents to the harmony of the Living. If experimental immersion in the 'pre-life' period of this correctee is successful to even the slightest extent, any information we receive as a result will be invaluable;
– the correctee is not connected to *socio*: therefore, in order to visualise his immersion for him, it would be necessary to introduce additional equipment. However, such a measure seems excessive and potentially harmful. In this case the results of retrospection are entirely unpredictable. In order to avoid any psychological trauma for the subject, and as a result of security concerns arising in connection to the threat which the subject may pose, we are planning to carry out a 'closed immersion' without demonstration to the correctee. In order to avoid misunderstandings and technical blunders the correctee will be put into an induced sleep.

P.S. Poor Lot is very stressed about the experiment. I played him at wonder-chess. He refused a head start, lost, and heaped abuse on me. We were about to fall out. I had to offer a rematch and lose on purpose.

Sometimes Lot behaves like a child.

Zero

Inside there were things like scanners with cylindrical cell-chambers. I knew the set-up well: as a child I had a lot of brain scans. They wanted to find some defect in me, something organic that made me different from the others...

They told us to get undressed and lie on the trolley. I don't remember the experiment very well.

I think the surface of the trolley was cold and smooth. I think they strapped us down and put some kind of medicine into a vein. From then on I only have fragments of memories.

Professor Leo, he says that the ray won't hurt a bit.

My friend Cracker, his neck covered in crimson spots, he whispers something about the Five Seconds of Darkness.

Ef's mirror face, his monotonous voice breaking into a deafening racket. He wants to stay, but the scientists take exception, and they have some sort of advantage in this dispute.

The Butcher's Son, he whimpers, he does not want to lie naked on the trolley. Professor Lot thanks us for our contribution to science and says 'no death'.

Our trolleys go into the dark maws of the scanners...

It's like I'm in a container...

I'm a blind worker termite...

darkness...

The Scientist

Document No. 25 (leaseholder's private entry) –
access via SPO guest entry

6th September 451 A.V.

Crossposted to the Association of Laboratory Workers

We have just completed the first experiment with the directed Leo-Lot ray. We did not get the results we had expected. Our experiment is a mistake, and therefore we are cancelling all the remaining sessions we had planned. The directed ray is not operational. In the future we should look for other, more optimal methods for incarnational retrospection. We consider our method to be dangerous. It should be banned.

Zero

Afterwards, when Ef was asking me about what happened during the experiment, I didn't remember anything. I told him that I had had a dream, but that was a lie. I didn't remember anything, even any dreams, I just wanted him to leave me alone. He said tell me your dream, and I told him about a dream that I used to have quite a lot. I'm little and Hanna and I are sitting by a river and I'm building a lovely castle for Hanna out of sand and stones. My castle is finished and she looks at me and laughs, and I destroy it, and then I start rebuilding – and then I knock it down. I build, then knock down, build, then knock down... I'm happy, I could build and knock down this castle my whole life long, as long as Hanna is laughing...

'What next?' Ef asked.

'Nothing. I woke up and realised that she's gone.'

'She is still here,' Ef hummed. 'But that's not important right now. And your dream isn't important either. When you woke up, while you were getting dressed and all that... The correctees and Leo and Lot – what were they saying?'

'Nothing. Only thing was Cracker said that he was wrong.'

'What did he mean by that?'

'He thought that during the experiment they would put us on pause. But that didn't happen.'

Cracker was wrong. He thought that during the experiment they would put us on pause, but that didn't happen.

Something else happened. I lost him forever.

We were separated immediately after the experiment. We weren't even allowed to share a few words, to say goodbye. I was calm. At that time I hadn't yet realised why the planetman was preparing to move Cracker in a separate van. They had taken us to the experiment together, and I would have suspected that something was up when Cracker was led off down a white corridor, but they also immediately took the pre-pauser off somewhere – he hadn't managed to cut his PTC in half – and the one from the middle group (I think he was called Joker) was taken off on his own as well. So they took me to the House of Correction with only the Butcher's Son for company and I thought anything's possible with all their rules and regulations.

On the way back the Butcher's Son did not play with his chains anymore but looked somehow despondent. A couple of times I tried to do the 'piggy' for him, pressing my nose up with my finger like Cracker did, but he didn't react at all and I left him in peace.

Only when I had gone back to my group, at daily roll call, did I realise that something was up with Cracker. The group warder didn't read out his name and I got scared that she had got angry at him for some violation of discipline, but I explained it to myself by saying that they just hadn't brought Cracker back from the lab yet. She looked at me like I had pissed myself in front of everyone. And the whole group stared at me like an idiot too. Then someone started cackling with laughter.

'Correctee Cracker is no longer a member of our group.' As she looked at me the warder smiled slightly at the corner of her mouth, as if she wanted to laugh along with everyone else, but was still restraining herself. 'What are you lot up to?' She looked round at everyone. 'Why haven't you explained to your friend what has happened?'

They probably said something back to her in second layer because her face suddenly went strict.

'He's not connected to *socio*,' she said. 'But that doesn't mean that he's not your friend. Or that he's not every bit as good as the rest of you. He's just different. And it's your job to show him care and kindness. Otherwise I might register your behaviour as *cruel*.'

There is nothing worse for a correctee than being accused of cruelty. Cruel behaviour brought with it corrective measures. It was written down in the 'Rules of Correction' which hung on the door of every dormitory:

'First-degree cruelty (oral or social mockery of the physical defects of correctee friends, oral rudeness to a pet): one-off disconnection from *socio* for forty minutes.'

'Second-degree cruelty (physical violence towards correctee friends): daily disconnection from *socio* for seven days.'

There weren't many people who exhibited second-degree cruelty, only total psychos. Even first degree didn't happen that often: they all suffered so badly when they were disconnected. They cried, begged for forgiveness or rocked from side to side, staring at a fixed point. Those that had been disconnected even once became affectionate and attentive, like the nannies from the infant group.

Third-degree cruelty (physical violence towards a pet) was quite unthinkable. The sentence for that was confinement to a solitary chamber with life-long minimisation of *socio*. No one had ever gone as far as the third degree... Except Cracker.

My groupmates told me everything. They were very kind to me.

They said it was all about the snail, Cracker's pet.

They said that, poor thing, she had got an infection under her shell. While Cracker and I were being taken to the lab, she had ceased living.

They said that the entomologist had taken the snail for an autopsy. A foreign object was found under her shell – something made by Cracker.

They said that Cracker was cruel, that he was being put in solitary. They said they didn't know what the object was.

But I knew, I knew all too well: it was a little piece of paper with a diagram on it. A week ago Cracker had pushed it inside the snail's shell: he thought it was a 'natural hidey-hole'. I've mentioned already how he would set up hidey-holes every-where... Of course I've already mentioned it.

He was accused of third-degree cruelty for violence towards a pet. But I knew, I knew very well, that this wasn't just about cruelty. The House administration could hardly have been thrilled about the 'foreign object' itself.

growth of the foetus = great reduction

birth of the monster = number of livings becomes unchanging

Perhaps it was irony on the part of the House administration or evidence of some sort of favour, or even sympathy; whatever it was, they set up Cracker's solitary chamber in his favourite place. In the special maximum security unit, on floor minus two, under the fluorescent lights. In the blindingly white hall, opposite the Son's chamber.

I went to visit them there every day.

After the experiment the Butcher's Son became depressed and apathetic. He was probably not sleeping well. Grey-blue shadows like spread wings had formed under his eyes. As if a moth had settled on the bridge of his nose... Later, when I found out what happened during the experiment, I started to think that the way the Son had changed was totally under-standable. If he had really seen *what* he had done back then, then he must have been horrified. It's unlikely that the Son really realised that it was him who carried out this slaughter. But he probably sensed that it had something to do with him. In any case the very sight of it would be enough to give anyone sleepless nights...

...It turned out that I didn't get a chance to ask any of the other subjects of the experiment about what they had been through. On that very day, immediately after the experiment, the pre-pauser Ivanushka was taken off to the Pause Zone at the Festival for Assisting Nature. I tried to look for correctee Joker, but the warder of the middle group told me, with no little irritation, that the correctee with that nickname had temporarily ceased to exist. He had hanged himself in the shower cubicle, without leaving a note. They didn't like suicides in the House of Correction, their warders didn't get a pat on the head. Unmotivated premature pause is, firstly, very stupid (what can you possibly change by doing that?), and, secondly, it is evidence of some pedagogical error on the part of the warder, and thirdly, and this was the main thing, it made life difficult for the staff. He was a healthy man, not that old, he could look after himself – and now, there you go, a screaming baby, feed him, wash him, change his nappies. So the warder's irritation was entirely understandable.

I never again crossed paths with any of the scientists that had run the experiment. They never appeared at the House of Correction and completely different people took us on the next trip to the Farm.

And Cracker, what about Cracker...? He couldn't say anything to me. Sitting next to him, on the other side of the soundproof glass, I remembered with bitterness that not long ago, in this very place, we had swapped secrets.

Now I was searched before I could enter the Special Unit – to be sure that I didn't have any writing implements or any other materials which I could use to give Cracker information. I had to cover the lower half of my face with a mask so that Cracker wouldn't be able to read my lips.

The information vacuum was the chief corrective measure for Blacklisters.

At first Cracker seemed surprisingly lively, almost happy. He gesticulated animatedly, smiled, did the 'piggy' for the Son, moved his lips inaudibly (I only managed to understand one thing: 'cracker can break any password cracker can break through any defence') and waved to me when I came and when I left.

After a few days this unnatural jollity was replaced by complete despair. He spent whole days lying on the floor of his cell, hunched over, his slender legs tucked under his stomach. He started to look even more like a spider – stock still, pretending to be unliving on the brightly lit floor. When he saw me, he emerged from hibernation, seemingly grudgingly, as if against his own will, and slowly got up and came over to the transparent wall. There was an emptiness in his eyes: I had seen something like it before somewhere. Hanna's eyes used to get like that when she was in deep layers. But Cracker couldn't be in deep layers. His access to *socio* was minimal now, like all the Blacklisters. Only music and shows – oh, and maybe some adverts.

And then he stopped reacting to me. Completely. As if he didn't see me. As if his chamber were covered on the inside by some light-resistant film.

I still kept coming. I would sit and look at Cracker in his torpor, at the Butcher's Son and his 'black moth'. I also started sleeping badly. Without Cracker and his snoring, without the familiar game of pistons. I needed that rumbling noise; I was used to sneaking off to sleep in the little periods of quiet. When Cracker was moved to the Special Unit, I started listening to the breathing of the other correctees, trying to feel for their rhythm and tune into it. I actually did manage to hear it – their shared rhythm, rapid and fussy, all scrunched up like a ball of thin barbed wire, strident, like the buzzing of a swarm of bees. I got caught up in it, stuck in it, and, as I drifted off, it was like I was tearing off my skin. I tried to take my mind off it, to block out their breathing with my own breathing, or coughing, or fidgeting, I even whistled quietly – useless. Their uneven rhythm. I could no longer not hear it.

Part 2

Report

(Transcript of conversation between correctee Triton and SPO officer, dated 17.07.471 A.V.; extract)

Triton: He went up in flames instantly. Why are you asking? Everyone saw it, not just me.

SPO officer: We're asking everyone, don't worry. Tell me what else you remember about the fire.

Triton: He was like a pillar of fire. So bright. It was this colour... All these colours like 'feeling lucky'. It's probably not very nice to say this seeing as how Zero ceased to exist and didn't get reproduced, right...? But it was really beautiful, I kind of even liked the way he burned.

SPO officer: Perhaps it is not actually very nice of you to talk like that about your dead friend.

Triton: He wasn't my friend. Smin, he wasn't even on *socio*.

SPO officer: But you were friends in first layer.

Triton: No, he wasn't my friend. Zero treated his pets badly. We always had a live feed from the termite mound, usually I didn't keep it in my memory, because the video files take up too much space, but the last few minutes... before he ceased living... I decided to keep that bit in my memory forever. It's a really sad video. The way the soldiers stuck their heads out of the termite mound to try and stop the fire getting in. The way the workers crawled on top of the queen, trying to cover her enormous body under their bodies, protecting her from the fire. And the way the nymphs gnawed off their beautiful wings...

Zero

The final straw, perhaps, was my trip to see Hanna in her boarding house – though there is no point in calling her that. Better to call her Mia 31.

When Ef asked if I wanted anything for Nativity and I replied that I would like to see Hanna, I didn't think that he would say yes, I just gave him an honest answer. But he said, 'Why not, if it will calm you down?' The administration only let us go grudgingly. They don't really like it when correctees go wandering about outside the House. As far as I could tell Ef was very insistent, even put pressure on them somehow. They gave us three hours: two for the trip, there and back, and one hour for the 'meeting with a former Darling'. They strongly recommended handcuffs ('This virus... anything's possible'), but he didn't make me wear them ('Personally, I trust the lad'). I was touched by that. I almost started trusting him too.

Why did Ef take me to see her at the boarding house? To calm me down? Ha. Probably he wanted to provoke me from the very beginning. Perhaps he even hoped that I would try to run away. I didn't try... But, one way or another, I still broke free, but that's exactly what he had been waiting for. Hey, I even sort of understand him. All that fuss about me, all that spam, those thousands of infected messages and mails which they keep sending each other like crazy, as if they don't even know what they are doing themselves, as if it's because of some goddamn virus, which keeps reproducing itself constantly... You should go along and check – maybe someone's already been doing it *by themselves* for ages, of their own accord, maybe someone likes doing it, maybe some-one has some sympathy for me, maybe there really have been dissidents all this time. Maybe the Service for Planetary Order already thinks the boundary between *socio* virus and *socio* revolt seemed too fragile. They hoped that they would lock me up in a House of Correction and everyone would forget about me. And that there they would be able to quietly poke about inside me, study me like some newly discovered pet, grab at my wings and tug at my antennae – and that I would stay there for life stuck on inviz mode, an unknown but harmless correctee animal... And that's how it went. For many years that's exactly how it's been – but now I am thirty-one and the whole world has suddenly remembered that I exist. The 'o threat' – that's what they've called the virus that has brought me my fame; there is no anti-virus yet – I hope that there will be one by your time.

By the way, it's funny that I'm the only one who doesn't get a chance to see all that spam myself. But certain rumours have still reached me and I've put together a short list of 'chain letters' that I've heard about in case you're interested:

1. 'You've got a stupid job, and before the pause you had a stupid job, and after the pause you're going to have a stupid job. But you want to be a screenwriter or a game rater... Follow Zero – he was born to change your life ☺.'

2. 'You're fifty and you don't like all these recommendations to visit the Pause Zone. Follow Zero – he will give you long life ☺.'

3. 'You're a woman. The Living requires you to mate regularly, but you don't want a Darling. Follow Zero. He will let you take precautions ☺.'

4. 'You're a woman. The Living requires you to give your Darlings away to a boarding house, but you want to stay with them. Follow Zero. He does not consider your maternal feelings a deviation from the psychic norm.'

5. 'You want a dog. A real, living dog in first layer. Follow Zero, and animals will love you like they love him ☺.'

6. 'You read the Book of Life. But the number of the Living has changed, and there's not a word about it in the Book. Don't believe everything you read in the Book ☺.'

Sorry, it seems I got a bit distracted. I wanted to tell you about Mia 31.

Mia. Hanna. A fat, listless twelve-year-old girl. My mother's second inc-successor (the first, a little boy, only lived for eight years; they say he was a dwarf). Mia's forehead was covered in pustules and her eyes were so dull and cold that it was like some ancient-ancient pet was living in her skull and watching us all dispassionately through the little slits on that spotty dirty-brown globaloid forehead...

For about fifteen minutes Ef and I waited for her in the director's office. She finally appeared, or rather, the director led her in, holding her by the arm: The Eternal Murderer was on at the time and that idiot, as far as I could tell, struggled to keep up two layers and could have easily tripped on the stairs, transfixed by the Butcher's Son.

She seemed slightly disappointed by the fact that she was being distracted from the film, but she still tried to be polite. When I said hello, she offered to friend me 'so we can chat normally', but when I replied that I wasn't connected to *socio* something flashed in her eyes and burned there like a broken lamp, something like surprise. She said practically nothing throughout our entire meeting, except to say that she liked serials and 'like, yeah, second layer is so awesome', and I wasn't even sure if she understood why I had been brought there.

I imagined Hanna, so beautiful, with her velvety eyes like the wings of a tortoiseshell butterfly. Hanna, with her pure, pale face. Hanna, who could hold three layers effortlessly. Hanna, whom I had lost forever.

When our silent 'meeting' came to an end, Ef asked me:

'So then, are you happy? Are you convinced that everything's alright with your little Hanna?'

My 'little Hanna' and the director laughed in unison at something I couldn't hear. The planetman in The Eternal Murderer had obviously made a good joke.

I replied to Ef's question:

'She's not Hanna, she never has been her and never will be.'

Ef got up and took a step in my direction. Something predatory appeared in him – not in his cold mirror face, but rather in his movements, in his posture. The director of the boarding house stared at me, gurgled excitedly and then screwed up his face, as if what I had said had caused an attack of heartburn and he had choked on stomach acid.

'What did you mean by that?' Ef asked. 'What does that mean, "not Hanna"?'

'Hanna died.'

'Wow, did he just say that...' Hanna whispered, looking at me with something like awe. 'That's a bad word. You're not allowed to say that.'

'Let's put some handcuffs on for the way back, eh, buddy?' Ef buzzed. 'Looks like you don't respect the Living. Like you don't agree with Him. You just insulted Him, and it's all been recorded on this device.' He pointed at the chatterbox. 'As a member of the Service for Planetary Order I am obliged to inform the Administration at the House of Correction about your behaviour. And recommend that you be moved to the Special Unit.'

Of course he'd been planning on it ending up like this from the very beginning.

...Do I really disagree? Am I really a dissident? I always wanted to be like everyone else. I still want to. Not now, so then, after the Pause.

Hey, you, there, in the future! I hope you really will exist. I hope that you will be me. I hope that I will be. If you are my continuation, if I am you, then sorry about this idiotic incode that you got from me... Personally it's ruined my life, but I really hope you'll cope with it. That you won't get put in the Special Unit. That I won't get put there... That I will become a part of the Living.

It's probably cowardice. It's running away. It's not fair. But if you will exist, if you do exist, sorry for what I'm about to do. I'm planning on killing myself – yes, yes, sorry about that, sorry one more time, I shouldn't say that, I should put it differently. I am planning on 'temporarily ceasing to exist', 'taking a pause', but I'm no fool, I know: they all get pauses, but all I get is a 'stop'. So if you do exist, if you will exist – then we've won, you and me, because it means that we're like everyone else. I'm like everyone else. I am a part of the Living.

I always wanted to be like everyone else. But they have made me a god. They have made me a devil. They have made me a fruit fly for them to do experiments on. They have made me very dangerous. They did not even know what they were doing.

They have forced me into a corner. They have left me completely alone. They have taken away my best friend.

Today he will come again. Ef, the man in the mask. They will pronounce judgment on my case. Look for defects, ask nasty little questions, start digging about inside me like I'm a heap of common property.

And then I'm going to set myself on fire. Then they'll all see how a wonder-sunshine burns!

And here's another thing. If you exist, then, please, visit Cracker at least every now and again. He's very lonely there in his chamber. He's completely stopped moving. They say he fell into a coma and can't see or hear anything anymore. But I'm sure he'll be able to tell that you are sitting there with him.

That I am sitting there with him.

The Man with No Face

cerberus: you distract him and i'll grab him from behind
ef: let's try it the nice way first
cerberus: pointless. but you give it a go if you fancy

Very slowly, trying not to make any sudden movements, Ef moves up to the broken window and carefully raises his hand in greeting.

cerberus: watch don't frighten him

'Happy Birthday, Matthew!' Ef says.

Matthew shudders and gingerly crawls off inside the shop window, crunching on shards of glass. The blood has already clotted on his hands and face – he probably cut himself when he broke the glass.

They had found Matthew in district R 800, on the third floor of the Megalopolis shopping centre. It is one of those hideous abandoned malls which are listed in the 'to be demolished' column in the local office of Plan for a More Beautiful World, but still never get demolished because they're located in uninhabited districts and no one gets round to it. When it comes down to it, Megalopolis is not spoiling anyone's view, because no one, except crazy Matthew, comes out to R 800. At one time activists from the movement 'Memorial' wanted to turn shopping centres like this into museums of antiquity and run tours to them as part of the 'Let's Go for a Walk in First Layer' initiative and show people what commerce looked like before *socio*. However, they didn't manage to get even a single tour group together, so the project was shut down.

...Matthew had taken a shine to one of the women's clothes shops. Actually there had not been any clothes there for a long time, but naked mannequins pranced elegantly in the window.

When Cerberus and Ef came across him, Matthew had adorned the brown plastic girls with swathes of costume jewellery evidently plundered from the neighbouring boutique. When he saw the planetmen he got nervous and tried to hide behind the mannequins, then started building something like a barricade, throwing the women's bodies into a heap, but after a minute he had already calmed down and seemed to have entirely forgotten that anyone else was there.

Now, as Ef gets closer, Matthew looks more perplexed than frightened.

'Happy Birthday,' Ef repeats. 'We've come to congratulate you, Matthew.'

'It's my birthday?' A dreamy expression appears on the old man's face. 'Have you brought me a present?'

> *cerberus:* looks like he's almost conscious
> *ef:* yeah he's responding well

'Oh, of course we have a present for you, Matthew. You turned sixty today. It's an important day.'

'Sixty…' Matthew repeats and then winks, first with one eye, then with the other. 'Sixty. Sixty. Sixty. We strongly recommend.'

'There you go. You even remember that you got a message… We've come to give you something very valuable. A new life.'

'Men with mirrored faces,' Matthew starts mumbling, 'men without faces, men without voices… tremble for he is coming… thine twine swine…' Suddenly, with unexpected deftness, he dashes off to one side towards a jagged hole in the window and quite nimbly jumps out of the shop into the atrium of the shopping centre.

> *cerberus:* going to have to flatten him after all

'...Ye shall all be cast down! For you shall be cast out!'
Matthew breaks into an uneven old man's trot and his
bare feet leave brown bobbles of blood on the dusty floor.
'For the Saviour died for our sins! His name is Zero! Zero!
Died!'

They catch up with him in three bounds, throw him face
down on the floor and inject a tranquilliser into his neck.
Matthew clicks out almost immediately. Cerberus pulls the
handcuffs out of his inside pocket and then immediately
chucks them down on the floor next to Matthew in irritation.

cerberus: damn my contact glove has ripped

He gawps at his hand. A hole has opened up in his right glove.
Cerberus nods towards the handcuffs.

cerberus: ef go on you do it. i can't with bare skin
ef: i don't have any gloves myself. oh ok alright then

Ef leans over Matthew, fusses about with the handcuffs and
clicks them onto the old man's wrists. Matthew's hands are
hot. Which is unpleasant. It somehow doesn't tally with his
immobility and the fringe of black under his nails.

'It's not working!' Cerberus jabs at the lift button. 'We're
going to have to drag him ourselves.'

They haul the limp body down the stairs. The old man is
sticky with sweat and he gives off an overpowering, fermented
smell of gone-off perfume.

cerberus: he's a heavy old sod
ef: why's he put on all this perfume?
cerberus: he didn't put on the perfume he drank it
ef: perfume?!

cerberus: yep... hey, what happened at the end of
festival passions last night? did that virgin put out
for everyone?

They load Matthew into the truck; he quietly belches up a
flowery stench.

ef: dunno i was watching murderer

my adverts: This world... My world in first layer...
So beautiful, so full of variety, so full of life. Nature
feeds it with fresh air and sunlight. Architects fill it
with extraordinary buildings, landscape designers
carve out breathtaking gardens...

ef: turn off adverts

INVALID REQUEST
YOU CANNOT 'TURN OFF ADVERTS'

my adverts: Architects fill it with extraordinary
buildings, landscape designers carve out
breathtaking gardens, space designers take care
to make the layout of the streets alluring and
enchanting, artists strive to produce interesting
colour patterns. And it's all for me...

ef: ban 'my adverts'

you cannot 'ban my adverts'
it looks like you are trying to do something slightly
incorrect

my adverts: ...It's all for me. Because I have always
known how to value the beauty of the world and
I never forget about the importance of first layer.
I choose 'Let's Go for a Walk in First Layer'. I leave
my house at least twice a week. I love my world.
We love our world. We are the Living.

Musical interlude:

I'm going on another walk today,
Down Harmony I'll start to wend my way,
I'll stride along Consensus Boulevard,
And I'll forget that life was ever hard,
Then I'll take a left down Living Street,
It feels so good to move my own two feet,
I know there'll be adventure in the air
On Golden

'...Golden, Golden, Go-o-o-lden Mean Square!' Cerberus
sings along cheerily.

my adverts: Recommended by thousander Aelita!
The best walking route in area R 514 of region EA
8: Harmony Avenue – Consensus Boulevard –
Living Street – Golden Mean Square.
Let's go for a walk in first layer!

'I'm sick of these adverts. I get bombarded morning, noon
and night,' Ef grumbles, looking out the window of the van at
the street.

They are, as it happens, going across the utterly deserted
Golden Mean Square, carving channels in the golden sand. The
concretion of a fist rises up in the middle of the square. It's like
he is in the ring waiting for a rival the right size for him.

> *cerberus:* ah shut it it's a good song and the route's
> really nice
> *cerberus:* right we're here let's get him out
> *cerberus:* ef!

'Ef!' Cerberus's chatterbox glugs excitedly.

> *ef:* sorry i must have drifted off for a second

> *Ef has left a message for Cleo: 'let's go for a walk
> in first layer?'*

> *CAUTION! user Cleo is busy right now, you might
> be disturbing them*

The Festival for Assisting Nature greets them from afar with sonorous salvoes of fireworks and as soon as they drive onto the premises a song comes on in second layer, 'Listen to my pulse!', the latest musical hit from Festival Passions.

They unload Matthew; Cerberus sings along out of tune. He loves the festival and the sense of celebration. Matthew shakes his head, as if he is trying to force the loud noises out of it, and groans weakly. He has already come to, but he's groggy, like a fly in summer, and he barely resists as they unload him.

> *listen to my pulse baby*
> *listen to your pulse baby*

In the foyer of the Pause Zone the song comes across worse than outside, in snatches, and it sounds muffled. Matthew calms down. He even smiles when he sees a clown holding a bunch of balloons.

'It's my birthday,' Matthew tells the clown. 'Is that a present?' He nods at the balloons.

The clown leaps up and spins round on one leg, tweaks his own squeaky red nose, nods happily and holds out the balloons. Matthew tries to take the string in his hand; the handcuffs clink quietly. He freezes, staring at the clown in surprise, as if he is trying to tell by the sound what is stopping him accepting the present.

mo-o-ove to the rhythm
of our pulse

The clown winks a painted eye at the planetmen.

'Compulsory,' Ef whispers with his mirrored lips. Cerberus nods irritatedly. The clown hunches over and pulls his head down into his shoulders, miming horror. Behind this exaggerated, jokey fear, there is, it seems, real fear hiding in the corner of his multi-coloured eyes. He had not spotted the compulsory. He had not noticed the handcuffs. A good professional should always notice things like that.

Meanwhile Matthew is starting to get seriously nervous. It would seem that he has finally remembered how he got here and why. He is about to dart off towards the exit, but Cerberus and Ef take him by the arms and grip from both sides.

mo-o-ove to the rhythm

'Hounds of hell!' Matthew screeches. 'Men with mirror faces! Men without faces…!'

The pre-pausers, clustering excitedly around Souvenir Photos and Everything's Going to Be Alright, start to look around. Quickly scratching the mirrored masks of the planetmen with his gaze and clarifying something for himself, the clown screws his painted face into a grimace of pain. He starts to weep loudly and squirts out two little fountains of artificial tears. Matthew breaks off in the middle of his sentence and looks pityingly at the clown. He stops crying, flashes his white teeth in a smile, gives his hooter nose another squeeze, hands the balloons to Ef and takes a sweet out of his pocket. He takes off the rustling wrapper. Matthew holds his breath as he watches him.

'Let's have a little vitamin!' the clown announces solemnly. Matthew obediently opens his mouth wide and the clown puts an opalescent black sweet on his tongue. Then he bows and, as if showing Matthew what to do, marches cheerfully off to the far end of the foyer, towards the entrance to the Zone. Once there he waves to Matthew.

listen to my pulse listen to my pulse

'Don't go in there, multi-coloured man,' Matthew whispers, looking at the clown in fascination. 'Don't go in there, your paint will get washed off in there…'

I know one thing
there'll be a Darling
listen to my pulse listen to my pulse listen to my
pulse listen to my pulse listen to my pulse

There's something strange going on with the sound – it suddenly comes blaring on at full power. An invisible orchestra strikes up with a subtle electronic tremble, the anonymous singer pushes her screechy mantra from her throat in multiple spasms. Cerberus snarls and nods along obediently, Ef rummages through 'services' on the festival settings, hoping to switch off the soundtrack (an error has occurred: you are probably trying to do something slightly incorrect), Matthew writhes about, going limp in their hands. The pre-pausers who have crowded together in the foyer look around – some resentfully, some happily – and automatically drum out the rhythm with their feet. The ones that were talking out loud break into shouts, trying hard to yell over the noise of the deep layers.

my pulse listen to my pulse listen to my...

At last the music is turned off. The conversations die down. Only a young-looking pre-pauser, who has got all dressed up especially for the occasion, done up head to toe in 'feeling lucky' glad rags, is blaring away to the whole Pause Zone like a deaf-mute and flashing his greasy little eyes.

'...I never needed any accompaniment, it always worked like clockwork for me, I tell you I've sired a fair few Darlings here in my time...!'

The person he is talking to makes 'scary' eyes, the young-looking pre-pauser looks around and shuts up embarrassed. Total silence reigns – both in second layer and in first, as if something thick and sticky has been poured into his ears from inside and out. Matthew concentrates on sucking his sweet, he's not shouting and jerking about anymore, and Cerberus and Ef sit him down on the colourful sofa. The old man immerses himself in studying the design.

> user **clown** wants to become your friend on socio
> add him as a friend? yes no

Ef turns round. The clown is standing at the opposite end of the foyer in the company of another four men with faces painted like him and is waving both hands at him joyously. The rest are studying him with strange, playful smiles; one, in a jester's hat with little bells on it, is giggling. Only now does Ef realise that he is still holding the clown's present. A planetman in a mirror mask with balloons... That's a laugh.

Like in ancient times. No one could laugh at the king's guards except the king's jesters.

cerberus: don't pay any attention to those freaks
ef: ok

The jesters keep the Living jolly, so He doesn't get bored. They cheer Him up in all sorts of ways – even laughing at His own power.

*reminder: user **clown** wants to become your friend in socio*
add him to friends?
*yes **no***

The clown's face is twisted in a grimace of disappointment. Two fountains of artificial tears soak the foyer.

*user **clown** <u>really wants</u> to become your friend on socio*
you and clown have 1 mutual friend on socio: cleo
add clown as a friend?
***yes**_no*
*hooray! you and **clown** are now friends*

Silence bursts in his ears like popping bubbles. The music turns on again in second layer – quiet and subtle, without words. Info-fest is launched in third layer. For those poor creatures that can't hold third layer, the message is repeated in first layer through a loudspeaker. It turns on with a crackle and a cough, as if someone had cracked open a nut with their teeth and then choked on it.

'Dear guests and friends of guests! The festival administration is pleased to welcome you to the Pause Zone. There are thirty minutes remaining until the next Pause. We would like to draw your attention to the refreshments on offer: coffee, tea, hot and cold drinks and snacks. If you are in need of entertainment, one of our festival clowns is sure to lift your spirits with their fun tricks. If you are feeling sad or experiencing any distress, please ask one of the clowns about tranqvitamins...'

> *clown:* ef thanks for friending me

'...Dear guests! We would like to remind you that our pavilion offers a Souvenir Photos service. Your festival snaps from today will be transferred to your cell in the Renaissance Global Databank along with any other keepsakes; you can pick them up when you turn eight and have access to your cell.'

> *ef:* no worries
> *clown:* i've always dreamed of being friends with
> a planetman

'...Dear guests! We would like to remind you that our pavilion offers an Everything's Going to Be Alright service. If you have any unfinished business – if you have forgotten to tell someone something or to give them something, or if you have not had time to take your pet to the local Available Shelter, or if you would like to write something right now for your bank deposit cell, or anything else – don't worry. Our managers will accept your requests, take into account your wishes and tie up all your loose ends. Everything's going to be alright!'

'I want to pass on a message,' Matthew says.

> *clown:* listen sorry i screwed up there with your
> compulsory. i didn't realise at first what was going on...
> are you going to make a complaint about me?
> *ef:* not if you do me a favour
> *clown:* no probs what do you need?

'I've got a message. I have to pass on a message. My message.' Matthew rocks from side to side.

'Dear guests! We would like to remind you that the same hygiene code applies in the Pause Zone as in the Reproduction Zone. Before the Pause guests are obliged to take a disinfecting shower. The shower booths are exactly the same as those in the Reproduction Zone, so we hope that there will be no difficulties.'

> *ef:* i want to see cleo
> *clown:* she's right here on chat! she's 'busy'
> *ef:* not on chat. in person. in first layer
> *clown:* what have i got to do with it?
> *ef:* you work together, at the festival. she's a manager. you must know where she is
> *clown:* yeah, i know
> *ef:* show me
> *clown:* but... have you agreed to meet? she really is busy right now
> *ef:* are you going to do me a favour or what?!
> *clown:* hey don't stress out. do you want a little tranqvit?

'...A set of towels and a bathrobe will be provided for you as you enter the showers, which are situated immediately inside the entrance to the Pause Zone. We would like to express our heartfelt gratitude for the assistance you are giving to nature. There is no death!'

> *ef:* i'm filing a complaint
> *clown:* hang on. The seventh everything's going to be alright booth.

Ef slowly turns his mirrored face towards the seventh booth. A worried pre-pauser is dallying in front of the reflective glass of the little booth. He's explaining something, gesticulating wildly. He's sticking some bit of paper into a drawer that is sticking out. The drawer creeps back, the pre-pauser tracks it jealously and looks beseechingly at his own reflection.

Ef looks with mirrored eyes at Cleo's mirrored booth. She looks at him from inside. He can feel her watching him.

Cleo

I like the fact that I'm also behind a mirror. Not just my face, but all of me, entirely. I try to imagine that in the booth I'm safe. That I'm a snail in my shell. That I'm someone's pet and my owner won't let me get hurt.

> clown: some planetman's looking for you kiddo

I can't stand it when a needle is poked under my shell to make me stick my head out.

> cleo: the one with the balloons?

I never doubted that he would come to me in first layer. Ef's not the type to make empty threats. He's brought a compulsory. There are two of them in masks, in identical uniforms, but for some reason I guess immediately which one of them is Ef. It's like the balloons are his emblem.

> clown: that's the guy. he's asking me what booth
> you're in
> cleo: don't tell him
> clown: what do you take me for!? of course i'm not
> going to tell him!!

At that very second Ef fixes his gaze on my booth. He tells him.

> cleo: thanks a lot clown. i knew i could count on you
> clown: no worries! i'm as quiet as a larva ☺

I, by the way, never had any doubt that Clown would give me away. He's a nasty piece of work, I didn't like him from the moment I saw him. There's something rotten about him. And under the paint his skin is the colour of a rotten banana... A lot darker than usual globaloid skin.

Clown was transferred to us a month ago, allegedly from some distant region. Allergies – that's how he explained the transfer. 'An allergy to local grasses.' Clown brought a whole nursery of house flies with him and took one of the terrariums into the festival's Available Corner. He's just like those flies – intrusive, clueless and he gets everywhere. Literally. Once he was my partner in the Reproduction Zone – I still feel sick when I remember that act. He stuck his tongue in my ears, my eyes, my nostrils. His tongue was stiff and sticky and his breath smelled of rotten fruit.

Then it turned out that the flies were not his pets, but food for his pets. Clown's pets were these disgusting beetles, some of which had two heads. A week ago he brought in six beetles (five females and one male) and put them in the terrarium. Within a couple of hours the female beetles had devoured all the flies, then the male inseminated them and they devoured him too; he didn't resist. The next day they produced larvae and ceased to exist...

> **Subject: chain letter**
> *You are a woman. The Living demands that you mate regularly but you don't want a Darling. Follow Zero. He'll let you take precautions* ☺
> *!warning!* **this may be spam**
> *mark this message as spam?*
> **yes** *no*

Ef stares at me, right in the eyes, as if he can see me through the mirrored wall of the booth. That's impossible, I tell myself, but my sense of invincibility disappears anyway. As if someone had just injected citric acid under the snail's shell.

The pre-pauser client is still banging on like before. I look in his profile – he is sixty tomorrow. He came by himself – but at the last moment. Once I used to feel pity for people like him –

the unfortunates, fitfully attempting to mumble away their fear of the Five Seconds of Darkness with absurd requests and instructions. Now there's nothing but irritation. With an effort of will I force myself not to look at Ef and to concentrate on what the client is saying.

'...the idea, you know, only just came to me, but I've always been a creative person... I've jotted down the main points here, on this bit of paper... and if you could just give my project to the Association of Screenwriters... today, so that everything's, you know, sorted by the time I...I'm able to join the team...'

The 'profession' entry in his profile reads: arc welder. And I know that he'll be a welder in his new reproduction too; that's the best case scenario. Guys like him never join the Association of Screenwriters after the pause – however much people blather on about the flexibility of your invector.

Guys like him never make dizzying leaps forward in their careers. No one ever does. Everyone either stays on the same level or falls lower. Like I did. From being who I was before, before the pause, to turning into an 'everything's going to be alright' manager.

'Everything's going to be alright,' I tell the pre-pauser from inside my shell. 'We can guarantee that your project will be handed to the recipient.'

...Ef finally looks away. And leans over to the compulsory that they brought in. He says something in his ear. He nods like a rag doll being shaken. He's clearly on tranqvits: he is obedience itself.

'...the main thing is that it gets to them... Because this idea, I've got to say, can't fail... Everyone's going to love it...'

The compulsory gets up slowly; Ef supports him, holding him by the arm.

'...And if everyone loves it that means the Living is going to love it too... I'll just quickly tell you, young lady, what it's about...'

And they walk in my direction. Ef and the old compulsory.

'...my working title is The Eternal Nobody, but if the
Association of Screenwriters comes up with something of their
own I'm not going complain... I called it that because the idea
is sort of part of the same project as The Eternal Murderer...
The thing is that this Zero, or rather, Nobody – he's, like, not
part of the Living, he doesn't have an incode, and he's trying
to destroy the harmony of the Living...'

Ef and his compulsory stand behind my client. They're
waiting their turn – even though there are a few free booths.
The compulsory rocks from side to side, his face is calm, his
eyes closed. Ef holds him by the arm. It's just idyllic.

'...The SPO find out about this. And they try to eliminate
Nobody... So far it's based on real events... Well, Zero, you
know... And that's when the made-up bits start... Then it
turns out that it's not that easy to kill Nobody, and he actually
survives, and sort of starts carrying out his revenge plans...
Nobody hides in...'

'Very interesting,' I say. 'I have no doubt that everything's
going to be alright with your project.'

'Really?' The welder's face lights with a smile that's so
happy that I activate the external camera in portrait mode.
For an advertising stand. 'Our clients are pleased because
everything's going to be alright.'

'Absolutely,' I say. 'Your project will be given to the
Association of Screenwriters today.'

'And once it's there, do you reckon, that everything's going
to be...'

'We are only responsible for prompt delivery.' I turn off
portrait mode.

The smile is falling from his face and that wouldn't do for
the stand.

'Are there any other tasks or will that be all?'

'That's all,' he looks at me with sickly eyes. Previously I used to feel sorry for people like him...

'OK then, thank you for using this service today. Everything will be alright, until we meet again, there is no death.'

'No death...'

...Now I don't feel sorry for them. He makes fitful attempts to find something else to latch onto. To avoid going off into the darkness, even for five seconds. Just to be in a place where everything is always alright.

'Ah yes... the towels...'

'You will receive a towel and bathrobe when you enter the shower room, which is situated immediately in the Pause Zone. You can use an additional Everything's Going to Be Alright bonus and choose the colour of your robe and towel right now.'

'Of course! Of course, I want to choose right now!' He's positively trembling with relief. 'What colours do you have?'

Decent managers call it the 'bathrobe trick'. It works ninety times out of a hundred with worried clients. It's amazing how cowards like my welder grasp at the offer of choosing the colour... You know, the illusion of control over the situation; they don't know what's in store for them in the Pause Zone, but they know that they'll be wearing a stripy bathrobe; I have some idea how it works, I understand the psychological mechanism, but I continue to be surprised. Your spectrum of possibilities has collapsed to the chance to choose the colour of a bit of material. Isn't that humiliating?

'We would like to draw your attention to the plain *socio* coloured bathrobes – free, unavailable and inviz, as well as blue and black robes with orange stripes and checked robes done in feeling lucky tones.'

'Feeling lucky!' he chooses. They all choose that.

'No death!' The welder leaves almost happy.

'No death.' Ef leads his compulsory up to the booth.

'This is the Festival's Everything's Going to Be Alright service,' I chirp.

> *ef:* hi cleo. are you sure everything's going to be
> alright?
> *cleo:* what do you want from me?!

I say out loud:
'We would like to remind you that all our services may only be discussed in first layer and will be recorded on video and audio. How can I help you?'

> *ef:* information

Out loud he says:
'This is my friend Matthew. He would like to use your services.' Ef gives me the compulsory's incode and shakes him gently, like a tank with a sleeping pet inside. Matthew slowly opens his eyes. His huge pupils, the irises wide open, are two round burrows leading down into the dark of his skull. Tranqvitamins. Two or three times the normal dose. This creature is hardly in any condition to use any services, except, of course, the pause itself.

'Everything is going to be alright,' I tell the empty black openings. 'How can we help you?'

I am not expecting any reply, but by some miracle Matthew switches on:
'I want to pass on a message.'
'Fantastic. Is it some photographs? Documents? Some kind of object?'
'A message.'
'If it's just a message, you can pass it on yourself through *socio*. Right now.' He can't see me, but just in case I smile my most radiant smile as I open his personal profile in third layer.

The compulsory silently screws up his empty eyes. He's strange – too strange even for someone on tranqvitamins. And his profile is opening too slowly...

> *cleo:* <u>request to TSS:</u> a document's frozen on me in 3rd layer, what's going on?
> *TSS_195:* checking in progress...please wait, checking in progress
> *TSS_196:* access is temporarily forbidden. your *socio*-activity is limited or absent
> *cleo:* ???
> *TSS_195:* all bugs will be fixed in a few seconds. we would like to apologise for any inconvenience...

'My head can't,' Matthew tells me dreamily and presses his face against the booth.

I see his dilated pupils right in front of me. They are pulsating slightly, as if the darkness is pushing them open from the inside. As if they're going to burst open any second now and coat the walls of the booth in splashes of black... He's barely managing to stand upright. Too high a dose. How is he even talking...?

'Your correspondent cannot receive the message? Do they not have *socio*-activity? The thing is we're having a few slight bugs with *socio* right now, in a few seconds they'll all be...'

'Impossible,' Matthew quietly knocks his forehead against the wall of the booth, as if he's asking to be let in. 'Connection is impossible. Impossible...'

'...Maybe your correspondent is not yet three years of age...?' Clown makes faces at me from the other end of the foyer. Matthew smiles at Clown's reflection in the cabin wall. Ef smiles too. My confusion clearly amuses him.

'Whatever it is, Matthew, let's proceed as follows. I'll give you a piece of paper and a pen, and you can write your message and also...'

'Won't work,' Ef finally speaks up.

TSS_195: bugs fixed...

'Why not?'
'Matthew can't write.'

cleo: what on earth are you talking about?!

'You are perhaps not quite right,' I say. 'The educational program Living Fingers is installed at the age of five...'
'He's forgotten how to write, go onto the "info" section on his profile, it says on there...'
Even before Ef manages to finish his sentence, I see myself: '...at the age of thirty numerous errors were discovered in the program. Diagnosis: inoperable system failure. *Socio* cannot be reinstalled due to organic violations in the brain...'
'Which is why Matthew is not able to send and receive messages,' Ef says.
'But... I can see he's got activity in fourth layer. Right now!'
'In fourth?' Ef smiles. 'This fellow can't even hold second! Phantom activity flashes... They don't have any meaningful content. You will have to write the message out yourself, by hand. And give it to the recipient – if, of course, he remembers who he wants to send it to.'
The compulsory continues to bang up against the wall of the booth like a moth.
'Matthew,' I say as gently as possible, 'everything's going to be alright. Now I'm going to write down your message. You read it out and I'll write it down, OK?'
His eyes roll up into his head, he presses his cheek and the corner of his slobbering mouth against the booth and begins to slide down slowly. I catch sight of two long, dirty teeth beneath his top lip as it is pulled back. Ef catches Matthew

before he falls and takes him in his arms like a little Darling. I look at his limp body: the tranqvitamins have finally done their job... Then something happens which cannot happen. I still hear – we both hear – Matthew speaking, dour and dispassionate:

'Write down this message. Subject of message. To the saviour from the apostle. Beginning of text. You have come to save the world. The monster must die at your hands...'

Ef's mirrored mask wrinkles with lines of surprise on his forehead. He leans his head over Matthew and the old man's face is reflected in his. His rolled eyes reveal a stripe of white and an inflamed hatchwork of blood vessels. His parted lips have yellowish drops of drool in the corners. It is just unthinkable that this man can talk right now, but still he is talking, dragging the words out of his recalcitrant mouth:

'...You will be a captive, but the servant will elevate you, if you serve him. End of text.'

'Everything's alright,' I say to myself, 'everything's going to be alright. Even if your client is ranting away, just do your job. Carry out your duties, and that's all.'

'Who should I give the message to?'

'The Saviour,' Matthew replies.

'There is no one with that nickname on the *socio* base,' I say. 'But everything's alright. There's a Saver, a Saver1, a Saver33... Shall I pass your message on to one of those?'

'To the Saviour. His name is Zero.'

>   *just do your job...*

'Unfortunately, we cannot carry out your request. The person who you are talking about, Zero, he... is no longer living. He was not reproduced.'

'Everything is going to be alright,' Matthew says in a singsong voice. 'Yes, he died for our sins. But give him the message when he rises again.'

We wait for him to continue, but Matthew does not say

another word. For some reason Ef rocks him gently in his arms, as if he were singing a lullaby to a Darling.

The loudspeaker plays an announcement:

'The next pause will begin in one minute. We would like to encourage all guests to make their way into the Pause Zone! Dear guests! We would like to remind you that the same hygiene code applies in the Pause Zone as in the Reproduction Zone. Before the Pause guests are obliged to take a disinfecting shower. The shower booths are exactly the same as those in the Reproduction Zone, so we hope that there will be no difficulties. Could all those who have come to say goodbye to their friends please leave the foyer. Thank you for assisting nature. Until we meet again. There is no death!'

'You have to leave, officer,' I say to Ef, trying to hide the gloating note in my voice.

'Matthew can't walk. I'll carry him into the Pause Zone.'

> *cleo:* are you trying to wind me up? all this is being recorded. so you're only compromising yourself, not me

In first layer I say:

'Unfortunately, that is not possible. There is no provision in the Festival programme for those coming to say goodbye to Pausers to enter the Pause Zone. You are saying goodbye to him, right?'

'Yes...'

'Don't worry, everything's going to be alright with your charge. I have already called for a wonder-trolley...'

...He lays Matthew on his back on the wonder-trolley. Matthew opens his eyes. His pupils are not so enormous anymore and you can see what colour his eyes are. Blue. Murky blue, like a new-born Darling.

'Everything's going to be alright,' I say to him. 'The wonder-trolley is fitted with the latest navigation systems. It will deliver you to the shower room quickly and directly.'

> ef: look at him! what does he need with a shower
> room?! he can't even stand up. he can't even get
> undressed.
> cleo: that's not a problem

'My present...' Matthew whimpers quietly. 'Birthday... my
present... present...'

'Here's your present.' Ef ties the bunch of balloons to one
of the wonder-straps.

Matthew obediently immerses himself in observing the
balloons. He doesn't even notice the wonder-trolley moving
off. Ef, stooping over, watches him go. Something's wrong
with him, with Ef. The Living is, without doubt, full of love,
but I've never seen a planetman being so kind to a compulsory.

> ef: is someone going to help him in there?
> cleo: ??

'Will someone help him get changed and leave the shower?'
he asks out loud.

Only now do I finally realise that there's something not right
about him.

> **FESTIVAL INFO:** This evening's pause has been
> successfully completed. All Pause Zone employees
> are free for the day.

'Everything's going to be alright,' I say.

Then I turn off the light, switch off the audio and video
recording, clamber out of the booth into the empty foyer and,
my lips almost touching his lifeless mirror neck, I whisper:
'They don't leave the shower.'

Report

(Transcript of conversation with Staff Entomologist at House of Correction No. 3578, 'Harmony', conducted by SPO officer, dated 17.07.471 A.V.; extract)

Entomologist: ...Like a pillar of fire, yes. He burned down to the ground, right in front of our eyes. And you know what I've got to say? I don't care. I don't feel sorry for him. He wasn't a part of the Living, the Living would never have shown such cruelty to his little brothers. And I begged him, the creep...

SPO officer: I would ask you to choose your expressions carefully: this conversation is being recorded for the case file.

Entomologist: Sorry. I begged him not to set himself on fire by the pets! I even feel some responsibility for what happened. I didn't protect them! I asked all the correctees to save the last minutes of the feed from the termite mound in their memories. It's a very sad video. The way the soldiers stuck their heads out of the mound, trying to stop the fire getting in. The way the workers...

SPO officer: Thanks, I've heard that already. I am talking to you now not in your role as an entomologist, but as a witness. I'd like more details about when correctee Zero set himself on fire.

Entomologist: He was holding a wonder-sunshine...

SPO officer: Where did the correctee get hold of that device?

Entomologist: He stole it from the Special Unit. We use wonder-sunshines there in the fluorescent lights.

SPO officer: So, what, any correctee can just come along and take the wonder-sunshine out of the light?

Entomologist: No! Of course not. The lamps are put high up. Plus to unscrew the panel and get the wonder-sunshine out you need a special tool.

SPO officer: Then how, in your opinion, did correctee Zero get hold of the wonder-sunshine?

Entomologist: I have no idea. Maybe he had an accomplice. I don't know. Why are you asking me and not the House security service? They can at least show you the footage from the cameras in the Special Unit.

SPO officer: We believe that we have good reason to ask you. We have already questioned the guards. And watched the footage from the cameras. Everything there checks out – if, of course, you don't count the thirty minutes on the day before the fire when the cameras were turned off due to an unexplained technical error. By the way, how good are you with technology?

Entomologist: What are you implying? I am good at what I do. Insects.

SPO officer: Alright then, let's go back to the fire. How exactly did the wonder-sunshine start burning?

Entomologist: I have no idea! Correctee Zero was holding the wonder-sunshine in his hand and then he just... went up in flames. I don't know how it happened. Wonder-sunshines don't explode just like that. It requires a really strong blow.

SPO officer: I am aware of that. And there was no blow?

Entomologist: No, there wasn't.

SPO officer: Then how do you explain what happened?

Entomologist: I... don't know. Maybe the Living performed a miracle. Destroyed that which was not a part of Him.

Cleo

The brilliant sand crunches under my feet. Unlike most people I like going on walks: walking in first layer helps keep you fit. At least I don't weigh eighty kilos like the majority of women that come to the festival to shake their flabby bodies...

He follows me out of the festival complex. Golden Mean Square is empty – there is no one here but us and that stupid fist... I don't like concrete art.

> *cleo:* why did you need to meet in person?
> *ef:* to ask you a personal question
> *cleo:* you can ask me a personal question in a deep layer
> *ef:* in a deep layer i won't see your face
> *cleo:* what do you want?!

He replies out loud, with the chatterbox switched off – when it's not distorted by the device, his voice sounds unpleasantly animated:

'I want to know how sincere your answer is.'

> *cleo:* that's crazy! what's my face got to do with anything??

He says nothing. I can't tell anything from his face, that's for sure. I am so envious of his mask.

> *cleo:* so then, what's this question?

'Do you know the formula for the injection? The one used in the experiment with the directed Leo-Lot ray?'
'Is this an interrogation?'
'No. You can see. The conversation device is switched off.'

'Then gopz. Why do you think I'm going to answer your question?'

'Because I have a couple of documents in my memory. And if I forward them to my bosses, then you're going to be put under investigation.'

> *cleo:* can i see what these documents are before
> i reply?
> *ef:* of course

'Only now I'll put the question differently,' he adds out loud.

> *cleo:* ???

'The formula for the injection?'

> *cleo:* i told you i don't know
> *ef:* then why are we talking

He brings his mirrored face up to mine so that I see my reflection.

'You have very expressive features, Cleo.'

He turns away and walks off through the square, the golden sand rustling under his feet.

> *hi,* cleo!
> *you have a new message from a friend*
> *open message now?*
> **yes** *no*
>
> *from: ef*
> *to: cleo*
> *subject: none*
> *text: none*
> *attached files: Cleo.doc; Beetle.doc*

Not turning back, he waves at me.

ef: sorry if i offended you at all

Ef

'I'm cold,' Ef says, 'I shouldn't sleep on the snow anymore.'

He doesn't look good. Worse than two days ago. Back then it had even seemed to me like the swelling had started to go down slightly but I probably just didn't notice it in the bad light: all I had was some smelly wax candles which I'd got from Megalopolis. Now that I've finally fixed a Nativity garland to the bars with tiny wonder-sunshines and the cage is awash with golden light, it's horrible to even look at him.

His right eye has closed up almost entirely, the left is a bloodshot crack glinting in the folds of his livid eyelids, like the shell of a mollusc just opening in the heat. His hair is sticky with sweat, blood and pus and is standing up in a funny tuft, his lips have become dry and cracked. He hasn't eaten and hasn't drunk the vitacomplex that I left him: the white bottle and packet of dry food are untouched. The haematoma sprawls over his face in an uneven patch: it is like the juice of crushed blackberries has soaked through his skin. The wound itself – at the top of the forehead, right in the middle – doesn't look so bad now and is kind of heal-ing... But it's giving off a bad smell. The smell of rotten cheese.

'Let's redo this wound,' I say, opening the first aid kit.

'No need. Just put a bit of snow on it.'

'It's summer now, Ef.'

His dry lips give a weak smile:

'Who are you trying to fool, Cerberus? The whole place is covered in snow. You're standing up to your knees in a snow drift.'

For the first couple of days he just whimpered in pain and kept losing consciousness, but the rest of the time he was able to think more or less clearly. Now he is almost permanently delirious. He thinks I am Cerberus. In his rare moments of insight he asks who I am and where we are, but he can't concentrate on the reply.

'Request to TSS, check my connection to *socio*... I can't see my friend list...'

I inject him with something to reduce his fever. I pour a few thick mouthfuls of vitacomplex into his mouth. I look over the wound and change the bandage. Ef does not resist and doesn't even groan, as if he isn't in pain anymore.

'Cold,' he repeats.

I cover him with another rug. It's twenty-five degrees outside and here in the cage it must be as high as thirty, but Ef really is shivering from the cold.

'Did he really leave us here to freeze?' I can hear despair and hurt in his voice.

'Who is "he"?' I am curious.

'The Living, who else. It was him who sent us here to look for the antivirus... No connection to *socio*... But he is right. We are now infected and we are a threat. We should stay away until the pause... I can't see my friend list... The crystalline structure of the snowflake is the source of infection. It's no surprise that there is no antivirus yet. That's what harmony is like: any snowman can become a traitor...'

I figure that there is more going on here than just the wound and the fever. He's going mad because he's got no connection. Like a warrior termite that's been moved to a separate container.

Ef's face is covered in a beaded film of sweat. The beads are slowly swelling... I touch his forehead with my hand – not so hot any more, the jab is starting to work – and look at my wet hand. The skin on his forehead is so purple that it's amazing that something clear can ooze out of it.

'Where am I?' Ef asks me. I reply:

'In the old zoo. You're sitting in a cage which used to house a pair of orang-utans.'

This is the absolute truth. That's what it says on the sign.

'Who are you?' Ef asks me.

I reply:

'A friend.'

That's a lie.

'I can't see my friend list,' he says in despair. 'Where's my friend list gone? I can't remember their names... who did you say used to live here...?'

'Orang-utans.'

'I don't remember what orang-utans are...'

'Tree-dwelling apes,' I swiftly open *Wikipedia* in second layer. 'Until the beginning of our era they lived in the rainforest of the islands of Borneo and Sumatra, in what is now region A3 6. The majority of the population was exterminated during the Great Reduction; the remainder died out as a result of migration into regions with an unsuitable climate...'

He listens to me so attentively, his mouth hanging open, that I feel ashamed. I shouldn't have made fun of him.

'And my praying mantis...?'

'I'm feeding your mantis.'

'You are Cerberus, right? There's something up with my memory,' he says. 'I've got no access. I can't get into my memory.'

So many times over these days while I have been keeping him here an almost irresistible desire has risen up inside me to give back to him that which I have taken from him and which I have no need for. His friends, his shows, his pleasures, his games, his circulars. The magic box containing his memory and his reason. But it's too late. It's all gone too far.

I've gone too far...

'I understand,' Ef looks me right in the eye with his murky, bloodshot eye. 'Finish me off.'

His voice sounds calm, almost matter-of-fact, and for the first time for many days his face looks aware.

'Just finish me off. One more blow to the head.'

A horrible feeling rises up inside me, as if someone is digging through my hair. And crawling up my back. At that moment the *autodoctor* bursts into my skull with helpful comments

> perhaps your instincts are suggesting that there is some threat of danger: piloerection and adrenaline release detected.

Piloerection…? *Wikipedia* obediently pops up with a definition: a basic reflex, the contraction of the muscles of the hair follicles, resulting in the hair being raised. In response to danger raised fur makes animals seem larger and more frightening… *Descriptive Illustration* flashes up: some little animal looking like an angry ball of fur…

All this noise. All these flashes, bubbles, voices, windows, boxes. An endless party inside my head. A crowd of well-intentioned strangers, they reply and ask questions, talk and demonstrate, interrupt and cajole, they ask me out for a walk, they force me to be friends. Fofs, they've exhausted me! But there, sitting opposite me, is a man who cannot live without them… Danger? How can this castrated cripple be a threat to me: even if his mind has cleared for a moment…? So, no: my piloerection does not come from fear. Tell me, autodoctor, can you get piloerection from shame? From regret? From guilt and self-disgust?

> *autodoctor:* in very rare cases

Well then, what we have here is a very rare case. Extremely rare. I would even say unique.

Ef looks up at me, tilting his head strangely, as if he was planning to charge at me and gore me.

'I'm wounded,' he states with inexplicable joy.

I suddenly realise what this look of concentration of his means: he's not looking at me at all, he's examining his reflection in my mirrored face. His bruise, his swollen eye and the bandage on his head...

He feels his wound through the bandage, presses it a few times with two fingers, somehow too roughly and sharply, and every time he gasps in amazement, as if he's surprised that it might hurt.

'...I'm wounded right in the *socio* slot. Did you do this to me?'

I look at his unavailable watering eye, I look for a long time, trying to figure out why there is this strange exhilaration in his voice again, but his eye doesn't express anything except patient expectation of an answer and I reply, 'Yes, Ef, I did that to you.'

What now? He will ask why, he will promise that I'll be put on the Blacklist, he will go crazy, he will try to mutilate me in return, he will demand a connection, a doctor and details. I will say that it's his own fault, I'll say that I'm sorry, that I'm really sorry, but I had no other choice, I will say 'forgive me', and then, probably, I will do what he asks. I will finish him off. One more blow to the head. Or maybe two or three. I can't keep him here forever.

Instead of that he says, 'You're awesome. You're a total legend!'

He says:

'This new game is just mind-blowing! "The Mean Streets of First Layer", right? Isn't that what it's called? A proper no deather!'

He says, 'I've got to send my thanks to the Association of Game Raters right away! Those guys have done a great job! At first I didn't even realise that I'm in fifth layer... Total illusion of first! Visually, and with sensations of pain, and... Cerberus, have you given it a rating? The sensory stimulation is better than in *luxury*, no? And especially this whole thing with the broken *socio* slot,' he pokes his fingers right into the wound again, wrinkling his forehead with pain and pleasure. 'Smin, I was completely convinced that I had actually been disconnected from *socio*! I only guessed when I saw my reflection...' He laughs and then is overcome with wheezy coughing. '...At this beaten meat in the place of my face and no mask, hardly realistic is it? And that's when it hit me: if my *socio* slot has blacked out, why is the cerebron not backing it up...? And this snow... it's also a sort of signal... of alarm... I've sort of... lost track... what was I just saying?'

He looks around embarrassed. Licks his dry lips. Gawps at me with his mollusc-eye, trustingly, waiting for a hint.

Who am I to take away his final consolation? To explain to the termite that he's now in a separate container. The termite really wants to believe that he is still building the mound along with everyone else, like before. So I give him a hint.

'You were saying that you like this game. "The Mean Streets of First Layer." Everything's really realistic.'

'Right, exactly!' He's happy again. 'The game. Well, I, basically, give up. One–nil to you. I can't for the life of me figure out where the escape is here... Everything's done so cleverly... So finish me off. Looks like that's the only way out of here.'

'You're right,' I say. 'There's no other way out. Everything is done so cleverly.'

Zero

The first time it was Foxcub. A year before the fire. He came up to me on the Available Terrace and looked at me damply for a long time with eyes the colour of rotten potato. Until I realised that he was trying to talk to me in second layer and stopped giving him the cold shoulder:

'It's not going to work. I am completely *asocial*.'

I turned away from him and set off walking alongside the rows of pets, but for some reason Foxcub shambled after me. I changed direction a few times but he just meandered around after me, like a fly following a slop-bucket, so I turned round to face him again:

'What do you want, Fox?'

His expression was so blank, even for him, that I had to grab him by the shoulder and shake him.

'Hey, Fox! What are you after? Say it out loud!'

'Hi. It. Is. Me,' Foxcub announced slowly, with evident effort.

'I know it's you. Fox, are you sick or something?'

'No. I. Am. Not. Fox.'

'Wait, I'm going to call a warder...'

'No. No. No. No.'

'Hey, calm down...'

By the way, he seemed absolutely calm. Too calm even.

'Just in silence. Follow him.'

'Who?!'

'Foxcub,' said Foxcub.

'Why are you talking about yourself in the third person?'

'About myself,' Foxcub whispered barely audibly and set off towards the exit from the Available Terrace.

His movements were slow and strangely fluid, as if he were walking underwater. It all looked so crazy that I followed him. In silence.

We floated unhurriedly down the corridor, went out into the yard, crossed it and entered the Special Unit. We were searched at the entrance; the guard took a gnawed pencil from somewhere under Foxcub's clothes and shook it in front of his nose:

'Writing implement: what's this for?'

'What for,' Foxcub fixed his potato eyes on the writing implement and froze.

He stood motionless for a little while, blinking, his mouth slightly open, entirely immersed in observation. It seemed like he was carefully studying the tooth marks on the wooden surface in order to attempt to comprehend its deep pencilly essence, its destiny and meaning.

'What's up with him: is he one-layered?' The guard nodded at Foxcub. 'Retarded, like you?'

'Alternatively gifted,' I replied. 'Like me. He loves drawing.'

'You can't take writing implements into the Special Unit. It's...' – the guard shook the pencil in the air, and Foxcub's pupils darted from side to side obediently – 'it's a violation. Who've you come to see?'

'To minus two,' Foxcub reported unexpectedly brightly. 'To visit Cracker he's probably really lonely there our friend let us through please.'

'Your mate Cracker's been a vegetable for a while now – he's not bored. And you are breaking the rules. You have a writing implement. I will let you through if you...' – the guard jabs Foxcub with his finger – 'sing me a song. On camera. And I'll put it up on FreakTube. My rating's started to go down... So, sing.'

'What should I sing?'

'Something from Festival Passions, goon.'

'Festival Passions is blocked for us,' Foxcub replied after thinking a bit.

'Oh yeah. Then something from The Eternal Murderer.'

'While you are laid in bed at night, who keeps you safe from harm? It's the planetmen! Who shows what is wrong and right, the Living's strong right arm? It's the planetmen! And who will always be right there to rescue you and me-e-e? It's the planetmen! Whose eyes are everywhe-e-ere and who is always the-e-ere, protecting stability and harmon-ee-ee...'

On the final 'harmoneeee' Foxcub squeaked and his voice wavered. The guard started applauding warmly.

'Good lad, nice job. Now tell us who you are and how old you are. The FreakTube viewers will want to know.'

'I'm Foxcub. I am twenty-eight. I live in a House of Correction. I used to be a criminal, but now I've got a low PTC, so soon I'll be corrected.'

'And tell us how many layers can you hold simultaneously?'

'One,' Foxcub explained. 'Sometimes one and a half.'

'Brilliant!' The guard gave a broad grin. 'You can go through. I will give you back the writing implement when you come out.'

Slowly, as if he were afraid to stumble, Foxcub walked towards the lift.

Cracker was lying still with his eyes closed, as usual. He had been lying like that for a long time now. Three times a day a nurse fed him and changed his nappy. Twice a day she turned him over. Once a day, before he went to sleep, she wiped his face and crotch with moist sanitary wipes. He was given a bath once a week.

The rest of the time he just lay there.

Sixteen years ago, when Cracker stopped moving entirely and his diagnosis was changed from 'apathetic stupor' to 'first-degree coma', the question of an artificial pause had arisen all by itself. After several consultations, the House administration decided to carry out a pause on Cracker as soon as his basic reflexes disappeared and he lost the ability to breathe and take food naturally. Until that time, as long as he did not burden the staff any more than the infant correctees, he would be looked after. Liquid food, nappies and sanitary wipes. Nothing more. No check-ups, no medicine, no life-support machines. No additional actions. Nothing more than what he would have got after a natural pause.

They had not counted on him lasting so long. They gave him between one and six months. After no more than half a year, they said, correctee Cracker will forget how to swallow and how to breathe. After no more than half a year, correctee Cracker will temporarily cease to exist.

But the years passed and he continued to exist. Quietly and unassumingly, like a pet in its cocoon.

He was thirteen when they put him on the Blacklist and transferred him to the Special Unit. He was sixteen when he turned his head and looked at me through the glass for the last time; after that Cracker went into total stupor and I stopped visiting him. He was thirty-two when Foxcub sang the song about the planetmen and took me back to minus two.

During the first year he spent in the chamber under the correcting light, Cracker dried out, turned yellow and curled up, like an unliving little friend fixed to a piece of card with a pin and placed under glass as a memento. Old age had eaten into his child's body like a poisonous fungus, not giving his organism the chance to go through the appointed cycle of transformations: age, maturity... When I visited him for the last time, when he was sixteen, he looked like both an old man and a teenager simultaneously. He reminded me of one of those optical illusions which the psychologists used to shove under my nose when I was a kid (look: it looks like a beautiful woman with a hat with a feather... And then – ta-da! – it's a witch with a long nose!).

Back then the nurse, I remember, called him her little pupa. And I started calling him that too. To myself.

He was a broken, sick little pupa which would never hatch into a winged being.

When Fox and I arrived, Cracker was lying still with his eyes shut. He had barely changed.

The same sleeping pupa.

Foxcub went right up to Cracker's chamber and pressed his face against the glass. He stood there for about half a minute and then turned to me, pulled himself up to his full height and opened his mouth, as if he was about to start singing again.

For sixteen years I hadn't been to minus two. In that time the Butcher's Son had lived up to the pause and been reproduced and had learned to crawl and even stand up on his little legs, holding on to the glass sides of the chamber with his hands. When he spotted us he did this little trick, and then stood there, swaying slightly in his natty 'feeling lucky' trousers and sucking a yellow dummy, and looked carefully at me and Foxcub in turn. I pressed my finger up against the tip of my nose, like before, but he didn't even smile. After the pause, he must have forgotten that the 'piggy' is funny. Or perhaps he just couldnt't smile – probably no one had ever shown him how to make this face. Why go looking for trouble? A Blacklister's smile is a very bad omen... I let go of my nose and stretched my lips out in the kindliest grin possible. The little fellow recoiled from the glass, fell down and hunched over, weeping without a sound.

I was sorry I came.

'Hey, Fox. What have you dragged me here for?'

'I am not Fox I already said,' Foxcub droned; his pupils spread out like spots of mould on the skin of a potato. 'I missed you so I summoned you. You haven't come for so long. No death. Friend.'

'No dea...' I started and choked on the words.

Something – maybe my gag reflex, maybe my tear reflex – was preventing me from talking; my throat went tight. Something – maybe happiness, maybe fatigue – swelled up inside me and made me very heavy. I felt an overwhelming desire to sit down on the floor and lean against the see-through wall.

There, behind the wall, lay my friend, motionless, hunched over; my friend who I had not seen for so long.

'Is that you...' I whispered through my spasm, through the soundproof glass, 'you, Cracker?'

'Of course, me, who else?' Foxcub replied flatly. 'Who, apart from Cracker, can break any password, get through any defence? I am pleased to see you. Friend. Although you look stupid. Ha. Ha.'

Foxcub licked his dry lips and continued, painstakingly articulating himself: 'Hee. Ho. Ho. Like I'm laughing. Shame can't manage. To make this idiot laugh naturally.'

'How did you... But Foxcub... What have you done with him?'

'Nothing special. I just broke into his cell. His defences were totally weak.'

'But you... I mean he... he is you...'

'Hee. Ha. You're still funny,' Foxcub said indifferently. 'He is him. I am just in him. I've just played about a bit. Turned off some things he didn't need. Installed a new "outloud" mode. Set up some simple algorithms. Where to go. Intermediary points. The final destination. It's only for a while. I'll let him go. I'll wipe everything. He'll forget.'

'It's impossible,' I thought. 'Impossible. Impossible. No way.'

'It is possible,' Cracker replied with Foxcub's lips, as if he had read my mind. 'It's nothing. You can't even imagine. The things I've learned to do now.'

'Can you hear what I'm thinking?!'

'Of course not, but it's not hard to guess. Your face is very expressive. Ho. He. Hee. Come on, Foxcub, laugh normally you bastard.'

Foxcub hiccoughed. His face was empty and tired. As if he was struggling to remember a dream but couldn't. I looked at Cracker. A dried-up, motionless pupa.

'Open your eyes,' I asked. 'Look at me.'

'I am looking at you,' Foxcub replied obligingly.

'Not like that. Yourself.'

'No.'

'You can't?'

'Unnecessary action. Takes a lot of energy. And memory. Will lose control over him. I no longer overload my brain with pointless commands.'

I became sad and wistful.

'Please!'

'No. Stupid. We do not have much time. Soon the cameras are going to come back on.'

'Are there cameras here? In our secret place?'

'There are cameras everywhere. But I've switched them off for a while.'

'You've switched them off?' I looked over from Foxcub to the motionless Cracker and then back again. 'You?!'

'It was nothing,' Foxcub said again. 'Compared to what I can do now.'

The Butcher's Son – I had completely forgotten about him – unexpectedly collapsed on his back and started twitching all his limbs excitedly.

'I have downloaded the first season of Baby Bubbles for him,' Foxcub reported wearily. 'The creeps hooked up the four hundredth straightaway. Without the backstory he is not going to understand anything.'

'And with the backstory he will?!'

'Yes. Now he's going to understand everything. I am training him. He will see a lot of layers.'

'Teach him to smile,' I asked.

'No. It is a bad omen.'

'Do you really believe in omens?'

'Me no. Them yes. Do not want. Them to see him as threat.'

Foxcub fell silent for a long time; his face became still and dark, like a used wonder-sunshine. Cracker just stayed lying there not moving. For a fraction of a second it seemed to me like the corners of his lips tensed slightly into the promise of a smile, but it was a trick of the light, or Cracker did not keep his promise; a trick in either case.

The Butcher's Son opened his mouth and drooled and starts gawking at me. Then he waved, not at me, but at someone sitting in my stomach. I wanted to wave to him too but then it hit me. He can't even see me. He's in second layer. With the baby Bubbles and Livvles. He's watching the first episode.

I remember that episode, they showed it to me in the natural development group. It was called 'Getting to Know Everyone'.

Who lives in our house?
Hi, I'm Duckles.
Hi, I'm Monkles.
And who are you, little fellow?

The Butcher's Son pointed at himself and waved again.

Everybody let's hold hands,
Let's all join the circle dance!

The Butcher's Son reached out his hands to his invisible new friends and started spinning around his axis. I knew what this meant. He had to become a part of the ball. A part of Livvles. But something went wrong. Something happened. Something bad, something evil: the Butcher's Son jerked to the right, fell down as if pushed, covered his eyes with his hands, trying to block out something I couldn't see, threw his mouth wide open and wept.

'I fixed a little something,' Foxcub started talking unexpectedly. The Butcher's Son crawled off to the far wall of his chamber, lay on the floor and pulled his knees up to his chin; he was shivering violently.

'I changed the way Livvles looks. Livvles is a monster.'

'That's cruel!' I went up to the Son's chamber; he looked at me with pained, moist eyes. 'That's cruel, Cracker! Look at him, he's terrified! Why do you have to torture the poor child?'

'He will fear the Monster. He will not want to become a part of the Monster. From childhood. He will be on your side.'

'But I don't have any...'

'You do. The Monster is on one side. You are on the other. Separate. Outside him. In the future. You will need friends.'

My future 'friend' had rolled up in a ball on the floor, his whole body jerking rhythmically as he tried to fall asleep. Before his pause this was how he would rock himself to sleep. The light. This empty white correcting light under which it must have been hard to get to sleep. But easy to lose your mind. I turned round. Another wave of fatigue came over me – not the sort that pins you to the floor and stops you breathing, but a different sort, the sort that fills your whole body with invisible cotton wool, that poisons you and takes away your pain. That makes you indifferent.

'You're insane,' I said, trying not to look either at Cracker or at his 'hostage'. 'What sort of future can I have here, in the House of Correction? What friends? You and the Son sitting in your impenetrable test tubes...'

'...retrable tes tubs...' Foxcub rasped.

Fox looked bad: his face became pale and damp, like a peeled potato. He stood like before, pulled up to his full height, and his legs shuddered noticeably.

'Would you like to sit down, eh, Fox? Or lie down?'

'Mnt Fx. Bn lying dn lng tme.'

'Give him a break, Cracker! He's in a bad way. Let him go finally!'

'Soon e-nough,' Foxcub said with effort, sounding out the syllables. 'Help hm st...'

I sat Foxcub on the floor, leaning his back against Cracker's chamber. He half-shut his eyes and said nothing for a little while. Then he started talking again, quietly, but fairly clearly:

'You are right. There is no future in this house. That is why I invited you here. You have to get out of here…'

'That's nonsense, Cracker!'

'There is no time. Do not interrupt me. Listen.' Foxcub coughed up short phrases in bursts. 'You will get out. Not now. Later. I will help. For now info. Must know. Above all. Chatterboxes. They are cleverer. Than it seems.'

And then Cracker told me about the chatterboxes using Fox's disobedient tongue, his numbed vocal cords, his dry lips.

About the way the chatterbox, which hangs from every planetman's belt, is not just a device for recording and conducting conversations.

About the way the chatterbox conceals a marvellous secret. Inside the chatterbox there hides a tiny cerebron. Not invasive, like they were before. The final model, the last type that was used before the Nativity. About the way the tiny cerebron duplicates all the information from the planetman's *socio* slot: how, in other words, it is a copy of his cell. And in a force majeure situation, if the planetman's *socio* slot is turned off, his cerebron continues to function.

About the way the *socio* slot is usually turned off after a planetman's physical pause. In this case an external cerebron proves to be very useful: the Service for Planetary Order can download all the information from the temporarily non-existent planetman's cell through his chatterbox.

About the way that theoretically – purely theoretically – a different sort of force majeure is possible. For instance, if the planetman is alive, but his *socio* slot is damaged. Let's say, an injury. A head trauma. It's unlikely – but anyway. Then the planetman can take the cerebron from this chatterbox and, in order to stay on *socio*, can get hooked up to that. Through an external port...

...Inside Foxcub something started gurgling.

'...tterbox...ternal ort... fox you res... digra...'

Fox flopped his tongue, which was covered in a grey film, out of his mouth and vomited on the shiny floor.

Cleo.doc

10th June 471; 5:00

…Again those questions in the wastes. And she's quite a piece of work this one. I'm going to have to feel her out a bit better ☺

Right, let's get going.

10th July 471; 15:30

I think it is necessary to instigate independent surveillance of subject:

current name – *cleo*
eternal name – *leo*
current sex – *female*
invector – *generally positive.* Predominant specialisation over recent reproductions: 'research scientist' and 'head of research'. Previous reproduction: Leo – professor, doctor, one of the creators of the infamous 'directed Leo-Lot ray' experiment.

However, the current reproduction has seen serious professional demotion following the shameful failure of the experiment carried out prior to the pause. Despite her high intellect coefficient and excellent multilayer receptive capabilities, *cleo* has not been permitted to do scientific work and is employed at the festival service Everything's Going to Be Alright and is not happy with her work, a fact which she has mentioned more than once in personal *socio* chats.

type of relationship formed between myself and subject under investigation: erotic connection in deep layers

NB. I do not believe that the 'personal aspect' can have a negative effect on surveillance in this instance, because I feel no emotional attachment to the subject.

Basis for instigation of surveillance: subject's suspicious behaviour. It was *cleo* who initiated an intimate relationship in deep layers. Despite my insistence on entirely <u>cruel</u> and one might even say <u>sadistic</u> conditions for the act in *luxury* mode, subject *cleo* nevertheless <u>continues to insist</u> on repeating it. On the conclusion of the act *cleo*, it would seem, <u>tries to take advantage</u> of my *relax* status and <u>extract confidential information</u> concerning the correctee under my control, *Zero* (who himself took part in the Leo-Lot ray experiment and was, without doubt, the most important object of inquiry). The subject tries to pass her interest off as common curiosity (I am looking after a celebrity ☺), however, I think that my answers interest her a great deal more than the *acts* themselves ☹. More than once *cleo* asked me about a personal (!!) meeting with Zero in first layer (cf. video recording of extract of our act in *luxury*).

I suspect that *cleo*'s plans may be criminal in nature.

We cannot rule out the possibility that she is planning to pursue, or has already pursued, independent, unsanctioned scientific activity in relation to the directed Leo-Lot ray (and in this sense with the 'mysterious' genesis of Zero – a very tasty little morsel). Her aim is obvious: to return her 'good name' in scientific circles and restore her invector. I would evaluate actions of this sort as a threat to the harmony and peace of the Living, as the Leo-Lot ray experiment was acknowledged as 'unsuccessful and harmful' and further experiments were forbidden at the highest level, and contact between citizens and Zero is strictly forbidden.

Moreover, taking into account *cleo*'s clear dislike of the specialisation given to her in this reproduction, it is impossible to exclude the possibility that *cleo* is a member of the criminal group the Dissidents. In this case her interest in Zero, who was born, according to the Dissidents' absurd doctrine, to change their lives, is entirely harmful in nature.

<u>11th July 471</u>

Yesterday I instigated surveillance on *cleo*'s cell using 'beetle' spyware. I installed the 'beetle' in the fashionable *dog socio-*toy, after which I sent a free gift link to the game directly to the subject. On receipt of the link to the game by the subject the *dog* was unpacked and launched.

Ef: memory F: Hunter's Living Journal: private entries:
<u>**Beetle1.doc**</u>

<u>11.07.471:</u> no suspicious data found

<u>12.07.471:</u> demand by user *cleo* No. 108 (!!!) for *socio* communication with hidden user *lot* granted in accordance with statue 470764 'On the rights of citizens for a final *socio* meeting with a pre-pauser'.

<u>13.07.471:</u>
9:00 *cleo* invites user *lot* to her cell in order to chat in *socio*. No reaction in reply.
11:00 *cleo* invites user *lot* to her cell
Lot accepts invitation
I cite the transcript of the conversation made by *dog*:
cleo: hello there
lot: hi! who are you?

cleo: i'm leo

lot: should that name mean something to me?

cleo: yes, *lot*. we used to work together. we were scientists. don't you remember?

lot: i don't remember... the doctor says i have this illness. No memory ☹

cleo: ☹

lot: but i'm looking in *socio* now. so... leo and lot... oh, i found a photo straightaway! it's handy this *socio*! are you the one with a beard or without?

cleo: yes, i had a beard. the one without a beard is you...

lot: and what was it we were doing?

cleo: we were trying to look back into the past. to overcome the five seconds of darkness.

lot: five seconds of darkness!! sounds lovely.

user *lot* has updated his status: 5 seconds of darkness

cleo: do you not remember anything about the directed Leo-Lot ray? about the formula of the injection?

lot: i don't remember. sorry, i need to go to the dining room. it's breakfast time. we're having stewed fruit. my favourite.

16:00

lot wants to enter cleo's cell and chat in *socio*

cleo: hey!!

lot: you tricked me

cleo: ?

lot: you are not my colleague. You are not leo

cleo: who told you that?!

lot: my doctor. he tells me what i don't remember. my friend leo no longer exists

cleo: you've just misunderstood!!! i am leo – just in his next reproduction ☺

lot: leo died

cleo: what are you saying! there is no death!!!

lot: really?

leo: of course not. have you forgotten THAT too? what is this illness you've got, what's it called?

lot: lot's drowsy demon ☺

cleo: ?

lot: my doctor says that i am the only person with this illness. every night – while i am asleep – my deep layer memory is completely wiped. everything i've saved in my memory over the course of the day is wiped. all that's left is my basic reflexes and skills.

cleo: and your memory in first layer??? is that wiped too?

lot: no

cleo: then you should remember loads! our experiment: we conducted it partly in first layer!

lot: first layer memory is unreliable ☹ it's too fragile. without the support of deep layers it's mostly blocked off. try and go off *socio* and remember the names and details of your best friends! try and remember what you did a day before, let alone a month ago... it'll never work. without *socio* memory we've all got dementia ☺ not just me ☺ ☺

cleo: how strange. you're talking completely differently. not like you did this morning

lot: maybe i got smarter? ☺

cleo: something like that ☺

lot: so much time has passed since then! i try to fill my memory as actively as possible over the course of the day. the bigger your *socio* memory the better your first layer memory will work... i hope that by evening i'll be a wise man ☺ but tomorrow i'll forget it all again ☹ by the way, madam, what is that animal of yours that's so inquisitive?

cleo: it's a dog. a game app. she's very good with people.

lot: she's sweet. but a bit pushy. please don't take offence, madam. i don't like being sniffed all the time. i'm going.

cleo: pop in in the evening, when you are a wise man ☺ and by the way why are you calling me 'madam'? we're friends, aren't we?

lot: leo was my friend. probably. but you are a woman that i don't even know. it would be impolite not to call you madam

cleo: but i am leo, what's the difference!! there's no need for these conventions!

lot: let's drop this conversation, i really have to go

cleo: so are you going to pop in?

lot: your dog has worn me out a bit. if you like, come to my place. today or tomorrow

cleo: tomorrow's not going to work

lot: why not?

cleo: erm... you've got a pause. haven't you been told?

User *lot* has left chat

20:00
cleo wants to enter *lot*'s cell and chat in *socio*
No reply.

21:00
cleo wants to enter *lot*'s cell and chat in *socio*
No reply.

22:00
cleo wants to enter *lot*'s cell and chat in *socio*
No reply.

23:00
cleo wants to enter *lot*'s cell and chat in
lot: come in
(further content of conversation is unknown as dog remains in *cleo*'s cell)

The Man with No Face

'Meerkat' 'Badger'. 'Jerboa'. 'Mountain Goat...'

As I go past the empty cages and tanks, I automatically whack the names into the search engine and *socio* spits useless information about non-existent animals into my skull like it were a bin.

I know a little bit about bears myself, without any wikipedia. Cracker told me about the bear – a long time ago, long before he was put on the Blacklist and stopped moving. He would tell me that the bear was a terrifying monster that lived in the forest and ate everything it came across, ripping apart the living flesh of its victims with long curved claws. It was a fierce and unpredictable beast with stinking breath and only the bees knew how to calm it down: they would feed it their sweet floral honey, and then the bear would curb its anger for a little while. When the monster was tired, it would crawl beneath the earth and temporarily cease to exist – it would fall into a deep sleep from which it could not be woken for half a year and then it would be reborn and go back outside, once again thirsty for blood and honey.

The ancients thought this beast was the god of the forest. In the pre-global dialect of region EA 8 the word for 'bear' was 'medved', which meant the 'master of the honey', but that was not a name so much as a term of respect used instead of a name. It was forbidden to say the name of the god out loud.

Cracker talked about this tradition with great excitement. He liked that unbridgeable, respectful distance which people tried to use to separate the mindless god from themselves. 'Not like us! They weren't a part of the monster, you see?' Cracker rubbed crazily at his spots. 'They were separate. And the god was separate. And if he wanted to devour them, they killed him.'

'Elephant'. 'Giraffe'. 'Camel'. 'Ostrich'.

I like the abandoned zoo. Empty cells, the doors thrown wide open, ponds filled with oozy mud, the dry, branching trees for climbing, the brown boulders, the decayed little huts, the rusty troughs, the burrows in the petrified sand: everything here was in a strange state of half-collapse, as if everything was not completely finished, as if it had begun to die and then frozen in surprise. There was none of that smell here, that thick smell of fear and hate which permeated the Farm. They died quickly here, the imprisoned beasts and ancient gods. They did not have time to get really scared, let alone start to hate. People just brought them their food in the evening and they ate it as usual. And then they fell asleep and didn't wake up.

...By the way that's an idea. I'm thinking about my prisoner, whom I have left again, locked up, surprised and bewildered in the apes' cage. 'What's up with you, mate? Finish me off,' Ef begged me. 'Stop, you're not playing fair,' he whispered hoarsely as I left. It's cowardice. Cowardice is preventing me from finishing him off, although, of course, it would be easy and fair to do so. It would be good to use a gun – I do have a gun, but a shot might draw attention to the zoo... With my bare hands then, or with some object? One hit or two? Will his little oyster eye close up or will it bulge out? And what will the noise be like? A crunch or a splat? A croak or a groan? A groan or a scream...?

So maybe I could poison him? A good method for cowards... Indirect. Sprinkle poison in his vitacomplex, or not even poison, where would I get poison from, I could just feed him something that's gone really bad, Megalopolis is full of stuff like that... No, that's rubbish. I could just go and never come back, and without medicine and water he would cease to exist in a few days, but I'm not ready to do even that for him. Cowardice. It won't let me temporarily take his life. But I'm not just afraid of killing him – after all what does it mean to kill someone who lives forever? I'm afraid of what will happen after I kill him. They will detect his pause. They will close his cell. What will happen to me? No. No. I can't do without the mask and the cell so soon… It's too convenient to be impenetrable and mirrored. Too convenient to have access to private files…

So I go back. Two or three times a day I go back to the apes' cage and extend his torture. And I leave him there on his own.

I left him on his own again today.

But he's not going to last long… What are you hoping for? Again and again, like an anthill in a state of alarm, panic spreads through me. It poisons my blood with the acid of poisonous bites. Poisonous questions… Oh, my panic has a hundred thin little voices and each one is striving to be the first to squeak out their question, to leave their comment. My panic is my own *socio* but there is no way to 'exit'… *Or do you think that you can keep him in this cage for years?* I don't think so. The planetman is giving up with every passing day. Even without my help he will die soon. I mean, sorry, he'll temporarily cease to exist. *What if he doesn't even die? How long will you last, eh,* 'socio *user ef'? How long will you last in this role?* Not for long. No, no, no, not for long. Until the first med-exam, which, by the way, the *autodoctor* has already been gently inviting me to. In a week he will invite me strictly. I won't go and then they will come to me and they'll take off my mirrored mask – and after that it goes dark; the end… *So, maybe you could make a run for it? Right now?* Uh-huh, pull out this cerebron, chuck it away right here, in the zoo, and run off somewhere far away in the middle of nowhere – I've thought about it a lot… I'll live in the woods, collect roots and berries… *Will you live there all by yourself?* I won't be able to get used to the loneliness. *Will you just be surviving? Clinging on to your pathetic life?* That's a normal instinct for someone like me. For a mortal animal. *OK, but in winter? When there are no roots or berries? When the snow starts to fall? I'll live in one of the shopping centres. And medicine, food, water? You have to order them through socio, how else are you going to get them?* There is food and clothing in shopping centres. *But hasn't that food gone off?* For the most part, but… *And aren't they tearing down the shopping centres soon?* Yes, yes, yes. The food there is spoiled. The winters there are severe. And they're going to tear down the shopping centres. *Turns out you're doomed?* Turns out I'm doomed. *What were you thinking when you ran away from the House?* But I wasn't thinking. I was just saving myself, I was afraid of ending up in the Special Unit. I just wanted freedom. It's a normal instinct for a mortal animal…

But you have to have a plan! Do you really not have a plan?! Cracker had a plan for me. A crazy, ridiculous plan, dreamed up by a correctee who had spent several hundred years in the House, who didn't have a clue about what first-layer life was like. He wanted me to fight his Monster. He wanted me to be like him, to sacrifice myself. *And you didn't want to?* And I didn't want to. I don't have anything against the Living. I don't want to threaten His peace and harmony. On the contrary I could even protect Him. I like protecting Him, I could become a planetman… *And take old men who call you the Saviour to the Pause Zone?* Yes, I would take the old men. I would be a part of the Living… *But you are not a part of it. You are not a protector, but an enemy, your duty is to commit apoptosis, to destroy yourself so that the organism can remain healthy.* I am not an enemy… *You are an alien cell!* How do you know? *Oho, you're still hoping that something will happen?* I hope that if we repeat the Leo-Lot experiment… *Don't make me laugh. Are you talking about that anonymous letter? That's just spam…* 'Don't believe the lies. The Leo-Lot ray can shine in both directions, backward and forward, and it has revealed your great future. But they have taken away your future, they destroyed the discovery, they forced the scientists to keep silent, just so you would remain a nobody. So that you might not become he who you must be, for the greater glory of the

Living... But I will right the injustice.' Signed – 'A Dissident Well-wisher'. Just spam? This letter came on the third day of my life in the mask. No one knew that I was me. No one knew, but the person who sent it knew.... Just spam? I ran that 'well-wisher' through all the SPO databases, but I couldn't determine the IP address. So it's someone very serious. Someone who seriously doesn't agree. A serious dissident.

So what now? So you are just going to wander about, shining away with your mirrored pie-hole? I prefer being impenetrable and mirrored until I figure out what is actually going on. *And what if they catch me?* Well, so be it.

Well, so be it.

I walk away from the zoo on foot. Across some wasteland, marked by the black outlines of the metallic skeletons of a gigantic wheel, carousels, swings and a rocket leaning to one side and some absurd little railway carriages... The naive entertainments of the ancients. They would go spinning and whirling around there before the Magical Attraction Parks were launched in deep layers – with their miracles, transformations, flights and battles, with their first-class sensory stimulation...

...Three kids of pre-boarding house age swathed in inviz rags are hanging about on the wasteland: one is lazily trying to snap the crumbling wings off the rocket, the other two are unsuccessfully attempting to spin the wheel. They're obviously from the roboslums, otherwise they wouldn't come here. Either they don't have physical access to those *socio* layers in which the Magical Parks buzz and flash away, or they do have access but don't have enough *socio* money for entry. I can understand why they come here.

I used to come here myself. When I was a kid.

For me there was no way to get to the Magical Park. So I used to beg Hanna to let me go 'to the swings'; she grudgingly let me go. She didn't like the fact that it was next to the robo-slums, but she took pity on me because I was deprived. She thought that I came here to play about on these rusty stumps. But I didn't play. Like them, I came here to break things.

...Beyond the wasteland is the beginning of the roboslums; my path lies through them. It's not dangerous here: Hanna was worried for no reason, the robots are harmless. They almost don't notice me, they don't even notice themselves. Some are, despite the summer, wrapped up tight in torn inviz rags, others are sitting on the doorsteps of their fraying cardboard houses almost naked; many of the women are wearing bikinis taken from electronic cleaners. I hear hoarse cries coming from beneath a heap of rubbish:

'Yeah, mantis, yeah, mantis, yeah...!'

'Hor-net! Hor-net!'

'Come on! Come on! Come on!'

'Fofs! Fofs!'

'Do him! Come on, mantis! Come on, fellah!'

...I hurry up and a wave of nausea rises to my throat. Like that time, a week ago, when I was digging about in Ef's memory and I came across the file 'Violence'. With video clips: a mantis against a centipede, a mantis against a stag beetle...

...In first layer the robots are not interested in anything but cockroach racing and insect fights. They don't have the memory or the attention span for anything else; the robots are completely absorbed in the little they can make out in second. Morning, noon and night they root about in their *socio*-trash, picking fragments of series out of it, bits of second-layer shoot 'em ups and adventures, stupid chats, half-installed educational programs. Like allergy-sufferers scratching at their inflamed skin, they keep trying to *load*, *save to memory*, *reinstall* and *add to list*. It's pointless. Their cells are not fully functional: numerous installation errors and system failures. So the fragments of the shows don't form a consistent storyline. The adventures break off right at the beginning of the journey. Chats are blocked after five orthographic errors

> *sorry, this application has been closed. in order to avoid repeating this error, you must reinstall happy letters.*

But the robots aren't able to download Happy Letters or Happy Numbers either.

> *before the download starts, please enter the code which you see in front of you. this is necessary to confirm that you are not a robot.*

They don't have the brains to enter this code. They can't. That's where their name comes from.

…Someone comes diving out of a heap of dirty boxes and rags right at my feet. He strikes his forehead against the toe of my boot, rolls onto his back and lies there, looking up at me with festering eyes and arms waggling tiredly, like an upturned pet beetle. I ask automatically:

'Are you in pain?' But then I realise that he probably hasn't noticed me at all.

I walk round him in a wide arc so I don't hurt him by accident again, but he suddenly flips briskly onto his stomach, leaps up onto all fours, scampers over to me and takes a tight grip of my trouser leg.

He's about thirteen, his face is lopsided, asymmetrical. This face seems vaguely familiar.

'Pwease, pwease, pwease,' he splutters and tugs at my trouser leg. 'Mister pwanetman! Don' tay'!' He kneels in front of me. 'Pwease!'

That 'pwease'… Suddenly I recognise him.

'Mark? Are you Mark?'

My voice, monotonous from the chatterbox, does not frighten him. He looks at me, tense and thoughtful, as if he is trying the name out on himself, then nods seriously:

'Yeth, Ma-ak.'

In development group he could never say his name either. So he still hasn't learned...

...They, the robots, can never get to *luxury* mode. In filth, in delirium, on the bare earth or on the polyethylene-cardboard floor, not clambering out from beneath the fragments and crumbs of second layer, slaves to blind instinct not knowing what they are doing, they mate and in pain do they bring forth children.

If the children are lucky and installation goes well, the *socio* service sends them to ordinary boarding houses. But quite often they are not lucky. There's nothing surprising about this: in the roboslums, with the overcrowding and the residents' poor health, they die and mate practically constantly; the whole place is like a hideous parody of the Festival for Assisting Nature... Thus the robots are reborn as robots and remain in the slums. If the children can hold first layer, they visit the natural development group. Like the one I visited. And Mark too.

Our teacher said that the group is a chance to break out of the slums and become a fully fledged part of the Living. She said: if you can hold first layer, you can take up a useful and necessary profession. For instance, you could become a toilet cleaner or a bin man, or go to work at the filling station or take dung from the farm or skin the corpses. Mark wanted to work at the farm....

Only very few manage to break out of the slums. The slums drag you down. And first layer becomes a pale memory.

That said, Mark can hold first layer pretty well.

'...Pwease! Don' take 'er! Iss, iss, iss her birfday today, mummy is stiw young! She don' need to go to festival!'

I wonder whether I should turn off the recording function on my chatterbox, but no, that would arouse the suspicion of the SPO. I didn't record anything for an hour already back in the zoo. So I ask strictly:

'How old is she?'

'I don't remember.'

'Her name?'

'I don' remember.' Mark shakes his head. 'I don' remember. She don't remember either.'

I go through the database of today's compulsories in this area. There are five of them, of which three are women, but none of them is Mark's biological mother.

'Not today,' I state. 'It is not her turn today.'

Mark smiles, revealing his dirty teeth, and starts jerking his head strangely – either trying to bow to me, or trying to *create* something in his pathetic second layer. I turn around and walk off.

> *please wait, conversation currently being processed...*
> *interlocutor mark, perhaps, manifested signs of*
> *perverted attachment to a Darling*
> *interlocutor mark, perhaps, is suffering from psychic*
> *distress*
>
> *officer ef, would you like to report this to the*
> *Psychological Service for Assisting the Population?*
> *yes **no***
>
> *caution! PSAP strongly recommends that citizens*
> *inform them about all instances of psychological*
> *deviation*
> *do you want to report this deviation to the Psychological*
> *Service for Assisting the Population?*
> *yes **no***

caution! the roboslums are considered psychologically unsound. information you provide could be important for statistics.

do you want to provide information?
*yes **no***

caution! persons with perverted attachment to their Darlings often belong to the 'Familials', a radical group. This group is a threat to the peace and harmony of the Living. Your inaction is not rational. As an SPO officer you must send an alarm signal to the PSAP.

please wait... automatic alarm signal is being sent...

...complete.

thank you for your vigilance!

I've got fairly far by the time Mark calls to me.

'What is she called?' he cries. 'What is my mummy called? Maak wants to remember!'

I look in the database. It's all I can do for him now. In the next three hours a team from the Psychological Service is going to come and pay him a visit.

'Your mother is called Rosa,' I say. 'A beautiful name.'

I keep going, trying not to think about Mark, about what I have just done to him.

Right in the very centre of the slums a naked robot, aged about forty, with a peaceful face and, strange as this may seem, showing no signs of degeneration, is sitting in the middle of the road in the lotus position. He is thin and all angular like a mantis. His eyes are wide open. For some reason I am reminded of Cracker.

To my own surprise I lean over him and clap loudly a couple of centimetres from his face. He doesn't blink. Not even the slightest movement of his facial muscles…

…They say that, in addition to the robots, the slums are also home to 'drowners'. They are divers, *socio* geniuses, who have reached the deepest, twelfth layer and have remained in the depths, either willingly or because they are unable to withstand the pressure. They say that when this happens all the drowner's surface layers are destroyed. So there is no way of telling the difference between a drowner and an ordinary robot… So they say. But those are just rumours. A legend which is impossible to verify. No one knows if twelfth layer exists or if drowners even exist. Because only they can get so deep.

Well, except the members of the Council of Eight.

And, maybe, Cracker.

My friend Cracker, the best diver in the world.

Zero

The second time it was the entomologist.

Half a year had passed since Fox had led me to the Special Unit to see Cracker's motionless body and then nearly done himself in. Back then I had had to go up to the guard and ask him to call a doctor; they only just managed to resuscitate him. When he came to he could not explain how and why he had ended up on the Blacklisters' level. He stared at me in surprise and licked his dirty lips spitefully. The cameras didn't help either: there was a spontaneous recording malfunction. The only witness, the guard, confirmed that Fox had come of his own will and had even insisted on visiting his 'sick friend'. They diagnosed it as 'over-exhaustion'. His song became a hit on FreakTube.

His health soon improved, and only once, a few months after the incident in the Special Unit, did Foxcub have another small attack. He was found unconscious on the Available Terrace.

And on that same day I found something else there on the terrace. In the box with the paper rubbish: I was asking everyone to throw any unwanted cellulose in there – envelopes, used tissues, sweet wrappers or unwanted draft letters for Renaissance, so they could be used as feed for my termite... On that evening, when Foxcub collapsed in a faint, I fished out of the box a piece of paper folded over three times, with two skewed, uneven diagrams full of uncertain, shaky lines. Under one of them something was written in pencil in the trembling handwriting of someone without Happy Fingers installed: 'plan for getting cerebron from chatterbox'. Under the second there was: 'plan for installing cerebron on zero'.

I was scared. I was angry at Cracker. I hated him. A crazy risk. Putting me in danger. Putting Foxcub in danger. I was drenched in warm sweat, thick like rancid oil, which smelled so strong that I thought: they'll catch me, they'll unmask me and they'll put me in the Special Unit, even without figuring out what's going on. Just because of this smell of curiosity and fear.

I decided that I should feed the drawings to my termite immediately, right that minute. But instead I tucked the drawings under my clothes. Then put them back in the box.

Using the paper feed box as a hidey-hole was typical of Cracker: 'hide in plain sight'. It was dangerous but much less dangerous than carrying the drawings round with me.

They didn't catch me. Either the camera had another 'malfunction' that day or Fox's scrawl didn't look suspicious to whoever processed the data.

...Half a year had passed since Fox had taken me to see motionless Cracker. In that half a year Fox had not remembered anything. In that half a year I didn't go to the Special Unit to visit Cracker once. In that half a year I had memorized the tiniest details of the two wiggly diagrams and fed the drawings to my termite.

Half a year had passed, and the entomologist came up to me:

'No death. Friend. Need to talk. Follow him. In silence.'

The entomologist proved to be a much more durable medium than Foxcub, and more gifted: he gave voice to Cracker's words for a whole hour, occasionally even with expressions and gestures, and he didn't faint – all he did was go slightly pale and try to yawn – and he left the Blacklisters' level of his own accord. True, he didn't turn out to be as obedient as Fox. In the middle of the 'séance' he even found a way of throwing Cracker out, but not for long: he just had time to ask 'What's going on...?' and then collapsed back into unconsciousness.

'His cell is resisting,' the entomologist said through gritted teeth, jabbing his forehead. 'Good defence system. But it is still nice to work with him. He has more functions than that cretin Foxcub. Lots of layers. Lots of possibilities. I will make him help you.'

As if not agreeing with what he was saying, the entomologist twisted his lips. There was boredom in his eyes. He opened his mouth wide and crooked and tried to yawn, but couldn't.

The Butcher's Son stared unhappily at us from his chamber. He wasn't sucking a dummy anymore, not falling over, not squinting into the light and not crying. He was watching. His face was smooth with chubby cheeks and his eyes looked very old.

This time, under the correcting light, under the fixed gaze of the Son, my friend Cracker laid out his plan to me via the entomologist's bloodless lips and twisted mouth.

The plan for my escape.

This time, when I had heard him out, I said:

'Cracker. You are completely insane.'

'I am a genius,' the entomologist replied and was overcome with yawning. 'I will work this miracle.'

He started laughing, a little gruffly, but overall realistically.

'They will see fire.'

Cleo

…She, of course, is not to blame. They forced her. They made her like this. But it's still a betrayal. *Dog* was created to love me, to entertain me and to be devoted to me. And not to spy on me. And certainly not so hypocritically. So deviously.

I force myself to look at her – and she immediately switches to *play* mode. She finds a ball and chases it around the room, but only for show. She doesn't even look at the ball. Only at me. With such devoted eyes. Following me.

I send her the command *heel* and at that moment she charges towards my legs. She sits and cheerily cocks one ear. And waits for encouragement. The dog-owner window which pops up suggests that I choose a *reward*: 'bone', 'squeaky toy', 'cheese' or 'sausage'. I cancel the reward. I go into the *punishment* menu. And I choose *hit the dog.*

> *!Caution dog-owner! You have chosen the wrong action for **dog**. **Dog** obeyed your command **heel!** and deserves encouragement. **Dog** has broken no rules and does not deserve punishment.*
> *You should now encourage **dog**. 'Bone', 'squeaky toy', 'cheese' or 'sausage'? Hint: your dog prefers the reward 'sausage'!*

I hit her again

> *Incorrect*

and again.

> *Incorrect*

Dog goes back to her place dejectedly and closes her eyes.

*!Caution! You have made 3 (three) basic errors in your training. Your trainer's rating has dropped by 6 (six) points. Your **dog** is now depressed and distressed. If such errors are repeated, your **dog** will start to be afraid of you!*

I start to regret hitting *dog* almost immediately. It's not about the points. She isn't to blame. Ef is to blame, that obstinate dick in the mask. 'Unhappy with her work'. 'Criminal character'. For the sake of all that's living, what crime can he see here?!

Yes, I *don't agree*. You could put it that way. I don't agree with the fact that freaks like him, limited, faceless, devoid of fantasy, people like him can decide to humiliate a DISTINGUISHED scientist and smear him with mud for the only serious mistake he has made in his whole career. That guys like him can rob me of my vocation – that is definitely not the will of the Living.

Yes, I am a scientist. Yes, yes, yes, science is what I do. It has always been that way. I have dozens of discoveries, hundreds of articles, thousands of laboratory investigations to my name! How can I be anything else if my box in Renaissance is full of reports, formulae, illustrations of the cross-sections of mice, dubious hypotheses and brilliant theories, notes in the margin, bits of advice and hints, questions and answers, and all those little notes – 'do not forget', 'consider', 'try to understand', 'check in case', 'be careful', 'continue'. What else can I be, if for hundreds of years I have been preparing myself for this…?

I know, I have known for a long time now: there's something dodgy about our experiment. About the results.

It's strange. So many months of preparation. Two brilliant specialists. Successful experiments with the *Heterotermes indicola* termite: consecutive immersion to a depth of twenty-six reproductions! And what do we get from it – nada? One failure and that's it? Something seems strange to me… OK then. Let's just say. OK. The experiment failed. But why is it 'harmful'? Why is repetition 'forbidden' if there was no result...? Surely it would make more sense to continue research in this field?

It's dodgy. We probably saw something. Something... bad. So bad that the designs for the experiment were completely destroyed.

...So bad that Lot and I evidently destroyed everything ourselves.

...So bad that the Leo-Lot ray has been banned by a decree from the Council of Eight (which means we did manage to send our results 'upstairs' and there, upstairs, someone thought they were dangerous).

...So bad that almost immediately after the experiment my colleague Lot was confined to a Nervous Disorders Clinic in first layer and became friends-only on *socio*.

...So bad, that a day after the experiment I temporarily ceased to exist for reasons mysteriously listed in the pathologist's report as 'poisoning'; with what substance, in what circumstances – not a word about that (an unfortunate accident, or, more likely, murder?).

...So bad that they *strongly recommend* that I should not continue my scientific activity in my new reproduction.

So what was it that was *so bad*?

No posts, a completely uncharacteristic, ridiculous, rushed pause; always pedantic, logical and careful I suddenly dive into the Darkness not leaving behind for posterity a single hint, lead or clue about what happened... I emerge in complete ignorance, and as a woman to boot. But, as a woman, I can say to hell with logic for a bit and trust my intuition. Put the question a bit differently. Change 'what' to 'which'.

Which of the five of them in the experiment was hiding this thing that was *so bad*?

The answer is obvious. Zero. The man with no incode. We saw something when our little ray shed light on the pitch darkness. Something which makes the Butcher's Son's worst crimes look like a harmless prank.

Something that I didn't want to get involved in.

Something that robbed Lot of his senses and his memory.

*You have not fed **dog** even once today*

Dog looks at me, sad and troubled, from her *place*. I give her a double helping of *wet food*. There's no point in starving her now. At the end of the day, it really isn't her fault that she has a beetle. She probably doesn't even know anything about it. She's just interested in everything to do with me, which is completely natural for her, that's the way she was born. She doesn't know that she is betraying me with her curiosity...

***Dog** does not want to eat wet food*

...Or does she know?

I cancel the *wet food* from her bowl and give her *dry*.

I remember how she whimpered and even growled that evening when I refused to take her with me to see Lot. Did she just not want to be left alone in my cell without me? Or was she annoyed that she couldn't spy on me?

...That evening I spent several hours in a row knocking on his door without success. Lot let me in towards night, joking, 'I've got my head together.' He had been coming to me in the neutral *shade* setting, now he had chosen himself a userpic. He looked young and was dressed exactly like he was in the photo of me and him from thirty years ago (the one in which he's got one squinting eye and I have a horrible thick beard). But his voice sounded the same as it had in the afternoon, dull and slack. Like that of a sixty-year-old. Which is what he was.

The cell's *premises* were fitted out hastily, without imagination or harmony; just heaps of disordered programmes and settings and open files and folders everywhere, like suitcases thrown open in a motel. His cell really did remind me of a messy hotel room that had a different guest every day, with each new guest bringing his own mess – all that remained was the bare walls; a null interface.

In the very centre of the cell there was an enormous chessboard – a heavy, pointless object taking up a lot of space and memory, which was nevertheless pretty much the only thing in the whole interior which hadn't just been downloaded with the original basic features but had been modified somehow. Over the course of the day Lot had evidently kept changing the look of his *wonder-chess* until he had made it into a real battlefield with miniature woods, rivers, plains and foothills, all broken up into quadrants; the horses playing the knights had real foam in their mouths and their riders had capes and armour; there were charging soldiers, kings, kings' wives, kings' castles, kings' gardens and kings' courtiers...

When I came in, the horseman in the black cape on E5 shouted something in a gruff voice, drew his sword, spurred on his steed and charged onto G6, where a snow-white horse was idling, its head bent over the water. When she heard the sound of hooves, the snow-white horse shuddered and neighed abruptly and rolled her eyes wildly. The rider in the white cloak stroked her withers, leant down to her trembling ear and started whispering tender, calming words in some ancient language, full of sibilants and sadness. The horse shut her frightened eyes obediently and the black horseman plunged his sword into her white breast. The blood spurted from the wound in a huge, clownish fountain, splattering the grass and the face of the killer in the black cloak. The white horse collapsed heavily into the murky quadrant of the river, pulling the white rider with him, who had put his hands together in prayer. A window floated up mournfully from the sludgy depths bearing the message:

black knight-e5 x white knight-g6.

'What colour are you?' I asked.

lot: white. it's a fantastic game chess. anyway, i've
been practising all day ☺ i started on 'novice' level,
and now i'm playing against a master! you do like
chess, don't you?
cleo: it was a hobby of mine before the pause. but
not now. it's a waste of time
lot: never. it develops logical thinking and memory.
just what i need. on the last day of my life
cleo: lot, your life isn't ending!! tomorrow you've just
got a pause! hasn't this been explained to you yet?!
lot: it's been explained, of course everything's been
explained... people like me, invalids, aren't even taken
off to the festival, they do it right here, in the clinic.
i was told that it will be a 'mercy pause'
cleo: great! that's the gentlest pause. in your sleep
lot: i'm pleased
cleo: do you remember anything about the
experiment?

white castle to g5
black castle to e7

lot: nothing worthwhile, i'm afraid... nothing more than
you've already...

?white's next move?

Lot fell silent absent-mindedly, distracted by what was
happening on the *field*. There a squat man in a white uniform
was butchering an enemy soldier, only a young boy, with his

bayonet with sadistic enthusiasm. Time after time he plunged the bayonet into his stomach – but every time he did not run him through and every time he stabbed him not in the same place, but just next to the previous stab. The little soldier writhed and after every jab whispered hoarsely: 'Finish me off, finish me off...' Lot probably wasn't sure if he had chosen the right move, and that's why he was taking his time.

lot: maybe... i remember what i felt when we saw
the result...
cleo: so there was a result??
lot: of course. so anyway, the feeling...

*player lot, you must make a move in the next
20...19...18...*

lot: not fear, but something more. grief, maybe? yes,
if you will. sort of like incurable grief. so huge that
i can't even find room for it. i also remembered that
i desperately wanted oblivion. to forget, to wipe it out,
to pull what i had seen out of myself...

...15...14...13 seconds...

He finally finished off the black pawn-soldier. In place of the corpse a huge grave mound rose up bearing the legend 'gxh5' and at that moment a window popped up blocking out half the field:

*player lot, your opponent would like to warn you about
an error:*
your move gives your opponent mate in three moves
*your opponent will allow you to retake the previous
move*

do you want to retake it?
yes no

Lot refused to retake the move.

do you want to give up?
yes no

Lot gave up.

The dead horses, horsemen and foot soldiers rose from the dead and, quietly jangling their weapons, wandered back to their original positions. The turrets that had been destroyed sprung back into place. All the gaps in the fortress walls were covered over.

play again?
*yes **no***

The pieces disappeared. All that was left was the fields, hills and quiet backwaters...

cleo: overall you were in quite a good position...
why did you refuse to retake that move?
lot: i don't like it when he is patronising
cleo: who? who were you playing against??

Lot looked at me with carefree eyes that were squinting at a sun that hadn't existed for thirty years.

lot: i was playing against leo.
cleo: against me???
lot: against leo. i found a 'play ghost' option. it's really simple: you can choose any offline player – the key thing is that he has to have no fewer than a hundred

games saved in *socio* – and you can 'summon' him.
His tactics will be based on the total of the games he
has played before... i summoned Leo. amazing! total
illusion of online. this ghost, he plays just like Leo,
and it's not just about his moves. it's about the way
he carries himself...

cleo: lot!

lot:...so arrogant and patronising...

cleo: lot, mate, why are you being like this

leo: ...he is 'letting me' replay the move – how very
like you, Leo!...

Lot dashed about his cell excitedly, randomly poking about
in some files, opening and copying nameless documents, loading and deleting *socio* updates... All the time he was squinting
at the distant sun and saying that he was tired of Leo giving
him freebies. Of Leo being generous. Of Leo looking down
on him.

And I begged him: calm down.

I kept saying: no, you've got it all confused.

I kept saying: it's just because of your illness, because of your
terrible illness, that's why you think that you remember, but it's
a false memory. Mistaken memories.

I kept saying: you and I were friends.

I kept saying: what do you mean looking down on you, what
freebies, I have my letters from Renaissance. Letters which
I have read and you are mentioned in them all the time, and
there's not a bad word about you in there...

And he would reply: how like Leo. How worthy. How noble.
No bad words.

He said that he was always in his shadow, the shadow of the
master Leo. The master would think something up and all he
would do was encourage him and help him realise it...

cleo: nonsense! how can you say that, you don't even REMEMBER!!

lot: it's already almost midnight and i've been loading my memory all day, i remember a lot! your envy. your anger...

cleo: maybe you can remember the formula for the injection better?

lot: ☺ ☺ ☺

cleo: what's funny?!

lot: to be honest it's more sad ☹ i don't remember the formula because i never knew it in first layer. I reckon that leo discovered the formula...

cleo: and the result? what you saw – do you remember that???

lot: i can't. i can't for now. i don't have enough memory. but i remember all too well that feeling of incurable...

00:00
Socio *reminder: today is user lot's birthday, help him celebrate!*
Do you want to give user lot a birthday cake?
yes *no*
do you want to light 60 birthday candles?
yes *no*

I chose the first cake I saw – chocolate with raspberry cream – and in my haste I forgot to regulate the brightness of the candles. They came on at maximum level, flooding the cell with a poisonous glow.

'Is it Zero?' I asked. 'Was there something incurable about him? Come on, remember!!'

lot: lovely cake, thanks...

He squinted at the birthday candles; their light made his skin seem pale, like an ant's egg.

> *cleo:* remember!!
> *lot:* perhaps... probably, something about him... i don't remember exactly. but i remember that it was a threat to everyone... a fatal threat... leo!
> *cleo:* ?
> *lot:* i'm scared, leo. i think that i'm about to remember... i need to go to sleep... i want to sleep, to sleep
> *cleo:* wait!!

Lot's lowly blew out the candles.

> *user lot has switched to sleep mode*
> *as usual, this will not get in the way of chatting in* socio
> *would you like to wish lot sweet dreams?*

> *cleo:* why did you fall asleep??
> *lot:* so i wouldn't remember
> *cleo:* coward!
> *lot:* you are right, leo. i am a coward. you know, it's my illness: i think i created it myself. i don't know, i don't remember how – but i did it to myself then so that i would forget. i am a coward, right. i killed my own memory. you had the courage to kill yourself entirely... then, later... i've lost my train of thought again... you were always... you were... what were we just talking about...?

> *user lot has turned on <u>delete all</u> mode*

...At first his face disappeared. The mischievous, young face with narrowed eyes froze for a second and then seemed to be sprinkled with glimmering dust; after his face his body and then his clothes crumbled into tiny fragments... For a moment a different userpic was revealed behind these fragments: a primitive anime face, probably from the early settings, but this too disappeared very quickly, leaving behind just the *shade*.

Then the cell started to change. The fields faded to black-and-white and then his *wonder-chess* disappeared completely. The photo albums, diaries, books and folders went pale and dissolved...

> this cell is obsolete
> you must immediately leave lot's cell

I stood by the *exit* and watched as the drowsy demon devoured everything that Lot had *created* in the day. His cell was stripped bare, turning into a standard inviz cocoon.

> caution! user lot <u>deleted</u> all his friends forever
> you are no longer friends with user lot, you
> are temporarily registered as a guest
> you must leave the cell immediately

> *lot:* don't go, guest!

His *shade* flew towards me, trying to block off the exit.

> *lot:* please! don't leave me here on my own!
> *guest:* i've got to go
> *lot:* i'm in pain! there's someone else here...
> *guest:* you are asleep
> *lot:* some pet bit me on the neck...
> *guest:* you are asleep, you are dreaming. try to roll over
> *lot:* i can't... it's hard to breathe

leave the cell immediately

guest: it really is time for me to go. no death!

I managed to say 'no death', but I didn't manage to leave. I stayed there.

I saw how his *shade* bent over and broke into two pieces. How these pieces crawled off in different directions like two halves of an earthworm.

I felt the cocoon of his cell pulsing and getting smaller, squeezing in and out around me, whistling like a punctured lung.

> *caution! mercy pause is underway*
> *lot's cell will be blocked*
> *your presence in* lot's *cell may be damaging to your health*

I heard him wheezing – not here, but *there*, in first layer.

Then everything froze – on a half-wheeze, half-breath – and the cocoon became dry and silent.

I crawled through the darkness. I had no mouth and no eyes...

> lot's *cell is blocked*
> *error k4u85n789*
> *ou will be automatically disconnected from* socio *if this error is repeated...*

I crawled through the darkness. I was the darkness. I smelled of unliving pets.

The Man with No Face

'A-a-ay, cross my cell with gold, mister planetman mister boss man...!'

A wide-hipped woman, like an elderly wonder-cleaner come to life, crawls over to me on all fours, dragging one leg behind her. She's wearing a bikini and a puffy brown nipple pokes out from one of the cups of the top; she has some baubles from Megalopolis round her neck and grey-black hair held back with a red ribbon.

'A-a-ay, I'll tell your fortune, you won't go wrong with me, you'll learn what was, what is and what will be...' She has a hoarse voice with a whining tone, and her mouth stinks of over-fermented cologne; it's the same smell that the pre-pauser Matthew had. '...I see beyond the pause, I see before, I tell all, of that you can be sure... I also remove curses and correct defects in your...' – she gives a long belch – 'in your invector.'

'Is there some kind of violation going on here?' I bark officiously. 'Conning people are we?'

'My inner eye can never lie, every word is true...'

Slum witches. Normally I only see glimpses of them: fortune tellers and palm readers, naturally, avoid me, a man in a mirror mask. But this one is shameless and drunk enough to go up to an SPO officer.

'...Every word is true, I will help you...'

> caution! your conversation device has detected
> speech activity from a subject who may be a witch
> is your interlocutor a witch?
> **yes** no
>
> do you want to report the violation?
> yes **no**

...Their activities are considered illegal, but forgivable nonetheless. For the fights between mantises, stag beetles, centipedes, scorpions and hornets you might end up with a pause with subsequent correction. But they don't normally punish the witches so strictly. Only occasionally, as a warning. In theory they're innocent enough, they don't do anyone any harm.

For the most part they are visited by their own kind – robots from the slums. People who have no other entertainment, no other prospects. The witches give them something different – ten minutes of excitement and romance and some hope for the future. Hope that after the pause they will be able to watch Festival Passions, have fun playing no deathers and live in crystal houses. For all that they don't mind parting with a little *socio*-money. They don't mind transferring the witch their monthly disability benefit...

But sometimes the witches are visited by clients from well-off areas. They are visited by naive little girls, dreaming of becoming the 'voice' of Festival Passions, the one who sings the title song. They are visited by unattractive women planning on casting a spell on the pedigree festival studs. They are visited by old failures who have dragged out their empty, boring lives pause after pause, so that they can finally get some comfort from an upcoming 'turn in their invector'. They are visited by the curious. And those looking for adventure. And the simply gullible.

'...what was, what is and what will be! Sterile procedure! I tell your future in contact gloves...!'

'Ah, get lost. And stop violating,' I grumble through my chatterbox, then put it on pause and ask: 'How much?'

'Only ten unics! Cheap...'

It really is cheap.

She beckons me with a finger and crawls off somewhere behind a heap of boxes, dragging her leg behind her.

'Sit down,' she points to a dirty blanket on the floor. I sit down.

'Money up front.'

She gives me a number and I transfer ten unics to her *socio* account.

The witch sits down opposite me, rummages around the blanket and pulls out an open box of contact gloves, which have clearly been used more than once; she pulls some on.

'Take off the mask.' Along with words the sepulchral smell of rotting flowers seeps from her mouth.

'No.'

The witch looks at me with a long, completely empty gaze, then nods.

'What do you want to know?'

'What happened before the pause. And what will happen afterwards.'

'Clients rarely take an interest in what has already happened. What, did you not leave yourself a letter in Renaissance?'

'You ask too many questions for a fortune-teller. Go on, do your job. Or give me back the money.'

She sniffs, offended, and stretches out a hand in a contact glove towards me. The glove smells of damp and earthy.

'I'll tell your future you won't go wrong with me... I will count to three... One, two...'

She places her index finger on my mirrored forehead – in about the place where normal people have a *socio* slot – and freezes, her eyes puffing out like a prawn.

caution! system may be under threat

'Right, let's go again... For some reason I can't see your past...'

...protocol error 067_3605...

213

'...You just relax, my little planetman friend, don't tense up... The main thing is to relax,' she hurriedly paws my forehead in different places. 'How about I sing you a song...? Sleeping are the calves and lambs, oo-oo-ooh... Sleeping are the newts, the rams, oo-oo-ooh...'

if this error is repeated, this application will be closed...

'...Dreams of waters dark and slow, oo-oo-ooh... Dreams of bitter, future woe, oo-oo-ooh... So, right, now I'm going to count to three... When I get to three you and I will discover everything... One, two... three! Right, I see... You have no past. And no present. Hey, you are not even alive...'

The witch pulls her hand away sharply and shakes it in the air, as if she had burned herself on my mask.

'Who is he?!' she screeches in my face, then twists her neck awkwardly and shouts into the emptiness behind her. 'He's no planetman! He was not, he is not! Who is he...?'

This witch has lost it. I should never have followed her...

'...Take your hands off me! Let me go, bastard!'

She starts jerking and tumbling about on the blanket, fighting off invisible demons. Then she rips off her top, screams and collapses on her back. She whines thinly and quietly:

'He is the one we have been waiting for. The one we have been waiting for. The one we have been waiting for...'

I would really, really like to get up and leave, but for some reason I can't feel my legs.

I crawl, I crawl slowly on my hands, dragging my numb legs over the dirty blanket.

it looks like you are trying to do something slightly incorrect

The fortune-teller gives a hoarse, gurgling sigh as if she is drawing water into her lungs and says:

'He has risen again.'

> *...do you want to exit sleep mode?*
> *yes no*
>
> *ef:* what the hell am i doing in sleep mode?!
>
> *invalid request...*

I died and rose again, in accordance with a precise plan.

The Miracle

Letter to Self

I died and rose again in accordance with a precise plan. In accordance with my friend Cracker's plan.

He worked a miracle for me – and that miracle cost him dearly. But he managed it. He made them all see fire. The correctees, the officers, even Ef – the entire household.

Everyone except me. I was the only one who could not see my own staged death.

At the set hour I went down to the Available Terrace, leaving my 'suicide diary' on my bed open at the last page. I still thought that it was dangerous and stupid, that nothing would work for Cracker, and that they would find this diary of mine while I was not in the dormitory, and then there was no way I would be able to avoid solitary in the Special Unit...

...It worked. He blocked off first layer for all of them, replacing it with a phantom, a realistic hallucination from second.

While they were standing there, staring blindly at the floor, their mouths gaping open, choking and groaning slightly, as if they were trying to cry out in a dream, while they watched a ten-minute clip of me being swallowed up by hellish flame on the Available Terrace, I followed Cracker's instructions, not trying to make sense of anything or over-thinking anything, but precisely, like a robot. I hit him in the front of the skull, right in the centre, with one of the trowels for loosening the sand which hung alongside every terrarium with desert pets. I pulled off Ef's mask. I opened up his chatterbox. Inside I found a cerebron – it was different from the skewed doodle which Fox had drawn in the diagram, but still recognisable – and took out two cerebral lenses. They were small, warm and slippery like pieces of a jellyfish that has died in the sun.

I put one in the left eye, and the other in the right, like in the diagram... They blinded and deafened me – and I collapsed. Into the buzzing, hundred-voiced, flickering depths, which bubbled like butter boiling in a pan.

There, in the depths, like a spider lurking in his web, sat my friend Cracker. He had four arms and four legs, and he grabbed me with his four slender, jointed hands as I wheezed and drowned and he pulled me to his chest and shouted:

> *cracker:* breathe! follow my breathing, otherwise
> you won't be able to hold first layer

When I learned to breathe again, he let me go, squatted down, bending the knees on all his four legs, and said:

> *cracker:* welcome to hell

He showed me Ef's cell – my cell. He explained how to hold first layer, which became quiet and ghostly, like the world as seen by a man drowning in murky water.

> *cracker:* however deep you go, don't lose sight of the
> surface. don't forget – here, inside is the WOMB of the
> monster. there, outside, is everything that is not him

He taught me how to talk in the depths and I said:

> *ef:* don't leave me
> *cracker:* then you have to friend me ☺

He was with me, as much as he could. Nearly ten minutes. It's terrifying to imagine how much effort he must have expended, keeping up the illusion that they were present at my death and still constantly staying with me, or, to be precise, in me. Helping me, supporting me, leading me through everything, protecting me, like a brainlesss, cumbersome queen who has to be saved from a termite mound besieged by enemies.

...Once I had pulled that mirrored mask on, with its sharp stench of blood, once I had *actually* set fire to the termite room and the reflection of the flame flickered in the eyes of the bewitched household, once Samson, the driver of the food truck, reeling and pale, with glassy eyes (*my guy*, Cracker explained in a business-like way when he appeared) had started dragging the impassive Ef from the terrace, Cracker said:

time for you to go

I took the cage with my worker termite and followed Samson, barely making out the contours of first layer, which were murky even without the smoke. Ef's friends were scrabbling around in my head, Ef's memory flared up in my mind as a ripe bunch of files and folders. In first layer I saw myself as if from the outside: a man in a planetman's mask, an officer in the Service for Order. That must have been when I started playing this game: thinking about myself in the third person. I liked calling myself Ef.

...The termite huddled against the wall of the cage, like it was a window. Almost the whole way to the old zoo, after every turn in the road he crawled along the wall of the cage to the point closest to his former home. To our former home. Then he suddenly lost interest in the turns, as if his invisible in-built compass had broken, and slowly crawled down to the floor and stopped moving. I thought: his castle has probably just burned down to the ground... I shook the cage with the tiny curled up body inside – it obeyed unwittingly, rolling back and forth.

my termite has died,

I said to Cracker and at that moment discovered that I could no longer see Cracker.

your friend cracker is no longer on socio

He left *socio* without saying 'no death'. He slipped off without a sound, like a thief.

We didn't say goodbye. I didn't even say thank you for the miracle. I never saw him again: not in first layer, not in *socio*. I will never see him again. My friend Cracker had abandoned me forever, but there, in the van carrying me off to a new life, I did not know that yet. My friend was dying, and I was crying for my termite, not my friend...

Because I could have guessed. By the way that the behaviour of 'his guy', the truck driver, changed. Samson was obviously trying to shake off his control. He drove nervily, jerkily, wobbling from side to side, accelerating and braking without reason, as if some invisible man was taking his leg off the pedals and turning the wheel. In the zoo he helped me unload Ef, who was groaning, but it was somehow grudging, as if he doubted whether he should really be helping. Before he left, Samson took a long look at the empty cages, then stared at me. Beads of white gunk had accumulated in the corners of his eyes, and suspicion blossomed murkily at the bottom of his boggy pupils.

'What...is...this...place?' Samson asked gruffly, although he was not supposed to ask.

Cracker had obviously lost control over him, he couldn't cope – though in comparison with the miracle which he had worked for me, managing a medium was nothing...! At that moment my friend Cracker was probably in agony. 'Lost ability to breathe and swallow independently,' I read in his medical records later. 'Cause of deterioration of condition unknown. Connection to artificial breathing apparatus does not seem expedient.' The cause is clear enough. He used up too much strength and energy dragging me to freedom.

He took everything through to the very end. There in the zoo he still managed to 'sit' Samson back in the van and make him leave without any unnecessary questions.

I can't even imagine how much effort this must have taken. Most likely, as he was driving Samson away, Cracker was no longer breathing.

...As I was dragging the planetman into the orang-utans' cage, he woke up for a little bit. Perhaps that was the last time Ef was fully conscious. He said my name and then punched me hard on the cheek. The mirror mask softened the blow slightly, but I tasted blood in my mouth...

...I dream that I am back in Samson's van. And that Samson is driving me back to the House of Correction. He is obeying Cracker, but Cracker has ordered him to take me to the Special Unit. Because now, as Cracker is no longer breathing, he is no longer my friend and is giving bad orders... I dream that I was asleep on the witch's blanket in the roboslums, and that Samson found me there, tied me up, flayed the skin from my face and poked out one of my eyes. And that then he loaded me into the van and drove me back to the House of Correction...

I often dream that I am going back there. I often have night-mares. To avoid nightmares you have to move in your sleep.

I touch my cheeks with my hands: they are hot and sticky and have no skin. The nightmare doesn't go away. Then I order myself to wake up entirely. I slowly and heavily slip out of *sleep mode* and into my cell and I bang up against bare walls. The settings have been wiped.

Something's wrong in first layer too. My nightmare is contin-uing: I hear the sound of a motor and feel it juddering.

'He's just not waking up,' someone's chatterbox states dispassionately. 'Gonna have to liven him up a bit.'

Someone hits me on the cheek. Hard, with the back of their hand.

I automatically try to protect my cheek with my hand, and I realise that I am in handcuffs. I feel my face with my fingertips – I'm not wearing the mirror mask, and my skin really sticky and sore. With some difficulty I unstick my eyes – the right one itches and stings – and I am looking at first layer. I am in the back seat of an SPO patrol car. Outside the window the golden lights of the empty streets and the enormous silhouettes of concretions flash by. A giant iron fork, a giant bronze table, a giant apple, a giant index finger...

...The fingers which I touched my face with are covered in blood. Cerberus is sitting to the right of me; his unblinking eyes seem angry even beneath his mask.

'Doesn't that hurt?' his chatterbox snarls, but Cerberus hits my face again, this time with his fist.

Ef is sitting on the left of me. He does not slouch in the seat only because he is tightly strapped in. His head is thrown back, his swollen face is covered in streams of sweat. He breathes hoarsely, unevenly – you would think he was snoring but his eyes are wide open. Beneath the old bandage his wound smells terrible.

'Look at him, look at him, don't you take your eyes off him,' Cerberus buzzes dourly. 'Look what you did to my partner.' He hits me in the face again. 'Killing's too good for you. Piece of shit. Bastard.'

'Quiet back there,' orders someone vaguely familiar from the front seat without turning round. 'We have to deliver him without any damage.'

The vaguely familiar man is driving. He's just sitting there – the vehicle is on automatic – his hands not touching the wheel while he examines the pet clasped in his swarthy hand. Then he breaks off from studying the pet and looks at me in the rear-view mirror. I recognise those eyes – a couple of festering olives. But last time his face was all painted, and now I can see his unhealthy dark skin. My friend Clown. From the Pause Zone...

He opens his palm and I see that what he has in his hand is not a pet. It's a cerebral lens – the one they poked out of my eye, all dried out, with a couple of little crimson veins inside.

'I didn't even know that the capillaries grew into it.' Clown contemplates the lens as he holds it up to the light. 'Looks like it broke. The techservice can get the other one out, I'm no good with these ancient devices... Correctee Zero,' he addresses me in a boring voice, 'you are accused of committing a series of serious and grievous crimes...'

The planned route and final destination flashes up on the instrument panel. The House of Correction. A waking nightmare. A silvery dot – our vehicle – is crawling up a curved orange line, sure and steady, like an ant marching along the path trodden by its kinsmen...

I close my eyes so that I don't see the way the silver ant is dragging me back to its nest. Now I only see the structure. The womb. It turns out that even one cerebral lens is enough to play about in it a bit. With one lens the womb looks slightly skewiff, but it's entirely suitable for a bit of playing about.

I don't want to play about. I'm tired of the flashing and the voices, of the music and films, of the spam and the useful advice, of the jokes and the sales.

I want to *leave socio.*

...failed!

You are right, womb. It was a failure. But the failures will end soon enough. In about half an hour they are going to poke out the remaining cerebral lens, and you will disappear, womb, you will crumble into nothing. And then I myself will disappear – the Council of Eight will hardly allow me to live after everything I've done.

I would like to leave the womb right now, but...

you cannot leave socio

...it won't let me go.

limited or no exit
this problem will be fixed – meanwhile you can chat
with your friends!

I try to imagine Hanna's face on the evening when she went off to the festival, but a sort of sad shadow thickens in front of my eyes, then nods and immediately loses its shape. I try to imagine Cracker, the way he was in the Special Unit, but instead of him his eight-limbed userpic crawls out of the cracks in my memory and scurries off into the depths like a thief. Then, unbidden and surprisingly distinct, the face of the madman Matthew floats up, the face of my 'apostle', whom I denied. Whom I caught, bound and sent off on his final journey on a wonder-trolley, so that he wouldn't make anyone suspicious...

Is this what you expected from me, Cracker my friend, when you performed the miracle, when a spasm gripped your throat? That I would become a creepy little bastard and spend my two weeks of freedom in a mirror mask, trying to find out what the great future that lay in store for me was...? And then I let myself get caught, asleep, without yet having figured anything out? Though that's not quite true: there's no doubt about my future now. Solitary in the Special Unit. Sentenced to pause. Darkness.

What did you see in me, my friend: a cowardly animal being taken to the slaughterhouse, eyes shut in mortal fear...? No, not that. You believed in me. You wanted me to turn the world upside down. You pushed me out of captivity, equipping me only with a nonsensical message: 'Fight the Monster.' You wanted me to find all the dissident lists in the Service for Planetary Order's database. Beneath the merciless corrective light, through the mouths of those in your service, you told me that you had created the dissidents yourself. All that spam, that virus that kept forwarding itself – you, Cracker, launched it all into *socio*... It was only later, you said, only later that they actually did appear. The dissidents. You just prepared the ground for them. Now the dissidents send out 'threats' themselves and call them 'chain letters'. And wait for me to come... You said that there were even some Thousanders among the dissidents. You wanted me to friend them and get them to follow me. You wanted me to get Thousanders, so that they would bring their thousands. You said: 'They'll get you of course, But you will injure Him.' You thought I would sacrifice my life for your obsession. Sorry, Cracker. My life is short compared to yours – sorry, I got selfish. And now I'm giving it away just like that... If you knew, you would probably unfriend me...

> *...Do you want to chat with your* socio *friends?*
> *yes no*

Ef's friends, some of them are my enemies, and all the rest are just strangers. His friends blink their pulsing, available mouths mockingly at me, inviting me in. Cracker's cell is not lit up, there is only a little timer counting down the time until the birth – 265 days remaining ☺.

> i have no friends

I say to the womb.

i am completely alone
incorrect

the womb argues,

you have 230 friends on your list

It's dumb, the womb. And stubborn. There's no point in arguing with it. I don't argue, I just delete the friends. In turn I plug up the hungry, greedy mouths.

I delete 229 friends from my list. Only one is left.

delete user cleo *from your friend list?*
yes **no**

No. When you are wearing handcuffs and you're about to cease existing, you really want at least one friend…
The entrance to her cell is getting smaller, evenly, drowsily, but it swings open as I come nearer.

your friend cleo is offering you an act in luxury?
agree?
yes *no*

Why not? She might as well be my final, one and only friend. Someone might as well love me, even just a bit, in *luxury* mode, as a final send-off.

user ef wants to be dominant in the act
cleo is taking the passive role

…I *create* the land, the grass, the flowers and the shrubs, the trees and the stones, the hills and the gullies, and the pine

225

cones and the moss, the fallen leaves, the mushrooms rotting beneath them, and a lot else besides...

I *create* myself – in the form of a white-eyed wolf, one I saw at the farm once.

I *create* her – in the form of a white-eyed female who loves my scent...

I'll have time to inseminate her before the end of the world begins.

...Before the man sitting to the left of me chokes on his coughing and snoring and temporarily ceases living. Before the womb, which believed that I was him, vomits me to the surface in disgust.

Cleo

Dog *refuses to eat dry food*

She hasn't touched her food for a day now. Because I don't play with her anymore, I don't stroke her or play fetch with her.

> your **dog** is depressed. you need to pay her more attention. your dog-owner rating equals 0.

I can't. I'm also depressed. I'm a rubbish dog-owner. I hope when they get the beetle out of her, everything will be like before. But until then I won't play with her whatever happens... Not now.

Not right now, when I'm looking at another document created with her help.

Ef: memory F: Hunter's Living Journal: private entries: Beetle2.doc

14.07.471

After the conversation with *lot*, which, unfortunately, took place outside the cell and was not recorded, the subject is nervous and clearly in a state of stress. From 9:00 unt il 11:00 she runs a series of requests – fairly chaotic – on themes like: 'Leo demanded...', 'Leo said...', 'according to Leo', 'Leo five seconds of darkness', 'Leo leo lot ray'. Then she creates the folder 'leo memories'. copies all the direct quotations she has found in it and saves the folder in her memory.

(*note: the search requests on their own are no threat, and are, of course,not illegal. nevertheless 'scientific investigations' of this sort must be automatically registered as 'suspicious'*).

<u>11:15.</u> Request sent to the Association of Laboratory Workers: 'please send me the articles I have written on the "Directed Leo-Lot Ray".'

<u>15:50.</u> An entirely logical refusal from the Association of Laboratory Workers: 'Unfortunately, we cannot distribute the requested documents. The Leo-Lot experiment was a failure. All research materials were destroyed either by the authors themselves or the Association.'

<u>15:52.</u> Another request to the Association of Laboratory Workers. This time the subject asks them to send all her research work not connected to the experiment.

<u>17:20.</u> The Association of Laboratory Workers sends out compressed files with a complete collection of Leo's research articles. The subject unzips the files and saves them all in 'leo memories'.

From <u>17:40</u> to <u>23:57</u> Cleo copies the texts of all the souvenir letters in Renaissance left during his previous reproduction into a separate file. She saves the file in her memory in the same folder.

<u>15.07. 471:</u>

<u>09:15.</u> Cleo downloads *wonder-chess*.

Something's up here. She certainly isn't planning on playing. Ah, there it is! She finds *master Leo* among the virtual players. She saves all the games he has played in her memory in the same 'leo memories' file.

<u>12:00.</u> Hello, something very interesting! The subject is closing or deactivating EVERYTHING in her memory except 'leo memories'.

Page designers determine the size of the font and the encoding of the text. If the encoding doesn't match the one set in the reader, what you see is

...see fire now
painf
ĕïåéäDàQ̄ş̦œǻdĕä?aʾQ̄

unable to display page

...I choose *visit to vet* from the menu and send 200(!) unics to the right account. The Association of Game Raters fleeces you pretty mercilessly for veterinary services, even though the quality is, to be frank, not great: the reception room loads without a right-hand wall, the vet isn't at all 3D – she's all dull and flat, like a squashed beetle, and her facial expressions are limited, like a slum robot.

'Welcome, dog-owner,' she says through the unmoving half-moon of her mouth. 'As you are here, you cannot be taking good care of your *dog*, which has led to her developing some illness. How can I help you?'

'My dog is healthy. She's just picked up a parasite. I want to delete it.'

'Oh!' Her face is stretched into a grimace for a second, so badly drawn that it could mean anything, from abhorrence to sympathy, and then straightens out. 'Picking up a worm is very bad. It is good that I can help you. Deleting worms is a simple operation. It is a paid service. 100 unics for every *socio*-worm.'

'It's not a worm.'

'Oh?'

'It's more like a beetle.'

'Really?'

'Yeah, really. Spyware.'

'I have never experienced a dog with spyware.'

'Now you have.'

The vet makes her mouth round – probably to spit out the next 'oh' – and freezes. My dog, emboldened, sniffs and licks her frozen face, then goes over to the non-existent right-hand wall and, cocking her head to one side inquisitively, looks into the endless blackness.

> Unfortunately, I am not able to carry out your request: my qualifications are insufficient.
> You might want to try our superpro – a top level professional. Consultation costs 300 unics. Pay for consultation?
> **yes** no

'What a con!' I say to the vet, but she just sits there, her rounded jaw hanging low, and doesn't come out of her paralysis, even to say goodbye.

The superpro looks like he could be her twin brother, only instead of a black thatch of hair, he has an oval pink bald spot and glasses on his nose. In contrast to his less-qualified colleague he casts a shadow, has better facial expressions and his study loads fully.

He examines *dog* and takes an x-ray (another 100 unics flows out of my *socio* account). He hangs a series of x-rays on the wall of his office. What's there on the slides doesn't look too good: a little patch of white in the dog's brain, absolutely tiny – but it has slender little legs extending out in all directions, shackling all her internal organs.

'Bad news, I am afraid,' says the superpro. 'It would be dangerous to delete the beetle. Look, it has grown into all the vitally important areas. It is involved in nearly all the *dog*'s active processes... But there's some good news too. The beetle presents no threat to the *dog*'s health. On the contrary, in a way it is even helping her. It is making the *dog* more active and intelligent. All your *dog*'s applications, such as vision, smell, intuition, curiosity, ability to learn and ability to sympathise are superbly well-developed... Judge for yourself, the beetle program is friendly.'

'It's spyware. It's not friendly to me.'

'In this game we look after the health of cats and dogs. We do not deal with the problems of *dog-owners* and *cat-lovers*. This is dealt with by the Psychological Service for Assisting the Population.'

'Can you at least say when information was last downloaded from the beetle?'

'300 unics,' the superprofessional replies, and an entirely first-layer expression of cynicism appears on his round face.

I transfer the money silently and he lights up with a pleasant smile.

'The last download was on 15th July 471, 12:00.'

The time of Zero's death. The time of the last message sent by Ef... Let's suppose Zero's self-immolation in first layer distracted the planetman from following me in second. Why then didn't he download the rest later, the most important bits?!

'How much will deleting the beetle cost?'

'I see no reason for the operation,' the superpro says.

'And what if I, say, triple your fee – will you see one then?' The expression 'deeply offended' appears on his face.

'The *dog* is inoperable,' he says hostilely through gritted teeth. 'Don't worry, she's completely healthy. All the best, no death, come again.'

The veterinary clinic shoves me and the dog back into the viscous between world. *Dog* tumbles about and yaps away – she loves going for walks in the depths, she likes the sensation of weightlessness. She twitches her paws playfully, inviting me to play with her.

'She is a spy,' I say to myself. 'My *dog* is a spy. She is not my friend. A sneak.'

I wait for *dog* to turn away from me and then I go back to my cell.

Alone, without her. I leave her tumbling in the *socio-emptiness*.

She will notice that I've gone, and get scared and start to look for me in the depths – but that won't last long.

She won't see me killing her.

And I won't see her ceasing to live.

Why did he not download the most important bits? The things I did when I was thrown out of the fresh grave that formed in place of Lot's cell? The things I did when the darkness swelled up inside me and burst like a septic boil. When I woke up in my cell and *dog* was licking me with its painted-on tongue. When I was turned inside out in first layer and the autodoctor was overflowing with recommendations: *you appear to have been an accidental witness to someone's socio-pause... this can cause considerable physical and mental stress... please consult a psychotherapist immediately... if nausea continues, call an 'ambulance'...*

I didn't call an ambulance. Instead I called up a ghost.

I collected everything left in *socio* by my predecessor into one file – everything that Leo had ever said, written, thought or worked out... I thought at the end of the day if a ghost can play me at chess, why can't he talk to me heart to heart? A ghost can make a move, based on the logic of his previously played games. A ghost will give me answers based on the logic of his previously lived life. Based on the make up of the brain that once invented the Leo-Lot ray.

I shut off everything in my memory except for the video function and 'leo memories', and I felt like I was losing my consciousness bit by bit. As if a voracious swarm of termites was gobbling up my thoughts, memories and habits, leaving yawning emptiness in their place... Then, devoured, empty, with fragments of someone else's memory in my head, I lurched randomly back and forth through my cell, unaware, unremembering, completely disoriented.

My *dog* – that part of her which was stored outside my memory – crawled after me sadly and tried to whimper. My *dog* became a skeleton again, through which I could see her internal organs. The form in which she had been downloaded initially. I had installed the fur and the whole exterior manually, separately, and now all those settings had been wiped...

...I had no childhood. No home. No body. My life was tiny, cold and precise, like a snow crystal. I was made of symbols. I knew a lot of scientific theories and chess openings. But I had no idea how to use all this, who I should play against and why.

Even now, when I watch the video, I feel *that* chill. It's like I'm standing in a breeze with my back to an open window. I'm standing and watching myself amble casually, randomly into my *socio* home cinema. The screen was turned off and my face was reflected in the twinkling black rectangle. The face of a man of about forty, whitish and half-transparent, as if pets had spun his skin from spider webs.

'Who's there?' I asked in a man's voice and replied to myself, 'Leo.'

'Why are you here?'

'I think you want to ask me a question.'

'I don't remember what it was.'

'Let's figure it out,' I said. 'Either you are interested in my scientific work, or my personal life, or my chess – that's all that I am made of. Personal life can be eliminated straightaway: those memories take up no more than five per cent, and they are all quite vague. As for chess: if you had wanted to play against me, you would just have started a game. Therefore, all that's left is science – but the records of my chess moves only answer for my logical thought. Which means that I have to *create* something for you. What is it?'

I hold the pause for a long time and then say calmly, 'The formula for the compound. The one used for the injection in the Leo-Lot ray experiment.'

I didn't know exactly whose words these were. Mine: could I rack his first-layer memory and recall why I summoned him, or perhaps they were his words after all? Probably his. He and his dead chess brain had probably worked out in advance what I expected from him.

Whatever it was, I froze for two and a half hours (158 minutes 37 seconds according to the clock on the video) and all that time the *dog*'s skeleton desperately nuzzled me with its bony nose. Then I started moving again, created a new file and wrote the formula in it.

I said out loud to my reflection, 'Sorry. There is a five per cent chance of a mistake in the formula.' After a little while *socio* suggests I restore all settings.

> *it seems your previous settings were more convenient*
> *restore them?*
> **yes** *no*
>
> *save new file 'Formula' in memory?*

I saved it.

Ef did not download everything from the beetle. Instead he came to me in first layer and asked whether I knew the Leo-Lot formula. And before that he asked if any of the festival employees might help a pre-pauser *after the shower*. You don't have to know hundreds of openings and middle games to realise that the man in the mask that quizzed me on Golden Mean Square, who did not know how pauses are carried out, is no planetman.

He is someone who has made too many mistakes recently. He is someone who has one message waiting for him in the

Everything's Going to Be Alright service. To the Saviour from the Apostle.

He is the one who has already destroyed me once before.

He is the one I need.

They say there's no better way of getting to know someone than *luxury* mode. They're lying. The best way to get to know someone is the directed Leo-Lot ray. I need a lab. I need to win his confidence, get contact up and running, convince him.

They say that there's no better way of getting close to someone than *luxury* mode. They're probably lying about that too, but I don't know any other way...

> *Error #47037*
> *your* **dog** *cannot find its way home*
>
> *cleo:* control panel: install and delete programmes: delete **dog**
>
> *...please wait... program will be deleted in*
> *60 seconds... deletion of program is in progress...*
> *unsuccessful!*
> *error #43048. it is impossible to delete 'dog': you*
> *do not have access to the application 'body of dog'*
> *if this error occurs again, please contact techsupport...*

I couldn't delete her here, in the cell. But I was afraid of looking at her fading eyes for a whole minute. Dog owner friends of mine have told me how naturalistic *socio*-animals are when they die... I didn't know that it would be like this. As the Living is my witness, I didn't want to drag out her suffering. I wanted it all to happen quickly and painlessly...

She will whimper, she will look for the way home, she will sniff around, trying to find my trail. But there are no trails in *the depths*. There are no smells and no sounds can be heard.

Without food, water or the attention of her owner she will be done for in two to three days. The beetle will write the chronicle of her solitude, and then they will both disappear.

> your **dog** is depressed
> we would like to remind you that she is an inside dog,
> and long walks outside the cell are harmful to her
> call **dog** back home?
>
> **yes** no
>
> let's call the **dog** back home... unsuccessful!
> unfortunately, your **dog** cannot find the way home.

...They say the only way to forget about sadness and shame, to silence the voice of your conscience, is to move to *luxury*.

I offer him an *act*, and he agrees. He wants to be dominant.

Luxury

He *creates* the earth, the grass, the flowers and the shrubs, the trees and the stones, the hills and the gullies, the pine cones and the moss, the fallen leaves and the mushrooms rotting beneath them, the fine suspension of rain in the air, the low, swollen sky, and the birds hiding their snakelike heads under their warm wings. He *creates* the animals – mice, badgers and racoons, squirrels and hares, and deer, and foxes, and bears.

He *creates* himself in the form of a wild dog or, maybe, a wolf.

He *creates* me in a form like his.

I draw his scent in through my nostrils and realise that in this world he and I have the same mother, that he is my brother and my husband, that we were born together and we will die together, and become a part of this earth and this grass, of these flowers and shrubs, of these trees and pine cones and leaves. And our children's children, as they track a fat hare on a rainy evening, will smell our scent as it seeps from the plants and the soil.

...He licks my ears, my eyes and nose, my stomach, my crotch and my nipples and then my eyes and ears again. In first layer I would feel sick with disgust, but here, in *luxury*, in the wet grass, in the body of an animal, I take pleasure in every touch. He licks me, and his mouth is hot with the scent of me, and of our mother, of the male he fought with over me, of the damp earth, of the blood and flesh of our prey, and of death, and, ever so slightly, of fear.

We know that there, on the far side of the blue-grey hills, where the animal marks on the tree trunks stop, there, beyond the line that binds sky and earth, lives the Dead God.

No one knows how he was born: he does not and never has had a mother or a father.

His body is not whole. The parts are not connected to each other and one part can crawl away from another over the line of the horizon.

He does not grow old. He will never die because he is already dead…

We fear him.

We will mate to try to fight this fear…

He is completely dominant in this *act*. He *created* this whole world, he *created* me and himself – all that is left to me is the details.

I *create* a home for us – a den on the slope of a hill. Its entrance is almost invisible in a thick cluster of tree roots, but just in case I *create* an outcrop of tall grass. For safety. So that no one will notice us… Inside the den I *create* a floor of warm branches and dry leaves.

I go inside and he sneaks in after me. He bites my neck with his teeth; it is not painful, but commanding. I break free, turn around and growl for show, but I give in almost immediately. I think about the pups, which will smell like me and him. He takes me, growling quietly.

When the *act* is over, he licks me again, but I snarl at him to make him stop. I clamp my teeth shut and whimper silently to myself, so that he doesn't hear. I think about the pups, which will smell like me and like him, when he and I are already smelling of earth and rotting meat. I think about the breeding seasons I have been through before – about the hundreds of squeamish pairings in contact underwear. I think about the festival which the Dead God needs to fertilize himself. I think about the *dog* which is scampering about in the emptiness and cannot find my trail. I think about the fact that something is wrong with my *luxury* programme: such melancholy is unnatural in the 'garden of delights'.

We lie in silence by the entrance to the den and look out. At the world he *created* for our *act*. The land is good, but the sky is tainted with pus-yellow and there is no moon. I wonder whether I should *create* it but I don't have the strength to change anything.

He quietly leaves the den and sits with his back to me. He is doing something to our world – and the pus-filled abscesses in the sky burst, not with rain, but with thick, dull snow.

I wonder whether I need to make our den warmer before the pups come.

He throws back his head and gives a long, throaty howl. And then disappears. His world turns into the Wastes of Solitude.

And I am all alone there.

Cerberus

No bargaining with his conscience, no worries, no doubts. He was lucky: he had been a constant guardian of order for the last 306 years, at the very least. But probably since the Nativity itself, it's just there is no record of it: Renaissance only appeared in 145 A.V. And in the first branch of the bank in the EA region, in the first letter he left for himself in his personal cell (in the old fashioned way, on paper), the first words on the first line are 'I am a planetman, I am proud of that and always will be.' It's a little cheesy, but forgivable: it's an Initial Entry after all. And a sincere one at that. Cerberus really had always taken pride in his work. He was a good professional: in all those 326 years there had been no serious fines or warnings – sure, some minor violations ('observed not wearing mask', 'assault of persons in custody', 'non-consensual copulation outside of festival zone'), but not a single penalty card for cowardice, not a single *socio*-bribe, and a whole gallery of awards. The first three, trinkets that still existed in first layer, were great rarities – 'For Vigilance and Valour', 'For Services to *Socio*' and 'Hero, First Class' – Cerberus kept them all in his cell in Renaissance. He liked to get them out and feel them in his hands every now and again: it was childish, of course, but Cerberus thought that it was better for someone with eternal life to be a child at heart rather than a complete cynic. At the end of the day, for guys like him Renaissance still existed in first layer. Like a cupboard full of toys, an old-fashioned chest of drawers with *tangible* treasures from his childhood, from his past...

From the Sixties of the second century onwards the awards had become virtual; Cerberus had hung a whole wall in his *socio* cell with 'Heroes' and 'For Valours', and, as a sign of its respect for his achievements, the Service for Technical Support had given him a complimentary Eternal Memory setting. The setting was not wiped after the pause – so when Cerberus was reproduced and entered an empty cell, his medals and awards were already there waiting for him, hanging on the bare walls.

And there had been a lot of pauses. Twice he was killed during arrests: in 149 and in 176; they had not yet perfected the Houses of Correction, it was a difficult time. In the Eighties these outrages came to an end and working in the SPO became much safer, but Cerberus still renewed himself regularly, preferring to visit the Pause Zone after the first gentle recommendation so that he could stay in good shape, so he had only reached sixty once.

Everything was right and proper. His life was precise, uncomplicated and orderly, like a pyramid of ice cubes. Yes, a pyramid of ice – that's how he had always thought of his life when he became a child. As if he was building it: cube – pause – cube – pause, building it up to the sky. Then, when he got a bit older, he would prefer the analogy of a chain. His life was like a strong, endless chain, with no weak links.

Other people's chains would break every now and again. Cerberus's friends would fall away after picking up five penalty cards, and new, inexperienced ones would come to replace them. Over the course of three and a bit centuries everyone he had started out with had been replaced, including the Servant of Order. Everyone except Ef, his constant partner and best friend: his partner's 'chain', like Cerberus's, had no weak links.

Over the course of three and a bit centuries Cerberus and Ef had been through a lot – sting operations and early pauses, first-layer injuries and cells deformed by viruses, dragnets for spammers and attacks by hackers. They had tracked members of familial sects who didn't give their Darlings to the boarding houses, they had searched the cells of heretic old believers who believed in the ancient three-headed god, they had ensnared dissident scum in all layers...

Justice has no face. 'The human factor' has no influence on planetary order. The mirrored distance should keep the SPO officer at arm's length from everyone, even other officers. So it is written in the Codex... But over the course of three and a bit centuries they had become friends, not only in *socio*, but in first, and occasionally they had broken the rules of the Codex, not seriously, but little things here and there. The previous Servant of Order had always forgiven them for their antics.

They had seen each other without their masks – different faces at different times. They had heard each other's voices without them being distorted by chatterboxes. They could recognise each other from a long way off by the way they walked, and from up close by their smell. By the way their standard inviz-coloured uniforms smelled at the armpit. At festivals they would share one girl. And when one of them was reproduced as a woman (which had happened a couple of times for each of them), they had become lovers.

...Over the course of three and a bit centuries they had grown together nicely and their 'chains' had become intertwined. So when Ef started behaving strangely, Cerberus noticed immediately. It began after Zero's suicide, he and Ef were sitting in a pub in first layer. Ef kept touching his mirrored cheek and Cerberus said show me. Ef reacted as if they were strangers. He was cold.

From then on it was easy, like in the training program for young guardians of the Living, 'Catch the Thief'. All future planetmen had this program installed when they were four. Cerberus remembered how Duckles, mirrored and opalescent, had once taken him by the hand and led him off into a patch of reeds. There, by the stream, he taught him how to hide and sit in wait. 'You suspect that Fishie has stolen something, right, little fellow?' Little Cerberus nodded animatedly: 'Fishie is a thief. I'm sure.' Duckles' magnificent mirrored bill smiled: 'Well done.'

'So I'm going to go and tell Livvles!' 'It's too soon,' Duckles didn't let go of his hand. 'First gather evidence. Make sure

Fishie doesn't realise that you know that he's up to no good. Let him think you are his friend. But instigate surveillance on him and start putting together a report. When the report is ready, give it to me. I am your senior officer. I will give the report to Livvles myself. And I will ask Him to reward you.'

Two words, two magic spells, full of sibilant sorcery: 'surveillance' and 'senior officer'; Cerberus didn't know what they meant. Backed by the songs of the cicadas, in the crackling clump of reeds, Duckles explained to him what they meant. At four years old Cerberus filed a report against Fishie and received his first gold star...

...It was so simple. He had shared his suspicions with his senior officer. The Servant of Order, like Duckles before him, had ordered him to gather evidence. Cerberus put together a report on the fake Ef over the course of a few days. He didn't include, of course, the refusal to take off the mask. But he did include:

– errors during arrest and transport of compulsory Matthew (completely amateurish, Ef would never have made mistakes like that with his experience and savvy);

– behaviour unbefitting of an SPO officer in the Pause Zone at the local Festival for Assisting Nature (a total rookie would have behaved better);

– partner's inability to complete password-response exercise ('Did that virgin at the festival put out for everyone?' – the correct answer should have been 'No, she's waiting for you and me');

– 'diagnosis' offered by conversation device (Cerberus had chosen 'interrogation' mode on his chatterbox when he and Ef were chatting during the arrest of the compulsory and later at the festival). The chatterbox's conclusions were beyond belief. 'Based on the *interlocutor*'s physical indicators, such as body temperature, arterial pressure, pupil dilation, and functioning of sebaceous, sudoriferous and salivary glands, the *interlocutor*'s condition can be characterized as *close to panic*, with frequent episodes of *fear, shame* and *remorse*';

– comparative analysis of user ef's *socio* speech before and after 15th July 471: '*socio* speech belongs to two different users...'

...QED. *Quod erat demonstrandum.* Which was to be demonstrated. This evidence was enough to arrest the fake Ef and bring a case against him for the kidnap of an SPO officer. And to start searching immediately: there had been no signal about Ef's pause, so he must be being kept captive. In these stable times of ours this is an unprecedented crime against the Living...

The last time the *real* Ef went on *socio* chat was when he was in the House of Correction. A few minutes before the suicide of correctee Zero. Cerberus kept the statements of the witnesses who had been present at the suicide in a separate file. The statements all matched. Matched a little *too* well. And there was no shortage of witnesses. *Too* many witnesses. There was not a single correctee, or warder, or member of the domestic staff or House administration who did not give a statement. It turned out that the ENTIRETY of the household was on the Available Terrace at the outbreak of the fire. Which is impossible, purely physically: they just wouldn't fit... That said, the chatterbox tracking the physical condition of those interrogated came to the conclusion that all the witnesses had answered Cerberus's questions sincerely enough.

He did not try to put together any versions of events. He just sent the report and the transcripts of the interrogations to his senior officer and awaited further instruction.

He was sure that his senior officer would instruct him to seize the fake Ef immediately. But his senior officer instructed him to 'hold on a bit for now'.

Cerberus was taken aback.

cerberus: do you have doubts about the information
i have given you?
servant: don't be silly?! but, you know, you can never
be too careful ☺
cerberus: there is an official *socio* speech analysis.
on the basis of that i'd like your permission for
compulsory unmasking of the suspect
servant: refused. just observe for now
cerberus: observe?! servant, ask for the video
recording from the festival! look at the way he was
acting. like an idiot. he treated that compulsory like
a woman feeding her darling! even the pre-pausers
were looking at him... you don't even need to turn your
chatterbox on to see how strange he is being!! i insist
that you give me permission...

...It turned out that the Servant of Order was handling this case personally. In first layer, undercover as Clown. With no mask.

Cerberus almost forgot to breathe in excitement. He noisily pushed the warm, celebratory air out of himself. Glap, he's involved in a Case of First Level Planetary Secrecy! His senior officer had taken his mask off in front of him. He had seen him – the Servant of Order, the head of the SPO; sure, he might have been wearing clown's makeup, but he had still seen him. He and the Servant were going to be working together on this case. What does that mean? It means they trust him. They really trust him. What else might it mean? Maybe an Order of the Living is not too much to hope for? He wondered whether he should hang it separately. Not on the same wall with all the other awards, but right there on his *desktop*.

The Servant of Order permitted the arrest of the pretender only after ten days. At first they recovered Ef – the scumbag was keeping him in a cage, like a sick ram at the Farm. His partner was in a very bad way. His temperature was over forty, he was groaning and ranting, begging for snow.

Interlocutor's condition can be characterised as pre-pausal – the chatterbox announced, although it hadn't been asked.

Cerberus felt that beneath his mask his face was wet with tears. A pause is fine. A pause is nothing. But his friend had spent so long in this state! He must have suffered so much…

cerberus: permission to finish him off?

he asked, already placing the cold barrel against his friend's temple.

'Ice, ice…' Ef smiled and closed his eyes.

servant: i forbid it. let's take him to the car

Cerberus took the gun away. Do it by the Codex, right. But there's something inhuman about it. The former Servant would definitely have let him finish him off. This new one wants everything to be strictly by the Codex… Fine, it would be stupid to pick a fight with him. The former Servant would never have worked alongside Cerberus.

They sat in wait for the fake Ef in the roboslums. It was a strange arrest. For some reason the Servant dragged along – literally dragged along, across the ground – a slum witch. He shook her like a dead bird that had fallen from the sky (Cerberus had seen that happen once) and jabbed his finger against her filthy chest:

'Are you really a witch or just a bullshitter?'

The woman drunkenly chanted her dumb first-layer spam in a drawl:

'Ay, I'll tell your future, you won't go wrong…'

'So who am I then?' the Servant barked.

'Thirty unics, dearie, just whack it in my *sociopurse...*'

The Servant kicked her withered, naked leg with the heel of his boot. He pressed the heel against her kneecap. Something crunched. The fortune teller howled.

'I said, who am I?'

She reached a trembling hand towards the Servant and he bent over so it would be easier for her. He touched his forehead with a grubby finger, and the Servant contorted in disgust.

'Fofs,' the witch whispered, and frowning in pain, tried to kneel. 'Forgive me poor sinner that I am, great Servant of Order.'

'Our friend will be here any moment,' the Servant responded with contempt, 'a planetman, in a mirrored mask. We want you to give him a surprise. Tell his fortune and then switch him to sleep mode...'

'Hypnosis?' the fortune teller enquired. 'I have to hypnotize him?'

'Yes, yes,' the Servant nodded irritatedly. 'Do you know how?'

'Of course.' The witch shook her dirty-grey mane.

> *cerberus:* why put him to sleep, boss?
> *servant:* we'll take him quietly, no shooting. besides, i'm curious
> *cerberus:* about what?
> *servant:* what she's going to say to him
> *cerberus:* but she... she's just a filthy robot...

The Servant's eyes smiled almost imperceptibly; they were glossy and black like the backs of African cockroaches.

> *servant:* the ancients used to listen to women like her

...The witch actually did put the fake Ef in sleep mode.

After that the Servant of Order instructed Cerberus to drag her to the other side of the boxes and temporarily end her life.

While Cerberus pulled on his contact gloves, she whimpered quietly but ever so sadly, like an animal at the Farm. He started feeling weird.

'No death,' he said as he leaned over her.

The witch stopped whimpering and suddenly spat – the yellow glob hung on his mirrored face. 'Sometimes you have to break the Codex,' Cerberus wrote in his *socio* blog and snapped the witch's neck. He could hear the groans of robots mating behind the rubbish skips.

They loaded the rat into the van and took him to the House of Correction. Cerberus beat him about the face, gasping with futile hatred. Where's the justice? The vengeance? Living, you are too kind! You are full of love, you forgive your errant sons, you do not punish them, you only correct them. And you are sentencing this freak, who tormented my friend for thirteen days and nights, to a simple pause. You are sending him off into the darkness. And if he comes out of it, you will patiently correct him...

...On the way poor Ef's agonies came to an end and he temporarily ceased to live and Cerberus felt better. Tiredness came – cosy and warm like a woollen scarf; it wound round his neck and shoulders. First layer shuddered pleasantly along with the car; in second Cerberus whacked on the soundtrack from The Eternal Murderer; in fifth – which was where he kept his illegal video (he could always say that he had just confiscated it) – he started playing an amazing battle between a scorpion and a stag beetle. He relaxed and started thinking about his Order of the Living. He wasn't just going to hang it on his *desktop*.

He would make it his wallpaper, thanks very much... He wondered, would Eternal Memory save that setting...?

...you are preparing to switch to sleep mode
would you like to sleep? yes no

Cerberus actually doubted whether he should go to sleep, but his eyes were already closed. He didn't see his senior officer aiming the gun at him.

In fifth layer the stag broke off the scorpion's left claw. The scorpion tried to sting the beetle in the stomach...

Servant of Order URGENTLY SUMMONS *Second*
second: ?
servant: officer cerberus has broken rank – he
arbitrarily carried out a witness's pause – at the
present moment he is making an attempt on suspect
Zero – he refuses to obey orders – he has received five
penalty cards in a day – request permission for pause
second: permission for pause granted. with subsequent
expulsion from the SPO

...Cerberus dreamed that he was building a tower from cubes of ice.

The gun had a silencer.

The cubes quietly collapsed.

Part 3

Eight

'Gwanda! Gwanda gwan-da gwan-da...' The youngest had only recently learned to talk, and she liked the sounds. '...dagwan dagwan da-gwa...' She laughed and held up her hands to clap and reached up to his beard. She also really liked this thick crop of twisted white springs.

'Second,' her mother said didactically. 'Granddad is Second.' The youngest fell silent for a second, opening even wider her coffee-coloured eyes, which were perpetually amazed anyway, and then started gurgling away again:

'Segun! Segun! Segun! Segun...!'

'Bzhdvang! Dz! Dz!!' Her five-year-old brother exploded in spit and sound as he played a no deather in second layer.

Second frowned wearily.

'Sh-h-h.' His mother put her finger to her lips. 'Darling, don't vocalise.'

The boy stared at her blindly, then squinted, aiming at someone in second layer; his right hand was clenched into a weak, shuddering little fist:

'Bzdva-a-ang!!!'

'Don't vocalise, how many times do I have to tell you. Don't vocalise the depths!'

...With an insidious bumble-bee buzz the Diver's wonder-chair rolled into the hall. The youngest, screeching in delight, hurried off towards him on all fours. She liked the way that the Diver was always so docile and still. You could push his arm off the armrest of the chair and the arm would just stay hanging there. You could pinch him and tickle the soles of his feet, he was not afraid of tickling. You could even poke about in his mouth when no one was watching...

'Wai!' She tugged on the Diver's trouser-leg. 'Wai? Wai?'

'Wise One,' her mother reminded her with a smile. 'Wuh-ize wuh-un. Say it.'

'Wai wa… Wai wa!'

'That'll do!' Groaning, Second leaned over and unhooked the youngest from the Diver's trouser-leg. The youngest was furious and lay on the floor and started screaming loudly and stroppily, waiting for the tears to come.

'Enough!' Second turned impatiently to the Servant of Order. 'Talk to your woman.'

'Take the kids, Layla!' The Servant examined the screaming Darlings strictly. 'There's only two minutes to go until the Conference.'

'And what have the kids got to do with that?' Layla snapped back. 'They're just sitting in first layer, they're not bothering anyone…'

'Idiot,' the Servant said good-naturedly. 'This is an Open Conference. It's broadcast in first layer.'

Layla snorted sceptically, but she took the children away, wiggling her enormous behind.

'She's got fat,' the Servant thought as she left. 'And insolent. I have to take another one.'

'That First is going to be the pause of me!' Second grumbled restlessly and squirmed on the new sofa, trying to find a comfortable pose and somehow stick in it; the sofa was doing a good job of resisting. 'I'm going to break my spine!'

Second hated the sofa. The sofa was from the latest 'Feeling Lucky' collection – bright, ridiculous and completely shapeless, like all of First's design fantasies; but not sitting on it during the Conference would mean showing disrespect to his colleague's work. And his colleague First took such things to heart.

Due to an excess of adolescent energy First got personally involved in creative projects. And the Association of Designers that he headed up (largely thanks to the efforts of their thirteen-year-old moderator; nevertheless, Second reckoned that they were all a bit soft in the head), instead of making attractive and useful objects which might tempt people into using first layer, developed completely impractical clothes and furniture which no one could ever use, even if for some reason they wanted to, and adorned the streets with concretal sculptures of forks, eyeballs and clenched fists. Only people who never left *socio* could dream up stuff like that! And then they are surprised that the general populace wander round in bedraggled hand-me-downs and sleep on the floor. It's a disgrace. I'd like to tell the idiot straight out that his sofa is nothing more than a pile of multi-coloured crap...!

'Not today, father,' the Servant replied quietly.

Second shuddered: he hadn't even noticed that he was talking out loud. He nodded, and poked at the sofa's upholstery with a trembling finger.

'Yes, of course not today, Darling...'

The Servant of Order looked at his father – the bald skull, the white beard, the wrinkled skin covered in liver spots – and was quietly horrified. Fofs, he's so old! The oldest person on the planet. A strange thought. Not so long ago Fifth had been the oldest...

Members of the Council of Eight normally live a long time. Until a natural pause: the experience gained in each reproduction is too valuable to just wipe it all out at sixty. And their natural pauses did not, as a rule, come until late. A 'clean' life: carefully checked, long-term partners (no doing the rounds with festival sluts), natural food from farms (even including protein!), medical treatment almost at ancient levels... But sooner or later the pause comes to everyone: Fifth temporarily ceased to exist at the age of eighty-seven, only just falling short of the sacred second eight; for two weeks now there had been a countdown on his cell, ticking down until the birth... So now the oldest is Second. His father. Eighty-two years old...

But his eyes are still lively and intelligent. Cunning. Black. The Servant concentrated on his father's eyes. He said:

'Don't worry, everything's going to go great...' Who was he talking to: his father, or, more likely, himself? '...The most important thing is you've got to distribute the transcript immediately. Don't lose the initiative...'

'Gopz,' Second barked. 'Don't tell your father what to do. And wipe the Wise One's mouth, he's drooling, it's embarrassing when there are other people around.'

...In eighth layer an eight on its side started shining – the emblem of the Council, the ancient symbol for infinity. Time to start. Second connected himself and Diver.

The other participants were already waiting in the conference-zone, each in two forms: their *socio* avatar and direct connection from first layer in a separate window.

They started according to protocol.

> '**First**, moderator of the harmony of first layer, welcomes the Wise One and all members of the Council,'

said the Golden Horse and swished its tail stupidly.

First's actual pimpled face nodded solemnly in the window.

'Next you'll be squeezing out manure, idiot,' thought Second. 'What's with all these vulgar farmyard motifs...' But out loud he said:

> '**Second**, moderator of the tranquillity of the Living in all layers, welcomes the Wise One and all members of the Council.'

His Octopus intertwined his tentacles respectfully (you see he had used his brain when choosing a userpic: a mighty, eight-armed beast from the depths, very fitting).

'**Third**, moderator of the harmony of deep layers, welcomes the Wise One and all members of the Council.'

Third's avatar, a winged creature which had fangs, horns and a tail and was wearing armour, smiled absent-mindedly; it was clearly doing something else in shallower layers at the same time. Third's sallow face twisted feebly in the first-layer window, trying, evidently, to smile like the Winged Beast. 'Didn't shave again,' Second looked into the window with distaste, 'and he's dressed in rags, how can he let himself go like that. He's gone to seed, got fat... Fofs, he's still a young man, only forty-two. Plus, he can hardly claim to be any good at cell design or tech-support...'

'**Fourth**, moderator of assistance to nature, welcomes the Wise One and all members of the Council.'

A blue-eyed athlete, flexing his muscles, raised his right hand. The grey-haired, sharp-nosed woman in the live broadcast window maintained a contemptuous silence.

Second looked away. Recently members of the Council had tried not to look at Fourth: she aroused something like superstitious fear in them. She was responsible for farms, medical centres and festivals. All the mating and pausing. Previously, when she had been rosy-cheeked and busty, she had seemed to the Council to be a goddess of fertility. Now, with hollow cheeks and thinning locks, devoured by some worm of an illness, she seemed like an old woman with a scythe.

'*Automatic secretary of the Council of Eight welcomes the Wise One and all members of the Council. I would like to inform you that Fifth, moderator of entertainment content and socio advertising,*

> *is undergoing rebirth. The Association of Screenwriters,*
> *the Association of Game Raters and the Association*
> *of Copywriters have temporarily been transferred to*
> *the control of Fifth's honoured deputy. Unfortunately,*
> *the deputy does not have the right to vote.'*

> '**Sixth**, moderator of the production of goods for popular
> consumption, welcomes the Wise One
> and all members of the Council.'

Sixth nodded rapidly, like a wooden bobble-head doll, from the window in first layer. His eyes, a little slanted, poured a meagre portion of unctuous bonhomie onto the members of the Council. The Dragon, his avatar, launched a volley of fire from its mouth.

> '**S..ve..th**, mod..r...'

A semi-transparent Duckles started vibrating and disappeared from the conference-zone.

The child's face in the live broadcast window scowled discontentedly and also disappeared.

> *'Automatic secretary of the Council of Eight welcomes*
> *the Wise One and all members of the Council. I would*
> *like to inform you that **Seventh**, moderator of sales and*
> *socio-monetary affairs, has currently reached the age*
> *of six. Unfortunately, it is difficult for him to participate*
> *in a Conference at this depth and he will not have the*
> *right to vote until he is twelve years old.'*

Eighth – the Wise One – said nothing, as usual. His face in first layer remained impassive. His avatar did not appear in the conference-zone.

His avatar resided in twelfth layer.

After the official greetings, they relaxed slightly, discussed the health of their Darlings, the last episode of Festival Passions (without Fifth the topic dried up), the design of the new furniture (everyone hypocritically lauded it; First, like an idiot, clopped his hoof proudly after every compliment), silly mistakes in programs (not to offend Third, but just for laughs). Then Second moved to the agenda.

'We have gathered together here at the behest of the Wise One,' he said, 'to discuss the Zero problem. The Wise One would like to make an announcement… Gentlemen! I would like to request that we all now dive.'

Golden Horse, Octopus, Winged Beast, Dragon and the handsome blue-eyed athlete all disappeared from the conference-zone.

Octopus returned first, after a minute. The rest pulled themselves up after him.

'I'm so embarrassed.' Second wiped his damp brow with a 'feeling lucky' napkin; the octopus's tentacles trembled nervily. 'You all heard, gentlemen, what the Wise One was proposing…'

Third nodded his horns darkly; in first layer his pale face was also covered in perspiration.

Golden Horse neighed smugly, but in the live broadcast window the look on First's face showed his dismay…

'You didn't hear anything, you fool,' Second thought spitefully, 'you struggle to even hold eighth layer, so what are you going to do with twelfth! And you can't even control your facial expression in first layer. Totally pathetic.'

He had to hurry with distributing the transcript, but Second could not say no to a bit of fun. He asked First:

'Did you hear everything clearly?'

The horse shook its radiant mane; First scowled, looking spiteful and harassed in the live broadcast window.

first: i heard everything

second: do you agree with what the Wise One said?

first: absolutely

Well, isn't that just marvellous.

'So, dear colleagues,' said Second, 'for your convenience I have, nevertheless, produced a transcript of the Wise One's announcement and sent round the document. I suggest that we move to a vote.'

In first layer First's eyes bulged and his mouth gaped. He was taking a look at the document.

Let's start the vote...

Do you agree with the Wise One's proposal?

yes no

Second clicked **yes** in open mode. Everyone might as well see that he agreed. It's bound to work, bound to! He was counting on a majority: everything was coming together nicely. First is definitely going to vote 'for', he has already blurted out that he agrees and he's not going to want to lose face, unless he is a complete cretin. He would probably be a 'yes' anyway, just to save himself both from diving and from universal derision. At the age of twelve he had been stupid enough to admit that he could not find the Diver and he had been teased ever since... Seventh and Fifth don't have a vote, which is lucky, Sixth and Third, most likely, will be against. But Fourth should agree – which means there are three of us. Against two. So it's a majority. And maybe Dragon will agree. After all he's a smart guy, Sixth, I don't know why he's having problems with *socio* marketing... And I'm in control of the SPO and the PSAP, the Houses of Correction and the looney bins, I can cause him problems... If he comes out against I'll stop half the deliveries – it's long overdue, by the way. Or else everything at his factories, whether it's pants, boots or toothbrushes – it's all going to be made from the same stinking shit...

...Voting over.
The Wise One's proposal has been accepted
with a majority of votes.

The Wolf

He wound a rusty lock of hair around his finger.

'I'm going to dye it,' she said. 'Black.'

'Why?!'

Cleo pulled the towel down to her face.

'Layla says that I don't look after myself. That in the Residence women have to take care of their appearance and comply with globaloid standards. And my hair looks like a run-down anthill in the woods. She promised she'd give me some black dye.'

'Your hair is like flowing honey.' He stroked her auburn crown. 'Layla's just jealous. No one has hair like this anymore.'

'Exactly. On the whole the Living has dark hair. I should look like everyone else.'

'I don't want you to look like everyone else. Anyway it wouldn't work.'

He carefully pulled the towel from her face. Such white skin. And under her eyes and on her nose, like the grains of sand on Golden Mean Square…

He ran his hand along her cheek and neck. With effort he pushed his hand under the towel – she had wrapped it tightly around her like a cocoon – and then pulled it away.

'You've got that on again?'

'It's a different suit…' Cleo hurriedly uncovered herself to convince him. 'It's not the same as yesterday. Skin-tight, ultra-thin, for the sensation of body contact. You'll like it… I mean… well, it really is properly, properly thin. And almost see-through.'

Eighth ran his finger along the cool surface of the sucs[6]. Thicker, thinner – what's the difference… He didn't like that smooth film. Which was heat-resistant and impenetrable to odour or moisture. Which made nipples and pelvis feel the same. Which kept their bodies apart.

Which let them touch properly, skin to skin, only at the genitals.

He lay down next to her, but not touching her.

'What's the suit for? What, am I physically unappealing?'

'Fofs, you know that I find you very physically attractive! Before you I had never felt pleasure in first layer at all.'

'I've just taken a shower. I'm not sticky, not contagious, not dirty. I don't have any skin diseases. You're clean and healthy too. I don't understand why you've put this sucs on.'

'Every time with you it's…'

'Every time I don't understand!'

'I put the sucs on because… for example, I might sweat.'

'I don't care.'

'It's an unpleasant physiological smell.'

'I like the way you smell.'

'Your temperature goes up during the act. Your skin gets hotter.'

'I like it when you're hot.'

'Listen!' she sat up, suddenly happy about something: she pulled her knees, wrapped in the sucs, up to her chin. 'I specially asked Layla. Just now. She says that she and the Servant always wear contact suits too. Everyone does. For hygiene and psychological comfort. It's… It's just nice. So, Darling…'

He shuddered: when Cleo called him that he would instantly remember Hanna.

'…so, let's try it in this one! They did this one for me specially. If you like it, Dragon will put it into production…'

'Dragon? Sixth?'

She nodded.

'What's Dragon got to do with anything?!'

'Well, he said that what with your predilections… I mean, seeing as how you like tactile contact… there's probably loads of people like you. Dragon said that it could become a massive trend at festivals – ultra-thin, see-through sucs… And Fifth's deputy promised to launch some ads on *socio* – only, of course, if you really do like this sucs...'

'Fofs...' the Wise One covered his face in his hands. 'Layla, Sixth, Fifth... Looks like you've managed to discuss our sex life with everyone already?!'

'Not with everyone. Only with my *socio* friends... And so what?'

'You really don't understand?'

'Smin.' She shook her honey-coloured hair irritatedly. 'Obviously I don't understand.'

She really didn't understand. Something about him didn't add up: this hypertrophic shyness of his, his pathological secrecy (as if the *act* were some sort of dirty secret), and this unbelievable, unnatural, shameless willingness to touch someone else's body. In *luxury* you can be a hot, stinking animal – and despite all that still *create* an incredible *act*. But not here in first layer! It's like he did not feel any difference... She peered across at him – he was lying on his side, his knees clasped to his stomach, bare-skinned, ridiculous, with no clothes, no sucs – and her irritation was suddenly replaced by pity.

'He's not connected,' she said to herself. 'He is alone, completely alone in his body, I have to remember that. He's not used to sharing things with friends because he's got no one in his friend list. He doesn't even have a friend list. An unbearable emptiness. I have to be patient with him...'

She ruffled his hair with her hand, which was sheathed in contact film. The thinnest sucs. She could almost feel the warmth of his skin... Why get annoyed? She should explain everything to him tenderly and calmly:

'It's totally normal to discuss these things with friends. The *act* isn't something intimate. You do it at festivals and in *luxury*. You do it in front of everyone. And with everyone...'

'I don't want you to do it with everyone,' the Wise One said. 'Promise that you won't.'

'I won't,' she struggled to keep smiling.

He was like a moody child. He poked her and whined: 'Mine'...

Well, as for first layer, that makes sense: members of the Council have to have long-term partners for 'personal use'. At first this shocked her a little, but then she had to admit that it really was more hygienic and convenient this way... It would never have crossed her mind to take another partner even if she had wanted to...

Eighth understood this and wasn't too worried about first layer. He was worried about third. He was jealous of *luxury* mode. He even asked her not to have *acts* with anyone there...

It was stupid. Absurd. A neurosis. Demanding that she re-strain herself in the *garden of delights*!

Demanding that she observe certain rules in this space of absolute freedom.

Having failed to convince him of the ridiculousness of these requests, she started making promises. It was funny – he had no way of checking, but it calmed him down...

He always noticed when she was *there*. By her face in first layer. Her face always looked as if she was in pain. As if she was shouting without a sound or was about to cry. She did not deny that she went into *luxury* but she obediently lied about the *act*. She said that she didn't do the *act* with anyone. That she was visiting her wolf cubs...

Eight was still lying on his side. She embraced him from behind, pressing her stomach and breasts against his back.

'So then, are we going to try out the sucs? If you like it...'

'I won't like it, Cleo.'

'But...'

'I liked how it was then. The first time. Without any sucs...' He still called that *act* 'the first time'.

They were both silent for a little while. From down below, in the garden, came snatches of a slanging match. It was Layla talking in first layer to the Servant of Order's new, additional woman, who he had taken a month ago. Layla's voice, which was angry but still somehow frightened, broke into a shriek. The new one's voice sounded quiet, but fairly assured. As well as Layla, Layla's kids were shrieking too.

'Tell me that you love me,' Eighth asked suddenly.

'The Living is full of love…'

'No, not like that!'

'How then?'

'Tell me that you love only me.'

'But it's not like that…'

She felt his shoulders shaking.

'Are you feeling alright?'

'If you can, don't press that film up against me. It's making me cold.'

She moved away.

A memory flickered, half-decayed, fragile, like the wing of a dead butterfly in the wind. Once – she was only fifteen – she had given birth to a Darling. The infant was ill and temporarily ceased to exist after a few months. But the whole time he was with her she looked after him using the My Little Living program: she changed his clothes, fed him, bathed him, gave him massages and so on. For every procedure, she used single-use contact gloves like you're supposed to. When she had touched him, completely naked, with her gloved hands, he had shaken exactly like that… *Don't press that film up against me.…* As if he was cold. Perhaps she even took the gloves off a few times so that the little fellow would calm down. She probably did. But she couldn't remember exactly. That's always the way with first-layer memories: they crumble like yester-day's dreams. And she had deleted the file 'Darling' from her memory a long time ago, on the advice of a psychologist. As soon as he temporarily ceased living. 'Send psychically trau-matic files to trash.' Everything disappeared: photographs, videos, diary entries. Everything was forgotten – his face and eyes, his crying and groaning. All that was left were vague memories of his body... The way he used to shake. And the warmth of his lips as they gripped her swollen nipple.

...Cleo slowly took off the sucs and pressed her bare skin against his bare skin. He turned to her and embraced her, strong and commanding. Hot panic flooded her stomach. She felt like a snail that had been ripped from its shell. He touched her nipple with his tongue. She shuddered and closed her eyes. Calm. Calm. It's only him after all. Her mate, the father of her dead children. The one she had been pining for all this time.

In third layer she dived with a jerk into *luxury*. She opened the forest and the den which were saved in her personal settings.

> *there is currently no one here apart from you*
> *invite friends for act **independent act***

She sneaks through the wet grass, weaving her way and making occasional sharp turns to one side to cover her tracks. At last she comes up to the den and pokes her head inside. It smells of decay, soil, fungus and her own musty fur. It does not smell of him. The white-eyed wolf, born of the same mother as her, has not come here without her...

...She has not been here for a long time herself. Not since they brought her to the Residence and she realised that he would never come back to their shared home.

But while hope still remained she came here often. She waited for him day after day, hunting and insulating the den, listening to the beating of four new hearts in her body. Then the time came, but something went wrong – she could not give them life. The cubs were born dead, although *luxury* promised all its users the fulfilment of their wildest fantasies. She gnawed through their slippery umbilical cords and went to dig a hole in the frozen earth. Then she dragged each of the four stiff, furry bodies there in turn. The bitter taste of carrion lingered on her teeth.

Then she *created* a putrid yellow moon, nibbled on the right side, and howled loudly. She hoped that he would still come. At least now. To weep for their children.

But he still did not appear and in despair she brought different partners from her list to the den a few times. None of them could give her the *act* the way he had given it to her then. When she took the form of a she-wolf, it got them going, but their fantasies were pathetic. They were limited to role-playing 'hunter and hunted' with a touch of S&M: some would turn themselves into idiotic mice or hares and throw themselves into her jaws, others would grab a gun... She would break off the *act*, return to the hole and give a long, protracted howl.

She missed him. She was his mate. He had *created* her that way.

Perhaps that was why she had agreed to live with him in the Residence. Because of that *act*, and not because of all the privileges there like the lab and *socio*-money.

...She *creates* the day at dawn, and the fiery sun, and the birds singing in the gleaming crowns of the trees. She *creates* sheaves of multi-coloured foliage and rolls around in them on her back. She lets herself hear human groans from first layer. Her own and those of the one who never comes to see her here.

When she is close to finishing, when her tongue is lolling out, and she is breathing rapidly, arching her back and stiffening her tail, when all her eight nipples are hard, she suddenly hears footsteps and sees someone's long shadow next to her.

SPO guest entry carried out

She lifts her eyes.

The guest's face is smeared with a layer of paint and powder, like a festival clown. The Servant of Order. He has access even here. He muscles in on her fantasy, insolently, as if he owns the place, as if it were his own cell.

She lifts her upper lip, baring her front teeth, and growls quietly and flatly.

> *servant:* no death!
> *cleo:* gopz
> *servant:* i have a message for the Wise One
> *cleo:* what am i, his electronic secretary?
> *servant:* don't get cross, little doggy ☺ this is to do
> with you too. when you finish tell the Wise One that
> I am summoning you both to the laboratory
> *cleo:* you cannot SUMMON the Wise One. only humbly
> request

Clown smiles and sits down next to her on the ground. He turns over the multi-coloured leaves with his hand in its brilliant yellow glove. He catches an earthworm, lifts it to his face and examines it, squeezing it between his thumb and index finger.

> *servant:* let's say this is the Wise One

The worm wriggles and coils in uneven rings.

> *servant:* watch. i can crush him with my fingers.
> or i can let him go

He opens his fingers; the worm falls into the autumn leaves. It lies there motionless for a few seconds, pretending to be unliving, then burrows in tentatively.

servant: but today i'm feeling nice. be in the lab in an hour

cleo: why?

servant: a repeat experiment

cleo: that's impossible!! it's too early to run the experiment right now. the ants and termites are giving bad results

servant: how many immersions?

cleo: not more than two

servant: that'll be enough

The Servant left suddenly – rudely, without even saying good-bye – and she was left alone. She tucked in her tail and crawled into the den. She did not want to finish the *act* anymore.

She wanted to summon the self-righteous ghost from her memory; tear his dead throat to shreds with her claws and fangs – because he lied... Because he left me with a good-for-nothing, defective formula.

She curled up in a ball and whimpered gently, through her nostrils.

She heard Zero's voice, distant and pathetic, coming from first layer:

'Are you happy...? Tell me, are you happy here with me...?'

Namesakes

From: Servant
To: Fourth
Subject: FW: L-L ray: results

text of forwarded message:

'2 September 471: in the Residence laboratory I repeated
the directed Leo-Lot ray experiment previously carried
out on people using the Marvel 4 device.

The following volunteers took part in the experiment:

1. Zero (the Wise One)
2. The Servant of Order

Both volunteers were placed in Roberts chambers (the latest
Marvel 14 model). Both were given a trial injection of the
experimental L-L drug.

This is the latest, most recent version of the L-L drug, which
I have been working on for a month. This version of the drug
has so far given only weak positive results in experiments with
Hermotermes indicola termites (I managed to trace up to two
reproductions for several adults), and I believe it requires
further development.

Experimentation on people was, it seems to me, premature
and was carried out only at the request of the Servant. As
we might have expected, it ended in failure. Neither in the
case of Zero (devoid of *a priori* incode), nor in the case of
the Servant (who has a standard incode) did irradiation in
a Roberts chamber immediately after the introduction of

a dose of the L-L drug, which facilitates the ray's penetration, produce any results.

I request that the laboratory be saved after me for further work on the drug...'

Fofs, how are we worse than termites ☹
But seriously what do you reckon?

Regards,
S.

P.S. In response to this report I am requesting the report on the results from the first experiment with the Leo-Lot ray in 451.

From: Fourth
To: Servant
Subject: RE: 'L-L: results'

Let her carry on for now.
(a negative result is still a result)

Regards,
4.

P.S. As you know the Leo-Lot experiment in 451 was unsuccessful; no reports were kept.

From: Servant
To: Fourth
Subject: who are you trying to kid

According to my information, back then you did receive
a report from Professor Lot about the ray experiment.
So please share it with me, if you'd be so kind!

Regards,
S.

From: Fourth
To: Servant
Subject: RE: who are you trying to kid

Dearest Servant,
The so-called 'report' by Professor Lot is a classic example
of an entry in the 'diary of a madman'. What would be
the point in sharing it with you, I don't understand.

Regards,
4.

From: Servant
To: Fourth
Subject: RE:RE: who are you trying to kid

But still this 'diary of a madman' was enough for you
to ban all research in this field and make it classified.
Cf. subj. of mail.
Share it.

From: Fourth
To: Servant
Subject: RE(3): who are you trying to kid
OK, by all means.

'dust – five seconds of darkness – life – five seconds of darkness
– dust. All the little volunteer doggies gave the same result.
the continuity of death.'

From: Servant
To: Fourth
Subject: RE(4): who are you trying to kid

Gopz, what does that mean?!

From: Fourth
To: Servant ·
Subject: RE(5): who are you trying to kid

The crazy professor was evidently trying to say that man
is mortal ☺

At least you could read his report that way if you want to.
And as we know you can always find someone who does.

For this reason I thought it best not to publicize Lot's
document.

P.S. For my part, I am waiting for your report on the
'namesakes' for August.

For August 471:

In total five pairs of 'namesakes' (cf. July: 3; June: 2).

1) 3 Aug.; 14:03
No. 2 690 460 437: mutated namesakes in embryo with time difference of 2 seconds; apoptosis of older after 8 hours (not noticed); younger dvlp. normally.

2) 8 Aug.; 23:45–23:52
No. 0 639 443 649; mutated namesakes in embryo with time difference of 7.6 minutes; no apoptosis for 24 hours; younger eliminated (by default) in embryo after 24 hours along with biological carrier. Carrier repros. normally.

3) 16 Aug.; 19:22
No. 0 000 009 254: mutated one-off reproduction in presence of mature namesake; no apoptosis over course of day; older namesake eliminated (age 56, gender m.) after 25 hours; younger dvlp. as normal.

4) 26 Aug.; 15:40
No. 0 004 727 556; mutated namesakes in embryo after stalled p. (3 hours of darkness) simultaneously; apoptosis of both after 30 mins.; subsequent stalled p. (4 hours of darkness), further repro. in sing. as normal.

5) 27 Aug.–30 Aug.
No. 0 000 000 203: 27 Aug. mutated one-off reproduction in presence of mature namesake; no apoptosis over course of day; older namesake (age 37, gender f.) eliminated 28 Aug., after 24 hours. Warning: after 5 seconds 28 Aug. REPRO. (!) despite presence of antenat. namesake; no apoptosis for one day. Older namesake eliminated 29 Aug. during regular

medical check (no repro.), biol. carrier saved by conducting doctor). 30 Aug. – official complaint by bio. carrier (loss of Darling resulting from staff negligence). Measures taken on that day: conducting doctor eliminated (repro. normally), biol. carrier eliminated (p. remains stalled).

From: Fourth
To: Servant
Subject: RE: Report
Note: (!)

Extremely disturbed by case No. 5 dated 27–30 Aug.
Too many complications. Servant, be more careful!
The involvement of third parties is unacceptable!!
A secondary namesake is unprecedented.

The Wise One

As he walked past the Diver's see-through blue cell, Zero stopped. The Diver was sitting in his wonder-chair, facing the door. Artificial seaweed twisted together behind his back, forming an available-brown web. Zero always thought that the Diver, like Cracker had once, reminded him of a spider – a big, immobile spider, lurking in the shadow of his devious trap awaiting his prey – and his cell was like the solitary confinement chamber in the Special Unit... But he always dismissed this thought. You couldn't leave Special Unit solitary, but here the door was open. True, the Diver still could not make use of his freedom, get up and leave... *He just doesn't want to*, the Wise One quickly corrected himself. *He considers external movement unnecessary...*

The Servant had explained once that he and his father had specifically asked the designers to do up the cell as an 'underwater world'. It is symbolic: the Diver has turned his back on everything external and transitory and immersed himself in the *depths* that are inaccessible to all livings (except the eight moderators) so that from there, in the deepest layer, he can look at the world with an unclouded, all-seeing eye, publishing wise decrees and giving the other members of the Council of Eight instructions when they come down to him for advice. At least, that's how it used to be.

That's how it was until the Diver gave the moderators his final piece of advice...

...Exactly a month ago, on the very day when Zero was delivered to the Residence (he did not know where they were taking him or what for, but he was sure that he was going to be executed), the Servant of Order read him the words of the Wise One's Final Decree:

'My friends, I am desperately tired. My time has come: I want to *drown*. I am leaving worldly affairs behind and immersing myself forever in thirteenth layer. You will not be able to visit me there, because no living has ever returned from there. The place of the Wise One should not lie empty, so for that reason you should replace me immediately, but do not seek my replacement amongst my kind. In these difficult days of ours, when the *threat* comes from the outside, it is not a Diver who should provide leadership. Not a Diver, but someone who is very familiar with first layer, someone who knows their way around outside as well as I do in the depths. That is why you should make Zero the Wise One. He sees that which you who have lived so many lives do not see. He will give you wisdom, and it will be the wisdom of a child.'

The Council passed the Diver's decision, although – for the first time ever – not unanimously. Five voted. Three 'for', two 'against'.

'You got lucky, you son of a bitch,' the Servant had said then, as he brought him into the Residence. 'One more vote against and I wouldn't have been taking you here, but for a pause. Now take a look at this…' From under his clothes the Servant pulled out a sheaf of papers covered in large round handwriting. 'Recognise these?'

'Yes. They're my letters to myself.'

'We're going to set up a cell for you at Renaissance Bank,' the Servant said. 'We will put your diary in there, the one you left behind in the House of Correction. And we'll put these letters of yours in there too. All of them except…' – the Servant pulled a piece of paper from the pile – '…except this one. "The Miracle".' He shook the paper in the air irritatedly, like it was a slimy pet and it was attempting to wriggle free from his fingers. '"…I died and rose again, in accordance with a precise plan. In accordance with my friend Cracker…" We're going to destroy this letter of yours, you and me. Too many details, explanations... There's no need for them. We'll just content ourselves with the "miracle". You died and rose again. Full stop.'

The Servant tore the letter up into tiny pieces. To Zero the sound of ripping paper seemed deafening.

'You died and rose again to take up the high office of the Wise One. Repeat after me.'

'I died and rose again to take up the high office of the Wise One,' Zero responded obediently, not hearing his own voice. The words dropped from his lips like empty, rustling husks. There was no meaning in them. There was nothing in them.

Zero thought that from the outside the Residence seemed horribly reminiscent of the Farm.

The same four-metre concrete fence. The same blue glow from the electromagnetic barrier. But there, beyond the fence, things were completely different. It did not smell of fear there, but jasmine, mint and citrus fruits from the Available Garden. The main building in the Residence – an opulent palace of coloured stone, glass and wood – was drowning in flowers.

and forgive him his trespasses, for he is as a child

This building was like the castle from his childhood dreams. The castle which he had always wanted to build for Hanna... Zero smiled and followed the Servant inside. Snatches of phrases swirled and rattled in his head like a confused whirlwind – ... *you will be held captive, but the Servant will elevate you...*

He will give you the wisdom of a child... the ray has revealed your great future... – they swirled and swirled until only one was left. *You died and rose again, repeat. You died and rose again, repeat. You died and rose again, repeat...*

...When he left his post as the Wise One, the Diver left his cell behind. His successor was given apartments next it, and for thirty whole days, as he walked past it down the corridor, Zero would stop to stare at the still, serene face of his predecessor. Today, on the day when he was presenting his first piece of legislation and his report on the 'dissident problem', the Wise One stood in front of the cell for an especially long time. The Diver sat there, slumped feebly to one side; his slender, dried-out neck could not support the weight of his head.

Zero pressed his forehead against the cold blue glass.

'There is no death, Diver,' he whispered. 'I know that you can hear me. You are like Cracker. You hold all layers, you just don't want to waste your energy… Today is a special day. My first conference. Before it begins I would like to say… I would like to thank you for all you have done for me. Wasn't it you who sent me that anonymous letter? I know it was you. I remember it off by heart. "Don't believe the lies. The Leo-Lot ray has revealed your great future. But they have taken away your future, they destroyed the discovery, they forced the scientists to keep silent, just so you would remain a nobody. So that you might not become he who you must be, for the greater glory of the Living…" Glap, you helped me get my future back! What do you expect from me now? What do you think my service to the Living can be? What should I say today to the members of the Council? I hope I will do everything right, and you'll never have to regret your decision… You know, I didn't sleep all night. I was writing the First Speech for my presentation… Why don't I read it to you now? It's short, smin, it won't take a lot of your time…'

The Wise One looked at the Diver's half-open rolled eyes, and it seemed to him as if the narrow stripes of the pupils flashed slightly. That must mean he was still interested. The Wise One cleared his throat and started talking quietly, almost touching the glass with his lips; his words sprawled over the blue wall of the cell in warm, smoky patches:

'Eighth, the Wise One, welcomes all members of the Council. Unfortunately, I am still not connected to *socio* and must address you in first layer; however, I hope that by the time of the next session this problem will have been resolved... My friends! I am grateful for the trust you have shown me. And, smin, I'll do everything in my power to justify it. However terrible the mistakes I've made are, I swear, that all my short life I have dreamed of becoming a fully fledged part of the Living. Now my dream is destined to come true. Today, friends, I will share with you my thoughts regarding the "dissident problem". I'm not going to abuse your attention and will get straight down to business. To solve any problem you must first of all establish the reason for its emergence. To cure a patient, you must diagnose the illness and not just try and nullify the symptoms. I am sure that the appearance of the Dissidents is only a symptom of the fact that the Living is suffering. So what is the cause of this "illness"? My friends! I have been thinking about this every day for the thirty days I have spent within the hospitable walls of the Residence. I had probably thought about this before – subconsciously, instinctively – in my previous life, before I was resurrected. In the House of Correction. And this is what I've realised: the Living is suffering...'

The Puppet

'...from a lack of love. Even though we say that the Living is full of love and every part of him loves every other, in practice it is not like that at all... so then... there is no point in supp... what's this word? I can't make it out... ah! in suppressing the instinctive attachment... Hey, lad, give me that magnifying glass!... that biological Darlings have for each other... love between a man and a woman... revive ancient family values... institution of marriage... hmm!... bla bla bla... and fofs! reform of the Houses of Correction... responsibility for pre-pause crimes seems...heh-hem!... doubtful...' Second put down the magnifying glass and the piece of paper covered in the Wise One's writing. 'I haven't read in first layer for a hundred years, goodness me, my eyesight has really gone... Well, what can I say? It's fantastic!'

Second flopped back in his chair and was about to burst out laughing, but instead launched into a wet and crunchy cough – as if inside his chest someone was kneading half-melted snow covered in a brown crust. 'He's so old,' Zero thought, 'unnaturally old; the body of the Living shouldn't have to support guys as old as him, and definitely not in the leadership, in the, "brains", so to speak...' But out loud he said:

'So, do you like my speech?'

'Of course I like it!' Second pressed a napkin to his beard and hawked up the remnants of laughter and coughing. 'It reads like a treatment for a fantasy show...'

The Wise One was seeing the old man for the third time in his life. Their first meeting had taken place a month ago, on the day Zero had been brought to the Residence. Back then he had been shocked by how incredibly dilapidated the old man's body was (Second did not just look old, he looked *unliving*) in comparison with how absolutely sharp his mind was. Second was gentle with him, like a father, and congratulated him sincerely on his appointment and even extended his freckled and wrinkled hand in its contact glove, which was lined with swollen veins, in order to perform the ancient rite of the hand-shake. When he heard that the Wise One liked the scent of first-layer flowers and herbs, Second immediately arranged for him to be given apartments with windows facing the garden... You couldn't really call the second meeting a meeting – after a few days the old man had collapsed with pneumonia and Zero had gone round to visit him – Second was lying with his eyes wide open and whistling and squawking as he breathed; he didn't notice his guest – he was probably resting from his suffering in deep layers... 'He's not going to come out of it,' Zero thought then. 'It's cruel to torture him like this, he should be given a mercy pause...'

But the old man was stubborn. And today, on the day of the conference of the Council of Eight, he had found the strength to get up and go through to the conference hall. However, his thoughts were obviously getting confused this time:

'...If you like, I'll send this text to Fifth's deputy so that he can forward it to his guy in the Association of Screenwriters, it's a brilliant idea, they should take it up, they're going through a bit of a drought over there...'

'He's just blathering away,' Zero realised with sadness. 'Old age has, finally, taken its toll. Or perhaps he's delirious from his fever. *Like Ef, back in the zoo...*' The Wise One frowned and chased the thought away. He had died and risen again. The planetman, raving in his orang-utan cage, was from another, *previous* life. Now everything was different. He has died and risen again. He is a member of the Council of Eight. He is as a child, and all has been forgiven...

'What have screenwriters got to do with anything...?' Zero looked meaningfully at the Servant of Order, as if to say, it's not looking good.

The Servant was silent. Somehow strangely silent.

'I think there is something you have not quite understood,' the Wise One tried to speak loudly and clearly, so that his words would break through the crust of senile confusion. 'This is not an idea for a show. This is the text for my first speech at the conference of the Council of Eight. It's starting in fifteen minutes. With a live feed from here, from the first-layer conference...'

'Gopz,' Second said sharply; behind his white beard his face went crimson with coughing and fury. 'I know what is starting and where and when. But there is something which you have really not understood, sonny. This thing here...' – Second grabbed the piece of paper with the Wise One's speech on it from the table and shook it in the air – '...there's only one thing the members of the Council of Eight might need this for: wiping their behinds. Now listen to me very carefully. Listen carefully...' Second suddenly realised that he had lost his train of thought. 'Listen up and memorize this in that first-layer brain of yours...'

'Father!' The Servant of Order shook his head reproachfully.

> *servant:* you're going too far!! you'd do better to behave politely and properly!
> *second:* gopz

Second closed his eyes a little – his short grey eyelashes drowned in his swollen eyelids – and created a new document on his *desktop*. It is easier to formulate your thoughts in *socio* than straightaway out loud. He saved the document under the name 'o' and punched in there, point by point, everything that he wanted to say to this idiot. Then he read out loud:

'Right then, number one. You will never be connected to *socio*. You have been brought in as a professional first-layerer – and you will stay a first-layerer forever. So please don't go pestering either the sysadmins or the members of the Council.

You will use an external *socio* slot with a monitor through which you will be able to send and receive certain messages. That will suffice. Number two. You have not been brought in to share your crazy ideas with members of the Council. Seeing as it is now...' – Second jabbed Zero's speech in irritation – '... absolutely clear to me that you are not capable of offering anything practical, henceforth at conferences of the Council of Eight you will read out the text I give you...'

'With all due respect... what are you... how dare you?!' The Wise One physically sensed the anger flood into his head and face in hot, pulsing waves, and then subside along with his seething blood, leaving behind only a sonorous silence.

'The Diver appointed me to the Council of Eight,' Zero said with white lips. 'Second, you have no right either to take that tone with me or to lord it over me. I am the Wise One. My ideas...'

'You are a big fat nothing!' Second started coughing, whooping like a crow.

> *servant:* father, stop it! there's no need to provoke him!
> *second:* gopz! i don't have time to be messing around with this little prick. can't you see my pause is coming any minute now!
> *servant:* all the more reason to be careful
> *second:* with this nobody?! he's so stupid he doesn't even realise why he's here. fofs! he's got IDEAS!!!!
> *servant:* he is not a nobody. we ourselves have elevated him to a level where he can cause problems. so you should just stroke his fur. say you're sorry, say that you overreacted. we don't need this conflict over nothing

'I outrank you, you have to treat me with respect,' Zero mumbled and shuddered with self-disgust. His voice sounded quiet and somehow begging, as if he were scrounging seconds of lunch in the House dining hall.

Second grunted – something between a cough and a laugh – but said nothing.

'I am Eighth and the Wise One,' Zero tried to give his voice a hardness. 'I was appointed by the Diver. To take his place.'

servant: just don't say anything unnecessary

'...And your job is to be a puppet, just like him.'

servant: just shut up will you!!

'Father, you have a fever,' the Servant said out loud. 'You are insulting the Wise One and the Diver. You don't know what you are saying. I am afraid it's not worth you participating in the conference today.'

'What does that mean, "puppet"? What is he trying to say?' the Wise One asked in an alien, somehow mosquito-like voice. 'I will make what you have said public at the conference of the Council...'

servant: see what you have done you old fool move to plan b

Second opened his mouth slightly – a small dark hole in the grey curls of his beard – and broke down in a coughing fit. His whitish tongue would poke out for a moment, like a curious worm from its hole, and then hide back inside.

'He's just delirious.' The Servant of Order patted Second on the back sympathetically. 'He's still not well, I shouldn't have got him out of bed...'

'Gopz,' the old man jerked his shoulders in disgust to make the Servant take his hand away.

The coughing fit passed, but Second was breathing heavily. The pinkish-white worm crawled out of its hole again and rubbed up against the old man's parched lips, leaving a sticky, slimy trail on them.

'Hey, sonny...' Second looked at Zero, and the Wise One noticed that his eyes had cleared. 'It was wrong of me to be so rude to you. Forgive an old man. Sickness and worry are eating me up from the inside, like unfed pets. That's why I lose control sometimes and can be slightly... out of sorts. So... can I count on your magnanimous forgiveness, Wise One?'

'Of course,' Zero replied crisply and without colour. Like a puppet. *Like a mechanical talking puppet...*

With great effort the old man pulled himself up and extended a shaking, bony hand towards Zero. 'Just like that, no glove. Very touching,' Zero thought, just as mechanically, and shook the proffered hand. It was dry and hot.

Overcoming his disgust, Second held the Wise One's icy hand in his. His son was right. Rude, but right. There was no need to lose his temper.

'Well, no harm done,' he said. 'Now take this.' Second opened a desk drawer and pulled out a dirty, well-thumbed piece of paper, covered on both sides in crooked scribbles. 'Sorry about the handwriting,' the old man hunched over apologetically. 'I don't get any practice in first layer... Not like you, Wise One.'

'What is this?' the Wise One asked for some reason, even though he knew perfectly well *what*.

'It's my version of your First Speech,' Second replied.

'I'm not planning on...'

'I'm begging you...' The old man raised his hand in conciliation. 'First just read it. If you don't agree with my version, well then, propose yours to the Council of Eight. Although, in my opinion, that would be a huge mistake.'

'Alright.' Zero picked up the paper and ran his eyes over the text crossly.

'Eighth, the Wise One, welcomes all members of the Council. Friends! I am very worried and will get straight down to business...'

'Out loud if possible,' the Servant asked and rocked back in his chair, crossing his arms comfily across his stomach and half-closing his eyes, as if getting ready to hear his nightly lullaby. 'I'd also like to find out what's in there.'

...The Dissidents present a direct first-layer threat to the Living. It is our sacred duty to fight this attack in all its forms. Practically all categories of dissident are extremely dangerous:

Antivectorites (who disagree with the dictates of their invector) threaten the Living's principle of professional continuity.

Old-Livings (who disagree with age limits for each specific reproduction) threaten the Living's health and youth.

Precautioners (women who disagree with the necessity for compulsory conception after copulation) – perhaps the most dangerous category, they threaten the very principle of the Living's reproduction.

Familials, group A (who disagree with the need to be separated from their Darlings) threaten the Living's intellect, mental health and progress. These people (primarily women) see their 'continuation' in their Darlings, and not in themselves. In so doing they drive society into the primordial savagery based on grievous perversions and animal instincts.

Familials, group B ('couples' who do not agree with the necessity for regular changes in partner and remain 'faithful', as it is known, to each other) threaten the Living's freedom of choice, imposing artificial and harmful proprietorial instincts on him.

Tritheists (who disagree with the fact that there is no god but the Living, who is one in three billion) threaten the cultural heritage of the Living with their absurd belief in a hideous god with three heads (the head of the father, the head of the son, the head of the bird) and strive to sabotage belief in the sacred text of the Book of Life.

The 'Available World' society (who disagree with the absence of contact between the Living and Our Little Brothers) are perhaps the only ones who do not present a threat. The Living is actually very interested both in establishing contact with animals and in domesticating them.

Dear friends! To aid us in the battle against first-layer threats I propose the following:

1. Introduce tougher penalties for Dissidents. Compulsory pause with subsequent correction in the relevant institutions seems to me to be an adequate and sensible measure.

2. Increase accordingly the number of Houses of Correction (at least double).

3. Introduce a State of Emergency. I will tell you about that last point separately.

Until now it has only been the Wise One who has, before every pause or final immersion, chosen a new Diver to replace him (this time he appointed me). However, the State of Emergency makes it possible for all members of the Council to pass down power not on the basis of invector, but by appointing a successor. This radical measure is designed to help us, in these difficult days for the Living, avoid so-called 'memory lapses' – the long and inevitable periods during the reproduction of members of the Council (gestation, infancy, and childhood until eight years old) when it is impossible to access their cell in Renaissance Bank. My friends! At such a critical moment as this, such lengthy losses of memory – and, consequently, of experience and know-how – for several members of the Council is unacceptable.

As a consequence, I have a very serious request to make of my respected colleague Second (and I humbly ask that all members of the Council support my initiative). My request is that he should – in all seriousness – sacrifice himself on behalf of the

Living. I ask that Second, the moderator of the tranquillity of the Living in all layers, refuse his office immediately after the onset of the pause and hand the reins over to an heir.

The moderation of tranquillity (including the Service for Planetary Order, the Psychological Service for Assisting the Population, the system of Houses of Correction and much more) is the sort of area of government in which there must be no such 'lapses' at such a critical and unstable moment for the Living. For the post of Second I'm picturing an experienced young professional who is up to speed with all aspects of tranquillity and has already garnered invaluable experience as a moderator. I'm talking about the Servant of Order – the head of the SPO and the biological son of our present Second. He is the one who should take up his father's place after the pause – which is, as tragic as this may be, according to the consulting physician, quite close at hand...

'An excellent speech, I think,' Second surmised with a look of contentment. 'Turned out nicely, right?'

'You want to refuse your post in the Council in favour of your son?' the Wise One said dumbly.

'For the good of the Living,' Second nodded; for greater solemnity he opened his beetle-like eyes so vigorously and so wide that it looked like they would crawl out of his eye sockets any minute and fly away, buzzing and bobbing, into the Available Garden.

'For the good of the Living,' the Servant echoed, looking cheerily at his father and bending over in a clownish bow. 'So how about it, Wise One? Will you read this speech?'

'Of course not,' the Wise One tried to laugh, but ended up with a sort of squeaky whimper.

'Why, if I may ask?' the moderator of tranquillity enquired with genuine interest.

'Because I don't think the threat is that great. Because I don't agree with these harsh measures. And I don't agree with such... such hypocrisy. You've got double standards. You live... here, in the Residence we all live like familials. You are both antivectorites. And you, Second, are an old-living too...' The Wise One looked carefully at the old man out of the corner of his eye, expecting the next outburst of anger in response, but he listened carefully and even nodded in approval, as if agreeing. 'According to your own logic,' Zero continued, 'for every one of these "crimes" you should be forced to undergo a pause with subsequent correction...'

Second snorted in approval – as if he was not averse to sentencing himself to eternal correction – and coughed briefly.

'You're almost right, Wise One,' he said. 'About everything except the most important thing...'

'...The threat is great,' the old man continued. 'You have no idea how great. And as for our hypocrisy. I wouldn't use such a harsh word. Yes, the members of the Council and their... heh-hem...Darlings live a little differently from everyone else. But the logic behind that is entirely practical...'

Second closed his eyes and dug around in the archive from his previous life. He used to have a fantastic recording there in his Favourites, on this very subject. But what was it called? Probably something completely nonsensical... come on, remember. The old man launched a key word search. He remembered the key words well: 'bare ass'. The search promptly offered up a dozen 'arses' – for the most part photographs and only one document containing both elements. The document did indeed have an obscure name, completely unconnected to the context – 'Jupiter and the Bull' – probably some sort of code, but Second didn't have time to figure it out.

'You have to understand, sonny,' he said to the Wise One and started reading expressively. '"The Living is like a giant organism, a single body made of different parts. You must realise that the head and arse cannot live in the same conditions. The head is in control – the arse takes orders from it. The head breathes, eats, drinks and thinks a lot and takes care of the well-being of the arse. The arse defecates regularly, and with gratitude, ridding the organism of waste products... If you give the arse oxygen, it's still not going to learn to breathe. If you stick food up the arse, it's not going to be able to chew it. All these benefits will just make the arse clog up, stop doing its job, get sick and then quickly poison the whole organism. Which is to say, equal rights would be very damaging for the arse and all the other parts of the body..." Do you follow my reasoning, sonny?'

servant: he's not following anymore

Second broke off from his reading and focused his eyes in first layer.

second: i asked you to wait!

The Servant of Order was dragging the Wise One from the conference hall, his hands thrust under his armpits.

servant: it's time

The Wise One's straight, unbending legs rustled quietly on the floor. The Wise One's fingers were splayed wide, as if he was showing a deaf person the number ten. The Wise One's eyes were white and covered in little red veins, as if his eyeballs had rolled over in their sockets, turning their blind side to the world. The Wise One was like a big plastic doll that had broken as soon as it was bought because someone didn't play with it properly.

bakugan?

Second asked when the door closed behind the Servant and the Wise One.

servant: indeed

second: i can't stand those creatures

the old man squirmed.

well that's it, it's starting, let me know what happens. and, listen, don't overdo it with him with those bakugans. try to talk him round nicely

...First, moderator of harmony in first layer, welcomes the Wise One and all members of the Council...

servant: it's hardly going to work now, you've seen with your own efforts ☹ how stubborn he's got

second: you should show him the Malfunction
servant: what???!!!!
second: not the whole thing, obviously, just the stalls…
right my turn

The sideways eight, the ancient sign of infinity, pulsed and gave off a panicked squeak somewhere in its centre:

…awaiting greeting… awaiting greeting… awaiting greeting

'**Second**, moderator of the tranquillity of the Living in all layers, welcomes the Wise One and all members of the Council…'

The Malfunction

'Come on, little fellow...' the Servant whispered tenderly, putting the white bakugan larva on the Wise One's skin, '...over here, by the elbow, you'll like it there... and there's a nice big vein there...'

The little round white ball shuddered as it felt the warmth of the human body, then shyly plunged its tiny proboscis into the Wise One's skin. It carefully injected its juice and, nearly overcome with thirst, waited for it to take effect, and only then drew the warm, magical blood into itself.

The Servant of Order adored bakugans – wonderfully useful little monsters, a miracle of insect selection. When they have had their fill of blood, they undergo an instantaneous metamorphosis, moving through the pupa stage in a couple of seconds...

...A two-headed, pinkish-available coloured, winged beetle started scurrying down the Wise One's arm, heading from his elbow down towards his fist, gradually picking up speed for take-off. The Servant of Order caught him and crushed him: once transformed a bakugan is useless. There was blood, shot through with white bakugan juice, left on his fingers; the Servant licked it off: a natural vitamin... His chest got warmer and started thumping; the walls of the lobby became brighter and thicker, as if someone had increased the colour depth in first layer or put on a 'feeling lucky' filter; and after a couple of seconds or so his penis became engorged, like an insatiable bakugan larva – he got the urge to call for his new woman, right now... Now that's what the natural product gives you – you don't get that with vitacomplex. Vitacomplex is full of harmful impurities and all sorts of preservatives...

With a click Layla opened a window.

layla: where are you, darling?

servant: busy. at the conference

His desire disappeared immediately. Still, that bint must have some sort of animal instinct...

layla: whatever, gopz, you can take a break, gopz, when your woman asks!!

For some reason she closed her window and then immediately opened it back up again. Click. Click. Like being flicked on the nose. The Servant frowned: recently Layla had taken to getting hysterical within seconds, whether in first layer or on *socio*. 'You've given her too much slack, way too much slack,' the Servant thought with irritation. 'Absolutely anything goes...'

layla: i feel so terrible and you just don't care

Irritation mingled unpleasantly with pity and some strange wistful feeling, as if he hadn't fed his pet in a long time...

servant: hey sorry little one i really am busy right now
layla: do you call that bitch 'little one'
servant: that's it, gopz! take a tranqvitamin and give me some peace

Click.
Zero twitched.
...His consciousness was still there, it had never even gone away. He was just cold. So cold that he could not breathe, look or move. And it was very quiet, it was quiet in his chest, as if his heart was no longer beating.

It seemed to him: now he was made of ice. His eyes had rolled up into his head and frozen to his eyelids; his arms had gone stiff, his legs had gone stiff and stuck together.

It seemed to him: he was hard and icy, he could not be broken. But if you took his body out into the sun, it would melt and soak into the ground like watery lymph...

But there was no sun. Some warmth came from his left arm and spread through his arteries, veins and capillaries. He inhaled – his chest felt prickly and ticklish. As if a female mosquito had bitten him right on the heart... He tried to move his arm and heard a crack... *The ice has snapped*, he thought in a panic, ...*a bit of me has snapped off*...

'Careful there, Wise One,' said the Servant. 'Don't make any sudden movements. First wait until your whole body has relaxed, and then stretch your muscles. And don't jump up suddenly either: you'll get dizzy... So, that feel better?'

'Wht...hppn...m...' The words stuck in his throat like shards of ice.

'What happened to you? Oh, you made friends with a couple of my marvellous beetles! The black bakugan and the white bakugan. Those are ancient names, I don't even know what they mean... But the pets themselves are the product of many centuries of insect selection. Have you seen "extract of white bakugan" on the list of ingredients on vitacomplex? Most ordinary people think that it's some sort of plant... but no! it's a beetle...'

Zero sat down, slowly, with difficulty – the walls of the lobby shifted and started swaying back and forth, like pieces of cardboard attached to a gigantic pendulum. The sofa underneath him started jiggling unpleasantly, trying awkwardly to adapt to his new pose, but it could not cope with its sycophantic task and sagged sadly, leaning over to one side.

'...And have you seen "extract of black bakugan" on the list of ingredients for tranqvitamins?' The Servant of Order peered at the Wise One and, not waiting for a reply, continued his lecture regardless. 'In small doses the venom of the black bakugan larva calms you down and takes the edge off, so to speak, and the venom of the white one perks you up. It sharpens the senses, the libido and everything else... But if you increase the dose a little... by which I mean, if, for instance, a black bakugan beetle releases its venom under someone's skin, then that someone will be completely incapacitated, and will temporarily cease to exist after about an hour, and his pause will look entirely natural: paralysis of the muscles of the heart. That is, of course, if no one administers the anti-venom, which is the extract from the white bakugan. The white bakugan is good at neutralising the effect of the black one...'

'So that's what you did to the Diver,' the Wise One pronounced severely. 'Tranqvitamins... Extract of black bakugan... You stifled his free will, you made him a puppet... You kept putting those beetles on him... that's why he can't move at all in first layer... and in *socio* he just dumbly said everything you ordered him to say... I'm right, no? No?!'

For some reason the Servant of Order found this very funny and giggled ridiculously. His pupils were narrowing and widening, pulsing, like the hungry black bakugan larvae.

'...And now he's been poisoned with so much venom that soon he's going to temporarily cease,' the Wise One continued, wiggling his toes and noticing that warmth had, at last, got to the very bottom and was seemingly wrapping his calves and heels in prickly wool, '...and you want to turn me into a puppet like him...'

'Smin, he can think logically!' the Servant said excitedly; after a dose of white he was predisposed to being upbeat. 'He can construct chains of logic, in first layer, *by himself*, without a *socio*-analyser or the Brain Storm program... He makes conclusions: sure, they're wrong, but the logic!'

'You're talking nonsense, Wise One,' the Servant replied good-naturedly. 'Bakugans are valuable little beasts. How many would we have to produce to keep that poor bugger Diver quiet day after day? They are single-use, you know... The larva injects its

298

venom and that's it, after the metamorphosis it doesn't bite anymore.'

For the purposes of demonstration the Servant showed his interlocutor the crushed beetle.

'But the Diver...'

'But the Diver what?! Out there in the roboslums Divers are as common as flies on shit. They lie there, cretins, drooling and gawping at the heavens. You could pick any one of them, bring them into the Residence and make him the Wise One.'

'So what, anyone can sit in twelfth layer?'

'Now that is unlikely.' The Servant burst into screeching, girly laughter, and then broke off on a high, tuneless note. 'There's no one there. No one gets to twelfth. There's probably no such layer.'

The Wise One's face went crimson with indignation. This Servant doesn't even think he needs to lie properly! His thawed heart started jumping, as if it wanted to break through his ribcage. Barely holding back his hot rage, the Wise One said:

'Do you take me for a dribbling idiot?! I have personally received a message from the Diver! That's right, there's no need to act so surprised, he wrote to me once. He promised me his support and he kept his word.'

'What letter is that you're talking about? It's not this one is it by any chance...?' The Servant rifled through his *sent* folder looking for what he needed. '"Don't believe the lies. The Leo-Lot ray can shine in both directions, backward and forward, and it has revealed your great future, bla bla bla, but I will right the injustice." That one, right? Sorry I sent it without signing it. We didn't really know each other properly anyway...'

'Why...?' Zero whispered.

'Well... To stop you probably going and doing something stupid to yourself, Wise One.' The Servant found the file 'psych o' in his memory. 'The expert psychological analysis of your diary – the one you left in the House of Correction – had some worrying outcomes. "The author of this text is experiencing considerable stress and suffers from manic depression. This text, judging by certain psycho-lexemes, was conceived as a decoy (most likely the author has not yet committed the self-pause he warns us about at the end), however, overall, the text is *genuine*. There is an 87.3% probability that the author of this text is capable of self-pause if his condition becomes more severe." So we decided to cheer you up, so to speak... It would have been very upsetting to lose such a promising young man as yourself.'

layla: if i mean anything to you, get rid of that tart

'So you knew from the very beginning that I had run away...?'
'Come on, Wise One! I think you are underestimating your humble Servant.' The Servant gave Zero a comedic bow. 'Of course I knew.'
'Then why didn't you pick me up straightaway? Why did you let me go free?'
'Well, I'd put it this way: we were waiting for the stars to align.' The Servant of Order drew a sweeping smiley in the air with his index finger. 'Our old friend Fifth, moderator of ents and ads, was a nasty old bugger. He would never have voted for you to join the Council and he would have talked the others out of it, he had quite a lot of authority... You would have been sentenced to a pause if we had "picked you up" earlier. Before Fifth's pause. He was really in a bad way, poor fellow, so we decided to wait until he temporarily ceased. Plus it was interesting to watch you "in the wild", so to speak... I was, by the way, happy with you by and large. That's why in the Final Decree I mentioned your "wisdom of a child", and I wasn't lying. You have all the basic qualities of a real lead...'
'You wrote the Final Decree?! You forced the Diver to give up his position as the Wise One?'

'I told you' – the Servant absent-mindedly scanned around looking for the caps lock so that he could put the next reply in capital letters, then remembered with irritation that in the monstrously impoverished surroundings of first layer there was no caps lock for conversations – 'there is no Diver.'

> *layla:* i gave you my youth. i'm the mother of your darlings! seven years i didn't go to a festival, not once! but you, bastard, now you're going to take a second wife just like that?
> *servant:* gopz, stupid cow! what WIFE, where did you get that word from!
> *layla:* from the encyclopaedia of the ancient world

The Wise One struggled up from the shapeless, nauseating sofa. The walls of the lobby started swaying even faster, dragging the floor along with them. It was like the Wise One was standing on the swings in the ancient attraction park. He stumbled, and was about to try and grab the back of the sofa but it ducked down like a traitor, sinking into the seat and turning the sofa into something like a lumpy bagel.

'I told you not to stand up too quickly...' The Servant of Order took Zero by the arm obligingly and sat him back down on the sofa. 'None of the members of the Council can hold twelfth layer. No one, except Third, can even hold eleventh. They are just determined not to admit that they can't hear what the Diver says... Once, when he was young, First said that he couldn't see the Wise One. The rest almost tore him to pieces, like hornets round a lame grasshopper. They laughed, but they were all afraid. They could see a bit of themselves in First and were scared of being exposed and disgraced. Because the Council of Eight can see all twelve layers – so it is written in the Book of Life. No one dares question the Book, thus is it written, so that's how it must be...' The Servant of Order absent-mindedly deleted unwanted icons from the desktop; he felt spent – he wasn't used to giving such long speeches outside of *socio*. '...They say it actually was all like that before,' he muttered. 'Twelve layers and Divers, real ones...'

He hadn't meant to say that: the words had somehow crept out of his mouth on their own. They had slipped from his lips, like wet, defenceless slugs. 'Tiredness and nerves,' the Servant thought, 'first layer tension. As if being honest with this loser wasn't enough. Bloody first layer! You can't see what you are saying and you can't concentrate properly so you end up blabbering away when you shouldn't.'

'But that's all junk,' the Servant summarized decisively. 'There are no Divers and never have been. You shouldn't interpret what's in the Book literally. It's just an allegory... As far as I understand it it's about how any of the members of the Council can become the "Wise One". You need to search around for the "Diver" inside yourself... Because you know what the most important thing is? The most important thing is to be the first to give a voice to the "will" of the Wise One; the rest will pretend that they were also there at his consultation in twelfth layer... My father realised that a long time ago. But he's not the only one. Sixth has also bluffed us a few times. It took a lot of effort for father to force through the Final Decree. That slitty-eyed dung beetle knows there's no Diver...'

The Servant of Order fell silent. In an instant the scintillating cheeriness of the white bakugan somehow disappeared completely and all that was left was an unpleasant shivering in his limbs and an indistinct sadness, like the sort you get when the act is interrupted in *luxury* mode.

something is getting you down,

– the socio psychotherapist started worrying –

'There are no Divers and there never have been,' the Servant hurriedly wrote on the wall of his cell in font size 20: the psychotherapist recommended this sort of relaxation technique in stressful situations. But his mood was utterly ruined. Just as it had been ruined the two times he had brought brainless 'wise ones' from the roboslums. 'There are no Divers.' Both times he had written that phrase all over the walls of the cell. But he still couldn't quite fully believe what he had written. Then there was the letter in Renaissance...

The letter to self from the middle of the second century – it was like a splinter stuck under his nail. In this letter he wasn't yet called the Servant or even Cyborg 17. In the middle of the second century he had had the name Goblin and he had worked as a *socio*-virologist. In that letter he described his brief immersion in twelfth layer ('...I dived! How can you give a name to what you experience in the deepest of deeps? Global language is not rich enough to find the right words... Pleasure, wisdom, a sense of soaring and endless peace...? None of that's it, that's not it... Love? Holiness? That's not it... Perhaps, Death?') and he wondered whether he should disappear forever off into the roboslums for an eternal immersion. Goblin did not leave any more letters in that reproduction. Most likely – judging by the fact that after the pause he was reproduced in the roboslums and received the name Cyborg 17 – he had gone through with his plans.

There was no way now, of course, of checking whether this was junk. Was he a real Diver or had a virus just damaged his memory and judgment (that sort of thing happens to virologists the whole time)? Whatever happened, whenever he looked back, the Servant of Order shuddered in horror. He didn't like to talk about his past – his invector was too shameful. For almost three centuries, right up to his current reproduction in 430, he had been a stinking slum robot. He would still be one now if his biological mother had not been born under a lucky star.

His mother, big-eyed and hungry like a dragonfly, had been a slum witch. Her name was Mara and she was sixteen when Second noticed her as he toured the roboslums, in the company of six bodyguards, on a charitable 'visit of loving care'. He gestured for her to come over and she crawled over on her knees. 'Stand up and tell my fortune, little one,' Second said. 'Today I am giving you official permission to tell my fortune.' 'You should get down on your knees next to me,' Mara replied. 'Have a seat, you might need one.' The moderator of tranquillity frowned in surprise at this unheard of impudence. The bodyguards raised their machine guns in unison. But Second shook his head to say no and slowly kneeled down opposite Mara. She pressed her hand in its contact glove against his swarthy forehead: '...I see beyond the pause, I see before, I tell all, of that you can be sure. I see you, moderator of tranquillity in all layers... And I see myself, naked, next to you in bed...' Second laughed, unzipped his trousers and right there, not moving from the spot, performed the act with her in first layer. His bodyguards held her down – she, however, didn't put up any particular resistance. Then Second got up, kicked the witch and walked off, surrounded by his guards.

The next day he summoned her to the Residence.

He kept her as his long-term partner. She had already got pregnant with Cyborg 17 back there in the slums. 'It is just not done to give birth to robots in the Residence,' the moderator of tranquillity said. 'My Darling will be a man to be reckoned with.' 'He will be the Servant of Order,' said Mara, placing her hand on her stomach. 'Why not,' Second replied thoughtfully, 'why not...?'

'...his place.'

The Wise One's words came as if from afar. The Servant of Order suddenly noticed that he had got distracted from first layer and lost the thread of the conversation. Limited attention syndrome is one of the Living's chronic external illnesses...

'What did you say, Wise One?'

'I said: because the Diver did not become your puppet, you decided to take me in his place. A first-layerer with no access to *socio*. You could frighten me with your black and white beetles and train me up so that once a month I would read your words off a piece of paper... Am I right?'

'Only in the broadest terms...'

'"To the Saviour from the Apostle",' Zero said flatly. 'It was you who wrote that, to "cheer me up a bit"? Of course. Back there, in the Pause Zone, you fed Matthew a tranqvitamin. And then you slipped him a text in deep layers. "You will be held captive, but the Servant will elevate you if you will serve him."'

'Incredible,' the Servant of Order thought spitefully. 'He can quote the text off by heart without having access to memory...' Servant stared into the Wise One's crazed pupils, which pulsed from excessive white bakugan juice, and he suddenly became, if not scared, then distinctly out of sorts. Uncomfortable, as if he could feel the fixed gaze of a poisonous insect on the back of his head.

'That wasn't me,' the Servant replied, to his own amazement: it sounded as if he was justifying himself. 'That was your mate Cracker.'

'My friend Cracker was capable of that sort of thing,' the Wise One replied provocatively, 'but he had already temporarily ceased a week before Matthew left his message.'

'I know,' the Servant said quietly and angrily, and, for some reason, honestly. 'We did an autopsy on Matthew's cell. Cracker had put that text in his memory long before his pause, even before you ran away, Wise One. With the instruction: "activate before pause".'

The Servant of Order felt about in his memory trash for Matthew's message and picked at it, as if he were poking a sore tooth with his tongue, and kept fighting the strong desire to delete it permanently. But no, he mustn't. He had to keep this document as a reminder of his, the Servant's, personal and professional disgrace. As evidence of the fact that even his cell, the Servant's, was accessible and vulnerable. That some cunning little common or garden creep could get into his cell, the cell of the Servant of Order, and then crawl along the most delicate, most intricate web of neurons, and sneak into, infiltrate, his consciousness, his, the Servant of Order... The Servant frowned as if someone was tickling the back of his head with a cold metal stick. That rat Cracker – he had figured out a way of unpicking more than just his *socio* memory. He had read his *thoughts*. His secret plan, that he had never expressed in any layer, to do whatever it took to change his invector...

'So I'm supposed to serve the Servant?' Zero burst out laughing with a strange, quavering laugh, as if it wasn't him that was laughing but someone old and evil who had taken up residence behind his breastbone.

'You must serve the Living loyally,' the Servant responded ritually, as if he had been waiting for this question and prepared his answer in advance. 'Especially now, in these difficult days of ours, when the stability of the Living is under threat... Wise One...' The Servant sank his gaze into Zero and held a long pause. '...What you're about to see is quite something.'

The Servant strode towards the table and solemnly pulled an inviz cover off something square and bulky that was jutting up strangely in the middle of the lobby.

'A present for you.' The Servant made an expansive gesture; he seemed extremely pleased with himself.

'A Crystal Xo?' The Wise One stared hard at his 'present'. 'You wanted to surprise me with a Crystal XO, that old piece of crap that they use in natural development groups so that the hydrocephalics get to watch Baby Bubbles somehow?'

'Well, excuse me.' The Servant pulled closed the dark threads of his lips in offence. 'There wasn't a lot of choice. Crystal Xo is still the only first-layer monitor. There's no demand, you see. Maybe Sixth and First will develop something specially for you later, something more... elegant. But for now we've ordered you three monitors, and everything else you might need. One is in the conference hall – you, Wise One, wouldn't have noticed this with all this fuss, one here in the lobby, and one will be installed in your apartments – and each will have an in-built *socio* slot with limited connectivity! Great, right? You will have limited access to certain second-layer services. For instance, the members of the Council will be able to send you letters and messages... You will even be able to watch adverts and series!'

'What, am I supposed to say thank you?'

The Servant of Order twisted his face in irritation and turned on the Crystal. Something squeaked thinly. The screen flickered like a million swarming silver midges.

'There's a little something I need to show you,' the Servant said.

He closed his eyes and established a *socio* connection with the Crystal. The set-up was unpleasant and rough somehow – like he had been whacked in the forehead with a wooden baton. The Servant plunged into eighth layer and went into the *System*; on the way in, as ever, he felt a momentary falling sensation and a simultaneous shortness of breath. The *System* was not good at accepting those it had not chosen itself, those to whom it had not chosen to reveal itself. The *System* currently only allowed Fourth, the moderator of assistance to nature, to see it directly. The Servant of Order and the other members of the Council had to content themselves with a shared copy of the *System*, which was, however, sufficiently sensitive and aggressive to bite into their brains on the way in and the way out.

servant: **command:** share System with external user
Crystal X0.
caution! **System** *is a completely secret program
and should not be viewed by unauthorized persons.*
cancel command 'share' **continue
with command**

caution! user Crystal Xo *may threaten the
secure running of the System
cancel command 'share'* **continue
with command**

caution! **System** *will be shared with external user*
Crystal Xo
...processing...
...everything is now operational...

He got a headache from the stress, unavailable spots started
dancing in front of his eyes. It's so slow. Gopz, it's slow! It's like
trying to share a program with an unliving friend... 'In a way
that's exactly what he is,' the Servant suddenly realised. 'A
Crystal *socio* slot is unliving, external. My nerve cells are going
crazy trying to link up with its mechanical neurons... Ah right,
at last... It's got going...' The Servant wiped the sweat from
his brow.

...On the Crystal monitor the *System* looked unusual and
somehow almost innocuous, not like in eighth layer. Like a
funny animated little guy, sort of like Livvles, made of flashing,
multi-coloured numbers and letters twisted into tiny spirals.
Nothing at all like a nightmarish beast, unwittingly ingesting
you into its dark, sticky, greedy, calculated, calculating,
constantly self-renewing, living womb.

'The Living = 3 000 000 000 livings': the legend shone from
the bottom of the screen.

'Look, Wise One. Look and tremble,' the Servant said in a whisper, and, it seemed, without mockery. 'You see before you: the *System*.'

Zero stared at the little man made of numbers in disbelief.

'Do you at least know what the *System* is?' the Servant asked contemptuously, misinterpreting the Wise One's stare.

'No one knows what the *System* is,' replied the Wise One, and the Servant gave a satisfied nod.

That was the correct answer. The password for all those who knew.

What is the *System*?

The soul of the Living.

Or the body of the Living.

Or the mind of the Living.

What is the *System*?

The most precise model of the Living.

What is the *System*?

The nativity gift of the magi.

What is the *System*?

The restless ghost of the Living that appears to the chosen few.

But even the chosen few probably don't know what the System is.

Not in Wikipedia, or in the Encyclopaedia Socialia, or on AnswerNet are there any articles about the System. Not a word about it – as if the System does not exist. But every living sooner or later finds out about the System. Some a bit more, some a bit less; some see a little bit of it in a dream and some just catch the end of some first-layer rumour...

In this sense the Wise One had, one might say, got lucky. He had heard about the System from the person who knew more about it than anyone. From the very first person to see it. From Cracker.

'The System is *alive*,' his friend had explained to him. 'It has consciousness and free will.'

It is a program that was never written by anyone – at the least, by any living – and which it is impossible to control. It appeared immediately after the birth of the Living, and since then it has always been in inviz mode and shown itself only to the chosen few. Members of the Council (not all of them) and the very best Divers too. When a Diver drowns, it swallows him forever... As he talked about the System, Cracker scratched the scabby patches on his skin until they bled: 'I didn't create it, it installed itself in eighth layer, it did it *itself*, you see! When I first *saw* it, it looked perfect to me... Then, much later I realised that it's a sort of virus. Not a gift, but a curse...

'It exists separately from all the artificial *socio* systems for controlling the population. It never makes a mistake and never lies. It shows three billion incodes in their constant development. It precisely detects every reproduction and pause in the world...

'Precisely detects...' Cracker squeezed his spidery, slender-fingered hands into fists. '...But I wonder... Maybe it controls them?'

'You're crazy,' was Zero's response to that. 'You're paranoid, Cracker.' He didn't want to think that the System was a curse. He wanted to believe that the System was the nativity gift of the magi. And that one day it would accept him. Someday, after one year, two, three, ten, someone's pause would take too long. Someone's five seconds of darkness would accidentally turn out to be an eternity. Someone – some absolutely terrible person, some pathetic screw-up... some correctee with a terrible invector – would quit the System forever and it would then invite Zero to take up the vacant spot.

And he would stop being surplus to requirements.

Zero imagined the System as something solemn and sad. Like the temple in which the ancients used to pray to their three-headed god. Like the fiery underground world which the ancients went down into to live in after death.

...The little man made of numbers had nothing in common with how the Wise One had imagined the System. He was funny and ridiculous.

'In *socio* the System is different,' the Servant responded to what he was thinking. 'Like an ancient temple...' The Wise One felt an unpleasant chill.

'Actually it wasn't the System so much I wanted to show you...' The Servant faltered strangely. 'So much as... the Malfunction. A malfunction in the System, yes.'

The Wise One shivered. An idiotic, childish hope hit him somewhere just above the stomach. Like an imago struggling to break free from its cocoon. A system malfunction.

Someone's pause will take too long...

servant: **command:** *show Malfunction-1.*

'Look, Wise One.'

The funny little man on the screen slowly lifted both arms – as if he was surrendering himself to the mercy of an unseen enemy. Several twisted spirals of numbers on his body – in his armpits, on his palms and around the navel – turned unavailable and started to look like bruises.

'One, two, three... five... Fofs!' The Servant looked properly scared. '...seven, eight... eight of them. More than ever!'

'What is that...?'

The Servant of Order zoomed in on one of the 'bruises': a tiny patch of letters and numbers unfurled to reveal someone's eight-digit incode. At the bottom of the screen a timer came on with a panicky ping:

15 seconds...16 seconds...17...18....

'A stalled reproduction,' the Servant replied quietly. 'That timer is counting the seconds of darkness. After the pause there

311

should be, as you know, five seconds. And here – well, see for yourself...'

...19...20...21.

The Wise One felt a strange weightlessness. The imago of hope hatched somewhere in his stomach and flew up towards his throat on an acid wave of nausea.

Someone's five seconds of darkness might accidentally turn out to be an eternity...

'At the moment eight livings have not been reproduced at the correct time following the pause. That's a lot. Usually it's two or three...'

'Usually?!'

'Recently... The malfunction in the System was discovered nearly half a year ago. Someone's incode was reproduced late by all of two tenths of a second, but the System noticed and sent an alarm signal in *socio*. We decided that this was a unique and overall acceptable exception from the rule, and we didn't treat what had happened as significant. But a week later the situation happened again, only now the reproduction 'stalled' for two further seconds... Then suddenly two incodes stalled in two different regions. One was reproduced after ten minutes, the other... after a day. That's when we realised that the stability of the Living was under threat. He is sick, Wise One. The Living is seriously ill.'

...At second 108 the incode on the screen winked, changed colour from unavailable to grassy-available and dashed off somewhere to the right.

'What... what happened to him?'Zero shuddered.

'He was finally reproduced... *So far* all the stalled reproductions have gone through sooner or later. Our task, Wise One, is to prevent...' For some reason the Servant moved to a whisper, '...is to prevent any reduction... It's terrifying to think what would happen if someone's reproduction was just can-celled. Because the Number of the Living is unchanging, the Living is three billion livings... You must protect Him. We believe the system malfunction is connected to the destructive activity of the Dissidents. That is why the First Speech should be devoted to bringing in harsher measures and the introduc-tion of a state of emergency, you see? Wise One...? How are you feeling?'

'I'm fine,' the Wise One replied.

The walls and floor had stopped swaying in front of him. Everything became precise and incredibly bright, like *feeling lucky*. 'Feeling lucky,' Zero said to himself and got up. He felt a strange agitation in his whole body. His legs and arms were trembling – not from weakness, but from a strange foreboding of strength. As if some unseen and powerful engine had started working inside him. Right now he could run ten miles without stopping. Right now he would tear anyone who tried to block his path to shreds. He was like a rabid farm dog that had broken out of its cage. Now he's going to go and defend himself and his territory. He is going to defend his Master. He, Zero, will be the one to cure the Living of this sickness – and after that the Master will accept him... He is not afraid, he is no longer weak, he is the lord of first layer. Right now he is stronger than any of these bloated, clumsy, *socio* people that can't string their thoughts together. Now he is stronger than the Servant of Order standing next to him. Stronger than that clown, screwing up his face like he's got toothache.

'Gopz,' Zero said with an inscrutable smile; insane joy was ticking away in his head, like an explosive device gone mad. 'You, and Second, you can both gopz, alright? The Living does not have enough love, that's the reason for the Malfunc-tion. I am sure of it. I've come up with a good First Speech, simple and kind. I will not give *your* speech to the Council of Eight...'

'He's still stupid,' the Servant thought and shuddered as he left the System. 'In the grand scheme of things. Stupid and stubborn, like an owlet moth bashing against the window at night...'

'You've already given our speech, idiot,' the Servant replied wearily. The Wise One stared with eyes full of blood and venom at the darkened screen of the Crystal and then at the Servant.

'Did you really think that there is even a single corner in the Residence that's not fitted with video surveillance and recording?' The Servant suddenly got the urge to gather his saliva and spit in those stupid eyes. 'We filmed you while you read *our* speech. It's a shame it was without expression, but hey, the members of the Council hardly ever listen out for intonation in first layer... But if you want I'll ask Second if anyone in the Council was upset by the fact that you read off a piece of paper...? No, he says no one was upset. They all believed in your "direct connection"... So, I can congratulate you on a successful First Speech, Wise One: a First Speech is a big responsibility... You caught them unawares with your radical ideas... But on the other hand, the members of the Council have been planning on "clamping down" for a long time now. The discussion is now underway. What a shame that you can't take part in the general debate yet. Second is saying that all the members of the Council are terribly worried by your illness. You lost consciousness after all, and I literally carried you out of the conference hall in my arms... Sorry, lad, I had to do a little editing and after the speech cut straight to "the faint"... But they all hope that it's just the result of stress. It's entirely possible, you were just overly anxious, Wise One: the First Speech is a big responsibility... They hope that you feel a bit better and will come back to the conference hall to take part in the discussion... Are you feeling a bit better, Wise One, what do you reckon? In a way everything depends on you...'

'You scumbags,' the Wise One was trembling with anger and passion. 'I'm going to tell them all right now.'

The Servant of Order started laughing in surprise at how childish the threat sounded. 'I'm going to tell mum on you!' was how his Darlings usually reacted when he locked them in the unlit store cupboard as punishment for some misdemeanour...

The Servant watched Zero pulling at the gold-plated handle of the locked door in a frenzy.

'I'll break it down!' The Wise One took a few paces back and slammed himself against the door at a sprint.

...The Servant's Darlings also always tried to smash the door down. For some unknown reason they were terribly afraid of the dark in first layer. Layla thought that there was no point in punishing them with darkness, but the Servant wasn't particularly interested in what Layla thought. If his little livings want to achieve something in this life then they are going to have to be strong, devious and fearless. Like their father. They need to work on themselves, because neither of them has a particularly great invector, and no one knows how long this dolce vita behind the walls of the Residence is going to last. He, of course, smin, will try to keep them there forever. But there are no guarantees. He didn't even have any guarantees himself for now, so they would have to fight for their place in the sun. The Servant loved sitting in his office and listening to the sounds coming from the cupboard. To the children weeping and banging on the door. Good, good, let them develop their strength and overcome the ancient fears. One day – soon – they will realise that the door and the hinges are only wooden on the outside and that inside there is a core of high-carbon steel, and that there is no way of breaking the door down. One day – soon – they will try to trick him as he takes them to the cupboard. Interrupting each other, they will start urgently saying that last time, there, in the cupboard, they saw a rat, a real, live one, with fluffy fur and eyes like buttons... in the far corner, smin, father, smin, go have a look... And he will go in and they will lock the door behind him, and he will let them do it – as once, long ago, his father let him. Because you can't deny them that lesson. It will be their first serious act of deviousness... They will run away, laughing and whooping, and he will open the cupboard door from the inside with his key. He will find them in the garden, give each of them a slap on the face, and then hug them tight. Like his father once hugged him, tenderly, painfully...

...The Servant grudgingly paused the clip 'Darling_childhood_reconciliation_in_garden' from his family archive and said:

'Save your strength, Wise One. First off, there's no way of breaking down that door. Second, another two or three more sharp movements and you'll be unliving... Do you not feel how close your pause is, eh, Zero?'

Oh yes. He felt it alright. It was as if someone had jabbed him through the heart like a mounted butterfly, and was now toying with him, moving the needle back and forth, and with every movement cold sweat poured over his face and the taste of iron spread through his mouth.

The Servant bent over, scoured the floor with his eyes, picked up the little corpse of the recently deceased beetle, and shoved it in the Wise One's face.

'Two heads, see? That means a double dose of white venom. The first portion...' – The Servant of Order casually ripped one of the heads off the insect – '...neutralised the venom of the black bakugan... The second portion...' – He ripped off the other head, and a meagre pinkish droplet came out of the post-occipital suture – 'is killing you right now. Your pause will come in an hour – that is if you calm down and you're as good as gold – or quicker if you carry on acting crazy like this. Any physical effort, any sudden movement, any disturbing thought will speed up the process. Did I not tell you what happens to people that overdo it on white bakugan venom...? Anaphylactic shock. Paroxysmal tachycardia. Rupture of the heart muscle. Brain haemorrhage. Your blood vessels will swell and burst like a rotten grape...'

The Wise One was sitting on the floor, slumped with his back to the locked door.

His breathing was fast and hoarse and his whole body was trembling slightly – like a farm animal when a person has gone up too close to it.

The Servant of Order went up closer and wrinkled his face at the acrid smell emanating from the Wise One. Disgusting. He really does stink like an animal – of fear and sweat.

'Yes, yes, I know, it's bad news...' The Servant noticed that this farmyard stench had even given him a blocked nose. 'But there is some good news too. I can neutralise the effect of the venom. Ta-da!' Like a conjuror, the Servant pulled a transparent capsule containing a little shivering black ball from his inside pocket. 'The larva of the black bakugan. It's already excited, it's been warmed by the heat of my body, it's trembling with anticipation. It's ready to share its magical calming juice... You have to decide, Wise One. If you want, you can die here; the Council of Eight will be extremely upset at this sudden death as a result of nervous stress... Or, if you want, you can *cooperate*. You'll take a little break, you'll return to the conference hall and you'll join in with the debate. Don't you worry, Wise One, I'll be sitting next to you, giving you hints. So then, have I persuaded you?'

'Can...I... have...the...black...now...' Zero wheezed, as he gasped for air, and extended his hand, palm up, to the Servant, like a hungry robot begging passers-by for food on the outskirts of the slums.

It seemed to Zero like some *wise* stranger was watching him from inside. Disinterestedly recording every stage of dying and disgrace. Just now he had noted dispassionately that the strength and anger, the virtue and intelligence, the loyalty to his Master – all this had gone from Zero; all there was was deathly sadness, the ancient, childish fear of being left locked somewhere in the dark.

And the thumping too. The uneven, exhausting thumping of his raging blood.

'Not now,' the Servant of Order put the capsule back in his pocket. 'But if you are a good little boy, and repeat after me everything that you have to say, then in half an hour you will get your black bakugan. Just remember, deep breaths, not too fast… And the main thing is: remember that you are protecting the interests of the Living, even if you are under a little bit of pressure from us… You see, we, Wise One, know what we are doing. Some day you will realise that we are right.'

> *layla:* right that's it, i'm moving into the annexe with the kids, alright? i'm not going to live under the same roof as that bitch of yours
> *servant:* don't you dare involve the kids in this!
> *layla:* oh! remembered your kids did you you old tomcat

> **From:** *Electronic Secretary*
> **To:** *First, Second, Third, Fourth, Fifth, Sixth, Seventh, Eighth [mass mail]*
> **Subject:** *results of vote*
>
> *Following a debate, the proposals of Eighth (the Wise One) have been passed with a majority of votes. The members of the Council believe the introduction of a state of emergency to be a reasonable and timely measure.*
> *The members of the Council believe the introduction of harsher penalties to be a reasonable and timely measure.*
> *The members of the Council would like to express their high esteem for the generosity and courage of their colleague Second and will gratefully accept his sacrifice when his time comes.*

I would like to remind members of the Council that the subject of the next meeting is 'Socio advertising as a means of combating the Dissidents.'

Second

Welcome to Renaissance, the global historical database
Caution!
This cell contains only personal letters and documents.
This cell has been leased for 120 years with optional
extension on request.
Access to this cell is available only to the leaseholder.
Access to this cell is not available to leaseholders
under the age of eight.
Enter your incode.

Thank you, incode accepted.

Please place your plastic incode e-card against
the illuminated section of screen.

Thank you,
e-card accepted.

Please place your left hand against the illuminated
section of the screen.
Identification complete.

There is no death, Second!
You may open your bank deposit cell.

Caution!
You have just removed all the letters to self stored
in the deposit cell.
You have placed 1 (one) new letter to self in your
deposit cell.

Caution!
You have forgotten or do not wish to return the letters
to self you have removed to your cell.
Caution!
Your deposit cell now contains only 1 (one)
letter to self.

Until we meet again!
There is no death.

Letter to Self
4th September 471 A.V.

Gopz, my friend! Sorry about that, but I did make you ☹

You are now eight, so you probably already know that you should have been a member of the Council. And that you didn't get to be one.

You are not Second.

When you grow up, you will be, well, a *socio* worker... Yes, that's what we are going to do. So why don't I just go right ahead and sort everything out for 'me'...

...So that's it. Congratulations on your new job. They were all, of course, a little flabbergasted when I told them.

'A *socio* worker?!' Third even flapped his wings. 'And what exactly do you have your eye on?'

'Well, being a sysadmin, for instance,' I say.

'What?' he says. 'What – a sysadmin? Don't you want a decent job?'

So I go to him, grandly: 'And what exactly do you think is not "decent" about being a sysadmin?' And then I sort of soften up a bit and say: 'Well, maybe you're right at the end of the day. Being a sysadmin would be boring. I'd be better off with something creative... I'll do *socio* art. Pictures, you know, souvenirs, all those little bits and bobs for cell interiors... Or I'll develop the models for new presents: *socio* cakes and birthday bouquets... Or not. I'd be better off as a *socio-gunsmith*, that's it. Development and supply of weapons for shoot 'em ups and no deathers...'

'Maybe you'd like to create your own game?'

'Oh no,' I say. 'Why do my own? Too much responsibility. I'm tired, my friends, of responsibility...'

At first I was thinking of making myself the Servant of Order. Sort of like a reshuffle... But then I realised: no. Even an ordinary planetman – no. No positions of responsibility in first layer. No power. Otherwise, anything could happen, you probably have ambitions, you've been insulted, your sense of honour has been slighted... Why risk it? You'll still, probably, cause all sorts of hassle. So you're better off sitting in *socio* drawing handguns. I don't see any sense in risking my son's welfare for the sake of your pleasure. At the end of the day, I couldn't care less about you.

Yep, I couldn't care less. For me you just don't exist. You're surprised, right?

After all, you are me, my direct continuation. It's just five seconds of darkness and I'm alive again, bla bla bla... Tell me, matey, do you remember anything about me? Because tomorrow I'm going to pull all my previous letters to self out of Renaissance (I'm not going to leave behind all those state secrets for you to find ☹), and I'll leave only one, this one... Do you remember anything?

Maybe you remember how wisely I ruled in the Council of Eight? Or what I liked to have for lunch?

Or how my long-term woman smelled, my slum witch, when she was young? You don't remember, do you? I'll tell you: she smelled of fish and ginger... And later, how did she smell later, before the pause, do you remember? No, of course not. Because it wasn't you, it wasn't you but me who was there breathing in that sweet, boggy smell of decay which she breathed out in her groans...

Or maybe you remember the first time my son smiled? Or you remember how my grandchildren used to like to tug at my beard?

You don't remember anything. And without these crucial memories, are you really me?!

I couldn't care less about you. Just like my inc-predecessor couldn't care less about me. And just as you can't remember me, I couldn't remember him. I didn't know him and I couldn't feel him. His Darlings were completely alien to me. As an eight-year-old boy – just like you are now – I threw them, his women, his kids and his grandkids, out of the Residence. And, to be honest, I didn't care how and where they lived after that...

That's what everyone does. All the members of the Council, once they are renewed, throw 'their own' Darlings out of the Residence. Some harshly, with a kick up the behind, some politely, with respect. Some do it with no explanation, some with plausible excuses like 'repairs to the façade of the main building'.

And you'd do the exact same, right, mate?

You'd throw them all out, you, a snotty-nosed eight-year-old kid – my women, old and young, my son and my grandchildren... Everyone who is dear to me.

I am, you might say, a familial... What, have you pissed yourself? So then, off you go and make a complaint against 'yourself' to the SPO. A voluntary confession will reduce the punishment, they reckon... But nevertheless, I don't recommend it, my friend. We sentence guys like you to a Shameful Pause immediately... And a Shameful Pause – do you know what that is, my friend? It's a bit early for you to find out, but I'll tell you anyway. It's when they put you in solitary in the Special Unit – it's this sort of hermetically sealed, transparent chamber, like a terrarium, with twenty-four-hour video-surveillance – and in second layer they show all the livings how you slowly die from dehydration and starvation. They show you crapping where you sleep. They show you going mad and banging your head against the walls. And calling for your mummy. And writhing around in your own excrement...

So you'd be better off not telling anyone about me. *Quid licet Iovi, non licet bovi...* It's one rule for the powerful, and another for you animals. I can be a familial, but you have to live by the law and not go shooting your mouth off. And, perhaps, it'll work out, because the Living is all-merciful.

...You shouldn't think that I have always found the courage to call myself a familial. For a really, really long time I tried to believe in 'the life eternal'. I read my letters to self and struggled and struggled and tried to get into the role, to feel that I am *him*. I even sent his relatives some *socio* cash every month, seeking forgiveness for my sin...

And then I realised – I was already well past sixty then, other people don't live that long – I realised: it's all lies. Even before the Malfunctions, even before Fourth, I just knew it in my sick old stomach. I am me, the sum of my memories from birth until pause. Everyone who came before, everyone who will come after, is not me. And it doesn't matter if we happen to have numbers that match.

There are others who feel this in their belly too: to hell with inc-successors, your continuation is in your children... I destroy those bright sparks with absolutely no pity. The head and the arse can't live in the same conditions...

To my son, and my son's son, and his grandsons, that's who I want to pass down a quiet and obedient Living to. Manageable. Arranged by the Book...

The Heir

INT. FIRST LAYER. ANCIENT SUPERMARKET ABOUT TO
BE DEMOLISHED. At first we don't see anything,
absolute darkness. All we hear is some
mysterious rustling and someone's hoarse,
wheezy breathing. We are intrigued.

FROM BLACK sharply, with a characteristic click:
a wonder-sunshine floods the supermarket
in blinding light.

(NB. To begin with brightness at 8-9 – at first
we should instinctively shut our eyes – then
light to socio-STANDARD.)

We see a dishevelled elderly man, with a
very unpleasant, evil face, of an unhealthy
earthy colour. The man is squatting down
and his breathing is rapid and heavy. He's
an old-living. With a harsh, unfriendly
expression he peers across at the SPO officer,
who is walking up to him with quick, decisive
strides.

The officer is tall, young and good-looking.
His mirrored mask clings elegantly to his
handsome, wilful face.

PLANETMAN (through chatterbox): Don't move!

OLD-LIVING (in a nasty, screeching voice):
So you found me after all...

PLANETMAN: You thought you could escape the law, eh, violator?

OLD-LIVING (impudently): Yes, I thought I could escape the law. I do not agree with the law.

PLANETMAN: So you are a Dissident?! That's what I thought. What don't you agree with? Why did you not go to the festival at the appointed time? Why have you exceeded the acceptable length of life by three whole days?

OLD-LIVING: I don't agree with the compulsory pause or with age limits.

PLANETMAN (amiably): I'll explain to you why we have to have limits.

REDIRECT TO SOCIO (NB. The challenge for the cameramen and the editors is to create the sensation that we are moving to a deeper layer. The clip itself will only be broadcast in second layer.)

IN SOCIO
We see a cross-section of a human body.

PLANETMAN (VOICEOVER): Over the years our body gets worn out and ceases to be fit for purpose. We are poisoned by toxins and carcinogens. The heart, lungs, liver and kidneys no longer function properly...

We see these organs getting darker, as if covered in rot and soot.

PLANETMAN (VOICEOVER): ...Brain function deteriorates...

We see the brain 'decomposing' in the skull.

PLANETMAN (VOICEOVER): ...Plaque forms in the arteries...

Close up of artery: it is full of dark clumps, we see the blood pushing the artery out from the inside, unable to break through the blockage.

PLANETMAN (VOICEOVER): ...Cells stop regenerating. The skin becomes lined and covered in wrinkles, it loses its elasticity and healthy glow...

We see the hand, the skin on it is covered in liver spots, it becomes yellow and wrinkled.

PLANETMAN (VOICEOVER): ...Hair loses its pigmentation...

We see someone's black hair thinning and rapidly going grey at the same time.

PLANETMAN (VOICEOVER): ...The immune system weakens and the body comes under attack from illnesses.

The entire body shudders from coughing.
We somehow fly out of the body and see the
old-living again in first layer. He is coughing
violently. We realise that the tour we have just
been on was through his body.

INT. FIRST LAYER

PLANETMAN: The condition I have just described
is called 'old age'. People can survive quite
a long time in this condition, several years,
but is it really worth putting yourself through
this agony when the pause can solve all these
problems? All it takes is five seconds of
darkness and the Living will breathe a new,
young life into you, a life full of health,
stability and joyful discoveries.

OLD-LIVING (stamps foot): I still don't agree.

PLANETMAN (strictly): You are damaging the
health of the Living with your stubbornness!
You are a part of the Living and you are
poisoning His body with your old age. The
Living wants all of His parts to be renewed
at the right time. Otherwise the Living
will start to get old too.

OLD-LIVING: Ah, so that's what it is! Well, in
which case take me to the Pause Zone immediately.

PLANETMAN: As you are a violator, you can
expect a Shameful Pause.
OLD-LIVING: It doesn't matter, I agree.

PLANETMAN: Thank you for being so understanding. I hope that in the future you will be corrected and become a worthwhile part of the Living.

OLD-LIVING (with a hopeful smile): I promise to get corrected.

The clink of handcuffs being fastened.

We see the planetman and the old-living disappearing into the sunset along an avenue scattered with autumn leaves. Joyous, solemn music plays. In the background we hear, barely audible, the standard festival announcement ('...the Festival Administration is pleased to welcome you to the Pause Zone. We would like to draw your attention to the refreshments on offer: coffee, tea, hot and cold drinks and snacks.
If you are in need of entertainment, one of our festival clowns is sure to lift your spirits with one of their fun tricks...'), then we hear the sonorous cry of a new-born. FADE TO BLACK.

FROM BLACK:

A scrolling display on a black background with simultaneous voiceover:

VOICEOVER: The Council of Eight, the Association for the Assistance of Nature and the Service for Planetary Order would like to remind you: all livings must undergo the pause procedure no later than the day of their sixtieth birthday.

Those not in agreement with this law will
be subject to a Shameful Pause and sentenced
to indefinite correction in the relevant
institutions.

'...I'm going to puke,' Second said and shivered in a silent
cough to make the point clearer. 'With a hopeful smile, walking into the sunset, the cry of a new-born, the mirrored mask
elegantly clings to his wilful balls...' Second gave a wheezing
cackle, and First and Third followed his example.

Fifth's honoured deputy, assiduously goggling his eyes in
the live broadcast window, also wrinkled his expressionless
little globaloid face in obsequious cackling.

'I don't know what you're so happy about.' Second cut off
their laughter abruptly. 'Your screenplay is no good. What is
all this lovey-dovey crap you've put in? Why does the planetman try and talk the violator round, explaining and wriggling about like an earthworm? Why does the planetman even
talk to him at all? A dissident is an enemy, it only needs
a short chat. A dissident is a lost cause, there's no point having
some soul-saving conversation with him. What you've got to
do to a dissident...' Second's face twisted, either from pain or
from genuine hatred. '...is this...' Second clenched his trembling hand into a fist. 'Crush the rat. Teach the others a
lesson.'

'So then... if... if I have permission to speak...' jabbered
Fifth's deputy, 'what adjustments would the members of the
Council recommend...?'

> *second:* adjustments! you tell me, thickhead, what
> adjustments! i need a harsh, biting, realistic *socio* clip.
> and not this dialogue between two degenerates that
> you've just sent round!

'Make the conflict tougher,' First said didactically. 'Put the emphasis in the right places...'

'Who have you chosen to play the old-living?' Second asked seriously.

> *second:* send me a photo
> *dep 5:* already have

'Talk out loud!' roared Second. 'This conference is being held in first layer. You are showing disrespect to the Wise One!'

'The photograph is in your inbox, Second,' the deputy murmured.

'It's Prince G, a professional actor, he's been in all the shows... A familiar face...' the deputy fixed his gaze on Second's features as they darkened in rage and then played his trump card: 'Fifth's favourite actor.'

'A familiar face,' Second bleated, mimicking the deputy. 'His favourite actor... Idiot! The face of a traitor shouldn't be familiar, it shouldn't be someone's favourite! Plus, Prince is forty-five and this is about an old-living!'

'We'll give him makeup...'

'Silence!' Second cawed, 'Everything has to be realistic. When it's about an old-living the viewer has to see old age. Real, stinking, terrifying, rotten old age.' Second coughed wetly. 'The sort of age that when any cretin sees it he realises that it is poisoning the body of the Living!'

In their first-layer windows the members of the Council lowered their eyes in shame. The dark and wrinkled face of Second, covered in perspiration, fitted those criteria to perfection.

'A little radical for my tastes,' Sixth remarked. 'Why arouse negative emotions in the viewer? Viewers shouldn't have to feel disgusted when they see an advert.'

'Not when they see an advert, but when they see a criminal,' Second snapped back. 'We are, by the way, in a state of emergency, in case you had forgotten. Playtime is over.' Second flashed his eyes from beneath his swollen eyelids. 'This is what I think. We've got to do a documentary. Real violators. Real extracts from interrogations. Real punishments. Shameful Pauses broadcast on *socio*.'

'That's not possible,' Third intervened. 'Showing violence is banned on *socio*.'

'Who's talking about violence?' Second replied in a bored voice. 'No one's talking about violence... Wise One, what's your take on this issue?'

The Wise One nodded.

'"I like Second's proposal..."' whispered the Servant of Order.

'I like Second's proposal.'

'"There's a lot of common sense in it."'

'There's a lot of common sense in it.'

'"And seeing as the emergence of the Dissidents is partly my fault..."'

The Wise One inhaled deeply and held his breath. It helped slow his pulse, if only a little. The Servant said that if the second meeting goes smoothly then next time we'll manage without any venom...

'...And seeing as the emergence of the Dissidents is part...'

'Fofs,' Second suddenly sighed gruffly, and Zero stopped halfway through a word.

'Carry on,' mouthed the Serva nt.

'...ly my fault...'

Second gave out a short, sharp laugh. *I'm saying something wrong*, Zero thought in panic and immediately felt his pulse quicken. *What's he laughing at?*

The blood started splashing in his head, unbearably, deafeningly loud, striking his ear drums in taut streams, swathing first layer in sparkling tatters... Through this knocking, through the warm, sombre splashing he heard the old man's laughter –

332

he-hee, such a hideous laugh, unnatural, like in one of the dramas – and the voice of the Autosecretary ('Technical pause in conference') and the voice of the Servant again:

'...Can I trust you, Wise One? Can I trust you...?'

As if under a layer of water, blindly and slowly, not understanding anything, the Wise One nodded. And that moment he felt a slippery little lump bite into his wrist.

'I've given you the anti-venom,' whispered the Servant, somewhere there, beneath the water. 'After the break you can continue the speech yourself.'

'He-hee!' Second wailed.

what is he laughing at?

Sleep, sleep... Dozy and slow like a greasy bubble, silence stretched out in his head. And it dragged him, lulling him to sleep, somewhere downstream...

'Don't sleep, Wise One!'

...He so wanted to float away... With great effort Zero unstuck his swollen eyelids and sat up. It was quiet and sleepy in the conference hall and the old man was not giggling anymore, but had also fallen asleep, his grey beard sticking ridiculously into one of the hollows in the sofa. The Servant of Order was sitting next to his father and stroking his back.

'What was he laughing at?' Zero asked, suppressing a yawn.

'He wasn't laughing, he was dying.'

Zero looked into the old man's motionless grey face.

'So then,' – the Servant of Order examined himself in the dark screen of the Crystal like it was a mirror – 'will you manage without a prompt, Wise One?'

The Crystal blinked on with a dry crackle and split into eight squares. All for the convenience of the Wise One. So that at the conference he could see all the faces of the members of the Council...

The swarthy, tense features of the Servant appeared in square 2. He paused and then said:

'Second, moderator of the tranquillity of the Living in all layers, welcomes the members of the Council. Fifteen minutes ago, at the age of eighty-two, my father temporarily ceased. We would like to wish him a happy reproduction...!'

The members of the Council hummed in approval from the screen of the Crystal.

'...And I am, in hope and trepidation, taking over the reins. Dear friends! I am prepared to continue the conference and I maintain my previous position in regard to *socio* advertising. The Wise One will now tell us in detail about his vision...'

The Showman

'What is your name, woman?'
'Rosa.'
'A lovely name. And what are you called?'
Silence.
'Who is he, woman?'
'He is my son. He is called Mark.'
'Why won't he talk to me?'
'He is afraid.'
'Afraid of me?'
'Yes.'
'Why?'
'You told him to follow you, and now you want
to punish him.'
'And how did I tell him to follow me?'
'Follow Zero. That's what was written in the
chain letter.'
'The chain letter is a Dissident plot. How dare
you attribute their words to me?'

The Council of Eight, the Service for Planetary
Order and the Wise One would like to warn you:
the 'chain letter' is a Dissident plot. Every 'chain
letter' contains a harmful virus. If you have received
such a letter, do not read it, but erase it immediately
in order to avoid spreading the infection further.

'Do you know why you are here, Rosa?'
'Because we are familials.'
'And what does that mean?'
'It means that we love each other.'

'No, incorrect. It means that you are breaking the law. The law dictates that you send away your Darling at the age of seven. But many years have passed and you are still living under one roof as Darlings. It seems you do not agree with the law.'
'So it seems.'
'Which means you are Dissidents. Do you, Rosa, mother of Mark, admit that you are a Dissident?'
Silence.
'And you, Mark, son of Rosa, do you admit that you are a Dissident?'
Silence.
'In the name of the Living I sentence Rosa and Mark to a Shameful Pause…'
'Have mercy, Wise One…'
'…with subsequent correction. SPO officers will carry out the sentence live after the ad break. If you are younger than eight years old, you can't watch Rosa and Mark's pauses. If you are over eight, enter your name and incode to watch Rosa and Mark's pauses… See you after the break. This is the Wise One and you're watching Who Still Does Not Agree.'

The Council of Eight, the Service for Planetary Order and the Wise One would like to warn you: dissidence is punishable by Shameful Pause with subsequent correction. You can download the complete first series of interrogations and Shameful Pauses in second layer at dissidentwatch.net.tv

'And we're back!'

The Wise One pressed the touchpad with his finger, gently, almost tenderly. The Wise One's face froze on the screen in a triumphant, slightly twisted grin.

'So what do you think?'

He loved it when Cleo rewatched the show with him on the Crystal W.

'You're always faultless,' she said drily. 'Cruel, but just and artistic.'

'…And more and more cruel with every episode,' she thought to herself. 'If you watch Who Still Does Not Agree in second layer for some reason it doesn't seem so obvious. But the Crystal… The Crystal, with its flat picture, is cruder and more honest. It strips everything bare somehow…' Cleo looked at the motionless, self-satisfied face on the screen and then looked away. 'That cold, emotionless way he talks to them – for some reason this indifference seems like justice to the viewers; the calmer he is, the more "likes" the show gets… And that smile of his is unexpectedly touching, somehow childlike, when he just stands to one side and watches the Dissidents being put into the Chamber of Shame. Even Second once said that that smile gave him the creeps…'

But the viewers liked it. 'The Wise One's smile gives us livings hope and belief,' they muttered in the comments after every episode. 'Hope for the correction of those who have lost their way…' 'Belief in the complete extermination of the Dissidents…'

me and another billion of my friends like it <u>I don't like it</u>

They all like it.

But personally she preferred the way he had acted in the beginning. A year ago. When his voice would tremble and crack during the interrogations. When he was afraid to look the Dissidents in the eye. When he didn't dare smile when he was carrying out the verdict…

'No, I'm talking about the machine!' the Wise One said. 'How do you like my new CW?' Zero stroked the reflective body of the Crystal W. The latest model. An even more sophisticated design. Even more three-dimensional picture. Even thinner screen. Even more user-friendly interface. Even more sound and colour settings. The Crystal Wise One. Exclusive equipment especially for him. Better and better every time. And he rejoiced in every new model like a kid with a toy. How could you explain to him that there was no particular difference between the toys? That they were all crude, ugly, slow, clumsy imitations. Prosthetics for an invalid. Specially made for an invalid with no *socio*…

'The main thing is that you like it,' she said. It sounded false, but Zero didn't notice.

'I do.'

He laughed suddenly, abrupt and rattling, as if he were scattering a handful of pebbles on a marble floor. His crazed pupils swelled and narrowed in his chocolate eyes.

'Again?' she asked.

He said nothing.

With two fingers, Cleo carefully lifted the edge of his multi-coloured sleeve and pulled it up, baring his skin. An inflamed puncture trail of bites stretched from his palm to the joint of his elbow. Two bakugans were stuck to his wrist, a BW. She shuddered in disgust and let go of the sleeve.

'You're killing yourself,' she said. 'Which BW is this for today?'

'I haven't been counting,' Zero said amiably and closed his eyes.

'But I have! One BW in the morning. One before the show. And another one just now!'

'Er, not just one…'

'On the other arm too?!' she said in horror.

'So what. It's all under control, little one. I've got it under control.'

'You don't even know how many of these creatures you are plugging into yourself a day and it's under control?'

'Gopz,' he shrugged his shoulder irritatedly. She got up.

'OK, sorry Cleo, sorry little one,' he grabbed her by the arm and sat her back down next to him. 'Sit with me for a bit. It's just… don't bust my carousel right now, OK? Now, now…' he shoved his face against her shoulder and started breathing rapidly. 'Now, yeah…'

She hugged him tight, the way he liked. He shivered, then said: 'I'm flying… We're flying together…'

Zero invented the BW himself – an intravenous cocktail of black and white venom. 'The whole thing about it is that the bites are at the same time,' he said. 'If one larva is even a tiny bit late – it's already wrong, see, the high is broken. So you've got to pick larvae that are the same size and roughly the same age. Then they both release the juice at the same second and give you a carousel.' *Carousel* is what Zero called the effect of the BW – the fluctuating feeling of soaring and falling. And lots of other sensations which he couldn't explain. He suggested that she try it, but she felt sick when she so much as looked at those slugs digging into bare flesh.

At first he only took a BW before the beginning of the show, for courage.

'For indifference, more like,' he said. 'When I'm on the carousel, I couldn't care less about these Dissidents.' Then he started doubling the dose – one BW on each arm… then he started using every day, although he presented the show only once a week… And then that dreamy child's smile appeared – and he really couldn't care less about 'those Dissidents'. But it was still a lot of BWs. More and more all the time – now it was up to five or six doses a day. Even Second says he is overdoing it. It's bad for the heart and the brain.

'You're shaking. I'm going to put the blanket over you,' said Cleo. He always got cold after a carousel.

'Let's have a Darling,' said Zero. After a carousel he would become sentimental.

'But then when he turns seven are we going to send him away? Are you going to put us on your Who Still Does Not Agree programme...?'

She immediately regretted what she had said: it had come out rude and mean. He started shaking even more violently and covered his face with his hands as if he'd been slapped.

'Sorry.' She hugged him again. 'I'm sure, of course, that you would never touch your own Darling...'

'These people...' the Wise One droned into his hands. 'These Darlings... Familials... What, do you think I don't feel sorry for them?'

'I don't think you do,' she said honestly. 'Before – probably. But not anymore.'

He was not going to argue. He took his hands from his face and said:

'Maybe you're right.'

He reached over to the touchpad on his Crystal and went onto his docked network.

'...But whether I feel sorry for them or not, my show is saving the Living. Saving it, you understand? It's like shock therapy. Look at the System.' He opened up his little man made of numbers. 'Good progress, you see? After every Who Still Does Not Agree the number of scraps goes down. Then, by the next week, the scraps have appeared again, but every time there's fewer of them...'

'Scraps?' Cleo didn't understand.

'That's what Second calls the reproductions that have stalled... Like now, look, after the show there is only one, and half an hour ago there were dozens of them! Fewer dissidents means fewer stalled reproductions, you see! I don't know how it works, but it works.'

The Wise One stared sadly at one 'scrap'. A tiny unavailable little spiral flashing in the very centre of the System. He scraped his finger across the touchpad – then unwound the little spiral out into a ten-figure entry, stroked it with the black arrow of the cursor, like a pet which needs to be roused from sleep. *What are you doing, Cracker, my friend...? Why don't you come back to me, little scrap?*

But Cracker could not. Or would not. For more than a year now he hadn't wanted to come back. The first woman who carried him after the pause gave birth to him dead: he had choked on his umbilical cord. The second woman to get pregnant after that couldn't carry him for the full term: bleeding and a miscarriage in the twelfth week. And he dragged her down with him – she had lost so much blood that she temporarily ceased. And then he stalled. Went and stalled in the darkness, stubborn little scrap.

For nine days correctee Cracker had quite simply not been reproduced.

For nine days he had just been a collection of flashing figures.

For nine days he had simply not existed in the world...

Zero wound the little scrap, 'Cracker', back into a spiral, placed his head on the knees of his long-term woman and closed his eyes.

'I want a Darling with you,' he murmured sleepily and capriciously. 'I promise that I won't put you on the show. We will live together with our Darling like in ancient times. Like Second lives with his children... And then my Darling will become the Wise One in my place.'

'And are you going to take a second woman too, like Second?'

'No,' the Wise One frowned. 'I can't stand women getting hysterical.'

...Ever since Bagheera, the moderator of tranquillity's second long-term partner, had borne him his Darling not a day had gone by in the Residence without Layla shrieking and weeping.

She was terribly, monstrously jealous of Second and Bagheera and their new Darling…

'What, do you think I'd behave like Layla if you took another woman?'

'No… of course not. But I don't want anyone else anyway. I want you – and a Darling. By the way, I've already hired some first-layer designers to decorate a nursery.'

'Why do we need designers?' Cleo said mutedly.

'Because we need something special – I don't want him growing up in the standard feeling-lucky with anti-shock covering and hanging about on *socio* morning, noon and night. My Darling should know his way around in first layer – one day he's going to become the Wise…'

'Why do we need designers *now*? I haven't conceived yet…'

'So what? When are you ovulating?'

She grudgingly dug about in her memory:

'In three days.'

'So that means the designers have started work three days ahead of schedule…'

'Stop it!' she almost screeched, and it came out nasty and shrill, almost like Layla. 'Stop it…' she repeated more calmly this time; what annoyed her more than anything was when he pretended that everything was absolutely fine with her. 'You know… it's not going to work for me.'

'It'll all work out!' The Wise One waved it away. 'You'll see in three days. Smin, have faith, I've got a feeling! Everything's going to be alright.'

'Don't say "everything's going to be alright"!' Cleo snapped. 'That's what people say before the pause. If you want a Darling find yourself another woman. Something's wrong with me…'

'Rubbish. You're just not getting enough sleep. You spend your whole time in the lab…'

He stubbornly refused to believe. Every month the whole thing repeated itself: when are you ovulating – smin, this time it's definitely all going to work... And again – nothing. Something was wrong with the ovaries or the womb, that much was clear...

mother

...as clear as day. In her whole life she had only got pregnant once...

more than two million users already like mother

...and she had given birth to a Darling which was sick and which temporarily ceased shortly afterwards. And since then there had been hundreds of couplings at the festival, dozens of matings with Zero, but with no result. Infertility. An empty, barren uterus...

join the ravishing mother-queen in luxury *mode!*

...not like *there*.

But he doesn't want to believe it. He doesn't even want to hear about illness, about infertility.

The Wise One wants an heir. The Wise One is putting too much pressure on her, it's his own fault. Yes, his own fault. If he hadn't put her in this state of constant stress, if he wasn't insisting on a Darling, if he didn't force her to copulate with him naked, without a sucs, then she, probably, wouldn't have gone off *so far* into her fantasies in *luxury*. She wouldn't have started using a pseudonym, she wouldn't have become this Queen, covered in a layer of contact grease. She wouldn't have turned her woodland den into a termite mound, the Queendom. And she wouldn't be laying several thousand eggs in a day – in the world where she could produce offspring. Where all fantasies come true and delight you...

343

She entered the Queendom in inviz and opened statistics.

2 000 156 users are currently waiting for queen
in luxury
come on queen!

…A hundred more than four hours ago.

When she *created* her Queendom, she had not expected there would be so many who wanted to join. That everyone would come running: men and women, entomologists and members of the Council… 5,000 friends, that's what she had imagined at first, just to have a little distraction from first-layer problems. She hadn't thought that her Queendom would grow so big, that it would become a fantasy for millions.

2 000 163 users are waiting for queen
where are you, queen?

The Wise One nestled cosily on her knees, like a good lap-pet. He was dozing, smacking his lips funnily in his sleep. She carefully took his head from her knees and headed for the exit. Never in front of him.

mother_queen: just a sec

As ever before the *act*, she felt sick with fear and disgust.

With fear that the Wise One would find out, that he would find out and not be able to forgive her, and he would yell at her using all those stupid words from the Encyclopaedia of the Ancient World: 'faithful', 'cheating'…

And with disgust at herself, at what she had turned herself into, at what her millions of fans had turned her into: a huge, fat, clumsy, stupid, lustful…

mother_queen has updated her status: <u>available in isoptera</u>.

main menu

<small>larva</small> worker soldier nymph prince
<small>Who</small> will you be?
Join in!

Isoptera is a never-ending act in luxury created
by more than two million friends.

There was nothing – no up and no down, no thoughts and no body, no days and no nights. Absolute inviz. A thick, grey cocoon of peace. He was flying or floating, swaddled in blind nothingness. He had been lulled to sleep, he himself was nothing, just a part of inviz... And then, as always, a something stirred inside him traitorously and the emptiness thickened and started shaking, straining to expel this alien, *living* thing from itself...

His awakening was sudden and rough, like always after a BW sleep. Like he had been gobbled up and then spat in disgust out of a warm, soft mouth and into a buzzing beehive...

...There actually was something buzzing in first layer, dully and insistently. With difficulty the Wise One unglued his puffy eyes and sat up. No, not bees. Four fat bakugan beetles, overflowing with low-frequency buzzing, were ramming up against the Crystal, against a multi-coloured ad banner which was calling on him to love the Queen. The Wise One chased the beetles off the Crystal – heavy and glutted, they flew slowly off towards the wall; he squashed them and wiped their blood away with a cloth. Then he tried to close that damn banner, but instead it expanded to full screen. The Wise One cursed quietly. The Crystal would swallow all the ads that it found from second layer and play them on the screen. As if deliberately to tease the Wise One, offering him the chance to admire out of the corner of his eye what he could never have...

The Wise One went through into the bathroom, washed his face with cold water and treated the little wounds from the bakugans with disinfectant so they wouldn't go septic. Then he looked into the bedroom: Cleo was sitting on the floor, grasping her knees in her hands, doubled over, groaning quietly.

'Are you not feeling well?' he asked her, knowing that she wouldn't answer.

She didn't answer.

She rarely answered him when her face looked like that.

He sat down next to her and carefully stroked her eyebrows, which she had drawn towards the bridge of her nose in an expression of pain. Cleo started breathing noisily and collapsed against him, banging her face against his temple as if she were blind. He took her face in his hands and licked her on the lips, and she did not push him away.

She only let him kiss her on the lips when her face looked like *that*...

The screeching sound of a shrieking baby carried up from down below in the Available Garden. Cleo shuddered and wrenched herself free from the Wise One's embrace with disgust and lay on her stomach.

The shrieking broke into a raspy gurgling as if the baby was being tickled down there and was giggling inexpertly. For some reason Layla also started giggling with him, as if she were being tickled too. Bagheera started droning out a lullaby, plangent and out of tune... Never any peace. Why was that stupid woman always caterwauling outside our window...?

The Wise One went downstairs in irritation.

There, in the garden, Bagheera wasn't singing at all. She was whimpering, sitting on the ground and rocking her Darling in her arms. The Darling was grunting and choking on silent coughs, sticking out its bluish tongue; it had available spots on its neck...

But Layla really was roaring with laughter, wriggling in the arms of a guard. Second stood a little to one side with a pale, twisted face.

'Wise O-o-o-one,' Layla drawled through her laughter when she saw Zero. 'Make me your wife, Wise One, I'll give you a Darling! Wise One, don't think badly of me, I love kids! It's just this little toad I don't like, but I love all the others! Make me your wife, won't you? And I'll tell you everything! I know lots of things, Wise One, I even know about Malfunction number two! I even know that the Living's done for! And that your System is a fake and that they've been lying to you for ages!'

Second strode towards Layla and hit her in the face. She fell silent for a second, then started roaring with laughter again, her whole body shaking and her eyes goggling crazily.

'...They're lying, they're lying! And anyone who doesn't lie, my husband cuts open their head, right here.' Layla poked her forehead. 'Skin and bones, he cuts it all open and pulls out their memory and turns them into trolls!'

The guard dragged her away.

'...So will you take me as your wife, Wise One, when I become a troll? Because you're a troll too, Wise One – you'll be a troll and I'll be a troll and our kids will be trolls!'

The Healer

Dear Members of the Council! My eternal name is Healer 12, I'm an ordinary, run of the mill doctor and I work in an ordinary, run of the mill Centre for Population Control in region EA 8. I decided that I should write to you, and all other interested parts of the Living, here, in *socio*, in open mode, because I have recently been having more and more doubts about whether the wise Council is aware of the unlawful acts currently being carried out in ordinary, run of the mill centres like mine by SPO officers hiding behind the 'law'.

Do you know that, on the orders of those whose mission is supposed to be to defend the peace and security of the Living, on their orders dozens of unregistered pregnancy termination operations are being carried out every day, primarily on women in the early stages of pregnancy? That medical staff – ordinary, run-of-the-mill doctors like me and my friends – are being forced to carry out secret 'micro abortions' on women who have recently conceived – telling them that it was an ectopic pregnancy or that there was no pregnancy at all, and that the blood loss that's just taken place right there in the examination chair was caused by inflammation? Did you know that the 'conditions of secrecy' that have been imposed on us for carrying out these procedures in combination with the unplanned nature and urgency of the operations (instruction no. 2, as it is called, always comes unexpectedly) precludes the presence of assistants at the operation and forces us to work in premises that are not fitted with reanimation equipment? And that very often these operations lead not only to temporary cessation of existence for the foetus, but also to the temporary cessation or incapacitation of the would-be mother as a result of blood loss...

There is blood, blood on my hands and I will not keep silent about it! I have been a doctor for nine reproductions and I have, following the commands of the Servant of Order, stained my clean incode with the blood of innocents. After interrupting each existence, I clean up my office when I'm done and I wipe away the blood, but still it clings to my criminal hands. And when I leave my office and run into my colleagues in the corridor, I can tell by their faces, by the way they can't look me in the eye and hide their hands behind their back, I can tell that they're doing the same thing as me... Blood, blood on our hands. And we want to know what this 'law' is that forces us to spill the Living's blood.

That is all, my friends. At last I've done it. I've overcome my cowardice and written openly to the Council in Living Journal. I have confessed, and now you may judge me...

Dear members of the Council, judge me! As a doctor who has broken the rule of 'do no harm' or as a coward who has kept quiet too long, or even as a member of a criminal conspiracy, but do not judge me as a Dissident, in relation to the Defamation of Order act, because I have told you the absolute truth.

I like this   I don't like this

Hi, Wise One! You are viewing this page in reading mode. Unfortunately, you are not a socio-user so you cannot rate this LJ post. If you like, you can **view** *the ratings statistics for this LJ post.*

500 653 users **like** *Healer's open letter*

100 687 users **don't like** *Healer's open letter*

Leave a comment

spiderman: healer is a hero hooray

evelina_33: in april 471 i went to the district centre for control of the population. during my regular check-up the doctor announced that i had an 'inflammation of the womb', the ordinary regular check-up had somehow caused a haemorrhage. thanks, healer. now i know what really happened to me!!

milk-cap: what a load of nonsense, why would the planetmen destroy embryos. healer's a psycho

mongrel: +1 gopz

santa: healer is right, and it's actually a lot worse than he said.

sister_66: +100, what the planetmen are doing is an outrage. and it's not just embryos, go on orderisover. net, people there are talking about their pauses and their friends' pauses which have happened in the middle of the day without a trial or investigation

healer: thank you to everyone who replied: thanks to you guys i unexpectedly became a hundred-thousander, and that's a great honour and a great responsibility. my friends! i don't think of myself as a hero. i just said what someone had to say sooner or later.

second: Dear Healer, Thank you for your open letter and your timely alarm signal. The Council of Eight promises to carry out a very thorough inquiry in your centre, and also provide you with personal security for the duration of the inquiry.

healer: thanks

view whole thread (45 789 comments)?

healer: update: today I got an official invitation
to go to the Residence (!)
healer: update: I chatted to the Second member of
the Council and to the Wise One. Amazing, considerate
people who are devoted to the Living! They took what
I had to say very seriously and made copies of all the
Instruction No. 2's which I had kept especially for the
investigation. I have no doubt: with people like that in
power the SPO-ers' outrage will be stopped very soon.
healer: update: friends, I would like to share with you
all the findings of the inquiry. I am happy to report that
no violations or abuses of power were discovered in
the work of the SPO. The investigation revealed that
the Instruction No. 2's which staff at our Centre for
Population Control were receiving on the official
channel, seemingly from Order Service officers,
did not actually originate with the Order Service.
The Instruction No. 2's were the product of a harmful
virus which had been released into our Centre's
internal network. The creator of the virus, the dissident
Gnome, and also our system administrator, who
failed to trace the attack, have today been punished
with correction.
I would like to express my sincerest apologies to
the Service for Planetary Order for the unintentional
defamation contained in my Open Letter.
I would like to thank the Council of Eight for their
swift and timely response to my alarm signal.
spiderman: healer is a bloody stooge
santa: +1000. i'm deleting healer from my friend list

view whole thread (487 276 comments)?

The Wise One opened the whole thread and lazily scanned the final comments at the tail end of the discussion. There was nothing of interest – just the latest serving of nonsensical junk from Dissidents who stubbornly refused to believe in something that was plain for all to see.

For a while Healer's LJ had been a treasure house of interesting and unusual dissident types, 'slanderers of order', who looked fantastic on the show – real rebels. The episodes of Who Still Does Not Agree with Spiderman and Santa got the highest ratings in the history of the show, as did the broadcast of their Shameful Pauses...

Now it had all got so boring and predictable, no more breaths of fresh air. Once every few days another post would appear from someone who thought that Healer was right to agree and there would be another slack wave of indignation from a few dissidents. Something about 'manipulation of facts', 'bribing the author', a couple of links to *orderisover.net*.

The comments hadn't contained anything like the normal fully fledged dissidence for a long time now, and any attempts that the Wise One made to use 'slanderers' on the show usually ended in a fiasco: the slanderers would mumble something with a haunted look in their eye, immediately admit that they were guilty of everything, hurriedly delete their comments, repent blankly and promise to get corrected. Basically, there was no confrontation, no conflict...

But really, of course, he mustn't grumble. The wave of dissidence and mistrust of the SPO and the Council that had been produced by Healer's Open Letter had presented a pretty serious threat. And, glap, Second hadn't executed Healer in the heat of the moment (he had been planning on it at first, but the Wise One talked him out of it!), and they had got to the bottom of the problem properly and punished the guilty parties. If they had executed Healer then they would've ended up with a hundred-thousander martyr on their hands. And now they had a hundred-thousander friend. But friends are no good for the show... but then again, why not?!

'So I'll get him on too,' the Wise One realised with relief. 'Healer. He spoke well, I remember... And his face was so open and honest... A good face. I'll talk to him all theoretically, about slanderers of order, about dissidence as a phenomenon, and about his own story... And at the end of the show: an amnesty for all the "slanderers" who officially admit on Healer's page that they were wrong and that they made a mistake... The ratings are going to be just unbelievable...'

'Presenter to assistant,' he tapped on the keyboard. 'Invite user Healer to see me in the Residence immediately. Dress code "feeling lucky": we're going to film him for the show.'

Isoptera

hello, guest! we are pleased to see you
at the gates to the queendom of Isoptera!

Isoptera *is a never-ending act in* luxury,
created by more than two million friends.
If you wish to come in, please enter your
login and password...

Oops! Invalid login or password. Please try again!

...Congratulations, you have successfully entered
Isoptera. Please choose a role:
larva worker soldier nymph **prince**
Congratulations! You are a prince. The moderator
of Isoptera *will show you the way and explain*
our **rules...**

Hi, prince! You will live with the Queen and a million
other princes in the royal chambers. Isoptera is
based on a real termite mound. Follow me! The
royal chambers are located deep underground...
Right we're there. You see? The floor is covered
in rotting grass and moss so that the Queen will
be warm. And the ceiling here is low and arched,
it almost touches the Queen's back – so she simply
cannot leave the royal chambers and can hardly
even move ☺
Look how huge she is, the Queen! Ten times bigger
than you – what do you reckon, will you manage? ☺
As in nature, our Queen is mostly belly ☺
But she still has tiny little arms, a small head
and a pronotum, but these body parts don't matter

to you. Your place is right here, under her belly,
along with the other princes. While the Queen
is being satisfied by someone else, you can still
be involved. You can be constantly stroking her
and licking her: just try not to leave any deep
scars on her body (otherwise there's a fine ☹).
And when your turn comes, you will impregnate the
Queen. Your egg will definitely end up in her clutch
– and then you'll get a bonus!

The Troll

'...I am happy to report that no violations or abuses of power were discovered in the work of the SPO,' Healer repeated for the third time. 'The investigation revealed that the Instruction Number Two's which staff at our Centre for Population Control were receiving on the official channel, seemingly from Order Service officers, did not actually originate with the Order Service...'

'Stop!' The Wise One was furious. 'That's not the question! My question is: how did you feel when you were following Instruction Number Two?!'

Healer looked at Zero politely and slightly quizzically, then looked at the assistant, sighed dejectedly and stared at the floor. He tugged at his grey, greasy fringe with his fingers.

'Is he really so thick?' Zero thought. 'Or is he just shy? Or not used to first layer... No, that's not it. This is the man who produced the Open Letter. Last time he was with us at the Residence he could keep a conversation going fine. Maybe he's making fun of me? Some strange type of protest, or dissidence or something...'

'Would you like to be on my show?' he asked Healer ingratiatingly.

Healer nodded.

'Then answer my question clearly and precisely. What did you feel when you were following Instruction Number Two and terminating those pregnancies?'

'A great honour and a great responsibility?' Healer suggested hesitantly and looked up at Zero hopefully. 'Gratitude to the Council of Eight and the Service for Planetary Order?'

The Wise One shook his head darkly.

'The instructions were the product of a harmful virus...' Healer bleated quietly. 'Erm, I don't know... Which line? Which line should I choose?'

'Leave it, Wise One,' Zero's assistant whispered in his ear. 'Can't you see that he's a troll? He's not capable of keeping a conversation going, he just shuffles through a set selection of phrases recorded in his memory.'

'Are you a troll?' the Wise One asked loudly.

Healer sighed in relief and replied without even the slightest hesitation:

'Not a troll. Trolling is forbidden on *socio*. Trolling in first layer is impossible.'

'Do you remember writing the Open Letter?'

Healer tensed up again – the question was not precisely phrased. For a similar question – 'Did you write the Open Letter?' – there was a clear and unequivocal answer – 'Yes I did write it and I am grateful to the Council of Eight for their swift and timely reaction to my alarm signal'... But that 'do you remember' – it had confused everything somehow. It was a reference to something to which he no longer had access. To something murky, evil and terrifying, that happened before... before what? Before birth? Before the operation? Before what operation, now you mention it...?

'It happened before the operation,' came out all by itself somehow; he didn't understand the meaning of his own words, but he immediately understood that those words were *forbidden* because *punishment* burst in his head like a piercing pain.

'Before what operation?' the Wise One asked barely audibly.

Healer sank silently against the back of the chair and closed his eyes, waiting for the pain of punishment to pass.

'It's obvious what operation.' The assistant leaned over Healer, snapped on a contact glove and in a business-like fashion brushed the greasy grey locks from Healer's forehead. – 'Here, take a look, Wise One...'

and anyone who doesn't lie, my husband cuts open their head, right here

Zero saw a vertical pale-pink scar on Healer's forehead. Neat and very small – like a slender earthworm was sticking out of his hair. *Skin and bones, he cuts it all open.* 'Who did this...' Zero touched the worm with his finger, 'who did this to him?'

'Ooh, what are you doing, Wise One?' His assistant started fussing. 'Why are you touching it with your bare hand, here, take a glove, what is that, skin to skin, it's enough to make you sick...'

'Put that away,' Zero rejected the proffered contact glove; he actually did feel a bit sick, not from touching someone else's skin but from the awful feeling that on his own forehead, if he touched it, he would feel exactly the same scar.

'Who did this to you?' the Wise One asked, grasping Healer's hot face in his hands.

'Did what?' Healer frowned in disgust and broke free from Zero's arms.

'The operation. The scar.'

'What, a scar?' Healer absent-mindedly touched his forehead with his fingers. 'I hadn't even noticed... When I was a kid probably, I had a bad fall...'

'Uh-huh, you fell.' For some reason the assistant was overjoyed and whispered, tripping over his words, into the Wise One's ear: 'They say they do it in the clinics at Psychological Assistance... An experimental technique... Personally I've never come across it before in first layer, but I read, I read that... hang on I'll find it in my bookmarks... Aha, right. An operation to streamline the *socio* slot and partially erase pathological memory clusters, in conjunction with the pinpointed superimposition of false memories, can give fantastic results in the case of severe dementia, manic depressive psychoses and schiz...'

'Gopz!' Zero interrupted him halfway through the word. 'You can both gopz! In my show... there won't be...'

He wanted to say something else, maybe about trolling, which was unacceptable, about talking puppets which he would not tolerate on his show, but a wave of nausea rolled up to his throat, gluing all his words into a bitter, stinking lump. The Wise One tore the microphone off with wooden fingers and rushed out of the studio.

'No death,' Healer said politely to his back. 'I'm glad that you invited me here. I hope the viewers will like the show...'

Zero groaned and bent over the bath again in a dry, pointless spasm. There was nothing in him, not even foamy yellow bile, and he dry-heaved. When it had passed, the Wise One splashed his face with cold water. Then he pushed his whole head under the stream of water and started using his nails to scratch his inflamed skin, which was covered in painful goose-bumps – but carefully, only on the top of his head and behind his ears, so the larvae wouldn't be washed off from the inside of his elbows... He tensed up again and it was as if his tongue had swollen up in his throat, but this time the urge was not as strong. The Wise One gave a deep sigh. Now it's going to get much better. *It's going to pass any minute now, I've taken a good dose... Three white ones on the left and three black ones on the right, a triple BW...* It really was getting better. Not straightening up, feeling about with his hand, he ripped the towel from the hook. He rinsed his hair and wound the towel around his forehead right down by his eyebrows. He looked at himself in the mirror, which was smeared with cloudy splashes.

'Hi, you nobody, no death!' he said to his reflection. 'Well, go on, what have you got there, show us. Let's have a look at what you've got there under that towel?'

'No, don't look...'

we will be you are a troll and i am a troll and our kids
will be trolls

So what? It would all be so simple, yes, it would explain everything. A tiny little scar on the forehead – it would explain the last year. It would explain all the ready-made phrases rolling off his tongue on Who Still Does Not Agree, it would explain

the letters of happiness – are dissident plots.
how dare you attribute those words to me?

It would explain

do you, rosa, mother of mark, admit that
you are a dissident

It would explain

in the name of the living i sentence you to a pause
of shame...

It would explain

see you after the break! this is the wise one
and you're watching

That little pink worm would explain the Wise One's child-like smile.
The wisdom of the Wise One.
The intransigence of the Wise One.
The cruelty of the Wise One.

It would explain the Wise One's success as a showman.

It would explain how they made the Wise One into a puppet. Into a miraculous troll, swinging in a murky, forgetful mirage on his carousel...

All it takes is an operation to streamline the *socio* slot... hang on a minute... hang on a minute! But I'm not connected...! really? 'Is that what you think?' – his double swayed drunkenly there in the mirror – 'But maybe you just don't remember? Because, you know, trolls often don't remember important things... Partially erase pathological memory clusters plus false memories... Think, is it really possible that the Wise One would not be connected?'

'I am connected but through an external *socio* slot and only in second layer...'

'Yes, of course, through the Crystal. But what if that is self-deception...?'

False memories and false perception...

'...Where are you getting this idea from that the Crystal is not inside, but outside...?'

Nonsense, nonsense... That's all just the venom, the bakugan haze, too big a hit...

'What's that, Wise One, you have to love the bakugans, the bakugans are our friends! Look how they are swaying you right now, taking pity on you, keeping you warm...'

The walls suddenly shifted, the BW cradle started rocking.

'Let's fly, troll.' His pale double held out his hands to him. 'Let's you and I take a breather, die, suffocate... A triple dose! I've never flown like this before...!'

In the emptiness a sort of shadow hurried towards him. It crept up close, gave him a sniff and said:

'No death, my friend.'

'No death,' Zero replied. 'What, have I temporarily ceased?'

'Why do you think that?'

'Because I can see you.'

'No, neither of us has ceased yet... Although you, it seems, are really trying.' Cracker shook his fluffy yellow head in disapproval.

Actually, Cracker didn't look exactly like Cracker. He had too many limbs, mouths and an extra eye on the back of his head. But the Wise One knew somehow that it was definitely him...

'What is this place?' Zero asked.

'Let's put it this way,' the Cracker-like being scratched its big round belly thoughtfully. 'It's my personal inviz.'

'Are you not going to be born anymore?' Zero asked. 'Are you not going to come back to me in first layer?'

'Sorry,' his friend said. 'Maybe someday. But not right now.'

'Why?'

'You see, having a separate body only gets in my way. All that crap just takes up too much energy: digestion, respiration, excretion... A parasitic embryonic body is much more convenient, but even that is a burden at the end of the day: a heartbeat, this and that... But this stalled mode lets you preserve energy for action in *socio*. You can't even imagine what I am capable of, now I don't have a physical... By the way I broke into *Isoptera* today in *luxury*. Screwed the queen ten times in a row, without queuing... And at the same time I found out who she is in first layer. Do you want to know?'

'Not particularly,' the Wise One said honestly. 'I saw the advert. I think it's horrible.'

'Well you're right. What do you need with the queen, when you've got a wife like that... By the way, talking of horrible – you should be a bit more careful with those creatures. Six larvae at once – that could be a pausal dose! Though I'm glad you overdosed today. Otherwise we wouldn't have met. But still, you can't carry on like this...'

'Tell me, Cracker,' the Wise One touched the wet towel, which was still clinging to his forehead. 'Tell me honestly: am I a troll?'

Cracker doubled over and started shaking slightly, covering his little round mouths with his many-fingered hands.

'In a certain sense you are a troll,' he said, once he had finished laughing. 'Not in the sense you think, but in a technical sense... By the way, I can tell you as a specialist: a technical troll is not even capable of understanding or even having the idea that he is a troll. By default he has no doubt function.'

'So I wasn't given an operation?'

'You weren't my friend. And you don't have an internal *socio* slot...'

'Then why do I feel like a puppet?'

'Because you are a puppet?' his friend suggested and tittered into his hands again. 'Alright, alright, don't get annoyed. I will help you expose these puppet-masters. And fight the Monster...'

'The Living is not a Monster. I don't want to fight Him.'

'Am I asking the puppet what it wants?' the Cracker-like thing said in surprise. 'Go back right now, take off that stupid towel and turn on your Crystal. And, you know what, I want you to pray.'

'I don't know how to pray!'

'Give it a try, Wise One.'

The System

...Regaining consciousness was sore and difficult, as if he was flying and then fell. But this time it was from a much greater height than usual... He was lying curled up on his side, on the wet floor, shivering from cold. Bakugans were crawling over his face and back, dragging their hard, sharp wings across his skin, while one, the fattest, had slumped lazily on the floor beside him. Flipped over on its back, in a foul-smelling yellow puddle.

Gripping on to the side of the bath, the Wise One pulled himself up onto his feet. He shook the towel from his head – it fell on the beetle like a white shroud. He looked in the mirror. A clear forehead, with no scars on it. Where did he get the idea from that there should be a scar? After six larvae, anyway, he could have all sorts of hallucinations...

Swaying from lack of strength, he took a shower, drove the sluggish winged beetles off with the jet of water and drowned them in the bath. He crushed the one under the towel through the material with his foot and chucked it in the bin. A brownish-red stain was left on the towel.

His head was empty – but not in the same way as usual after a BW. The emptiness this time was not that soft, cosy ball of inviz which carousel would windup inside him, but a melancholy feeling that he had found out something important but forgotten it...

He put on what he had been wearing before – his presenter's 'feeling lucky' gear, which reeked of sweat – and walked out of the bathroom. Cleo was in the living room. She was lying on the floor, staring intently at the ceiling – she was probably watching a show or writing something in her Living Journal. Scattered all around her were crumpled food wrappers, an open pack of tranqvitamins, an unliving squashed bakugan – half-transparent, halfway through a metamorphosis – and an empty bottle of vitacomplex... He could never cure her of this stupid habit of throwing rubbish on the floor and then going to sleep in the exact same place. 'So what? Everyone does it.' 'So let's just have *everyone* do whatever they want then!' the Wise One said angrily. She didn't even bother to understand why he was so annoyed by this lack of respect for first layer. For his layer.

Everyone might as well just do whatever they want. There, outside, beyond the Residence and the Wise One's apartments. Let them lounge about on the soft, shaggy floors in their boring little first-layer boxes with their rounded edges, surrounded by sticky, springy, safety furniture, let them get fat and sleep, let them not wash for days, immersed in *socio*... That's not how it is at the Wise One's place. Here things are interesting. Here it's all like it was in ancient times – *hard* wooden furniture and a *hard* parquet floor. He has little multi-coloured poufs to sit on. He has pictures on the walls – real ones, with congealed encrustations of oil paint which he'd commissioned: three landscapes (a wood, the sea and some mountains, the beauty of first layer), depictions of wild animals... He has a pianola – you can make sounds on it in first layer. He has a library – seven real paper books, which smell of decay and mould... But she didn't care. She would go to sleep wherever she needed to on the hard floor or would move on to one of the poufs, if he reminded her. She never touched the pianola (why? I've got 'Wonder-Composer' installed), she didn't look at the pictures, she never opened any of the paper books. She didn't like the oak furniture – too many dangerous hard corners that gave her bruises ('Look where you're going, sweetheart!' – 'What, the whole time?!')... In first layer she was only interested in the lab. Those termites of hers. It still wasn't working with people, but the termites were giving amazing results – up to twelve immersions...

'What are you doing?' he asked, knowing full well that this question irritated her. *Socio* is private. Asking someone that question is no different from requesting the password to their inbox. But now her irritation suited him too – anything would. Anything that might somehow be able to silence this melancholic feeling that he had *forgotten something.*

'I'm watching the Shameful Pauses,' Cleo replied grudgingly. 'That woman just ceased, Rosa...'

'Let's watch it together,' he took the Crystal off sleep.

'No, gopz!' She squatted and gripped her knees with her arms. 'It's enough that you are here. And are you aware that watching the broadcasts of these pauses is now compulsory? Every day, for fifteen minutes, I have to see how they di...'

'Cleo!'

'How they die! What, don't you like that word?' Her voice broke into a shout. 'It's forbidden? But it fits very well. They are dying, suffocating, being killed in glass bell-jars! You don't know what it feels like when they cease – that gopzing Crystal of yours only shows the pictures! But I'm there!' She put her hands over her ears, as if she didn't want to hear her own shouting. 'Every day for fifteen minutes, with them! And I couldn't care less about "good progress"!'

'Stop shouting at me!'

She fell silent. She was sitting on her heels, rocking from side to side, her eyes closed and her hands pressed to her ears.

'Sorry,' Cleo said flatly. 'Sorry that I lost it. It's all the noise, it's driving me crazy.'

'What noise?'

'Those beetles of yours, they've got this horrible low-frequency hum... Or that redecorating you've decided to have done for our non-existent Darling... Or... Don't you hear it?'

He listened carefully.

'Cleo, it's quiet in this room. I always destroy the beetles after I... well, you know. And there is no redecorating happening yet. You just want to have something to blame me for.'

He turned away and sat at his Crystal, with his back to Cleo. He opened the System. His hands were shaking. His lips were shaking. She is being unfair. He is doing everything properly, wisely. He is doing his duty. He is helping the Living. He feels sorry for those Dissidents, but they are too dangerous to pardon. Only by harsh measures can they achieve good progress in the Living's recovery from illness... Only by harsh measures...

but once he had known: the Living does not have enough love

He is doing everything properly.

because he is a puppet. Because he is a coward

Because that is how it must be. He stared at the System: the good progress was evident. Three or four scraps, one of which, in the middle, was his stalled friend... He was hit with a wave of melancholy. He had to remember something important, something really important...

....A humble, primordial, ancient desire suddenly arose – the desire to pray to someone about something. Not the Living, but someone else – someone who could protect them both, someone who had ruled this world long ago, before the Nativity.

'Tremble for he cometh,' the Wise One mumbled; he did not know any pre-Nativity prayers, only the snatches he had accidentally overheard from the madman Matthew. 'Heavenly Three-headed God, thy will be done, thine twine swine...'

...CAUTION! SOMETHING IS ENDANGERING THE SYSTEM...

'...I am wandering in the darkness, I do not know who I am or where I came from...'

...SYSTEM MALFUNCTION no. 2 IS LOADING IN VIEWING MODE...

...and forgive me my sins, for I am as a child...

...analysing data...

CURRENT NUMBER OF DOUBLE-INCODES: 567 TRIPLE-INCODES: 253

'...Guide me, show me the way, for thine twine...'

...THE SYSTEM IS DETECTING UNCONTROLLED PROLIFERATION OF THE LIVING. THE METHOD OF ARTIFICIAL DESTRUCTION OF DOUBLES USING THE SERVICE FOR PLANETARY ORDER, WHICH WAS SUCCESSFULLY ADOPTED IN PREVIOUS CASES OF PROLIFERATION (40% 2nd c. AV, 70% 3rd c. AV, 20–30% 4th c. AV.), IS NOW INEFFECTIVE...

'...Tremble for he cometh, for thine twine swine...'

...THE SYSTEM IS DETECTING A SERIOUS THREAT TO THE TRANQUILIITY, STABILITY AND INTEGRITY OF THE LIVING...

'Fofs!' Cleo sobbed, as she looked at the screen, at the crazed, swollen 'little man'. 'Fofs! What, is he – dying?'

But Zero did not reply. Because he could no longer hear her. Because the System had broken through the border of the screen and appeared to him. And it had let him in, like an ancient, pre-nativity temple would let in sinners and wandering holy fools.

The Revelation of the Wise One in the Available Garden

Share this document <u>with everyone</u>.

My friends, we have been lied to. But today the time for truth has come. I have seen the System... Grieve with me! I am telling you in all honesty: I have seen the Darkness drawing near. The number of the Living has changed and continues to change day after day. Not all incodes are being reproduced in time, and some are not being reproduced at all. During reproduction others are doubled or even trebled...

From now on the System will reveal itself only to me. But I am telling you in all honesty: every day I will share it <u>with everyone</u>.

I can see the System... And I want you to see it too. You can read my New Commandments in the attachment.

1.

Henceforth the System is public property. Henceforth the System will be transparent for all.

2.

No more lies and no more liars in power. In the name of the Living I dissolve the Council of Eight.

3.

Henceforth livings are not responsible for their predecessors. In the name of the Living I grant an amnesty for all correctees.

4.

Henceforth everyone is free to choose their own vector according to their inclinations and talents.

5.

Henceforth everyone is free to live as long as nature allows.

6.

I legalise the ancient institution of marriage. Henceforth men may have women as long-term partners and make them their wives.

7.

I grant women the right to take precautions, but also the right to give birth and keep planned Darlings with them, according to their will.

8.

In all communities I will build temples to the Three-Headed God. I gently recommend that everyone visits these temples to pray for the health of the Living.

Part 4

The Wise Prophet

Letter to Self
17th September 479 A.V.

I haven't written a letter to self in a long time. A really long time. I thought there was no point – seeing as disaster has befallen the Living. But I changed my mind. There probably is a point – at the least, there will be if I do what I now believe to be right.

If I do what I have decided to do, reading this will prove useful to you, my friend.

And for me too: maybe it'll help me get my thoughts together somehow…

Today you could hear the rumble of explosions not far from the Residence, right from morning, and we had to spend all day in the bunker while a clean-up operation was carried out; the dog was going crazy. She's always been terrified of explosions or any loud noise. She is terrified of everything and everyone, apart from me. I have, of course, created a separate room for her in the bunker. I spent a bit of time with her, and I could feel how the air went rigid with the thick, acerbic, unbearable smell of her fear, and then I left and locked her in there on her own.

She's afraid of being alone too. Cleo and the Son and I were sitting at the opposite end of the bunker, but even from there we could hear her whimpering and thrashing about in there. The dog gets so distressed living here with us that sometimes I think it would be better if she ceased… I shouldn't have listened to Cleo and taken her from the Farm. Cleo hoped that we might be able to tame her.

Back then, immediately after the Revelation, lots of people hoped they would be able to tame farm animals. They thought that since the Living had died or was at least sick and weak, animals would stop being afraid... But the Great Taming was a failure. All the animals that had been brought from the Farms to be domesticated died in the first few days. Most ceased to exist from heart attacks – that is, from sheer terror... Others were shot because they behaved aggressively. The pigs, cows, chickens and rabbits were, I suppose, killed for their meat...

Our dog is probably the only animal which still *lives in a house*. Because I am here. When I am with her, she almost stops being afraid...

Perhaps she is the only animal from the Farm to have survived at all. Now that no one looks after the Farms...

Once a week I upload photographs onto *socio*: the Wise One and his faithful hound. Very optimistic. It gives people hope.

They don't hear, the people, how she whimpers, pines and thrashes about when I leave her. They don't hear how she overflows with yelping and barking when other people come up to her. My Son or Cleo. Or Layla. Or the General.

For most of the day, while the clean-up was going on around the Residence, me, Cleo and the Son played 'Gurners'. I invented this game myself – I wanted to create something personal and homemade which would unite the whole family in first layer... The game's not complicated – perhaps I'll tell you about it, maybe it'll be of some use to you. If my plans work out and quieter times do come, you can share the rules with everyone – I'd like that. So one person, the Gurner, has to act out a word or a whole phrase. By miming, gesturing or moving his body somehow (which, by the way, is good for developing children's coordination in first layer). And the others have to guess what he's trying to say. Really simple, right? And it's all fair, there's no *socio* to help you find the answer: you need to think for yourselves, with your own head, it's the only way... Cleo tried it once, as an experiment – she ran a clip of the Son's 'gurning' through an analysis program. The result was pretty funny: 'This person is frightened and/or aggressive. All indicators suggest that he requires the assistance of the Psychological Service.' But my son was only trying to get us to guess the word 'dog'... Cleo and I had a real laugh then, and even the Son groaned quietly along with us, his lips shut tight – that's how he laughs...

He was groaning like that today too, although it wasn't funny at all. The Son clearly went too far today. When it was his turn to be the 'gurner', he lay down on the stone floor, and grinning horribly, crossed his eyes and froze in that position.

'A pupa in metamorphosis?' Cleo asked wearily, looking off to one side.

The Son shook his head to say no.

'An unliving animal?' I suggested. Wrong again.

'We give in,' Cleo said. 'What is it?'

He said something to her in *socio*. She shuddered as if from a nearby explosion, and finally looked at the Son. With distaste and something like disgust, perhaps. And she said, 'Don't you dare.'

She rarely looks the Son in the eye. She rarely looks at him at all – normally she looks slightly to one side of him. When I ask her, she always denies it, but I think it's because she has never been able to learn to love him. The Son frightens her.

Because he can't pull his lips into a smile. Because he does not laugh, but groans.

Because he is not our Darling, but adopted.

Because he can't fall asleep without bright light.

Because he was a correctee.

Because when we took him out of the House and brought him to the Residence and he first saw my Crystal W, he poked the screen with his finger and started muttering, 'Sitem. Sitem. Sitem.' 'How does he know?' Cleo had asked then, calmly and evenly, and looked at him in that way for the first time. The System actually was open on the monitor. The Son was three years old. He couldn't have known yet.

He was three when we took him. Now he is ten.

Now he is lying still on the floor, grinning and goggling his eyes.

And I say, 'OK, go on then, spit it out, what were you thinking of?' He peers tentatively at Cleo, he doesn't know what to do. Because mummy has just said 'Don't you dare.' She looks away in silence.

He replies, 'I was doing "the Living". The unloving monster.'

Cleo says in a whisper, 'I'm calling Layla. Layla can take him off...'

Layla comes. Layla loves our Son. She loves everyone. She says, 'Alive or dead, the Living is full of love, and every part of him loves every other.' She is very placid, Layla. For a long time now, ever since she returned from the clinic, she has loved everyone. And her scar is absolutely tiny, and so neat...

She doesn't miss her own Darlings at all, she doesn't even remember them. Whereas I, paradoxical as this may seem, sometimes regret sending them away. They would have run around the Residence and they would have *laughed*, they would have played with the Son. And the Son, perhaps, would have learned to do what they do...

But back then I was afraid that the children of Second and Layla would start making claims – they might even have disputed the transfer of *wisdom* to my Son when I ceased... None of that matters now. The Son won't be the Wise One, you will be. But here, in the Residence, there is no sound of children's laughter. They have, probably, already ceased, Layla's Darlings. There's all sorts going on out there. I shouldn't have sent them away...

'Come with me, Butcher's Son,' Layla coos, leading him by the hand. 'Let's go to the temple. Let's pray to Threeheads for the Reduction to end and for the Living to rise again...'

We have a temple right here in the bunker – small, but cosy...

'He's still alive,' Cleo says to me, when we are left alone, and her eyes are absolutely crazy again, this has been happening a lot with her recently. 'The Living is still alive… But he's not well. I can hear him howling sadly…'

'That's the dog howling,' I reply.

'The dog is howling too, but quieter. You just can't hear it. You are the only one who can't hear these terrible noises!'

'Our Son doesn't hear them either.'

'No, he hears them. He just likes them…'

…Then my General comes. He says that the clean-up is over and we can go back up top. And that he has just sent me a dispatch from the front. With *bad* news.

Cleo

Suffering from tinnitus? Are you experiencing the
subjective sensation of noise in the ears without
an irritant? Are you in despair because the
autodoctor can't help you and are you dreaming
of a self-pause?
THERE IS A SOLUTION!!!
Just download the best music on socio!
Our tunes will drown out the sounds
on any frequency!
Our tunes will beat your neuritis of the auditory
nerve!

13:00

Music-makers – go screw yourselves. Why do they lie? Why do we all lie, pretending it's just tinnitus? 'Subjective sensation without an irritant…' A bare-faced lie.

There is an irritant.

We are just listening to the Living dying. His howls, his groans, his weeping, his roaring – with no end… We have been hearing Him dying for several years. You can't drown out those sounds with gopzing music. These sounds are driving me insane. They stop me from working. I haven't been to the lab for months.

And my research is extremely important for the Living… I am, as it happens, on the verge of a great discovery… The termites are giving a result of up to twenty immersions under the L-L ray… And what are my friends in *isoptera* if not termites…? At the end of the day the biological body is not important… When He dies, we'll all be able to live in *isoptera*, we'll make ourselves a new Living…

13:50

I reread my last post. The rantings of an absolute lunatic. It's all that noise. Fofs, He is howling so loud today!

But there is a small lull now and my head is clearer. I am saving the following in my memory as auto-reminders:

1. The termites in the experiment have no connection whatsoever to *isoptera*.

2. Experiments on people are still not giving any result.

3. Don't go mad, Cleo.

14:20

I ran myself through the autodoctor. My memory is partially destroyed. Everything seems to suggest I've picked up some kind of virus. There are a lot of viruses now. The noise is getting stronger.

My hair is the wrong colour. I have to change it. To support the Living.

15:00

Luxury is a good place to escape His howling. You can hear him there too, but it seems almost melodic. Like background music that you don't focus your attention on...

> mother_queen *has updated her status*
> *hi, I'm available again*

The Wise Prophet

The final dispatch of the Second Great Reduction:
17.09.479 A.V.

Committed in the past 24 hours:
- *acts of terrorism in first layer: 1,566 (dead: 12,456 pers.; injured: 9,342 pers.)*
- *acts of terrorism / virus attacks in socio: 11,569*
- *illegal organised self-pauses at underground Festivals for the Assistance of Nature: 14,980*
- *illegal self-pauses outside of festival zones: 11,934*
- *murders on streets: 5,750*
- *thefts and robberies: 25,875*
- *clean-up operations successfully carried out by the Army of the Three-Headed God: 4,965*
- *ceased to exist during clean-ups: 8,400 terrorists*
- *ceased to exist due to various illnesses, starvation and insanitary conditions: 68,411 pers.*
- *ceased to exist from previously received wounds: 12,784 pers.*
- *homeless children discovered on streets: 48,733*
- *temples of the Three-Headed God burned down / blown up: 421*

*Claim to region EA 1 restated by: Goldenhorse
(formerly, First member of the Council of Eight)
Claim to region EA 2 restated by: Goldenhorse
Claim to region EA 3 restated by: Goldenhorse,
Emperor
Claim to region EA 4 made by: Goldenhorse,*

Prince_of_Darkness
Claim to region EA 6 restated by: Emperor
Claim to region EA 7 made by: Goldenhorse,
Prince_of_Darkness, Emperor
Claim to region EA 8 restated by: Peacemaker,
Prince_of_Darkness, Emperor
Claim to region AS 1 restated by: Asiatic (formerly,
Sixth member of the Council of Eight)…
exterminated during armed territorial conflicts:
16,943 pers.
(of which, children: 2,570; women: 5,342)
sentenced to Public Pause of Shame as part
of Who Else Deceived Us: 1 pers.

Total *number to (temporarily?) cease to exist*
during the past 24 hours: **151,659** *pers.*

Reproduced during past 24 hours: 67 pers.

Number of livings *at present moment:*
1,000,476,117 *(one billion four hundred seventy*
six thousand one hundred and seventeen) pers.

'The figures look bad,' the General says dejectedly. 'The figures look very bad.'

As if he needed to say that. Every day it keeps getting worse and worse.

Don't make the same mistakes as me, pal.

I rescued people from a lie – but they could not handle the truth.

I gave them the right to a long life – and they die by their own hands. In illegal, dirty, vomit-strewn pause zones or just on the streets. Because, you see, they are not immortal.

I granted an amnesty for correctees, called on them to be who they wanted to be – and they became criminals.

I gave them a mighty new god in place of their weak, half-dead one – and they destroy the temples.

I gave them wise regents for their territories – and they rise up under the banners of the old stupid and deceitful ones.

I gave them the right to love their Darlings – and they throw them out as seven-year-olds.

I gave them the right to love each other – but they don't know how to love.

They blow things up, they burn them down, they get sick, they hang themselves, they weep, they beat up the weak. They pine away, they wallow in filth, they panic, they destroy themselves. They fight wars for empty spaces, they release *socio* viruses, they break into cells, they wipe memory, they rape, they die and they are not reproduced. They are reduced. And the Army of the Three-Headed God is no longer strong enough to hold them back...

'We can't hold them back any longer,' the General glowers, and his scar goes crimson, as it always does when he is agitated.

He is so devoted to me, he tries so hard to sense my mood and fulfil my desires that sometimes he manages to read my mind. It's good I agreed to keep him back then. He brought nearly all of the SPO into the Army of the Three-Headed God. And it's good that I streamlined his *socio* slot: after all, he had had his eyes on my position, the sneaky bastard...

Now he is meek and devoted. The operation was very successful: he kept all his professional skills and his entire contact list. But he doesn't remember being the Servant or being Second – except for some first-layer glimpses, fragments of nightmares... Now he is my General. He is the head of the Army of the Three-Headed God, he prays regularly and he does not question orders. And if his memory does play nasty tricks on him, he doesn't worry, because he knows the reason.

He clearly remembers getting wounded in the head in one of the first battles of the Reduction... No big deal, but his *socio* slot was grazed by a piece of shrapnel and it left a scar.

My General suddenly shudders with his whole body and groans, and covers his face with his hands.

'Three-Headed Lord,' he whispers, his face buried in his hands. 'Lord, Three-Headed Lord...!'

That's very unlike him. I put my hand on his shoulder – 'no sucs, just success: the Wise Prophet's hand works on demand!' – and quietly ask, 'General, are you not feeling well?'

Like a dog, he licks his dried out lips and slowly takes his hands from his face. The whites of his eyes are full of burst blood vessels. His teeth are chattering.

'Another terrorist attack in *socio*,' the General says. 'I am present there. We are all dying.'

The first reports appeared on the news feed after a quarter of an hour.

> *We are broadcasting live from the location of the incident. At the current moment the termite mound is overrun with fire, there are burnt insect bodies everywhere. Several hundred nymphs are circling in the air, evidently panicking. They are gnawing off their wings and falling to the ground, into the fire. There is some sort of movement by the exit from the burrow – it seems as if the surviving workers and soldiers are trying to drag out the charred body of the Queen...*
>
> *The explosion at Isoptera is the most horrific socio terrorist attack in the history of the Great Reduction: over the last few years nearly a billion users have worked together to create this resource. As yet no one has claimed responsibility for this monstrously cruel crime; however, it is evidently*

not the work of a lone suicide-bomber. To produce
an explosion of this magnitude in luxury required
a coordinated and well-organised fantasy on the
part of a large number of users.
The millions of friends of those who died today
in luxury are outraged at the government's
indifference and failure to act.
'The Wise Prophet will not help us.' This was
the response to the situation of Goldenhorse,
a former member of the Council of Eight, who
died today in Isoptera as a prince. 'Because he
doesn't understand us. He cannot share our pain.
The Wise One does not want to connect himself
to socio as a matter of principle – he has all sorts
of fine-sounding explanations for this behaviour
of his, but I have my own opinion on the matter.
He just doesn't want to be our friend on socio,
and that is all.'

'It's provocation.' The General has already almost calmed down, but his voice is still trembling a bit. 'To start a panic. I think Goldenhorse is behind the attack. Permission to terminate him?'

'Leave him.'

He looks confused, but still trusting, like a dog.

'Permission to capture him alive to take part in Who Else Deceived Us?'

I repeat: 'Leave him. We've taken enough lives.'

'So what are your orders?'

I say nothing for a long time. Then I say, 'You and your father were right.'

He rubs his blood-drenched eyes with his hands, like a Darling who has not had enough sleep. And he looks at me again – this time in entreaty:

'I don't remember my father. I don't understand you, Wise One...'

...The old man was right. And the Servant. And Fourth too. No one needs my truth. The whole world was held together by their lie.

Just a bit longer – and we will have been reduced completely, to nothing, to nought. Haha. To me. But I hope that the mistake can still be corrected.

Today I will bring the Living back to life...

My son will not be my heir. It will be you, my inc-successor.

But please don't have any illusions. In no way are you my continuation. This is just the only solution.

I am going to shut down the System.

How many of us are there now – a billion four hundred and something? – I'm going to take a slightly smaller figure. A billion. A nice, round number. So then: 'The Living equals a billion livings...' Sounds fantastic.

There, it is decided. The Living has risen again, and His number equals one billion. The rest will be reduced while we are establishing stability. Those that aren't reduced we will finish off. For their own good. For the good of the Living.

There is no other solution. I will force them to calm down. I will force them to multiply. If there are too many, I will terminate them. Then the System will sort itself out and start to work on its own.

At least, that's what happened last time. If you can believe Fourth. And the things she said on Who Else Deceived Us, before she was torn apart.

'Confess, Fourth, moderator of assistance to nature: when did you first lie?'
'My inc-predecessor first lied in the time of the first Great Reduction.'

At that time they moulded the Living from three billion, with three hundred thousand in reserve.

But it helped.

I sentenced her to a Public Pause of Shame – though she would have ceased within days anyway. She was like a skeleton. It was as if Death had stepped down from the ancient paintings to take part in the show…

…I say to the General, 'Don't worry. You don't have to understand anything. Now go and bring a good sysadmin to the Residence.'

'Why, Wise One?'

'When I resurrect the Living, I should become a part of him.'

The General smiles:

'Understood, Wise One.'

The Butcher's Son

…Father takes me over to the Crystal and says, 'Look, son. Look at the System for the last time. Soon I am going to shut off access.'

And I look, since he is asking, although I don't understand: why 'for the last time' all of a sudden?

Even if, for instance, he stops sharing the System with everyone, I will still be able to see it. It has always let me in, for as long as I can remember. Cracker promised me that the System would never turn me away.

Then he looks at the screen for a long time and says thoughtfully, 'My lucky number is eight. Incode no. 8 has been free for a long time, I'll take cell eight…'

And then I suddenly start having this attack, as if I'm saying someone else's words. I get it from time to time: it's as if someone has crawled into my head and is making all my decisions for me. I say to him, 'Well done, your intuition is good. That was your number after all.'

He asks what I mean by that, but I don't really even know myself. I don't know, but I say, 'In theory you should have been a double of incode 0 000 000 008. But Cracker managed to correct the last eight to a nought.'

And he shouts at me:

'Don't lie! Cracker was a child then! He's only two years older than me!'

I shrug my shoulders: 'Cracker is the founder. He will always be four and a bit centuries older than you.'

My father starts looking so stupid that I really want to laugh. But I mustn't. I bite my tongue painfully and squeeze my lips shut.

I mustn't laugh while the Monster is alive…

Then the sysadmin comes and gives him that capsule – they gave me one like that too, a long time ago, in the House… And he says to father, 'Connection is a great sacrament. I must read the Book of Life over you – or is your wisdom so great that you remember the text off by heart?'

'I remember it,' father replies. 'But I don't know what we should do with the opening. "The Living is three billion livings…" – because it doesn't tally with the truth.'

'What's truth got to do with anything?' The sysadmin gets scared. 'The text must be read out in accordance with the canon! Otherwise the program won't unpack and the *socio* slot won't go in right.'

'Fine,' says father. 'It might as well be in accordance with the canon for now. But remember – we are going to be changing the canon soon. "The Living is equal to one billion livings" – that's how it's always going to start…'

When the sysadmin leaves, my father takes the capsule and begins the rite. And I say to him: 'Dad, don't. The Monster must die!'

But he carries on reading. He gestures for me to go. And I leave.

my monster must die

I know where he keeps his black larvae.

The Troll

...And there in the Garden I meet the mistress, and her hair is all black, and there are bits of dye on her forehead and neck. She's dragging the dog along on a lead. The dog is wheezing, and shaking all over, and there is foam coming out of her mouth – she's ever so scared of all of us except the Wise One.

I say to her, 'Three-Headed Lord, mistress, what have you done with your beautiful honey-coloured hair?'

And she laughs, all strange like, and says, 'I was set on fire and now I'm all black.'

I say, 'What have you got the dog for?'

And she replies, 'What do you mean what for? For science. And you should come with me too, Layla. You do want to take part in an experiment, don't you, to contribute to science?'

Well, so I go with her to the lab, because I'm ever so pleased that I can be of use to science. And the mistress squeezed us into these long metal things, me in one, the dog in another, and before that she gave us some sort of jab too. Well, I got a little bit scared in there because it was dark and there was no air, and the dog was howling away all sad, but everything pretty much went alright. The mistress let us out fairly soon.

The dog puked right there on the floor and then ran off.

'I'll mop it all up right away, don't you worry,' I say to the mistress. 'But tell me, did we contribute to science?'

And she says, 'Of course! I'll send the result to your inbox now.'

And at that moment I got a mail from the mistress, but I couldn't make any sense of it.

This is what it said: 'Dust – five seconds of darkness – life – five seconds of darkness. All the little volunteer doggies have given the same result.'

And then she hugs me, just like that, without any contact gloves and says:

'Farewell, Layla.'

I ask her, 'Where are you going?'

And she says, 'I'm off to the Festival.'

'What are you on about?' I say, 'Mistress, stay here, there, outside, it's dangerous. You won't make it as far as the Festival, and anyway they're banned!'

But the mistress is stubborn.

'I make it, I don't make it,' she says, 'it makes no difference…'

On the doorstep she turns around and says, 'Do you hear that, Layla? The noise has stopped.'

And she leaves. And I'm left to mop up the mess the dog has made. And, smin, I listen closely, and the noise really has disappeared.

But it never really bothered me. It was just like the wind.

0

Dozens of fat, two-headed beetles fly about the room and crawl over my skin. I can no longer move. I can't chase them off.

My consciousness is still there, it never went away. It's just cold. So cold that I can't breathe, look or move. And it's very quiet. Quiet in my chest.

It seems to me like now I am made of ice. My eyes have rolled up into my head and frozen to my eyelids; my arms have gone stiff; my legs have gone stiff and stuck together.

It seems to me now that I am hard and icy, I cannot be broken. But if you took my body out into the sun, it would melt and soak into the ground like watery lymph...

But there is no sun.

My son is sitting at the opposite end of the room and sniffing. I hope that he feels at least a little bit sorry for what he has done to me... Somewhere nearby there is the rumble of gunfire.

The dog comes over. She pokes her face into my stiff body and yelps thinly.

Quietly and imperceptibly I am temporarily ceasing to exist, and after five seconds I will appear in the System again. With the number nought.

And then another nought will spring up. And another.

Small round holes in the body of the little man made of numbers, more and more of them all the time...

The dog howls over my corpse. Gunfire rattles the glass, but the dog stays by me. She licks my frozen hands.

She is so consumed by her grief that she lets the Son come up very close.

They both sit over the body. The dog's breathing is heavy and fast, and a hot, rotten smell comes from her mouth. An explosion makes the glass burst and fly out; the dog trembles in fear. The Son carefully reaches his hand out to her and strokes her raised fur. She growls limply, but stays where she is.

She lets him touch her.

'No death,' the Son says to her and smiles tentatively. The dog looks at him, cocking her head to one side.

His smile is utterly childlike.

Glossary

1. *FOFS*: 'Frightened Of Five Seconds'; popular abbreviation from *socio* chats. Entered first-layer lexis in the early second century AV.

2. *SMIN*: 'Swear on My INcode'. Popular abbreviation from *socio* chats. Entered first-layer lexis in the early third century AV.

3. *GOPZ*: Popular abbreviation from *socio* chats. 'GO to the Pause Zone'; used as a term of abuse, can be used as a joke in friendly conversation. Entered first-layer lexis in the first century AV soon after the first Festival for Assisting Nature.

4. GLAP: 'Glory to the Living and its Parts'; popular abbreviation from *socio* chats; entered first layer lexis in the early second century AV.

5. B2B: Brain2Brain

6. Sucs: Abbreviation: single-use contact suit

Biographical note

Anna Starobinets was born in Mosow in 1978 and graduated in philology from Moscow State University. She is a Russian journalist and internationally published author whose first book, *An Awkward Age*, is published by Hesperus Press.

James Rann is a translator and scholar of Russian literature, which he studied at Oxford University and University College London. A former winner of the Rossica Young Translator Award, he is also the translator of *It's Time*, by Pavel Kostin. He lives in London.

HESPERUS PRESS

Hesperus Press is committed to bringing near what is far –
far both in space and time. Works written by the greatest
authors, and unjustly neglected or simply little known in
the English-speaking world, are made accessible through
new translations and a completely fresh editorial approach.
Through these classic works, the reader is introduced to the
greatest writers from all times and all cultures.

For more information on Hesperus Press, please visit our
website: **www.hesperuspress.com**